ALONE

By Lisa Gardner

Alone

Lisa Gardner

Doubleday Large Print Home Library Edition

BANTAM BOOKS

This Large Print Edition, prepared especially for Doubleday Large Print Home Library, contains the complete, unabridged text of the original Publisher's Edition.

ALONE

A Bantam Book / January 2005

Published by
Bantam Dell
A Division of Random House, Inc.
New York, New York

ISBN 0-7394-5007-7

Printed in the United States of America
Published simultaneously in Canada

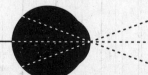

This Large Print Book carries the
Seal of Approval of N.A.V.H.

ALONE

Chapter
1

He'd put in a fifteen-hour shift the night the call came in. Too many impatient drivers on 93, leading to too much crash, bang, boom. City was like that this time of year. The trees were bare, night coming on quick and the holidays looming. It felt raw outside. After the easy camaraderie of summer barbecues, you now walked alone through city streets hearing nothing but the skeletal rattle of dry leaves skittering across cold pavement.

Lots of cops complained about the short,

gray days of February, but personally, Bobby Dodge had never cared for November. Today did nothing to change his mind.

His shift started with a minor fender bender, followed by two more rear-enders from northbound gawkers. Four hours of paperwork later, he thought he'd gotten through the worst of it. Then, in early afternoon, when traffic should've been a breeze even on the notoriously jam-packed 93, came a five-car pile-up as a speeding taxi driver tried to change four lanes at once and a stressed-out ad exec in a Hummer forcefully cut him off. The Hummer took the hit like a heavyweight champ; the rusted-out cab went down for the count and took out three other cars with it. Bobby got to call four wreckers, then diagram the accident, and then arrest the ad exec when it became clear the man had mixed in a few martinis with his power lunch.

Pinching a man for driving under the influence meant more paperwork, a trip to the South Boston barracks (now in the middle of rush-hour traffic, when no one respected anyone's right-of-way, not even a trooper's), and another altercation with the rich ad exec when he balked at entering the holding cell.

The ad exec had a good fifty pounds on Bobby. Like a lot of guys confronted by a smaller opponent, he confused superior weight with superior strength and ignored the warning signs telling him otherwise. The man grabbed the doorjamb with his right hand. He swung his lumbering body backwards, expecting to bowl over his smaller escort and what? Make a run for it through a police barracks swarming with armed troopers? Bobby ducked left, stuck out his foot, and watched the overweight executive slam to the floor. The man landed with an impressive crash and a few troopers paused long enough to clap their hands at the free show.

"I'm going to fucking sue!" the drunken exec screamed. "I'm going to sue you, your commanding officer, and the whole fucking state of Massachusetts. I'll own this joint. You hear me? *I'll fucking own your ass!*"

Bobby jerked the big guy to his feet. Ad Exec screamed a fresh round of obscenities, possibly because of the way Bobby was pinching the man's thumb. Bobby shoved the man into the holding cell and slammed the door.

"If you're gonna puke, please use the toilet," Bobby informed him, because by now the man had turned a little green. Ad Exec flipped him off. Then he doubled over and vomited on the floor.

Bobby shook his head. "Rich prick," he muttered.

Some days were like that, particularly in November.

Now it was shortly after ten p.m. Ad Exec had been bailed out by his overpriced lawyer, the holding cell was washed down, and Bobby's shift, which had started at seven a.m., was finally done. He should go home. Give Susan a buzz. Catch some sleep before his alarm went off at five and the whole joyous process started once more.

Instead, he was jittery in a way that surprised him. Too much adrenaline buzzing in his veins, when he was a man best known for being cool, calm, and collected.

Bobby didn't go home. Instead, he traded in his blues for jeans and a flannel shirt, then headed for the local bar.

At the Boston Beer Garden, fourteen

other guys were sitting around the rectangular-shaped bar, smoking cigarettes and nursing draft beer while zoning out in front of plasma-screen TVs. Bobby nodded to a few familiar faces, waved his hand at the bartender, Carl, then took an empty seat a bit down from the rest. Carrie brought him his usual order of nachos. Carl hand-delivered his Coke.

"Long day, Bobby?"

"Same old, same old."

"Susan coming in?"

"Practice night."

"Aye, the concert. Two weeks, right?" Carl shook his head. "Beautiful and talented. I'll tell you again, Bobby—she's a keeper."

"Don't let Martha hear you," Bobby told him. "After watching your wife haul a keg, I don't want to think of what she could do with a rolling pin."

"My Martha's also a keeper," Carl assured him. "Mostly 'cause I fear for my life."

Carl left Bobby alone with his Coke and nachos. Overhead, a live news bulletin was reporting on some kind of situation in Revere. A heavily armed suspect had barricaded himself in his home after taking potshots at his neighbors. Now, Boston PD had deployed their SWAT team, and "nobody was taking any chances."

Yeah, November was a funny kind of month. Wired people up, left them with no defenses against the oncoming gloom of winter. Left even guys like Bobby doing all they could do just to hold course.

He finished his nachos. He drank his Coke. He settled his bill, and just as he convinced himself it really was a good idea to go home, the beeper suddenly activated on his belt. He read the screen one moment and was bolting out the door the next.

It had been that kind of day. Now it would be that kind of night.

Catherine Rose Gagnon didn't like November much either, though for her, the real problem had started in October. October 22, 1980, to be exact. The air had been warm, the sun a hot kiss on her face as she walked home from school. She'd been carrying her books in her arms and wearing her favorite back-to-school outfit: knee-high brown socks, a dark brown corduroy skirt, and a long-sleeved gold top.

A car came up behind her. At first, she didn't notice, but dimly she became aware of the blue Chevy slowing to a crawl beside her. A guy's voice. *Hey, honey. Can you help me for a sec? I'm looking for a lost dog.*

Later, there was pain and blood and muffled cries of protest. Her tears streaking down her cheeks. Her teeth biting her lower lip.

Then there was darkness and her tiny, hollow cry, "Is anyone out there?"

And then, for the longest time, there was nothing.

They told her it lasted twenty-eight days. Catherine had no way of knowing. There was no time in the dark, just a loneliness that went on without end. There was cold and there was silence, and there were the times when he returned. But at least that was something. It was the sheer nothingness, endless streams of nothingness, that could drive a person insane.

Hunters found her. November 18. They noticed the plywood cover, poked it with their rifles, and were startled to hear her faint cry. They rescued her triumphantly, uncovering her four-by-six earthen prison and releasing her into the crisp fall air. Later she saw newspaper photos. Her dark blue eyes enormous, her head skull-like, her body thin and curled up on itself, like a small brown bat that had been yanked harshly into the sun.

The papers dubbed Catherine the Thanksgiving Miracle. Her parents took her home. Neighbors and family paraded through the front door with exclamations of "Oh, thank heavens!" and "Just in time for the holidays" and "Oh, can you really believe . . . ?"

Catherine sat and let people talk around her. She slipped food from the overflowing trays and stored it in her pockets. Her head was down, her shoulders hunched around her ears. She was still the little bat and for reasons she couldn't explain, she was overwhelmed by the light.

More police came. She told them of the man, of the car. They showed her pictures. She pointed at one. Later, days, weeks—did it really matter?—she came to the police station, stared at a lineup, and solemnly pointed her finger once again.

Richard Umbrio went on trial six months later. And three weeks into that, Catherine took the stand with her plain blue dress and polished Mary Janes. She pointed her finger one last time. Richard Umbrio went away for life.

And Catherine Rose returned home with her family.

She didn't eat much. She liked to take the food and slip it in her pocket, or simply hold it in the palm of her hand. She didn't sleep much. She lay in the dark, her blind bat eyes seeking something she couldn't name. Often, she held quite still to see if she could breathe without making a sound.

Sometimes her mother stood in the doorway, her pale white hands fluttering anxiously at her collarbone. Eventually, Catherine would hear her father down the hall. *Come to bed, Louise. She'll call if she needs you.*

But Catherine never called.

Years passed. Catherine grew up, straightening her shoulders, growing out her hair, and discovering that she possessed the kind of dark, potent beauty that stopped men in their tracks. She was all pale white skin, glossy black hair, and oversized navy eyes. Men wanted her desperately. So she used them indiscriminately. It wasn't her fault. It wasn't their fault. She simply never felt a thing.

Her mother died. 1994. Cancer. Catherine stood at the funeral and tried to cry. Her body had no moisture, and her sobs sounded papery and insincere.

She went home to her barren apartment and tried not to think of it again, though sometimes, out of the blue, she would picture her mother standing in the doorway of her room. *"Come to bed, Louise. She'll call if she needs you."*

"Hey, honey . . . I'm looking for a lost dog. . . ."

November 1998. The Thanksgiving Miracle curled up naked in her white porcelain tub, her thin, bony body trembling from the cold as she clutched a single razor in her fist. Something bad was going to happen. A darkness beyond darkness. A buried box from which there would be no coming back.

"Come to bed, Louise. She'll call if she needs you."

"Hey, honey . . . I'm looking for a lost dog?"

The blade, so slender and light in her hands. The feel of its edge, kissing her wrist. The abstract sensation of warm, red blood, lining her skin.

The phone rang. Catherine roused herself from her lethargy long enough to answer it. And that single call saved her life. The Thanksgiving Miracle rose again.

She thought about it now. As the TV blared in the background: *An armed suspect has barricaded himself in his home after taking numerous shots at his neighbors. Boston SWAT officials consider the situation highly volatile and extremely dangerous.*

As her son sobbed in her arms. "Mommy, Mommy, Mommy."

And as her husband bellowed from below: "I know what you're doing, Cat! How stupid do you think I am? Well, it's not going to work. There's no way in hell you're going to get away with it! Not this time!"

Jimmy stormed up the stairs, heading for their bedroom.

The phone had saved Catherine before. Now she prayed it would save her once again. "Hello, hello, nine-one-one? Can you hear me? It's my husband. I think he's got a gun."

Chapter

2

Bobby had been a member of the Massachusetts State Police Special Tactics and Operations (STOP) Team for the past six years. Called out at least three times a month—and generally every damn holiday—he thought very little could surprise him anymore. Tonight, he was wrong.

Roaring through the streets of Boston, he squealed his tires taking a hard right up Park Street, heading for the golden-domed State House, then threw his cruiser left onto Beacon, flying past the Common and the

Public Garden. At the last minute, he almost blew it—tried to head up Arlington straight for Marlborough, then realized that Marlborough was one way the wrong way. Like any good Masshole driver, he slammed on his brakes, cranked the wheel hard, and laid on his horn as he sliced across three lanes of traffic to stay on Beacon. Now his life was tougher, trying to pick up the right cross street to head up to Marlborough. In the end, he simply drove toward the white glow of floodlights and the flashing red lights of the Advanced Life Support ambulance.

Arriving at the corner of Marlborough and Gloucester, Bobby processed many details at once. Blue sawhorses and Boston PD cruisers already isolated one tiny block in the heart of Back Bay. Yellow crime-scene tape festooned several brownstone houses, and uniformed officers were taking up position on the corners. The ALS ambulance was now on-scene; so were several vans from the local media.

Things were definitely starting to rock and roll.

Bobby double-parked his Crown Vic just outside a blue sawhorse, jumped out the door, and jogged around to his trunk. Inside, he had everything a well-trained police sniper might need for a party. Rifle, scope, ammo, black BDUs, urban camo BDUs, ghillie hood, body armor, changes of clothing, snacks, water, a bean bag, night-vision goggles, binoculars, range finder, face paint, Swiss Army knife, and flashlight. Local police probably kept spare tires in their trunks; a state trooper could live out of his cruiser for a month.

Bobby hefted up his rucksack and immediately started assessing the situation.

In contrast to other SWAT teams, Bobby's tactical team never arrived en masse. Instead, his unit consisted of thirty-two guys located all over the state of Massachusetts, from the fingertip of Cape Cod to the foothills of the Berkshire Mountains. Headquarters was Adams, Mass., in the western half of the state, where Bobby's lieutenant had taken the call from Framingham Communications and made the decision to deploy.

In this case, a domestic barricade with hostages, all thirty-two guys had been activated and all thirty-two would arrive. Some would take three to four hours to get here. Others, like Bobby, made it in less than fifteen minutes. Either way, Bobby's LT prided himself on being able to get at least five officers anywhere in the state in under an hour.

Looking around now, Bobby figured he was one of those first five officers. Which meant he needed to hustle.

Most SWAT units were comprised of three teams: an entry team, a perimeter team, and snipers. The perimeter team had the primary job of securing and controlling the inner perimeter. Then came the snipers, who took up position outside the inner perimeter and served as reconnaissance—appraising the situation through their scope or binoculars, and radioing in details on the building as well as all people and movement inside. Finally, the entry team would prepare for last-resort action—if the hostage negotiator couldn't convince the suspects to come out, the entry team would storm in. Entries were messy; you prayed it didn't come to that, but sometimes it did.

Bobby's STOP team brought all those bells and whistles to the table, but they didn't specialize. Instead, given that they arrived piecemeal, they were cross-trained on all positions so they could get up and running the second boots hit the ground. In other words, while Bobby was one of the team's eight designated snipers, he wasn't looking at taking up sniping position just yet.

First goal—establish the inner perimeter. The inner perimeter was the area looking in at the scene. Establishing a good inner perimeter solved ninety percent of any tactical unit's headaches. You controlled and contained. It took at least two guys to form a perimeter, each standing on opposing corners, monitoring the diagonals.

Bobby was one guy. Now he was looking for a second. He spotted three other state police cruisers parked across the way, so he had teammates around here somewhere. Then he noticed the white van set up as command center. He jogged toward the van.

"Trooper Bobby Dodge," he announced five seconds later, climbing into the command center, setting down his gear, and thrusting out a hand.

"Lieutenant Jachrimo." The CO took his hand, handshake tight but quick. The thin-faced lieutenant wasn't from the state police, but from BPD. That didn't surprise

Bobby; the scene was technically Boston jurisdiction, plus the state police commander was probably still two hours away. While Bobby would've preferred his own LT, he was trained to play nice with others—up to a point, of course.

Jachrimo had a white board up in front of him and was making a Gantt chart in the upper left-hand corner. "Position?" the CO asked Bobby.

"Sniper."

"Can you hold a perimeter?"

"Yes, sir."

"Great, great, great." Lieutenant Jachrimo broke away from the white board long enough to stick his head out of the van and yell at a Boston uniform, "Hey. Hey, you. I need the phone company. Understand? Use your radio, call in to dispatch and get the goddamn phone company, 'cause nothing in this van is working, and you can't really have a command post if it doesn't command. Got it?"

The uniform went flying, and Jachrimo returned his harried attention to Bobby. "Okay, so what do you know?"

"Domestic barricade, male subject believed armed with a gun, wife and child also

on the premises." Bobby repeated the message he'd received on his pager.

"Suspect's name is Jimmy Gagnon. Mean
anything to you?"

Bobby shook his head.

"Just as well." Jachrimo finished his
Gantt chart, then started an overhead
sketch of the neighborhood on the lower
part of the white board. "So here's where
we're at. Woman called nine-one-one
shortly after eleven-thirty. Claimed to be
Catherine Gagnon, Jimmy's wife. Said her
husband was drunk and threatening her and
their son with a handgun. The nine-one-one
operator tried to hold her on the line, but
there was some kind of disturbance and the
call was disconnected. About sixty seconds
later, nine-one-one received a call from a
neighbor reporting sounds of gunfire.

"The call came into headquarters, but
our guys are already out on a situation in
Revere, so I kicked it to Framingham Communications, who contacted your lieutenant. Your unit's serving as the primary,
maybe for the whole show, maybe until our
guys wrap up the party in Revere. Don't
know. As of this moment, we have uniforms
securing the external perimeter. There are

men posted, here, here, and here, and cars positioned here and here to block off the connecting streets." Jachrimo made a series of Xs on his sketch, and that quickly, one block of brownstones was cordoned off from the surrounding neighborhood.

"The Gagnons occupy the top four levels of unit number four-fifteen. Uniforms have already evacuated the residents below their unit, as well as the residents of the brownstones on either side. We haven't had contact with anyone inside the residence yet, which, frankly, doesn't make me happy. As far as I'm concerned, we should've had the inner perimeter secured ten minutes ago and the hostage negotiators here eight minutes ago. But hey, that's just me."

"Manpower?"

"Troopers Fusilli, Adams, and Maroni are already on-scene. They're scoping the building now, looking to form a very tight perimeter, probably inside the building. I got one officer tracking down blueprints and another—hopefully—getting me the goddamn phone company."

"Intel from the neighbors?"

"According to the first-floor unit owner, the Gagnons did significant work on the place in the past five years. The top level of the brownstone was converted into cathedral ceilings for the fourth floor, where they apparently have one helluva master bedroom, with a walk-out balcony. Level one contains a small, one-bedroom unit, in addition to the lobby, which features an elevator that goes up to the second floor and the entrance to the Gagnon residence, as well as a staircase which reaches every level of the townhouse. The basement has been finished into a two-bedroom unit. We evacuated the couple that lives there and they told us exactly nothing; they have no idea about crawl spaces in the building, fire escapes, nada. It's an old building, though, so there's bound to be a few surprises.

"It would seem that the Gagnons keep to themselves, and whatever parties they've had, they haven't invited their neighbors. Couple has a reputation for its fights and we've been called out before for domestic disputes. First time there's been mention of a gun, though, so that's a fresh kick in the pants. Is it her? Is it him? Hell if I know. Mostly, it just sucks for the kid. So that's where we are and that's what we got."

The lieutenant's spiel ground to a halt just

in time. Phone company had arrived. Another one of Bobby's teammates as well.

"Perfect," the lieutenant declared. He stabbed one finger at the new trooper. "You, inner perimeter. And you," the finger moved to Bobby. "Find a position. I want intel on that house. Where's the husband, where's the wife, where's the kid? And better yet, is anyone still alive? Because it's been over thirty minutes now, and we haven't heard a thing."

Stepping out of the command center, Bobby picked up his pace. Now charged with a task, he had choices to make. He ran through them quickly.

First off, proper gear. He went with city camo, a battle dress uniform blended with shades of gray. Solid black provided too much of a silhouette. Camo blends, on the other hand, gave the eye a sense of depth, allowing the wearer to sink into the surrounding environment.

Over the top of his BDUs came soft body armor. The rest of his team would be wearing Kevlar with boron plates, but that kind of heavy body armor was too cumbersome for sniping. Bobby needed to be able to move quickly, while also maintaining an often uncomfortable pose for hours on end. For him, a flak vest and helmet would do.

Next up, rifle, scope, and ammo. Bobby slung his Sig Sauer 3000 over his shoulder, then went with a Leupold 3-9X 50mm variable scope. His scope was already zeroed to one hundred yards, standard setup for a law enforcement sniper, versus military snipers, who zeroed their scopes to five hundred yards. The military guys, however, were running around in ghillie suits and crawling through swamps. Bobby's job rarely got that interesting.

Briefly, Bobby debated night-vision goggles, but given that the area was lit up like the Fourth of July, he passed.

That left ammo. He selected two: Federal Match Grade .308 Remington 168-grain slugs, and Federal Match Grade .308 Remington 165-grain bullets with bonded tips. The 168-grain slugs were standard issue; the 165-grain bullets were better for shooting through glass. Given that it was a cold night and the residence in question seemed buttoned up tight, he'd start with a bonded tip in the chamber. When you only got one shot, you had to play the odds.

Next Bobby pared down his rucksack to three bottles of water, two PowerBars, a bean bag, his binoculars, and a range finder. He closed his trunk and turned immediately to the street.

He had his gear, now he needed a position.

Back Bay was an old, wealthy area of Boston. The tall, narrow brownstones boasted granite arches, elaborate wrought-iron balconies, and expansive bay windows. Broad shade trees, beautiful in the summer but now mere silhouettes, cast their skeletal canopies over BMWs, SAABs, and Mercedes, while in the glow of the police floodlights, gray veins of leafless ivy climbed up redbrick walls and caressed intricate window casings. It was a beautiful city block, grand, self-contained, slightly arrogant.

Bobby could work his entire life and still not be able to afford to *park* on a street like this, let alone live here. Funny how some people could seemingly have every advantage in life and still be so royally fucked up.

Distance would not be a problem, he determined. The brownstones sat shoulder to shoulder, with only fifty yards between one side of the street and the other. Angle was more of a consideration. Anything greater than forty-five degrees and the ballistics grew problematic. The brownstone in question appeared to be five stories, plus a daylight basement. The CO had commented, however, that the fifth floor had essentially become a vaulted ceiling for a fourth-story master bedroom.

That would fit what Bobby saw now—lights blazing on the fourth story, where there appeared to be a balcony with an elaborate wrought-iron railing.

He crossed the street, where he could get a better view. Space between the wrought-iron rails of the balcony appeared to be approximately three inches. No problem, given he trained monthly to nail a one-inch kill zone. Angle, however, became tricky; shooting straight through the three-inch gap would be a piece of cake. Trying to shoot up or shoot down more than thirty degrees, however . . .

Bobby definitely had to get off the ground.

Bobby eyed the four-story brownstone directly across from the Gagnons' and moments later was banging on the front door. While Lieutenant Jachrimo had told him uniforms had already evacuated area residents, Bobby wasn't surprised when a bright-eyed older man in a dark green robe immediately threw open the old wooden door; it was amazing how many people wouldn't leave their houses, even when surrounded by heavily armed men.

"Hey," the man said. "Are you a cop? Because I already told the other one I wasn't leaving."

"I need access to the top floor," Bobby said.

"Is that a rifle?"

"Sir, this is official police business. I need access to the top floor."

"Right. Top floor's the master bedroom. Oooh." The man's eyes went wide. "I get it. My balcony's across from the Gagnons'. You must be a police sniper. Ooooh, can I get you anything?"

"Just the top floor, sir. Immediately."

The man was dying to please. George Harlow was a consultant, he informed Bobby as he hastily led the way up a sweeping central staircase. He was almost always on the road, pure dumb luck he'd been home tonight at all to let Bobby in. His brownstone was smaller, not quite as nice as the others, but he owned the whole damn thing. Drove his condominium neighbors nuts speculating what the single-family dwelling must be worth. Why, just last month, a single-family townhouse in Back Bay sold for nearly ten million dollars. Ten million dollars. Yep, George's lush of a father hadn't left him such a bad inheritance after all. Of course, the property taxes were killing him.

Could George please touch the police rifle?

Bobby said no.

They arrived at the bedroom. The vast space bore hardly any furniture, let alone art on the walls. The man must travel a lot, because Bobby had seen hotel rooms with more personality. The front wall was all glass, however, with sliders right in the middle. Perfect.

"Kill the lights," he requested.

Mr. Harlow nearly giggled as he complied.

"Do you have a table I could use? Nothing fancy. And a chair."

Mr. Harlow had a card table. Bobby set it

up while his host rounded up a metal folding chair. Bobby's breathing had accelerated. The climb up four flights? Or the
adrenaline of a night that was about to officially begin?

He had now been on-scene for sixteen
minutes, not bad time, but not great. More
guys had probably already arrived. The
perimeter was getting fine-tuned. Soon
another officer would show up to serve as
spotter, providing two pairs of eyes. Then
would come the crisis negotiation team, finally making contact.

Bobby set up his Sig Sauer on the table.
He cracked the sliders one inch, just
enough for the tip of his rifle. Then he sat
down in Mr. Harlow's metal chair, turned on
the radio mounted in his flak vest, and
started to talk into the microphone/receiver
that was tucked inside his ear and worked
off the vibrations of his jawbone.

"This is Sniper One, reporting in."

"Go ahead, Sniper One," Lieutenant
Jachrimo answered back.

Bobby put his eye to the scope, and finally met the Gagnons.

Chapter

3

I see the back of a white male subject, approximately six feet tall, short brown hair, dark blue shirt, standing approximately four feet inside a pair of French doors on the front side of the building, which I'm going to call side A of level four. The French doors are approximately forty inches across, opening outward, and are the third opening across. Opening one of level four is a double-hung window, approximately thirty inches across and seven feet tall. Opening two is another double-hung window, approximately twenty-five inches across, seven feet tall. Opening four, side A, level four, is a final double-hung window, twenty-five inches across, seven feet tall."

Bobby reported in the details of the Gagnons' fourth floor while keeping his eyeon the lone male subject. The man didn't move. Watching someone, looking for something? Both of the man's hands were in front of him, so Bobby couldn't tell if he was armed.

Using binoculars now, Bobby scanned for a woman and child, but came up empty.

The room appeared to be a bedroom with a king-sized bed planted squarely in the middle of the space, lined up parallel to the French doors. The bed was one of those elaborate, wrought-iron affairs with gauzy white fabric draped every which way. Behind the bed he could see a row of white-painted folding doors. Probably a closet. Then, over to the left, he could make out an alcove where there appeared to be another doorway. Master bath? Sitting area?

The room was large, with many hiding spaces. That made life interesting for everyone.

Bobby tried to adjust his binoculars to penetrate the shadows of the left-hand alcove, without any luck. Briefly, he scanned the other lit windows of the brownstone, but didn't encounter any signs of other occupants.

So where were the wife and child? Hidden in the drapes of fabric swathing the bed? Tucked inside a closet? Already dead on the floor?

Bobby could feel his stomach starting to tighten with tension. He forced himself to slowly breathe in, then out. Focus. Be part of the moment, but outside of the moment. Detach.

Do you know the difference between a shooter and a sniper? A shooter has a pulse. A sniper doesn't.

Bobby prepared for the long haul: He fine-tuned his rifle stand, working the stock of his rifle into the bean bag until it achieved perfect height. He moved the chair until he could lean into the table, wedging the butt of his rifle squarely into the curve of his shoulder. When the rifle felt good, tight but comfortable against his body, like another appendage, a third arm, he leaned forward and found the spot weld—the place where his cheek met the stock and his eye met the scope in such perfect alignment that the entire world suddenly seemed to fill the crosshairs. He could see anything, he could shoot anything.

He studied once again the lone male subject, now peering over the edge of the wrought-iron bed.

Bobby chambered a bonded-tip slug and slowly placed the crosshairs of his scope on the back of the man's head. His breathing was shallow, his pulse steady. He lined up his shot without a single tremor in his hand.

Police snipers practiced one thing only— to immediately incapacitate a subject who may have his finger on a trigger. Basically, month in, month out, Bobby trained to sever a man's brain stem.

He was satisfied with his position. Angle was easy, distance manageable. He would incur minor deflection from the glass of the French doors, but nothing that couldn't be handled by the 165-grain ammo. With the target stationary, he did not need to worry about inducing lead, and at a distance this short, weather and wind were not relevant factors.

He pulled away from the scope, careful not to disturb the rifle, and with his right

hand made notes in his logbook. He detailed his ammo, his scope setting, and his
setup. Then he picked up his binoculars,
which provided a wider field of view, and
again, careful not to disturb his rifle, continued monitoring the scene.

The man had moved slightly toward the
foot of the bed. Bobby had a sense of growing tension, a force building to a crescendo.
He couldn't place why, but then he got it.

The way the man was standing, his
shoulders squared off, his elbows jutting
out, his feet slightly apart. It was a dominat-
ing pose, a man puffing himself up to appear even bigger and stronger. Bobby bet if
he could see the man's face now, it would
be wearing an ugly snarl, a red-mottled look
of rage.

Again, Bobby searched for signs of the
wife and child, and again came up empty.
Somewhere in that room, though, or the
man would be moving. Bobby wished he
could see the man's face.

With nothing immediately happening,
Bobby returned to diagramming the building for his team. Following protocol, he labeled each side of the brownstone with a
letter, A, B, C, or D. Given that the brown-

stone had adjoining units on both sides and the back, that left only the front, which he labeled A. Then he numbered each level of the townhouse, one through five, plus basement. Finally, he recorded each opening of side A, describing whether it was a window or door, giving its approximate size and numbering it left to right starting with the number one.

This yielded a uniformed chart for everyone to follow. The man was standing in front of French doors, side A, level four, opening three, or in quick shorthand when things got hopping, lone male A-four-three. No sorting through whose left or whose right. In three quick coordinates, boom, you got the job done.

The diagram completed, Bobby did his own personal check, things he'd learned from years on the job. Any sign of advanced preparation in the home? Doors barricaded, slats of wood nailed across windows? Any sign of someone trying to hide misdeeds? Blinds pulled, or furniture blocking the view, etc.? Advanced preparation was a warning sign. So were shots fired out the window or open threats of violence.

So far, everything remained quiet. No one

was visible in the entire building except a lone male subject, standing four feet inside French doors, A-four-three.

Bobby took the binoculars away from his eyes and returned to viewing the room through the scope of his rifle.

With the sliders cracked he was getting a cold breeze, chilling his face and stiffening his fingers. When a spotter showed up, he'd have the guy close the sliders, but sit close enough to crack them again at a moment's notice. For now, he was okay, though. His breathing was steady, his muscles relaxed. He was finding that zone. Calm but prepared. Alert but relaxed. Aim small, miss small. He wasn't even really thinking about the card table anymore, or the cold November wind, or the fact that Mr. Harlow still lingered in the doorway behind him, eager for some kind of show.

Soon, the hostage negotiator would arrive, get the subject on the phone, and try to work out a peaceful resolution. If no one was hurt yet, the negotiator would probably convince the man to quit now, while the worst he would suffer was a little embarrassment. If the family was injured, or worse, dead, then things would get trickier.

But the crisis management team was good. Just last year, Bobby had watched the lead negotiator, Al Hanson, convince three escaped felons to surrender peacefully, when all three criminals were facing life in prison and had nothing to lose by shooting it out.

Afterwards, Bobby's LT had gone up to each prisoner, clapped them on the shoulder, and thanked them sincerely for giving up.

These situations always started with so much adrenaline, testosterone, and generally nutty hype. Then Bobby's team showed up and worked on toning it all back down. No reason for rash action. No need for violence. Let's just go through the paces, my man, and it'll all work out fine.

Movement. Across the street, the suspect suddenly twisted, walking to the right in an agitated fashion. Bobby finally caught a glimpse of a handgun.

"White male subject, moving in front of French doors, A-four-three. I see what appears to be a nine-millimeter handgun in right hand. White female," Bobby declared suddenly, voice slightly triumphant. "Long black hair, dark red top, appears to be kneeling or sitting behind bed, fifteen feet inside French doors, A-four-three. White child, dark hair, pressed against the female. Small, maybe two or three years of age."

Lieutenant Jachrimo's voice came over the receiver. "Is the woman or child moving? Any sign of injuries?"

Bobby frowned. Harder to tell. The man cut in front of his view again, pacing rapidly now, right hand waving his gun. Bobby zeroed in on the man's weapon, seeking more details. Tough, with the man moving. Bobby zoomed back out, trying to get a sense of the lone male subject instead, how he held the nine-millimeter, how he moved around the room. An experienced gun handler? An agitated amateur? Also hard to determine.

The man shifted right and now Bobby could tell that the woman was yelling something. She had the child—a boy, maybe?—held tight against her, his face turned into her chest, her hands covering his ears.

Things were happening. Sudden, fast. Bobby couldn't tell what had sparked the commotion, but now the man was screaming. Through the scope Bobby could see the spittle flying from the man's lips, muscles cording on his neck. It was surreal: to watch such explosive rage and never hear a sound.

The woman stood up, child still clutched against her chest. Now she'd stopped yelling, seeming to have reached some sort of conclusion. The man screamed violently; she simply stared at him.

Abruptly, the man leveled his gun at the woman's head. He held out his left hand, as if motioning for the child.

"Male subject drawing down on female," Bobby heard himself report. "Male subject pointing a handgun—"

The man still had his gun aimed at the woman's head, but was now rounding the bed, fast, furious. She didn't say a word, didn't budge a step. Then the man was *right there,* yelling ferociously and, with his left hand, tugging at the child.

The boy peeled away from his mother's chest. Bobby had a sudden, fleeting glimpse of a small, pale face with dark, wild eyes. The kid was scared out of his mind.

"Male subject has child. Male subject is shoving child across the room."

Away from his mother. Away from whatever was about to happen next.

Bobby was in the *now,* part of the moment, but outside the moment. He worked the scope, minor adjustments as natural to him as taking a breath. Shifting slightly left, inducing a fraction of lead as the male subject pushed his son to the end of the bed, then stepped back toward his wife.

The child disappeared into the gauze of floating white fabric. Now it was just the man and woman, husband and wife. Jimmy Gagnon was no longer screaming, but his chest jerked up and down, breathing hard.

The woman finally spoke. Her lips were easy to follow in the magnified world of Bobby's Leupold scope.

"What now, Jimmy? What's left?"

Jimmy suddenly smiled, and in that smile, Bobby knew exactly what was going to happen next.

Jimmy Gagnon's finger tightened on the trigger. And from fifty yards away, in the darkened bedroom of a neighbor's townhouse, Bobby Dodge blew him away.

Panting. Breathing hard. Feeling an unbearable tightness suddenly burst, then deflate his chest. Bobby pulled his finger away from the trigger, jerking back the way a man might release a live rattler. His eye remained on the scope, however. He saw the woman rush to the end of the bed and scoop up the child, saw her turn the boy's head away from the spray of his father's body.

For a moment, mother and son stood entwined, one unit of curving arms and legs, the side of her cheek pressed against the top of his head. Then the woman's head came up. She gazed across the street. She peered into her neighbor's home. She looked straight at Bobby Dodge and he felt a tingle he couldn't explain.

"Thank you," the woman mouthed.

Bobby stood up from the table, realizing for the first time that he was breathing very hard and his face was covered in sweat.

"Holy crap," Mr. Harlow said from the doorway.

Then the rest of the world finally came into focus. Footsteps pounding. Sirens blaring. Men coming. Some for her, some for him.

Bobby tucked his hands behind his back, planted his feet, and waited as he was trained. He had done his job. He had taken a life to save a life.

Now the shit would hit the fan.

Chapter 4

The entry team descended upon the house, confirming one male subject, now missing half of his head. Then the entry team beat a hasty retreat. The residence no longer belonged to STOP. It had just become a crime scene.

The call went out to the DA's office, Suffolk County. An ADA got roused out of bed, assembled a task force of investigators, and arrived on the scene. Bobby's Sig Sauer was entered into evidence. His teammates were immediately sequestered and interviewed as witnesses.

Bobby got to sit in the back of a patrol car, technically not in trouble, but feeling very much like a truant kid.

Media was already gathering outside the yellow crime-scene tape. Television lights were blazing, while reporters vied for the best position. So far, the DA's office had everything wrapped up tight. The body had already been transported from the scene; Bobby was sheltered inside the patrol car.

Name of the game was never to provide too many visuals. Denied on the ground, however, the media would soon take to the air.

His LT, John Bruni, arrived at the scene. He came over to the cruiser and clapped Bobby on the shoulder.

"How you feeling?"

"All right."

"These things are always lousy."

"Yeah."

"Employee Assistance Unit will be here shortly. They'll explain your rights, give you some support. You're not the first guy this has happened to, Bobby."

"I know."

"Just answer what you feel like answering. If you get uncomfortable, call it a day.

The union provides a lawyer, so don't be afraid to ask for legal counsel."

"Okay."

"We're here for you, Bobby. Once part of the team, always part of the team."

Bruni had to go. Probably to check in with Public Affairs, which would soon be making a statement to the press: *Tonight an unidentified officer was involved in a fatal shooting. The DA has taken over investigation of the incident. No comment at this time.*

And so it would go. Bobby had seen it happen once before. A trooper was ambushed when making a routine patrol stop. Two Hispanic males in a beat-up Honda opened fire on the officer. He fired back, wounding one and killing the other. The officer had gone on immediate paid leave, disappearing from the barracks, disappearing from life, while the press tried his case in the papers and the Hispanic community accused him of racism. A month later, the DA's office ruled that the case didn't merit criminal charges—maybe the fact that the officer had a bullet lodged in his upper arm helped. The press never seemed to notice, though. A brother of the fatally shot man launched a civil suit against the officer, and last Bobby knew, the trooper was dealing with a million-dollar lawsuit.

He never returned to duty. And most people in Boston probably did think he was a racist.

Was it bad to have just killed a man, then sit here worrying about what that meant for your career? Was that totally self-absorbed? Inappropriate? Or was it just the way these things went?

Bobby was thinking of the woman again. Slender. Pale. Holding her child tight against her body. *Thank you,* her lips had said. He had shot her husband in front of her and her kid and she had thanked him for it.

Fresh knock on the window. Stupid, since the car door was open. Bobby looked up and saw one of his teammates, Patrick Loftus.

"Hell of a night," Loftus said.

"Yeah."

"Sorry I missed it. Just got here a few minutes ago. When all was said and done." Loftus lived on the Cape. Probably only an hour away. So the shooting had happened that fast. Bobby realized for the first time that he had no idea what the hour was. He'd gotten the call, jumped in his car, set up his rifle. The whole thing was already a blur in his mind, a series of actions and reactions. He came, he saw, he did. Holy shit, he had killed a man. Honestly, blown off half a man's head.

Thank you, the woman said, *thank you.*

Bobby leaned out of the car.

"Cameras?" he asked.

"Got 'em covered."

"Good." Bobby vomited onto the street.

"I'm really sorry," Loftus said quietly.

Bobby leaned back against the seat. He closed his eyes. "Yeah," he said. "So am I."

The EAU guys came next. Fellow officers, sort of like a peer support group. They walked him through the process. Investigators from the DA's office would be interviewing him shortly. He should answer the questions truthfully, but as briefly as possible. He had the right to an attorney—the State Police Association of Massachusetts, SPAM, would pay for his lawyer. He had the right to end questioning whenever he felt uncomfortable. He had the right against self-incrimination.

He should be aware that the guidelines for use of deadly force stated that lethal force was appropriate if you felt your own life, or someone else's, was in immediate danger. Something to consider, you know, when the investigators asked their questions.

The ADA would probably need at least two weeks to study the events. Bobby's gun would be examined, tapes of the radio conversation between him and the command post analyzed. They would do ballistic tests at the crime scene and take statements from everyone, including Bobby's teammates, the woman and child, and good old Mr. Harlow.

At the end of the investigation, it would be up to the DA's office to decide if the facts warranted criminal charges. If it was a righteous shoot, then Bobby was okay. Public Affairs would issue a statement, the DA would issue a statement, and Bobby would be back in action. If the DA did decide to press criminal charges . . .

Well, let's not put the cart before the horse.

From here on out, Bobby was on paid administrative leave. It wouldn't be a bad idea to use that time to come to terms with tonight. Maybe talk to some other guys who'd been through it—the EAU could arrange it. Maybe even, if he wanted, sign up for some post-critical-incident counsel-

ing. The EAU had a shrink they highly recommended and it would look good on
Bobby's record.

Killing someone was a big deal, even for
a cop. The sooner he faced it, the sooner he
could get on with his life.

Then the EAU guys were gone, and the
investigators took their place.

It was three-thirty in the morning now.
Bobby had been up for nearly twenty-two
hours. He followed the investigators to the
DA's office, where they all had steaming
cups of fresh coffee and sat around a
scarred wood table, like old friends shooting the shit.

Bobby wasn't fooled. He was bottomed
out and bone tired from buckets of adrenaline dumping suddenly into his blood-
stream, but he was still a sniper, a man who
could narrow the world down to a single set
of crosshairs, and maintain that concentra-
tion for hours.

They all began the dance.

Where was Bobby when he got the call?

Boston Beer Garden, he answered, and
immediately lost points. He added he'd
been drinking Coke, the bartender would
verify, and regained some ground.

He'd started work at what time today? He'd ended his shift at what hour? A fifteen-hour shift earned him a frown; the sidebar that he was trained to handle long hours didn't seem to rate him a second chance.

How had he gotten to the scene, how fast was his response time, what could he recall of his conversation with Lieutenant Jachrimo? They were searching here, looking for something, so Bobby's answers grew shorter. He felt the threat in the conversation, but couldn't identify the source. The investigators finally moved on, but the collegial atmosphere was fast eroding. Questions were sharper now, and answers harshly judged.

He had to explain how he'd determined to access Mr. Harlow's residence. He described his setup on the card table, why he chose to crack the window, why he went with bonded-tip ammo.

What did he see in the house, who did he see in the house?

Bobby did better here. White male subject, white female subject. Didn't give them names, and didn't give them presumed identities such as husband, wife, or child.

He was as neutral as possible. He'd shot a man, but it was nothing personal.

Finally, they got to the heart of the matter. Did he know the victim was James Gagnon?

And for the first time, Bobby paused.

Victim. Interesting choice of words. The man was no longer a suspect, someone who had pointed his gun at his own wife and tightened his finger on the trigger; he was a victim. Bobby thought now might be a good time to ask for that lawyer. But he didn't.

He answered as truthfully as he could. Lieutenant Jachrimo had identified the family as possibly being the Gagnons, but at the time of the incident, Bobby had received no verification of those names.

The investigators sat back again. Mollified? Suspicious? Hard to tell. They wanted to know if he'd met the wife, personally, socially. Had he spoken to her during the incident?

No, Bobby said.

Now it was time for the nitty-gritty. What made him decide to fire his weapon? Had he been okayed for use of deadly force by the CO?

No.

Had the victim made any verbal threats toward Bobby or another officer?

No.

Had the victim made any verbal threats toward his wife?

Not that Bobby had heard.

But the victim had a gun.

Yes.

Did he fire it?

There were reports of gunfire.

Before Bobby arrived. But what about afterwards? Did Bobby actually see the victim fire his weapon?

His finger was pulling the trigger.

So he fired his weapon?

Yes. No. Not sure. He was firing, I was firing; it all happened so fast.

So the victim didn't fire his weapon?

Not sure.

So possibly, the victim was just pointing his gun? Hadn't he been pointing the weapon for a while?

The man's finger was on the trigger.

But did he squeeze it? Did he try to shoot his wife?

I believed there was an immediate threat.

Why, Trooper Dodge, why?

Because of the way the man smiled.

Bobby couldn't say that. He said instead, "The subject stood two feet away from the woman with a nine-millimeter pointed at her head and his finger moving on the trigger. I perceived that to be an immediate and compelling threat."

Do you really think a man would kill his wife with his kid still in the room?

Yes, sir, I believed he would.

Why, Trooper Dodge, why?

Because sometimes, sir, shit like that happens.

The investigators finally nodded, then repeated the same questions all over again. Bobby knew how it worked. More times you made a man tell his story, the more he might trip up. Lies growing more embellished, truth more strained. They were giving Bobby rope and waiting to see if he'd hang himself with it.

At six-thirty they finally gave up. A new day was dawning outside the stifling conference room, and the collegial air returned. They were sorry they had to ask all these questions, you know. It was just a matter of procedure. Unfortunate night. Bad for everyone. But it looked good for Bobby that he was cooperating. They appreciated that very much. Everyone just wanted to get to the bottom of this, you understand. The sooner they got to the truth, the sooner everyone could put it behind them.

They'd have more questions. You know, don't go too far.

Bobby nodded wearily. He pushed back his chair and, when he went to rise, swayed on his feet. He saw one guy notice, narrowing his eyes suspiciously.

And Bobby had the sudden, disconcerting urge to sock the man in the gut. He left the room and found his lieutenant waiting for him in the hall.

"How did it go?" Lieutenant Bruni asked.

Bobby said honestly, "Not that good."

The sun was out, the sky bright, by the time Bobby turned into the building where Susan lived. The morning commute was already on. He heard squawks over his radio, describing congested traffic, motor vehicle accidents, and disabled cars parked in breakdown lanes. Day was happening. City dwellers emerging from their bolt-locked cages to crowd sidewalks and jam coffee houses.

He stepped out of his cruiser, inhaled a deep gulp of city air—cold, diesel-filled, cement-laced—and for one surreal moment, it felt to him as if the night had never happened. *This* moment was real, the building, the parking garage, the city, but the shooting had been fake, just a particularly powerful dream. He should change back into his uniform now, climb into his cruiser and get to work.

A guy walked by. Took one look at Bobby, standing dazed in his sweat-stained urban camos, and hastily picked up his step. That shook Bobby out of his funk.

He grabbed his trusty rucksack and headed for Susan's unit.

She answered on his second knock, wearing a pink chenille bathrobe and looking flushed from the warm comfort of her bed. Practices had a tendency to run deep into the night, and she often slept late the next morning.

She gazed at Bobby, all sleep-tousled blonde hair, rosy skin, and heavy-lidded gray eyes, and her face immediately softened into a smile. "Hey, sweetheart," she began, before the last of the sleep left her, and her instant pleasure gave way to immediate concern. "Shouldn't you be at work? Bobby, what's wrong?"

He walked into her apartment. There

were so many things he should say. He could feel the words building in the unbearable tightness of his chest. Susan was a concert cellist with the Boston Symphony Orchestra. They had met, of all places, in a local pub.

Bobby knew nothing about classical music. He was all sports bars, pickup games of basketball, and ice-cold beer. In contrast Susan was billowy skirts, long walks in the park, and tea at the Ritz.

He'd asked her out anyway. She'd surprised them both by saying yes. Days had turned into weeks, weeks into months, and now they'd been seeing each other for over a year. Sometimes he thought it was only a matter of time until she moved into his little three-story row house in South Boston. He allowed himself to think of weddings and babies and twin rockers at the retirement home.

He'd never quite brought himself to ask the question yet. Maybe because he still had too many moments like this one, when he stood before her sweaty, grimy, and covered with a night's work, and instead of feeling grateful to see her, he was shocked she let him through the door.

Her world was such a beautiful place.

What the hell was she doing with a guy like him?

"Bobby?" she asked quietly.

He couldn't find the words. None would move his lips. None would come close to releasing the pent-up emotions tightening his chest.

Oh God, that poor kid. To watch his father die.

Why had the bastard made him do it? Why had Jimmy Gagnon just ruined Bobby's life?

He moved without ever knowing he was moving. His hands were sliding under Susan's robe, trying desperately to find bare skin. She murmured something. Yes, no, he never really heard. He had her robe off, and was skimming his fingers across the thin lace that covered her breasts, while burying his face in the curve of her neck.

She had beautiful fingers. Long, delicate, but shockingly strong. Fingers that could coax a fine wooden instrument into the sweetest sounds. Now those fingers were on his back, finding the knots that corded his muscles. She had his shirt off, was working on his pants.

She was too slow. He was hungry, desperate. He needed things he couldn't name but knew instinctively she could give to him.

Funny how he'd always been delicate with her before. Her skin was fine china, her beauty too pure to tarnish. Now he ripped the gauzy nightgown from her body. His teeth sank into her rounded shoulder. His hands gripped her buttocks, pushed her up, lifting her against him.

They went down in a tangle on the hardwood floor. He got the bottom, she claimed the top. Her mouth was devouring his chest, her small, pale body writhing against his broad, dark frame. Light and shadow, good and bad.

She was poised above him, she was pushing down onto him. Her shoulders were thrown back, her breasts thrust out. She needed him. He needed her. Light and shadow, good and bad.

At the last minute, he saw the woman.

At the last minute, he saw the child.

Susan came with a guttural scream. He caught her as she collapsed upon his body, and he lay there withered on the floor, feeling a darkness that went on without end.

Chapter 5

Dr. Elizabeth Lane was thinking about getting a small dog. Or maybe a cat. Hey, what about a fish? Even a four-year-old could raise fish.

She had this conversation with herself once a year. Generally, right about now, when the holidays were looming and people were talking excitedly about upcoming family gatherings, and she went home each night to an empty condo that seemed much emptier than it did in spring-filled May or hot, sunny August.

It was a stupid conversation, which she of all people should know. For one thing, she had a very nice "empty" condo. Ten-foot ceilings, sweeping bay windows with original bull's-eye molding, rooftop terrace, gleaming cherry-wood floors. Then there was the furniture she'd spent the better part of her professional life acquiring—the low-slung black leather sofa, the bird's-eye maple cabinets, the stainless steel Soho lamps. She was pretty sure puppies and silk rugs didn't make a good mix. Cats and custom woodwork didn't sound like a good match either. Though none of that ruled out fish.

For another thing, if the upcoming holidays were really all fun and games, Elizabeth's schedule wouldn't currently be so overbooked. In fact, she'd spent the majority of the past four weeks working ten-hour days trying to help her various clients devise coping strategies for just this time of year. She had to get the bulimics prepared to face the groaning Thanksgiving table. She had to get the manic-depressives medicated enough to handle the candy-cane-fueled, festively wrapped frenzy, then the inevitable shattered-ornaments, dying-fir-tree, nobody-loves-me letdown. And finally, she had to get everyone—the self-destructive, the obsessive-compulsive, the neurotic, the psychotic, *everyone*—in shape to meet their families.

That alone should make Elizabeth grateful for her quiet home. Though again, it did not rule out fish.

Truthfully, Elizabeth had a nice life. She loved her condo, loved living in the city, and most days liked her job. She was starting to approach forty, however, and not even a trained psychiatrist could stare forty in the face without feeling the weight of her baggage. The marriage that had failed. The children she'd never had. The distance she lived from her family in Chicago, which hadn't seemed so much at first, but now they were all so busy and flying was so damn *tiring* that she made the trip less and less and her parents and sister's family made the trip less and less and now it had been so long since she'd seen any of them in person, it would be awkward to go home. She'd throw them out of their own rituals and routines. She'd be the outsider, looking in.

Maybe she'd get a Siamese fighting fish. Or better yet, a ficus tree. God knows a plant would probably be a lot less offended that she ate take-out sushi almost every other night. It was a thought.

The buzzer sounded out in the front office. Elizabeth ignored it, used to the random sounds of a city office, and the buzzer sounded again. Now she frowned. It was after five, too late for deliveries, and she didn't schedule after-hour appointments on Fridays; she needed at least the pretense of having a life. The buzzer sounded a third time. Shrill. Insistent. Elizabeth finally grew curious enough to leave her office for her receptionist's desk, where she hit a few buttons on Sarah's computer and promptly saw the view from the security camera posted above the outer door.

What she saw surprised her. But then again, maybe it didn't.

Elizabeth let the man in. Minutes later, he'd mounted the steps to her second-story office. The weather outside had turned cold—they might have flurries overnight—but that wasn't the only reason this man had a dark blue Patriots cap pulled low and a thick red scarf wrapped tight. Unfortunately for the man, his eyes still gave him away.

Elizabeth had seen the same cool gray gaze just this morning, staring back at her

from the front page of the *Boston Herald.*
"State Trooper Kills Judge's Son," the
headline blazed. "Late Night Shootout
Leaves Family Devastated."

The photo had most likely been taken
without the man knowing it. His gaze, peering off in the distance, appeared stark and
grim. Elizabeth had no idea what it must feel
like to kill a man, but the officer's expression
implied that it wasn't great.

"Good evening," she said evenly, and
held out her hand. "Dr. Elizabeth Lane."

The man's grip was firm but brief. Then
he buried both his hands back into the front
pockets of his jacket. "Bobby Dodge," he
muttered. "Lieutenant Bruni said he spoke
to you."

"He thought you might be interested in
coming in."

"Should I have made an appointment?"
Bobby frowned. "I didn't think about it.
Guess I should've called first. 'Course, it's
late now, too. Maybe I should just leave."

Elizabeth smiled. "Appointments generally
help, but it just so happens that you're in luck.
My plans have been canceled at the last
minute, so as long as you're here, let's meet."

"I don't know how this works," the officer

said in a rush. "I mean, I've never gone to any shrink. I'm not even sure I believe seeing a shrink helps. But the LT said I should come, and the EAU guys said I should come, so, well, here I am."

"What do you think?"

"I think I did my job. A woman and her kid are alive today because of me. I'm not ashamed."

Elizabeth nodded, and thought that anyone who asserted that quickly that he wasn't ashamed, probably was.

She gestured to her coatrack. "Please, hang up your things and follow me."

Bobby shed his jacket, hat, and scarf. Elizabeth gestured him toward the opened door of her office. She followed behind him, already making mental notes as she went.

She'd guess his age to be mid to late thirties. Not a huge guy. Maybe five ten, one hundred and sixty pounds. He moved well, though. Tight, controlled, a man who knew his way around. His jeans were well worn, same with his navy flannel shirt. She'd bet his family was strictly blue-collar, and that Bobby had been the first to attend college. Rather than follow his father's wish for a corporate dream, he'd split the difference and joined the state police—still moving up the economic rung from his father, but not drifting too far from his roots. He ran as a hobby and felt most at home when he was in the woods.

She was guessing, of course. It was a game she liked to play with herself whenever meeting new patients. It amazed her how often she got it right.

They entered her office and Bobby immediately spotted the small leather sofa.

"I'm not gonna have to sit there, am I?"

"You could take one of the wingback chairs." Elizabeth's office contained two hunter green chairs, tucked back from the desk, and not easy to see in the dim light. Most patients spied the sofa first and had their various reactions. Elizabeth often considered rearranging her office to make the chairs more prominent, but then again, a girl had to have some fun.

Bobby took one of the chairs. He sat on the edge, knees apart, long fingers braced in front of him. He surveyed the mahogany-paneled room with his dark gray stare, absorbing all the details—the textbooks lining the shelves, the brass plaques on the wall, the Zen garden that drove the obsessive-compulsives nuts.

There was something about him that niggled at her brain, but she couldn't quite place it. He wasn't just uncommonly self-possessed, he was preternaturally . . . quiet. No undue noise, no undue movements. She imagined he'd do very well with long stretches of silence. When talking to this man, he didn't come to you, you came to him.

"Comfortable?" she asked finally.

"Not what I was expecting."

"What were you expecting?"

"Something . . . not quite this nice." By "nice," he meant wealthy. They both understood that. "You really work for the state?"

"I started working with the state police fifteen years ago. My father's a retired Chicago detective, so let's just say I have a personal interest in the field." She shrugged. "Perhaps I've never changed my rates. Shall I explain to you how this works?"

"Okay."

"I am working for the State Police of Massachusetts, not for you. As such, I have a duty to report back based upon our conversations, which limits the confidentiality of anything you tell me. On the one hand, I never report specific details. On the other hand, I am required to give my conclusions and opinions. Thus, for example, you can tell me you drink three pints of whiskey a night, and while I wouldn't necessarily repeat that, I would have to recommend that you not return to duty. Is that clear to you?"

"Watch what I say." He grunted. "Interesting approach."

"Honesty is still the best policy," Elizabeth said quietly. "I'm here to help you, or if we decide that I can't, refer you to someone who can."

Bobby just shrugged. "Fine, so what do you want me to tell you?"

Elizabeth smiled again. Opening with blatant hostility. She would've expected no less. "Let's begin with the basics." She picked up her clipboard. "Name?"

"Robert G. Dodge."

"What's the G stand for?"

"Given the limited confidentiality, I'm not saying."

"Oooh, that good? Let's see, Geoffrey?"

"No."

"Godfrey?"

"How the hell?"

"Let's just say I also don't give out my middle name. Godfrey. Family name?"

"That's what my father says."

"And your parents are?"

"My father. His name's Larry. Lawrence, actually."

"And your mother?"

"Gone."

"Gone?"

"Yeah, gone. Left. I was four or five. No, maybe six or seven. I don't know. She left."

Elizabeth waited.

"I don't think marriage to my father was going so well," Bobby added. He spread his hands as if to say, *What can you do?* Indeed, at that young age, what could he have done?

"Siblings?"

"One. Older. Name's George Chandler Dodge, so yeah, the whole family's cursed with rotten English names. Now, what does this have to do with the shooting?"

"I don't know. Does it have anything to do with the shooting?"

Bobby was on his feet. "No. None of that. *That's* why people don't like shrinks."

Elizabeth held up her hands in surrender. "Point taken. Honestly, I'm simply filling in blanks on the form. And for the record, most people like to make a little small talk first."

Bobby sat back down. He remained scowling, however, and those keen eyes of his were narrowed, assessing. She wondered how often he used that stare on people and found them wanting. She added to her mental list: Lots of acquaintances but very few friends. Does not forgive. Does not forget.

And he had lied about his mother's leaving.

"I'd like to keep this simple," he said.

"Fair enough."

"Ask what you gotta ask, I'll answer what I gotta answer, and we can both get on with our lives."

"Admirable goal."

"I'm not thinking of a lifetime plan."

"Wouldn't dream of suggesting it to you," she assured him. "Unfortunately, this isn't single-sitting work."

"Why not?"

"For starters, you didn't make an appointment and we don't have enough time to cover everything in one night."

"Oh."

"So, I'm going to suggest that we talk a little bit tonight, then meet again on Monday."

"Monday." He had to think about it. "All right," he begrudged the professional headshrinker. "I can do that."

"Perfect. Glad we got that covered." Her

voice sounded drier than she intended, but at least he smiled. He had a decent smile. It softened the hard lines of his face and put bracket lines around his eyes. She was slightly surprised to realize that when he smiled, he was one very handsome man.

"Maybe instead of talking about last night, we can talk about today," she said.

"Today?"

"Today is the first day of your life after you've shot someone. Surely that's note-worthy. Have you slept?"

"A little."

"Eaten?"

He had to think about it, then seemed genuinely surprised. "No, I guess I haven't. I went out to fetch coffee when I woke up this afternoon, but then I saw the *Boston Herald* and . . . I never got the coffee."

"Did you pick up the *Herald*?"

"Yeah."

"Read the article?"

"Enough."

"What'd you think?"

"Massachusetts State Police officers don't target civilians, not even if they're judges' sons."

"Good piece of fiction?"

"Yeah, based on the three paragraphs I read, I'd agree with that."

"You didn't read more? I would've thought you'd be more curious."

"About what happened? I don't need some reporter's account, I had box seats."

"No. About the victim. About Jimmy Gagnon."

That drew him up short. She gave him credit. She'd caught him off guard, but he took the time to consider her point. "Information is a luxury tactical units don't have," he said finally. "When I pulled the trigger last night, I didn't care about the man's name, his neighborhood, his father, or his history. I didn't know if he beat his dog or gave money to orphanages. All I knew was that the subject had a gun pointed at a woman's head and his finger on the trigger. I had to base my actions on his actions. So I did. Now none of the rest matters anymore, so why torture myself with it?"

Elizabeth smiled again. She liked Bobby Dodge. She hadn't seen so many layers of denial and rationalization in years, but she liked Bobby Dodge.

"Exercise?" she asked. "Have you worked out today?"

"No. I thought about going for a run, but with my photo plastered everyplace . . ."

"I understand. Okay, this is your assignment for the weekend. You need to start taking care of yourself physically, so you can then tend to yourself emotionally. Is there anyplace you can go, maybe your father's, maybe your brother's, where you can escape and get some rest?"

"My girlfriend's."

"And she's doing okay with this?"

"I don't know. We haven't exactly had time to chat about it."

"Well, given what's happened, you're going to need a good support network, so if I were you, I'd talk to her about it." Elizabeth leaned forward. "Last night was a big thing, Bobby. It's going to take more than twenty-four hours for you to wade through it, so first things first. Eat three well-balanced meals a day and try to get a good night's sleep. If you're feeling tense and wired, engage in some light exercise to blow off steam. Be careful, though. There's a fine line between running six miles to help yourself relax and running fifty miles to grind your thoughts into dust. You don't want to cross that line."

"I promise not to run more than forty-nine miles," he said.

"All right, then. Have a nice weekend."

"That's it? Eat, sleep, work out, and I'm cured? I can go back to work next week?"

"Eat, sleep, work out, and we'll talk more later," she corrected mildly. "But not tonight; it's too late and maybe it's even too soon for you to know everything that's on your mind. I'm going to give you my phone number. You can call me if you do feel a sudden urge to talk, otherwise I'll see you on Monday. How does three sound?"

He shrugged. "They won't let me work, so I guess my day's kinda open."

"Perfect." She rose. He rose. He didn't bolt for the door right away, like she thought he might. Instead, he just sort of stood there, looking adrift.

"Sometimes," he said abruptly, "sometimes when I think about what happened, I get really angry. Not with myself, but with the subject, for going after his wife and kid. For making me shoot him. Is that weird? To kill a man and hate him for it?"

"I'd say that reaction falls within the normal category."

He nodded, but didn't lose that unsettled

look. "Can I ask you another question? A general psychobabble sort of one?"

"By all means, allow me to babble away."

"We get called out for domestic disturbances a lot. Seems three, four times a week I'm standing in someone's yard while the wife yells at the husband or the husband screams at the wife. One thing always strikes me—that we're gonna be back. That no matter how much these people pound on one another, they always stay together. And if you do get a little rough with the boyfriend while you're loading him into the squad car, nine times out of ten, the woman, the same one who called nine-one-one and is wearing the imprint of the guy's fist, will attack us for hurting her man."

"Domestic abuse is very complex," she agreed, wondering where this was going.

"So would it be strange to kill a woman's husband and have her thank you for it?"

Elizabeth paused. "That reaction would be less common," she said slowly.

"That's what I thought."

"But that doesn't necessarily mean anything."

"It's gotta mean something, Doc, or she wouldn't have said it."

"Bobby, did you talk to Catherine Gagnon? Did you know Jimmy's wife?"

"Nah, Doc. I can honestly tell you, we've never exchanged a word."

Bobby was already out in the reception area, donning his heavy wool jacket and rewrapping his scarf. Elizabeth trailed behind him, her radar working full power but unable to penetrate his screen.

"See you Monday at three. Gee, it feels good to have an appointment." Bobby rolled his eyes, gave her a little salute, headed for the door. Moments later, she watched him walk down Boylston Street, shoulders hunched against the cold, hands buried deep into the front of his jacket.

Dr. Elizabeth Lane stood at the window long after his figure had passed from sight. Finally, she sighed.

She hated what she had to do next.

Elizabeth picked up the phone.

"Hello." A few moments passed. "So sorry. My condolences. I realize this is very awkward." And then, "Again, I'm very sorry for the timing, sir, but we need to talk."

Chapter
6

Turning into south Boston, Bobby tried to figure out what he should do next. The doctor was right; he was tired, hungry, stressed out. He should call it a night, hole up at home and get some rest. He lived on the first floor of a three-family row house— rented out the top two floors for a little income, really little actually, since one of the tenants, Mrs. Higgins, had come with the house. The previous owner had been charging her one hundred and five dollars a month for the past twenty years, and Bobby hadn't the heart to change terms on her. People were like that in Southie. They took care of one another, and even if he was still an outsider, one of the new bloods buying into the old neighborhood, he felt he should live up to the spirit of the place. So he kept Mrs. Higgins and her three cats at a hundred and five a month, and in return, she baked him chocolate chip cookies and told him stories of her grandkids.

Mrs. Higgins was going to be disappointed with him now. She'd liked Susan, approved the way everyone else in Bobby's life approved. Susan was sweet, Susan was kind. Susan was grade-A wife material all the way.

And it was over. Bobby had lied to the counselor earlier, maybe because the knowledge still stung. As of five hours ago, he and Susan were through. It had been a fantasy, and now it was done.

He'd bolted awake shortly after one this afternoon, shaky and disoriented from the sound of traffic pouring through a sun-bright room. Ohmygod, he'd overslept his alarm. He was at the wrong house, he didn't have his uniform, oh shit, he was really in for it now—

And then it came back to him. The night, the shooting, the spray of a man's brains across a distant room. He lay in Susan's bed, feeling his heart pound, and for a moment, he was afraid he was having a heart attack. He couldn't breathe, and his arm was tingling, shooting pains going straight to his chest, which continued to heave and gasp.

Then it came to him. Susan's blonde head, warm and heavy on his shoulder. The length of her bare body, pressed against his. Her left leg, crooked over his hip. Her sheets, smelling of lavender and sex.

He'd eased his arm out from beneath her, and she'd stirred, rolling over, sighing deeply, then drifting back to sleep. He'd watched her a moment longer, feeling an emotion he couldn't name. He wanted to touch her cheek. He wanted to inhale the fragrance of her skin. He wanted to curl up against her and cling to her like a child.

And he'd thought, almost wildly, that maybe if he never got up, the day would never happen. He could stay here, she could stay here, and he'd never have to tell and she'd never have to know. His world could remain warm naked skin, tousled blonde hair, and lavender-scented sheets.

He'd never have to face what he had done. He'd never have to be the man who pulled the trigger. God, life was full of shit.

Bobby got out of bed. He made it to the bathroom, where he realized he hadn't had a chance to urinate since eight last night, and pissed for what felt like forever. Then he got dressed, found the lower drawer where he kept his extra things, and as quietly as he could, emptied the contents into his rucksack.

He paused at the doorway of the bedroom. He took in the flush of Susan's cheeks, the rumpled curls of her golden hair. And Bobby felt an ache that went on and on and on.

Bobby rarely thought of his mother anymore, but when he did, it was almost always during moments like this one. When he wanted something he knew he couldn't have. When he felt a little unhinged, a little undone, a permanent outsider, always looking in.

He remembered the way the woman had held her child last night, the little boy's head tucked against her chest, her hands tight

over his ears. And he found himself wondering, in a dark, foreboding sort of way, if
his mother had ever done the same.

Two in the afternoon on a bright, sunny
day, when he should've been cruising I-93
for speeders or drunks or motorists in need
of assistance, when he should've been going through the paces the way he'd been
going through the paces for years, Bobby
stood in the doorway of his girlfriend's bedroom and felt something inside him tear. A
sharp, hard ache. A genuine physical pain.

Then the worst of it was over, and all that
was left was an already fading ache, the
echo of a ghost pain, a soft mourning for
what might have been. He could live with
that. He had, in fact, been living with that for
years.

Bobby left.

When the front door clicked shut behind
him, Susan opened her eyes. She spotted
the empty space on the bed. She called out
his name, but he was already down the hall
and it was too late to hear.

The I Street Tavern was a bar's bar, herald-
ing back to the days of smoke-filled interi-

ors and drunken games of darts, the days before bars became smoke-free, family-friendly national chains and the settings of popular sitcoms. Lots of cops hung out here. Locals, too. It was the kind of a place where a guy could finally relax.

It was also crowded on a Friday night. Bobby thought he'd have to stand, but then halfway across the low-lit room, Walter Jensen from Boston PD spotted him and immediately slid off his stool.

"Bobby, my man! Get your ass over here! Have a seat, make yourself at home. Hey, Gary, Gary, Gary. I'm buying this man a beer!"

"Coke," Bobby said automatically, making his way to the wood-scarred bar, where lots of guys were turning now, some Bobby knew, some he didn't. Behind the bar, Gary had already started pouring a Killian's.

"Beer," Walt said sternly. "Pager can't get you anymore, Bobby. Remember? As long as you're on administrative leave, the four-hundred-pound gorilla is dead. So sit back, loosen that collar, and have yourself a cold one."

"Well, shit," Bobby said with some surprise. "You're right."

So Bobby had a beer. First from Walt, who had to congratulate him on a job well done.

"I heard it straight from the horse's mouth—Lieutenant Jachrimo himself. You did what you had to do. And through glass no less. Shit, Bobby, that's some serious shooting."

Then Donny, also BPD, wanted in on the glory. He refreshed Bobby's drink and contributed his own two cents.

"Just goes to show, money doesn't buy happiness. Walt, how many times have we been out to that place? Three, four, five? We're just sorry we missed the party."

It occurred to Bobby for the first time that both Walt and Donny were also part of Boston's SWAT. "How'd it play in Revere?" he asked.

"Same old, same old," Donny said. "Guy shot up the roof of his own house. Drank a six-pack. Shot up his house some more, and then, just when the LT was getting really pissed off at the lack of progress, passed out cold. We went in and wrapped him up tight while he snored. Kind of boring really. We didn't even get to yell."

"But you've been to Back Bay?"

"Sure, Jimmy and his lady liked to spark the fireworks. He'd get drunk, she'd get mad, and off they'd go."

"He beat her?"

Donny shrugged. "We never saw and she never said. They're not the ones who called it in anyway. It was always the neighbors who complained."

"Didn't like fighting in their neighborhood?"

"Jimmy liked to throw things," Walt said. "Once he hurled a chair off the balcony and onto his neighbor's Volvo. The neighbors *really* didn't like that."

"When you were called out, what'd you do?"

"Not much. Couple of uniforms would go by, talk to the happy couple. I caught the call once. Jimmy apologized and, being of a generous sort, offered me a beer. The wife never said much of anything. Cold fish, if you ask me, though maybe if you're married to a guy like Jimmy, you learn to keep your mouth shut."

"He was violent?"

"Time I was there, I saw a hole punched through the wall," Walt said. "Wife didn't say anything, but it looked to me the exact same size as a man's fist."

"And the kid?"

"Never saw him. I think they had a nanny. Probably better for the kid."

Bobby's second beer was getting low. Donny flagged Gary down for a refill and Bobby didn't complain. "You'd think a judge's son would know better," he said tersely.

Walt shrugged. "Way I hear it, Jimmy gets in a little trouble and the judge makes a little call, and it all goes away. If only we were all so lucky."

"Didn't go away this time," Bobby said sharply.

"Nope. Fine piece of shooting, Bobby. Honestly, if it wasn't for you, that wife and kid would probably be dead right now. That was some really serious shit."

More guys were coming up. Someone clapped him on the back. Someone else bought him another beer. Bobby could no longer feel the rim of the glass coming to his lips. He was aware of sliding a little, disappearing into a vortex inside the loud, overheated bar. But at the same time, he was hyperaware—of the guys who didn't come up to him, of the eyes that peered at him from across the room, of the way some people looked over, saw his face, then quickly shook their heads.

And now he noticed something he hadn't before: the way both Walt and Donny regarded him. With respect, yeah, and awe, maybe, but also with genuine pity. 'Cause he was a cop who'd killed a man. And at the end of the day, it probably didn't matter what the DA's office finally ruled or what the department issued as its official finding. They were living in the media age, and in the media age, cops didn't get to fire their weapons. Cops were honored if they got themselves killed in the line of duty, but they were never supposed to draw their guns, not even in self-defense.

Another beer arrived. Bobby picked up the glass. He was well on his way to being completely, shit-faced drunk, when his LT found him and gave him the news.

Jesus shitting bricks. What the hell are you doing, Bobby? Half this city is watching you and you go and get drunk?"

Lieutenant Bruni was dragging him around

the corner from the tavern. He had one finger crooked around the collar of Bobby's
jacket and was literally pulling him down the
street.

"Not . . . on the . . . clock," Bobby managed to slur out. Christ, it was cold outside.
The raw November night slapped him
across the face, making him blink owlishly.

"Camera crews are coming. Someone
leaked to the goddamn press that you were
holding court in a pub. But by God, you
must have a guardian angel somewhere,
because the chatter got picked up on the
scanner and I was sent to bail you out.
Bobby, listen to me."

Lieutenant Bruni suddenly jerked to a
halt. He was panting, his breath coming in
frosty clouds that floated across Bobby's vision. He had both hands on Bobby's collar,
shaking him.

"Bobby, you're in trouble."

"No . . . shit."

"Listen to me, Bobby. Today's been a
busy day downtown. Judge Gagnon is not
happy his son is dead, and he's not about to
listen to reason or circumstance. The judge
is gunning for revenge, Bobby, and he's got
you in his sights."

Bobby couldn't think of anything to say. The world was swimming around him. Air cold upon his cheeks. The stench of beer ripe in his nostrils. He needed to shower. Christ, he needed to sleep.

Thank you, the woman had said. *Thank you.*

And then it came to him: *What a fucking bitch!* Thank him? She shouldn't be thanking him. She should've left her drunken husband years ago. Or she should've said something to calm the man an hour earlier. Or never let go of her son. Or never taunted her husband in such a way to make him smile that cold, vengeful smile. She'd been the one in that room talking to Jimmy. She should've done a million and a half things differently, so Bobby would never have had to pull the trigger. So Bobby would never have had to kill a man and ruin his own god-damn life. So Bobby wouldn't be here now, drunk and exhausted and ashamed. What the hell kind of man killed a guy in front of his own kid anyway? Oh God, what had he done?

The bitch, the bitch, the bitch.

He pulled away from his lieutenant. He walked in small, random circles, still feeling crazy with rage. He wanted to take a bat and smash every fucking window in every fucking car on this street. And then he'd take a tire iron to every door and a blade to every tire. He wanted, he wanted, he wanted . . .

Oh Christ, he couldn't breathe. His chest had locked up. His lips were open, gasping, but nothing was coming, no air would draw in. He was having another heart attack. He was dying in South Boston because it was November and he'd always known it would happen like that. The summer was safe, fall not too bad, but November . . . November was a killer month. Shit, shit, shit.

"Head between your knees. Come on, Bobby. Bend over, deep breath. You can do it. Just concentrate on the sound of my voice."

Bobby felt hands on his shoulders, hands forcing his head down. Stars were building in front of his eyes, brilliant white spots blooming in a sea of black. The stars would burst soon, fade away, and then there'd be only the black, rushing to greet him.

Then, as quickly as it started, his chest unlocked, his compressed lungs suddenly gasped to life and inhaled a rush of oxygen.

He staggered into the middle of the street, barely missed a passing car, and gulped a deep lungful of icy night air.

Bruni was still beside him, dragging him out of the traffic and talking low and fast. "Pay attention to me, Bobby. Pull yourself together and pay attention."

Bobby found a streetlight to cling to. He wrapped his arms and legs around the cold metal. Then he hung his head and fought to get a grip.

"All right," he said. "I'm together."

Bruni looked skeptical, but he grunted in acquiescence. "Do you know what a clerk-magistrate hearing is?"

"A clerk what?"

"Clerk-magistrate. The clerk-magistrate reports to the Chelsea District Court of Suffolk County. That's the civil side of the county's judicial system, versus the criminal side. You probably didn't know— hell, I sure didn't know—but any person can seek a clerk-magistrate hearing for proba- ble cause that (a) a crime has been commit- ted, and (b) that the defendant did it. If the clerk-magistrate finds in favor of probable cause, then the clerk-magistrate can issue criminal charges against the defendant, *even though it's a civil court.* Basically, any civilian can run around the DA's office and, using the clerk-magistrate, pursue their own criminal case, with their own personal lawyer and their own personal funds. You might want to ask, Bobby, what this has to do with you."

"What does this have to do with me?" Bobby asked wearily.

"At four forty-five this evening, Maryanne Gagnon, wife of Suffolk Superior Court Judge James Gagnon and mother of Jimmy Gagnon, filed a motion for a hearing with the clerk-magistrate. She's arguing there's probable cause that a murder was committed, and that you did it."

Bobby made the mistake of closing his eyes. The world promptly spun sickeningly.

"Judge Gagnon's not waiting for the DA's office, Bobby. He doesn't give a damn what their investigators find, he doesn't give a damn what the hell our department finds. He's gunning for you himself."

"I thought . . . I thought as Massachusetts state employees we were protected from all that. The Mass. Tort Claims Act. As long as we're on the job, someone can only sue the state, not us."

"Yeah, nobody can bring a civil suit against you specifically. But this isn't a civil suit, Bobby. This is a probable cause hearing to press *criminal* charges. This is a *felony.* This is, *if you're found guilty, you go to jail.* This isn't some guy looking to ease his bereavement by collecting cold hard cash, Bobby. This is a guy looking to destroy your life."

Bobby's legs gave out and he went down hard, tilting wildly to the left, before Bruni caught his arm and brought him back to center. The lieutenant joined him on the curb. They sat, tucked hidden between two cars, and for a while, neither of them spoke.

"Jesus," Bobby said at last.

"I'm sorry, Bobby. Honest to God, I've never heard of anything like this. Do you have a lawyer?"

"I thought the union provided a lawyer."

"Union can't help. This is a case brought against you personally, not the State of Mass. or the department. For this, you're on your own."

Bobby placed his head in his hands. He was too tired, too drunk for this. He felt as if November had leached all the fight out of his bones, and he had nothing left.

"It was a righteous shoot," he said.

"No one I know is saying otherwise."

"The man was going to kill his wife."

"I listened to the tape of the command center's conversation this afternoon. You followed procedure, Bobby. You documented events, you detailed what was happening, and you did what you were trained to do. Maybe no one else will ever say this, but I'm proud of you, Bobby. You had a job to do, and you didn't back down."

Bobby couldn't talk anymore. He had to pinch the bridge of his nose to quell the moisture suddenly stinging his eyes. God, he was tired. Worse, he was *drunk.*

"Will it work?" Bobby asked at last. "Guy's a judge. He's got money, he's got influence. Shit, I can't afford a real suit on what I make. Does that mean he wins?"

"I don't know," Bruni said, but he sighed heavily, which meant he knew enough.

"I don't understand. Jimmy had a gun. Jimmy was pointing it at his wife and child. Doesn't that mean anything to anyone? To even his parents?"

"It's a little complicated."

"Why, because he's rich, because he's got a house in Back Bay? Beating your family is beating your family. I don't care how much money you got!"

The lieutenant grew quiet.

"What?" Bobby demanded to know. "For God's sake, *what*?"

Bruni sighed heavily. "In the court papers, the Gagnons aren't denying that Jimmy had a gun. And they're not denying that he pointed it at his wife. But they're saying . . .

"They're saying the wife's the problem in that house, Bobby. According to the court papers, Catherine Gagnon's been abusing her son. And if Jimmy was threatening her, it was only because he was trying to save his son's life."

Chapter
7

Nathan had been throwing up all day. He was finally asleep now, a pale, exhausted form that looked much too fragile against the pile of soft blue blankets. His eyelashes formed dark smudges against his cheeks. His sunken face appeared both too small and too old for a child who was only four.

When Maryanne and James had arrived first thing this morning, allegedly having bolted out of bed the minute they saw the news, but appearing strangely well groomed for a couple who had been wrenched from sleep by word of their son's death, they had eyed Nathan carefully.

Maryanne had been performing her favorite damsel-in-distress act, of course. All oversized blue eyes, pale face, and trembling hands.

"I simply can't bear it," she'd said again and again in her overwhelming Southern lilt. Forty years of living in Boston, and the woman could still sound as if she'd stepped straight out of a Tennessee Williams play.

In between all the theatrics, however, Catherine could see both Maryanne and James making mental notes: Boy is thin, lethargic, and obviously stressed. Boy does not move toward his mother, but clings to his nanny. Boy has fresh bruise on forehead.

Twice Maryanne tried to pull Catherine aside for "a quick word." Both times, Catherine held her ground. Prudence, the English nanny, was well trained and had been imported by Catherine for her dutiful nature and inherent sense of discretion. She was still new, however, so while Catherine had given her strict orders never to leave Nathan alone with his grandparents, she had no idea how the girl would hold up under pressure. James could be very charismatic when he chose.

For all Catherine knew, he'd convince the girl to fetch him a cup of tea, and that quickly, the war would be lost.

Catherine couldn't afford that kind of risk. Not these days.

Maryanne and James had offered to let her and Nathan stay with them, of course. After the "terrible events" of the night before, surely they needed someplace to stay, somewhere far away from this "tragic scene." *For God's sake, Catherine, think of the boy. Surely, he doesn't look well.*

Finally, James had lost his patience. The minute Prudence escorted Nathan from the room—most likely to throw up again—the judge had turned on Catherine in a terrible rage.

"Don't think you're going to get away with this. Jimmy told us what was going on. Do you think you won last night? Do you think killing Jimmy solved your problems? Because I'm telling you now, they're just getting started."

And for a moment, Catherine had honestly panicked. She thought wildly of Jimmy's new security system, installed six months earlier. The power light had gone off. She swore she saw the power light off.

Then she realized that the silence had dragged on too long, that James was still regarding her with that cold accusing stare, so she drew herself up to her full height and said as regally as she could, "I don't know what you're talking about, James. Now if you'll excuse me, I have to plan a funeral for my husband."

She'd swept out of the room, heart pounding, hands trembling, and a few minutes later, heard her in-laws storm out the door. Then the house was quiet again, except for the sound of Nathan dry-heaving down the hall.

Nathan hadn't cried. Not last night, not today. He probably wouldn't. In that way, he was Catherine's son. He faced everything—the doctors' appointments, the endless needles, the horribly invasive tests—dry eyed and solemn browed. The nurses loved him, but even when they touched him, he flinched.

He would have nightmares tonight. Horrible dreams where he would thrash wildly, then wake up screaming of pain and needles and demanding that the doctors leave him alone. Sometimes, more rarely, he cried out against the darkness, complaining of suffocating and needing every light to be turned on in the house. It both fascinated Catherine and frightened her that her personal nightmare had become her son's own.

Prudence would tend to him. As had Beatrice before her, and Margaret, Sonya, Chloë, and Abigail before that. So many faces, Catherine barely recalled them all. Of course she remembered Abby, who had been the first. Jimmy had hired her when Nathan was only one week old. Catherine hadn't wanted a nanny. Catherine had thought she'd care for her son herself, even nurse. But a week later, she roamed the house in a sleepless daze, the baby continuously vomiting on her milk-stained breast. She couldn't sleep, she couldn't eat. She compulsively turned on lights.

She held this creature, so small and helpless he mewed more than he cried, and she was overwhelmed by his sheer vulnerability, by all the things that could go wrong. Babies died. They starved, they were beaten, they died of the flu. They fell out windows, they died of SIDS. They were snatched out of cars, they were lured away from playgrounds, they were abused by priests. And there were fates worse than that. She knew of those, too. How some adults were actually excited by the cries of small children. How even a baby, a weak, helpless baby, could fall into the wrong hands and through no fault of its own, become a predator's toy.

How many babies were crying of hunger right now and being beaten for their trouble? How many babies were looking up hopefully into the eyes of their caretakers and receiving a smack to the side of the head? How many infants were born each day, innocent, boundless, sweet, only to be ruined by the very people who had given them life?

She wasn't going to be able to handle this. The world was too evil and Nathan too small. He would need her and she would fail him and that would destroy her once and for all.

She couldn't bear to hold him, but she couldn't stand to put him down. She couldn't bear to love him, but she couldn't stand to be apart. She was disintegrating into a million and a half tiny little shards, a sleep-deprived new mother, roaming the halls with her newborn son and quietly falling apart.

On the seventh day, Jimmy appeared with a young girl in tow. He explained it to Catherine gently, speaking slowly and using small words, which was about all she could understand. Abby would take Nathan now. Abby would feed him. Abby would tend to him. Catherine should go to bed. Jimmy had a glass of juice for her. And two pills. All she had to do was swallow and things would be better.

So that's how it happened the first time. Catherine traded her baby for a dose of Valium. After that, it wasn't so hard to spend a few days at a spa, then a week in Paris, two weeks in Rome.

The first nanny arrived, and Catherine had been visiting her child ever since.

Abby had done well by Nathan. Gotten him on a soy-based formula that briefly settled his finicky stomach. She read him his first story, earned his first smile, watched him take his first step. In the evenings, Catherine would hear them down the hall, Abby reading *Goodnight Moon* in her soft lilting voice, Nathan making small, snuggly murmurs as he curled up against her chest.

At Nathan's first birthday party, he'd fallen down. When Catherine tried to scoop him up, he'd screamed harder and, in front of all the parents, demanded his nanny. Then he'd flung his arms around Abby's shoulders and buried his face against her neck.

Catherine fired the woman the very next day. And Nathan had cried for a month.

After Abby had come Chloë, another one of Jimmy's choices. She was a petite, generously curved Frenchwoman, and Catherine hadn't even been surprised to come home and find her and Jimmy in bed. What did you expect when your husband brought home a "nanny" who by her own admission had never changed a diaper?

Catherine took over the hiring after that. She stuck to older women, true professionals who knew the ropes and could maintain a certain distance from their young charge. They were too mature to appeal to Jimmy, too respectful to comment on how much time Catherine spent away from her son, and too self-righteous to ever know of the nights Catherine stood in Nathan's room, watching her frail son sleep and feeling her heart beat wildly in her chest.

Nathan had made it all the way to four years old now, and still sometimes in her mind's eye, Catherine would see a beat-up blue Chevy turning down their street: *Hey, boy, I'm looking for a lost dog.*

Of course, Nathan didn't need a stranger to haunt his dreams. The danger for Nathan had come from right between these four walls.

Two a.m. She should go to sleep. She already knew she wouldn't. The press remained parked outside, impatient vultures still digging for dirt. From time to time, squad cars passed as well. Checking the scene, monitoring the press, staring up at the fourth floor.

She had given her first statement to the police within hours of Jimmy's death. She'd been proud of herself, cool, calm, and collected. *My husband has a temper. He drinks, he gets angry; this time, he found a gun. What had we fought about? Does it matter? Does anything justify a man aiming a gun at his wife? Yes, I was afraid. In all honesty, Detective, I thought I was dead.*

They had wanted to talk to Nathan as well. She'd put them off. *My son is too tired, too traumatized, too sick.* It had bought her some time. For now.

The investigators had spent most of last night and this morning in the master bedroom. Now the room was cordoned off with yellow crime-scene tape. Parts of the carpet had been removed. Shattered glass gathered. Bedding whisked away. Plastic sheeting covered the hole where the sliding glass door used to be. The cold wind sliced effortlessly through the plastic, however, and carried a host of smells to the rest of the house.

Blood. Urine. Gunpowder. Death.

Her neighbors probably thought she was crazy to stay. The press and police, too. Maybe she was traumatizing Nathan. Or maybe she was insane. Truth of the matter was, where else did they have to go? Her father didn't know how to handle these kinds of situations; arriving at her in-laws would be akin to stepping into the lion's den.

Or maybe there was something more sinister at work. Maybe she just wasn't ready to leave. This house, this room, it was all of Jimmy she had left. And though no one would believe her, least of all her in-laws, in her own way, she had loved Jimmy. She had hoped, she had prayed with what little faith she had, that it would not come to this.

Now she ducked under the crime-scene tape. Now she entered the master bedroom, a chill, ghostly chamber of black and white. Gauzy curtains stirred, while the plastic over the shattered slider heaved and sighed. The smells were richer here. A pungent rusty odor that made her nose recoil even as it triggered memory.

She crossed to the bed, running her hand over the bare mattress and staring at the darker splatters of blood. She lay down in the middle of the vast empty space.

Jimmy seeing her for the first time and flashing that crooked grin in the middle of the crowded department store. "Hey, perfume lady. What's a guy gotta do to get a little spritz?"

Jimmy making love to her, then, afterwards, realizing that she hadn't felt a thing and trying to be kind about it. "Hey, honey, you know what? We'll just have to practice more."

Jimmy fumbling the ring as he got down on one knee to propose. Jimmy staggering wildly as he carried her over the threshold. Jimmy promising her nine, ten children. Jimmy deliriously happy when she became pregnant with their first. Jimmy showering her with diamonds and pearls. Jimmy taking her on whirlwind shopping blitzes where he bought out half the city.

Jimmy sleeping with the maid, the nanny, her friends. Jimmy heading to the bar the first time she had to rush Nathan to the emergency room. Jimmy putting his fist through the wall when she dared to say he should drink less. Jimmy slamming his fist into her ribs when she dared to say something might be wrong with Nathan.

Then, six months ago, Jimmy coming upon the cache of letters written to her from her lover. He'd entered their bedroom at four a.m. He'd flipped her onto her stomach. He'd pinned her to the mattress, and then he'd sodomized her.

"Maybe I should've tried that in the very beginning," he'd said when he was done. "Maybe you would've felt something then."

Hours later, they'd sat across from one another at the breakfast table and made small talk about the weather.

Catherine curled up on the bare mattress now. She put her hand on the empty spot where her husband used to lie. And she remembered the last look on his face, during that instant right when the bullet found the tender spot behind his ear and right before it came shattering out the hard bone at his temple—an expression that was not handsome, not dashing, not charming, but totally, utterly betrayed.

And she wondered now, what had disappointed him most—his own imminent death, or the fact that he hadn't been able to kill her first?

A crash sounded from Nathan's room. Prudence started calling her name and Catherine scrambled down the hall, as surprised as anyone by the tearstains on her face.

At the hospital. Orders hastily shouted and promptly obeyed. One sharp needle and a nurse had drawn blood. Another sharp poke and the IV was in place. A third probing stab and Nathan had been catheterized.

Nathan's twenty-six-pound frame writhed in the middle of the hospital bed, jerking continuously as he fought to sit. His cheeks were on fire, sweat rolling down his limbs. His abdomen protruded painfully while his chest appeared concave as he gasped and heaved for breath.

A resident was reporting, "Severe epigastric pain—"

A nurse was shouting: "Temp one-oh-two. Heart rate one fifty, BP one fifteen over forty—"

Dr. Rocco was already barking out commands: "I need two milligrams morphine, cold compresses, TPN nutrition. Come on, people, *move!*"

The first time Catherine had been through this drill, she had trembled uncontrollably. Now, she was grim-faced as a combat veteran as two people pinned Nathan's writhing body to the bed and two others sliced off Nathan's cowboy-print pajamas and slapped on wires for the heart monitor. Nathan screamed in pain; they held him harder.

So it went, on and on and on, Nathan fighting for his life and the hospital staff fighting with him.

Afterwards, when the worst had passed, when the nurses and residents had moved on to more pressing cases, when only Nathan remained, unconscious, breathing strained, a tiny form lost in the middle of the metal-framed hospital bed, Dr. Rocco took her aside.

"Catherine . . . I know things must be difficult at home right now."

"You think?" The words came out too harshly. Catherine regretted her tone almost immediately. She turned her head away from Dr. Rocco and stared at the walls, which were really much too white. She could hear the beep of Nathan's monitor, faithfully counting out the rhythm of his heart. Sometimes, she heard that sound in her sleep.

"Jimmy, we have to do something about Nathan."

"Jesus, Catherine, can't you leave the poor boy alone?"

"Jimmy, look at him. He's sick. Really, really sick . . ."

"Is he? None of these fancy tests you order ever prove anything. Maybe the problem isn't with Nathan, Cat. I'm beginning to wonder—maybe the problem's with you."

"Catherine, he has pancreatitis again. That's the third time this year. Given his heart and the rest of his health, he can't keep battling these kinds of infections. His liver is enlarged, he's still showing signs of malnutrition, and worse, he's lost a pound since I saw him last. Have you been following the special diet we discussed? Lots of small meals, only soy products?"

"It's hard to get him to eat."

"What about favorite foods?"

"He likes the soy yogurt, but even then, after a bite or two, he's done."

"He's got to eat."

"I know."

"He must take his vitamins."

"We're trying."

"Catherine, four-year-olds don't get anorexia. Four-year-olds don't starve themselves to death."

"I know," she whispered helplessly. "I know." And then, more tentatively, "Isn't there anything else you can do?"

"Catherine . . ." The doctor sighed. Now he stared at the walls, too. "I'm recommending you to Dr. Iorfino," he said abruptly.

"You're sending me to another doctor?"

"He can see you on Monday. Three p.m."

"But another doctor will mean more tests." She was flabbergasted. "Nathan is tired of tests."

"I know."

"Tony . . ." The word came out as a plea. She was sorry the instant she said it.

Dr. Rocco finally looked at her. "The head of Pediatrics has formally asked me to remove myself from this case. I'm sorry, Catherine, but my hands are tied."

And then finally, Catherine got it. James. Her father-in-law had gotten to him, or had intervened with the higher-ups in the hospital, or maybe both. It didn't matter anymore.

As a doctor for Nathan, as an ally for her, Tony Rocco was done.

She rose steadily, careful to keep her chin up and her back straight. As gracefully as she could, she held out her hand. "Thank you for your assistance, Doctor," she murmured.

For one moment, he hesitated. "I'm sorry, Cat," he said softly. "Dr. Iorfino, he's a *good* doctor."

"Older? Balding? Fat?" she asked bitterly.

"A good doctor," Tony repeated.

She just shook her head. "I'm sorry, too."

She left the room, went down the hall where she could stand outside the window of ICU and watch Nathan's skinny chest rise and fall amid the sea of wires. In the morning, if his temperature was down and the worst of the inflammation past, she would take him home. He would sit in his own room, surrounded by his own toys. He would not ask many questions, this somber child of hers. He would simply wait, as they always waited, for the next crisis to occur.

She would have to think of a good time to tell him about the new doctor. Maybe she would have Prudence take him to a movie first, or make him some kind of treat. Or maybe it was better to wait for when he was already in a bad mood. She could layer on the misery and let him deal with it all at once.

Prudence would be there. Prudence would hold his hand if he finally cried.

Catherine couldn't stand being in the ICU anymore. She headed for the families' lounge, desperate for brighter lights, fresher air. People didn't make eye contact here or worry about some infamous widow whose husband had just been shot; they were too busy with problems of their own.

She was halfway right.

A man walked up to her the minute she appeared. He wore a brown suit and bad hairpiece and moved with a single-minded focus.

"Catherine Rose Gagnon?"

"Yes."

"Consider yourself served."

She took the sheaf of paper in bewilderment, barely noting the surprised glances of the other families. The man disappeared as quickly as he'd come, an intruder who knew he didn't belong. Then it was just her and a room full of strangers, all with loved ones battling for their lives down the hall.

Catherine unfolded the thick legal document. She read the heading, and even though she thought she'd considered everything, she was still stunned. Her stomach went hollow, she swayed on her feet.

And then she started laughing, the hysteria building like a bubble in her throat.

"Oh, Jimmy, Jimmy, Jimmy," she half laughed, half sobbed. "What have you done?"

In a darkened room of a darkened house, the phone rang once. The call was expected, but that didn't stop the recipient from feeling rather nervous.

"Robinson?" the caller asked.

"Yeah."

"Did you find him?"

"Yeah."

"Do we have a deal?"

"Keep up your end of the arrangement and he'll keep up his."

"Good. I'll wire you the money."

"You understand what you're doing, don't you?" Robinson blurted out. "I can't control him. He was a killer before he went to jail, he was a killer while he was in jail, and now—"

The caller cut him off. "Trust me: that's exactly what I'm hoping for."

Chapter

8

Bobby woke up blearily to the sound of a phone ringing. For a moment, he lay there, blinking his eyes at the ceiling and feeling the pounding in his head. Jesus, he stank of beer.

Then the phone rang again and the next thought flashed across his mind as a small hopeful flare: Susan.

He grabbed the phone. "Hello?"

The woman on the other end of the phone was not Susan and it amazed him how much he was disappointed.

"Robert Dodge?"

"Who's this?"

"Catherine Gagnon. I believe you shot my husband."

Jesus Christ. Bobby sat up. The shades were drawn, his room was dark, he couldn't get his bearings. His gaze scatter-shot around the room, finally finding his bedside clock and reading the glowing red numbers. Six forty-five a.m. He'd been asleep what, three, four hours? It wasn't enough for this.

"We can't talk," he said.

"I'm not calling to blame you."

"We can't talk," he said again, more emphatically.

"Officer Dodge, I wouldn't be alive right now if you hadn't done what you did. Is that what you need to hear?"

"Mrs. Gagnon, there are lawsuits, there are lawyers. We can't be seen talking."

"Point taken. I believe I can make it to the Isabella Stewart Gardner Museum without being followed. Can you?"

"Lady—"

"I'll be there after eleven. In the Veronese Room."

"Have a nice tour."

"Haven't you ever heard, Officer Dodge?

The enemy of your enemy is your friend. We have the same enemy, you and I, which means now we're the only hope either of us has left."

Eleven-fifteen A.M., Bobby found her in front of a Whistler portrait awash in vivid shades of blue. The artwork featured a lounging woman, nude, voluptuously curved and swathed in bright oriental fabrics. In contrast, Catherine Gagnon stood out as a stark silhouette. Long black hair, tailored black dress, skinny black heels. Even from the back, she was a striking woman. Slender, self-contained, oozing pedigreed wealth. Bobby decided she was too skinny for his tastes, too rich-bitch, but then she turned and he felt something tighten low in his gut. Something about the way she moved, he thought. Or maybe it was the way her dark, oversized eyes dominated her pale, sculpted face.

She looked at him. He looked at her. And for a long moment, neither took a step.

First time Bobby had seen her, he'd had the impression of a dark Madonna, a slender mother wrapping herself protectively around her young son. Now, with the allegations of child abuse fresh in his mind, he saw a black widow. She was cool. Ballsy, to call him up out of the blue. And probably, most likely, he decided, dangerous.

"You can relax," she said quietly from across the way. "It's an art museum. No cameras allowed, remember?"

"Clever," he acknowledged, and she flashed him a fleeting smile before returning her attention to the artwork.

He finally crossed to her, standing in front of the Whistler display, but leaving plenty of distance between them.

The room wasn't crowded yet; early November was off-season in Boston. Too late for leaf-peeping, too early for holiday shopping. Bobby and Catherine shared the opulent room of the mansion-museum with only four other souls, and those four didn't appear to be giving them a second glance.

"Do you like Whistler?" she asked.

"More of a Pedro Martinez fan, myself."

"Believe in the Red Sox curse?"

"Haven't seen anything to prove otherwise."

"I like this Whistler study," she said. "The long sensuous lines of the woman's body against that opulent blue fabric. It's extremely erotic. Do you think this woman was merely a model for him, or after posing for this, did she become Whistler's lover?"

Bobby didn't say anything. She didn't seem to require an answer.

"He had a reputation for being a dandy, you know. In 1888, however, just a few years after painting this piece, he supposedly married the love of his life, Beatrice Godwin. She died eight years later from cancer. What a pity. Did you know that Whistler's a local artist? Born in Lowell, Mass—"

"I didn't come for the art."

She merely arched a brow at him. "Shame, don't you think? It's a wonderful museum."

He gave her another look, and she finally relented. "Let's go upstairs. Third level."

"More Whistler?"

"No, more privacy."

They mounted the wide, curving staircase to the top level of the museum. They passed by more people, then several guards standing stony-faced in designated rooms. Fourteen years ago, two thieves disguised as Boston police officers had stolen thirteen

works of art from this museum. The theft
gave the museum a certain level of notoriety
that the security guards didn't forget. Now
they scrupulously studied each person
walking by, causing Bobby to avert his gaze.

When they finally arrived on the third
floor, he found that he was breathing harder
than necessary. Catherine Gagnon wasn't
as cool as she'd like to pretend either.
He could see both of her hands trembling
at her sides. As if sensing his gaze, she
stopped the motion by curving her fingers
into fists.

She walked all the way to the back and
he followed, noting things he didn't want to
note. Like the smell of her perfume, rich, almost cinnamony, like barely suppressed
heat. Or the way she walked, lithe, graceful,
like a cat. She worked out. Yoga or Pilates
would be his guess. Either way, she was
stronger than she looked.

In the back room of the third floor, no one
was around. Bobby and Catherine positioned themselves at random, close but not
too close, and Catherine started to talk.

"I loved my husband," she said softly. "I
know that must sound strange to you.
When I first met Jimmy, he was . . . amaz-

ing, generous, sweet. He took me on whirl-wind weekends to Paris and grand shop-ping tours. I . . . I had some trouble earlier in my life. Some sadness. When I first met Jimmy, for the first time, things felt right. He entered the picture and literally swept me off my feet. He was my knight in shining ar-mor."

Bobby wondered what *some sadness* meant. He wondered, for that matter, why Catherine Gagnon was telling him any of this. He'd killed Jimmy Gagnon; he didn't want to hear stories about the man now.

"I was wrong about Jimmy," Catherine said abruptly. "Jimmy wasn't a knight in shining armor. He was drunk and abusive, a manipulative, charismatic man who would smile at you when he got his way, and go af-ter you with a knife when he didn't. He was everything I swore to myself I knew better than to marry. But I didn't see it. I didn't un-derstand until it was much too late, and then I could only wonder. . . . I knew *better.* How had I still ended up married to the likes of him?"

She stopped abruptly, a person biting off an unspoken curse. She turned away again, but her steps were hard now, agitated as she paced the tiny room.

"He beat you?" Bobby asked.

"I can show you bruises." Her hands moved immediately to the belt of her dress. He held up his palm to stop her.

"Why didn't you tell the cops?"

"They were Boston cops. Jimmy's father, Judge Gagnon, had already handed down an edict: If Jimmy was in trouble, cops were to call him and he'd personally take care of it. Jimmy liked to brag about that. Shortly before he'd knock me unconscious."

Bobby frowned. He didn't like these kinds of stories, cops turning a blind eye, yet it fit with what two BPD cops had already told him. Jimmy Gagnon was a wild one, and he used his father as his own personal get-out-of-jail-free card.

"And your son?"

"Jimmy never touched Nathan. I would've left him if he had." She said the words too quickly; Bobby knew she lied.

"Seems to me a man knocking you around should be reason enough to grab the kid and run. Of course, life on the road wouldn't involve so much money."

"Oh, Jimmy didn't have any money."

"Yeah? What do you consider a home in the heart of Back Bay?"

"Jimmy's father bought it. His father bought most of the things we used. Jimmy's money is still tied up in a trust. His father is the executor and he doles out the money at will. It's from a clause dating back to Jimmy's great-great-grandfather on his mother's side. He hit it big in oil, then grew obsessed that future generations would squander the family fortune. His solution: he tied up the assets in trusts that don't dissolve until the inheritor turns fifty-five. Each successive generation has kept it that way. So the family has money—Maryanne inherited a positively filthy amount of money when she turned fifty-five—but Jimmy . . . Jimmy didn't have any wealth of his own yet."

"And now that Jimmy's dead?"

"The money goes straight to Nathan, also in a trust. I don't receive a cent."

Bobby remained skeptical. "But there are provisions for the boy's guardian, I'm sure."

"Nathan's guardian will receive a monthly allowance," she acknowledged. "But you're assuming I'm his guardian. This morning, I was served with court papers. James and

Maryanne are officially suing me for custody of Nathan. They claim I'm trying to kill him. Can you imagine that, Officer Dodge? A mother trying to harm her own son?"

She moved toward him, coming to a halt closer to him than strangers normally stand. He became aware of her perfume again, and the pale curve of her slender neck and the way her long, dark hair draped down her back, a rich, black curtain as erotic as the blue fabric in the Whistler portrait had been.

She made no other move, said no other word, and yet there was something about her that invited touch. Something about her that reached out to him as a man, and begged him to conquer her as a woman.

She was playing him. She was using her body as a weapon, deliberately trying to befuddle the brains of the poor, stupid state cop. Funny, even knowing that, he was still tempted to step forward, to press his body against hers.

"My son is in the hospital," she murmured.

"What?"

"He's in the ICU. Pancreatitis. Maybe that doesn't sound life-threatening to you, but for a boy like Nathan it is. My son is sick, Officer Dodge. He's very, very sick and the doctors don't know why, so my in-laws are blaming me. If they can make his illness my fault, they can take Nathan away. Then they'll have their grandson—and the money—all to themselves. Unless, of course, you help me."

Bobby let his gaze drift down the length of her body. "And why would I help you?"

She smiled. It was a fully feminine smile, but for the first time, Bobby also saw a spark of emotion in her eyes—she was sad. Catherine Gagnon was deeply, horribly sad. She reached up a hand and delicately splayed her fingers across his chest.

"We need each other," she said quietly. "Think about the clerk-magistrate hearing—"

"You know about the hearing?"

"Of course I know about it. The two motions go together, Officer Dodge. The custody battle is the foundation of the probable cause hearing. Basically, if I'm abusing Nathan, then you committed murder."

"I didn't commit murder."

Her fingers fluttered across his chest. "Of course. Just like I'm not the kind of woman

who would ever dream of harming her son."
She leaned closer, her breath whispering
across his lips. "Don't you trust me, Officer
Dodge? You should, you know. Because I
have no choice but to trust in you."

Bobby had to get some air. He left the museum, cabbed it home, and stood like an idiot in the middle of his family room. Fuck it.
He went for a run.

Down G Street to Columbia Road. Heading into the park, where traffic roared by on
his left, and there was nothing but ocean on
the right. Exchanging the Heights for the
Point, passing by the historic L Street Bath
House, and watching the homes go from
tidy three-levels to full-fledged mansions.
He hit Castle Island, where the wind gusted
into his face and the ocean pounded the
shore. Weather was wild here, the wind a
physical force, shoving against him as he
strained forward. He muscled his way
around the stone walls of the old lookout,
watching jets from Logan climb slowly into
the sky, looking as if they were barely going
to clear the island. Playground was here.

Kids out on the slide, bundled up against the weather.

He ran around again, picking up the sounds of kids laughing as the notes danced across the wind. Lots of families were moving into South Boston. Used to be working-class kids, walking up from the various housing projects to Castle Island. The families were more white-collar now, but the kids played just as rough.

He headed home, his lungs working hard and finally clearing the fog from his head.

Back in his house, he got out the yellow pages and, still dripping with sweat, started his calls. He found who he was looking for on the third try.

"We have a Nathan Gagnon admitted into the ICU," a hospital nurse responded to his query. "Brought in last night."

"Is he okay?"

"Well, we don't generally put the healthy ones in intensive care." The nurse sounded droll.

"I mean, what's his condition? I'm with the Massachusetts State Police." He rattled off his badge number.

"Serious but stable," the nurse reported.

"Pancreatitis," Bobby recalled. "Is that life-threatening?"

"It can be."

"In this case?"

"You'd have to talk to his pediatrician, Dr. Rocco."

Bobby made a note. "Has the boy been in before?"

"Few times. Again, Officer, you should talk to Dr. Rocco."

"Okay, okay. One more question, if you don't mind."

The nurse seemed to think about it, then must have decided that she didn't mind. "So?"

"Does the kid ever come in with other conditions? You know, broken bones, unexplained bruises?"

"Does he fall down the stairs a lot?" the woman asked dryly.

"Exactly. How's he doing with stairs?"

"Two broken bones in the last twelve months. You tell me."

"Two broken bones in the last twelve months," Bobby murmured. "No kidding. Thanks. You've been very helpful." He hung up the phone.

Bobby sat on the edge of his chair. Yellow

pages were open on his lap. Sweat trickled down his nose and dripped onto the thin paper. He could feel the darkness inside himself again, murky and deep. And he thought what he'd really like to do today, more than run, more than sleep, more than even speak with Susan, was go to a firing range and shoot the living daylights out of something.

So what did that say about him?

A smart man would forget about his encounter with Catherine Gagnon. He'd done his job, the best an officer could do. Now he should wash his hands of everything and walk away.

Of course, a smart man didn't meet a woman like Catherine in a very public museum. And a smart man didn't worry so much about a kid he barely knew.

Bobby snapped the yellow pages shut.

"Dr. Rocco," he repeated to himself. He headed for the shower.

Chapter
9

Bobby's cell phone rang the minute he left the house. He didn't feel like driving into Boston—just the parking would bankrupt him, and frankly, without flashing red lights to back him up, he wasn't stupid enough to brave the traffic. So he walked to the bus stop with his head down and shoulders rounded, feeling conspicuous in broad daylight, like a felon from *America's Most Wanted*.

Thank God Jimmy Gagnon had been white, Bobby thought, or he'd never be able to leave his home.

His phone bleated again. He flipped it open suspiciously, the wind already ripping the words from his lips.

"Yeah?"

"Bobby? Thank God. I've been trying to reach you since last night."

"Hey, Pop." Bobby relaxed, but only a fraction. He continued walking, his legs eating up the six blocks to the bus stop. "I called you this morning, but couldn't get through."

"Had to take the phone off the hook. Damn reporters wouldn't stop bothering me."

"Sorry 'bout that."

"I didn't tell them anything. Good-for-nothing sons of bitches." Bobby's father hated journalists almost as much as presidents from the Democratic Party. "You okay?"

"Working on it."

"On paid leave?"

"Till we hear from the DA."

"I did a little calling around," Pop said. Once upon a time, Bobby's father had gone by his real name, Larry, but then he'd set up shop as a custom pistolsmith to augment his retirement income. So many of his customers were Bobby's fellow police officers. They'd started calling him Pop, too, and now it had stuck. Bobby'd been surprised by the evolution, sure his gruff, hard-assed father would hate the familiarity. But Larry didn't seem to mind. Sometimes, he even appeared flattered. Things changed, Bobby supposed. In his own way, Bobby was trying to change, too. It was just a longer time coming.

"I'm hearing good things," Pop said quietly. "You did what you had to do."

Bobby shrugged. Saying "Thanks" would sound too cavalier. Saying anything else would be ungrateful.

"Bobby—"

"I know I should've tried harder to call you," Bobby cut in. "I shouldn't have left you so long to worry."

"It's not that—"

Bobby rushed on, quickly now, before he lost his courage. "I guess it all just hit me harder than I thought. I mean, I don't doubt taking the shot. I could only act on what I saw, and what I saw told me to shoot. But still, the guy's kid was in the room. Right there, not five feet away, and I blew his father's brains out. Now the boy has to live

with what I did, and *I* have to live with what
I did, and I . . ." Bobby's voice broke off,
sounded more ragged than he would've
liked. Jesus, how did he get into this mess?

Pop didn't try to say anything this time.

"It gets to me, Pop," Bobby said more
quietly. "I didn't think it would. But it gets to
me. And last night . . . last night I had a
beer."

His father didn't speak right away. He
said finally, heavily, "I heard it might have
been more like half a dozen beers."

"Yeah, yeah, you're right. It was probably
closer to five or six."

"Did it help?"

"No."

"How did you feel this morning?"

"Like shit."

"And tonight?"

"I'm done. I slipped, I learned my lesson,
I'm done." Bobby couldn't quite resist
adding, "And you?"

"I'm good," Pop said. "One asshole in the
family is enough, don't you think?"

Bobby had to smile. "Yeah, one asshole
is enough."

"And Susan?" his father asked gruffly.

"Now you got some time off, maybe you can bring her out for a visit."

"I don't know."

"What don't you know, son?"

"I don't know . . . a lot of things."

"Come visit me, Bobby. It's only a thirty-minute ride. You could spend an afternoon. We could talk."

"I should do that." Which they both knew meant that he wouldn't. Pop was trying, Bobby was trying, but there were still things both couldn't forgive and neither could forget.

"Hey, Pop, I gotta go." Bobby could see the small cluster of three people at the bus stop. An older woman stared at Bobby. He stared right back.

"Have you talked to your brother at all?"

"No."

"I'll give him a call. I'd hate for him to catch it on the news."

"Pop, George lives in Florida."

"Yeah, but these kinds of stories . . . they have a life of their own."

At the hospital, ironically enough, Bobby couldn't catch anyone's attention. He stood

for ten minutes at the registration desk before growing impatient and heading for the
hospital directory next to the elevator. He
found a listing for Anthony J. Rocco, M.D.,
on the third floor. Bobby took the stairs.

Arriving at the top, he was breathing
hard. He found a glassed-in waiting room
filled with children's toys and snotty-nosed
toddlers. Two kids were crying. One was
trying to cram a metal car down her throat.
Greater Boston Pediatrics, the sign said.
Bobby decided it must be the place to start.

The receptionist at the counter barely
glanced at him. She slid him a sign-in sheet
and a chewed-up pen while cracking her
gum and talking on the phone. Bobby had
to wait until she hung up to inform her he
wasn't a patient; he simply wanted to talk to
Dr. Rocco. This confused her greatly. He
flashed his badge, said he was with the police, and finally got a response. The girl flew
out of her chair and trotted down the hall in
search of the infamous Dr. Rocco.

Bobby didn't know whether to feel triumphant or vaguely ashamed. He'd put on
a pair of khakis, a button-down shirt, and
his best sports jacket for this occasion. He
was doing his impression of a homicide de-

tective, which probably only proved that even state troopers could watch too much TV.

Earlier in his career, six or seven years back, Bobby had debated making the transition from uniformed patrol officer to investigative detective. Uniformed officers were considered the grunts of the operation, the front-line troops even in an organization as elite as the state police. Detectives were smart; patrol officers, good at doing what they were told. Bobby had the brains, his sergeant had urged, why settle for driving a Crown Vic for the rest of his life?

Bobby had still been debating his options when he'd learned of an opening on the STOP team. He'd submitted his resumé and begun the rigorous selection process. He had to pass oral boards, prove proficiency with special weapons, and endure intense physical fitness requirements. Then came the special drills: scenarios involving swinging from ropes to see if the applicant was afraid of heights; scenarios involving a smoke machine to test how well the applicant functioned under extreme stress. They were tested with cold, tested with heat. Made to crawl through mud carrying eighty pounds of gear, required to hold a pose for up to three hours.

Always it was drilled into their heads: Tactical teams deployed anytime, anywhere. They could be called upon to enter any sort of situation and all kinds of terrain. You had to think fast on your feet, thrive under pressure, and be fearless. Survive the application process, and you received the honor of training four extra days a month while surrendering all your nights and weekends to be on call twenty-four seven. All this, for no additional income. Men joined the tactical team purely for the sake of pride. To be the best of the best. To know that as a team—and as an individual—you could handle anything.

Bobby'd survived the selection process. He'd won the open slot, and he'd never looked back. He was a good cop, serving with the best cops. At least that's what he'd thought until two days ago.

The receptionist was back, cheeks flushed, and breathless.

"Dr. Rocco will see you now."

A toddler screeched a fresh round of protest from the waiting area. Bobby pushed gratefully through the connecting door.

He found Dr. Rocco sitting in a small office halfway down the hall. The desk was buried under heaps of files, and the walls were covered with children's drawings and immunization schedules. A few things struck Bobby at once. One, Dr. Rocco was younger than he'd pictured, late thirties to early forties. Two, the doctor was a lot more attractive than Bobby'd imagined: thick dark hair, trim athletic build, and an oozy sort of country-club charm. Three, Dr. Rocco obviously read the *Boston Herald* and knew exactly who Bobby was.

"I have some questions about Nathan Gagnon," Bobby said.

Dr. Rocco didn't say anything at first. He was eyeing Bobby up and down. Wondering where Bobby got the gall to show his face in public? Preparing to cite doctor-patient confidentiality? Dr. Rocco finally glanced up again and Bobby saw something unexpected in the man's gaze: fear.

"Have a seat," the pediatrician said at last. He gestured to a file-covered chair, then belatedly grabbed the stack of papers. "How can I help you?"

"I understand you're in charge of Nathan Gagnon's care," Bobby said.

"For the past year, yes. Nathan was re-ferred to me by another pediatrician, Dr. Wagner, when she failed to make progress on his care."

"Nathan has an illness?"

"Officially, he's listed as FTT."

"FTT?" Bobby asked. He took out a small spiral notebook and a pen.

"Failure to thrive. Basically, from birth, Nathan's been behind the curve in size, weight, and key developmental bench-marks. He's not developing in a 'normal' manner."

Bobby frowned, not sure he was getting it. "The boy's too small?"

"Well, that's one element. Nathan's height of thirty-four inches puts him in the lowest one percent for a four-year-old boy, and his weight—twenty-six pounds—doesn't make the curve at all. His condition, however, has to do with more than just size."

"Explain."

"From birth, Nathan has struggled with vomiting, diarrhea, and spiking fevers. He seems constantly malnourished—he's had rickets, his blood phosphate levels are too low, same with blood glucose levels. As I said before, he's lagged behind almost all traditional benchmarks for development— he didn't sit up until he was eleven months old, he didn't cut teeth until he was eighteen months old, and didn't walk until he was twenty-six months old. None of that is considered good. And then, in the past year, his condition appears to have worsened. He's had several attacks of acute pancreatitis as well as two bone fractures. He's failed to thrive."

Bobby flipped a page in his notebook. "Let's talk about the bone fractures. Isn't it unusual for a four-year-old to have two broken bones in one year?"

"Not for a patient such as Nathan."

"What do you mean?"

"Nathan suffers from hypophosphatemia— low phosphate. Combined with the rickets, his bones are unusually brittle and prone to fracture. For the record, he also bruises quite easily."

Bobby looked up sharply. "Why do you say that?"

"That's why you're here, isn't it? To find out if Nathan was being abused. To prove to yourself you killed the right man." Dr. Rocco added quietly, "For the record, I think you aimed just fine."

Bobby scowled. He hadn't expected this turn in the conversation, to be called head-on. He felt overexposed and it pissed him off.

"Do you think Nathan was being abused?" Bobby asked tightly.

"There are a lot of ways to harm a child," Dr. Rocco replied.

"Did someone break Nathan's bones?"

"No. Rickets broke Nathan Gagnon's bones. I can tell from the X-rays."

Bobby sat back. Dr. Rocco's assessment didn't please him. In fact, it left him more confused than ever. "So what's wrong with this kid? Why does he have all these problems?"

"I don't know."

"You don't *know*?"

"That's essentially what a diagnosis of FTT tells you—we don't know. We can't pinpoint an exact cause, so the boy remains under the catchall umbrella of 'failure to thrive.' "

"Well, Doc, you must have explored *some* options?"

"Sure. We conducted initial tests—complete blood count, lead levels, urinalysis, and a set of electrolyte values. We've tested him for diabetes, reflux, malabsorption, and cystic fibrosis. One of the best endocrinologists in the country has examined Nathan for thyroid diseases, metabolic disorders, and hormonal imbalances. Then a nephrologist studied Nathan's kidneys and did more tests related to electrolytes, diabetes, and anemia. I've tested Nathan, I've studied Nathan, and I've sent him to the best experts I know. And I still don't have a diagnosis for him. Medically speaking, there's nothing majorly wrong with Nathan Gagnon, except for the fact that he's very, very sick."

Bobby was starting to hate this conversation. He twirled his pen between his fingers, then put it down and picked it up again. "You didn't like Jimmy Gagnon," he said bluntly.

"Never met the man."

"Never?"

"Never. Nathan's been in my office two or three times a month. For that matter, he's been rushed to the emergency room four times in the past six months. And not once have I ever met Jimmy Gagnon. That tells you something right there."

Bobby regarded the doctor's country-club looks. "So when did you start sleeping with Catherine?"

The man didn't bother to appear shocked. "She deserved better than him," he answered evenly.

"A neglected wife?"

"Worse." The doctor leaned forward, his face growing intent. "You're not asking the right questions yet. Maybe Nathan had a medical reason to bruise easily, but Catherine didn't."

"Jimmy beat her?"

"I saw the bruises myself."

"Black eyes?"

"Give the guy some credit. He never hit her where just anyone could see. I used to go to school with guys like Jimmy. They figured if they beat their girlfriends in private, it gave them some class."

"You could've reported it."

"Really? So some cop could look at me the way you're looking at me right now? I didn't even need to be sleeping with her. As long as I simply *wanted* to be sleeping with her, none of you uniforms would've taken me seriously."

"Ever consider dealing with Jimmy your-self?"

"I thought about it."

"And?"

"I went to the house once. When I knew Catherine and Nathan were away. I knocked on the door, but no one was home."

"And you never returned? Man's beating the woman you love, so you show up at an empty house and that's action enough?" Bobby's voice was cold.

"What would you have me do?" Dr. Rocco said tightly. "Threaten him with a gun?"

The barb was meant to hurt. Bobby merely shrugged and told the man honestly, "That's what I would've done."

Dr. Rocco finally flushed. He leaned away from Bobby, crossing his arms in front of his chest and staring at a spot on his desk. "I told her to leave him," he said at last.

"You'd take care of her?" Bobby glanced meaningfully at the doctor's left hand where he was wearing a gold band.

Again, the good doctor refused to be cowed. "I would've been honored."

"But she didn't do it. She stayed."

"She said I didn't know what I was saying. She said if she ever left Jimmy, he'd destroy her life and anyone else who tried to help her. She said my career would go down in flames."

"Did you believe her?"

"No. Yes. I don't know. I'd never met Jimmy Gagnon, remember? I'd just heard the stories. But then, six months ago, Jimmy found out about our . . . relationship. I had written some letters. I guess Catherine hadn't the heart to destroy them. Things were rough for her. The notes, I wrote them to give her hope."

Bobby waited.

"Next day, a private investigator was in my office, asking all sorts of questions about Nathan. He had a signed affidavit from Jimmy demanding release of his son's medical records. Within ten minutes, the investigator's strategy was clear. He wanted to know if Nathan's condition could be the result of prolonged starvation or some other form of parental abuse. Basically, he suggested that Nathan's illness had been caused by Catherine—that she was starving her son to death."

"Is that possible?"

"I don't believe so."

"You don't *believe* so?" Bobby arched both brows. "You just told me the kid has some kind of hard-to-diagnose disease. Now you're saying *she* could've done it?"

"Look, without having pinpointed a specific cause for Nathan's condition, medically speaking I can't rule anything out. Sure, one or more of his parents could be physically starving him. Or someone could be tampering with his food, or someone could be mentally manipulating him not to eat. As a doctor, I've followed up with Catherine, Nathan, and the various nannies about his eating habits. I've gotten answers assuring me that the boy is receiving plenty of food and plenty of the right kind of food. But at the end of the day, I'm still just the doctor. I go home to my family, and Nathan goes home to his."

"So someone could be abusing him?"

"It's *possible*." Dr. Rocco said it impatiently. "But I don't think it's *probable*. And that's what I told Jimmy's investigator. Anyway, it didn't matter. I stopped seeing Catherine, she made nice with Jimmy, and all the questions went away. *That's* what it was about. It was Jimmy making a point. If Catherine left him, she could kiss her son goodbye and say hello to the criminal justice system. Catherine's a smart woman. She did what she had to do. And for the record, I don't know what the hell else Jimmy did to her, but the day Catherine came to my office to end things, she could barely walk. *That's* the kind of man Jimmy Gagnon was. So I said it once, and I'll say it again. From where I sit, Officer Dodge, you aimed just fine."

Bobby narrowed his eyes. "With Jimmy dead, do you think Nathan might magically start to get better?"

"I don't know. And frankly, it's no longer my responsibility. As of this morning, I formally ended my relationship as Nathan's doctor. I referred him to Dr. Iorfino, as I was instructed to do by Dr. Gerritsen, the head of Pediatrics."

"You were fired as Nathan's doctor?" Bobby asked in surprise. "By your own boss?"

"You'd be amazed by the kind of power Judge Gagnon wields," Dr. Rocco said quietly. Then he got an odd smile on his face. "But don't worry, Officer. I'm not quite as helpless as you think. Dr. Iorfino is a geneticist. Call it a hunch, but I think I'm going to have the last laugh yet."

Chapter 10

Bobby was just leaving the hospital when he became aware of the footsteps behind him. He picked up his pace, hands jammed in his jacket pockets, head down as if staring at the sidewalk, though in reality the angle gave him a peek at the traffic behind him. Dress shoes, high-gloss black, he determined. Pimp shoes, his father would call them.

He rounded a left-hand corner sharply and gained a better view of his tail when the man belatedly tacked out wide. Long trench coat, beige, nicely tailored. Black dress pants, perfect cuff. Lawyer, Bobby thought. Then suddenly . . .

He drew up short, ramming his back against a storefront and catching his follower off guard. The man, older, heavy-set, with a scrap of neatly combed silver-brown hair brushing the top of his ears, promptly stopped, threw up his hands, and offered a beaming smile.

"Ah, you caught me."

"And now's the part when I throw you back." Bobby took a menacing step forward, but the man merely smiled again.

"What are you gonna do, Officer Dodge? Assault me in the middle of a street filled with people? We both know you're not the type to go head-to-head. Now, give you a rifle, fifty yards' distance, and a darkened room, on the other hand . . ."

Bobby grabbed the lapels of the man's coat. Three pedestrians noticed the byplay; they promptly scattered. "Try me," Bobby said.

"Now, Bobby—"

"Who the hell are you?"

"A friend."

"Well, *friend,* start talking, or in thirty seconds, I'm going to rip off your nuts."

The man laughed nervously. He'd tried calling Bobby's bluff once. He didn't look so certain about trying it a second time. "Just want to talk," the man said.

"Why?"

"Because I know things you should hear."

"Lawyer?"

"Investigator."

"For whom?"

"Come on, Bobby, you know for whom."

Bobby thought about it, and then he did. "James Gagnon."

"Technically, Maryanne Gagnon; the lawsuit's in her name. I'm Harris, by the way." The man tried offering his hand. Bobby ignored it. "Harris Reed, with Reed and Wagner Investigations. Perhaps you've heard of us?"

"Not a word."

"Touché. Would you mind letting go of my coat for a moment? Perhaps we could take a short walk. You look like a man who appreciates exercise. Then again, I imagine your meeting with Catherine Gagnon has already left you short of breath."

Bobby slowly released the man's collar. "You've been following me."

"More like taking an intense interest in your activities. Shall we?"

Harris gestured down the sidewalk. Bobby thinned his lips, but after a moment, grudgingly resumed walking. He was curious and they both knew it.

"She's beautiful, isn't she?" the investigator observed.

Bobby didn't reply.

"Would it be easier if she were ugly?" Harris asked. "I imagine it has to be disconcerting to meet the wife of the man you killed and already be fantasizing about fucking her."

"Get to the point."

"You've been asking questions, Officer Dodge. As long as you're asking questions, I thought you should hear all of the answers. May I?"

Bobby didn't protest; the investigator launched into his spiel.

"She was working at the perfume counter in Filene's," Harris began. "Did she tell you that? Yes, the fine, beautiful Mrs. Gagnon was a perfume spritzer for a living. She'd not only flunked out of college, but she had

no marketable skills to her name. She ped-
dled perfumes and lived in a rat-infested
apartment in East Boston, wearing the
same dress every other day. Until she met
Jimmy, of course."

"Was Jimmy eighteen?"

"Actually, he was twenty-seven at the
time."

"Then he was a big boy. He knew what he
was doing."

"You would think so," Harris agreed
mildly. "But with a woman like Catherine,
looks can be deceiving."

"She's the devil in angel's clothing, yada,
yada, yada. Get on with it."

"Jimmy Gagnon was a bit of a playboy.
I'm sure you've heard stories. He was a
good-looking man, fun-loving, free-spirited,
and of course, extremely generous. Lots of
women had come and gone in Jimmy's life.
His parents, I confess, were actually starting
to worry a little, wonder if he'd ever settle
down. Then he met Catherine. He grinned,
she spritzed, and the rest, as they say, was
history.

"My employers, James and Maryanne,
were delighted at first. Catherine seemed
lovely, quiet, perhaps even a little shy. Then,

of course, Jimmy told them all about her tragic life."

"Some sadness," Bobby muttered.

"Pardon?"

"Nothing."

"You should look up Catherine's name sometime. See 1980, any listings under Thanksgiving Miracle. That's what they called Catherine back then. After she'd been kidnapped by a pedophile and held as his personal sex slave for twenty-eight days in some pit he'd dug in the ground. Hunters found her by accident. Otherwise, God knows what would've happened to her.

"Jimmy found this story riveting. You had to see Catherine six years ago, when they first met. A little too thin, hollow-eyed, in a threadbare dress. She was not only beautiful, she was *tragic,* a regular damsel in distress. She told Jimmy he was the only chance at happiness she'd ever had, and Jimmy ate it up, hook, line and sinker. In a matter of months they were engaged, then married. Catherine Gagnon came, she saw, and she conquered."

They'd already covered one city block and were rapidly eating up the second.

"So Jimmy gained a beautiful wife and

Catherine gained a bank account." Bobby shrugged. "Sounds like half the marriages of the rich and famous. What's the problem?"

"Their son. Catherine and Jimmy had Nathan just a year later, and Catherine literally had a nervous breakdown. Frankly, she just couldn't cut it as a mother. And for the first time, James and Maryanne grew afraid. Not just of what Catherine was doing to Jimmy, but of what she might do to Nathan."

Harris abruptly switched gears. "Catherine was only twelve years old when Richard Umbrio snatched her off the street. I used to be a cop, you know, worked homicide in Baltimore. No matter how many cases you've seen, child kidnappings are the worst. Here's this poor girl, just walking home from school. Next thing she knows, she's being yanked into a car, probably screaming at the top of her lungs, but nobody hearing a thing. And Richard wasn't a small guy, not one of those sissy-looking child molesters you often see, the type who have to victimize children because they obviously couldn't handle anyone their own size. No—at the tender age of twenty,

Richard Umbrio was six foot four, weighed two hundred twenty pounds. His neighbors were already in the habit of crossing to the other side of the street just so they didn't have to make eye contact with him. Catherine, on the other hand, probably weighed eighty pounds. What was a little girl like her gonna do against a guy like him? Let me be the first to say, there isn't a hell big enough for some of the assholes we have walking here on earth.

"Richard took her out to the woods not far from his house. Set her up underground, where he could visit her as much as he liked and no one would hear a thing. She got a coffee can to use as a toilet, a jug of water, and a loaf of bread. That was it. No flashlight, no cot, no blanket to keep her warm. He kept her down there like an animal. And then for nearly a month, he did to her whatever he wanted, whenever he wanted.

"You have to wonder what that level of systematic abuse does to a child. You have to wonder how she must have felt. Left alone in the dark for long periods of time, then to finally have companionship in the form of a serial rapist. Makes you mad just to think about it, doesn't it?"

Bobby still didn't reply, but his jaw had gone tight and his hands were fisted at his sides. He had a feeling Harris hadn't gotten to the bad part yet. This was merely foreplay; Harris was still warming up.

"Maybe Catherine got lucky when she was found," the investigator said now. "Or maybe not. How does a person really recover from something like that? Is it ever possible for a girl to put all that behind her, to return to normal?"

Harris waited a heartbeat. Then he announced, "Catherine stopped sleeping the minute Nathan was born. Jimmy would find her pacing the house, frantically turning on lights. He'd bring her to bed, she'd spring out the other side. He'd turn off lights, she'd hunt them down again, including the one in the oven. And it wasn't just her strange compulsions. When she went to pick Nathan up, she'd hold him stiffly, away from her body. The more the baby screamed, the more she carried him around like a soup can she didn't know where to set down. The third day, Jimmy found her standing over the crib, holding a pillow. When Jimmy asked her what she was doing, she said Nathan had told her he was tired and needed to sleep. Jimmy called his parents, panicked. The Gagnons agreed he shouldn't leave Nathan alone with Catherine anymore, and they went to work finding a nanny.

"Now, granted, things calmed down a little once the nanny was hired. Mostly because Catherine handed over her son and never looked back. Literally. The nanny took the baby and Catherine headed for the local spa. Jimmy got a little frustrated, as you can imagine. He'd thought he'd married this lovely young lady, rescued her even, and this is how she repaid him, abandoning their child, jetting around Europe and consorting with a bunch of guys she liked to call her 'fellows.' For the sake of honesty, maybe Jimmy wasn't the most faithful of husbands, but this sure as hell isn't what anyone would call a happy marriage."

"So why didn't Jimmy just leave her?" Bobby asked. "Or was beating her much more fun?"

"Ahh, the infamous beatings. So you've already heard. Well, let's just say rumors of spousal abuse can be greatly exaggerated. Find me a police report. Find me a safe-deposit box filled with photos, or at least one corroborating witness. Stories are easy to tell; let's stick to the facts."

"Fact one." Bobby ticked off a finger. "If Jimmy was so unhappy in his marriage, why didn't he get out?"

"He did. That's the first time Nathan became 'sick.' "

"What?"

"You got it. Jimmy tried to leave Catherine, and Nathan became magically ill. Nathan was very sick, Catherine claimed. He needed special tests, he needed medical attention. She lined up the best experts money could buy, and Jimmy immediately returned home. His son was deathly ill, for crying out loud. He couldn't leave his wife at a time like that.

"And that was the pattern. Catherine would get caught sleeping with Jimmy's tailor, he'd get mad and Nathan would wind up back in the hospital. Sick, definitely—vomiting, feverish, malnourished—until the minute Jimmy toed the line. Then, Nathan would make a miraculous recovery. As you can imagine, James and Maryanne grew very concerned. Not only was Jimmy becoming a nervous wreck, but they couldn't bear to think what was going on with their grandson."

"And they started alleging child abuse,"

Bobby filled in. He stopped walking, looking Harris in the eye. "Got any facts to back up that story, Harris? Because Nathan's own doctor insists there's a medical basis for what's going on."

"Dr. Lancelot?" Harris snorted, also coming to a halt. "Ask him to say hello to his wife and kids. Catherine's got that poor sap so wrapped around her finger, he'd say the moon was made out of blue cheese if he thought it would make her happy. Six months ago, Jimmy found out she'd been sleeping with the fine doctor. And that's when I entered the picture. To start keeping tabs on Catherine. To try to figure out what was really going on with Nathan, and better yet to *protect* Nathan Gagnon, if it came to that. Because Jimmy had had enough. Six months ago, he started making plans for divorce."

They were at a street corner. Traffic picked up, the noise becoming loud. But all of a sudden, it didn't matter. All of a sudden, Bobby knew exactly what Harris was going to say next.

"James and Maryanne were right to be suspicious," Harris told him quietly. "Unfortunately, they underestimated how clever

Catherine can be. They focused their attention on Nathan, never worrying about poor Jimmy.

"Tuesday morning, Jimmy Gagnon formally filed for divorce from Catherine Gagnon. And just, what, sixty hours later, he was dead. You tell me, Officer, is that too much for coincidence?"

"Come on, Harris. It was a domestic disturbance call. She had no way of knowing what would happen next."

"Did you watch TV Thursday night, Officer Dodge? Hear the reports of how the Boston PD were already called out on a job, the same Boston PD officers who *knew* Jimmy and Catherine and might have shown a little more *finesse* in handling the situation? It makes me wonder if Catherine watched TV that night, too."

"She still couldn't have known that Jimmy would come home drunk, that Jimmy would get mad, that Jimmy would grab a gun—"

"Really? Because I know a lot of wives who know *exactly* how to push their husbands' buttons, the best way to pick a fight, the fastest way to burn his balls. Surely you've seen it before, Officer Dodge. There isn't a wife out there who can't make her husband fit to kill."

Harris gave him a meaningful look. This time, Bobby wasn't so quick to reply.

"She's going to call you again," Harris stated. "She's going to tell you her son is desperately ill. She's going to tell you that you're the only hope she has left. She's going to beg you to help her. It's what she does, Officer Dodge; she destroys men's lives."

"You honestly think she'd kill her own child just to get back at her husband?"

Harris merely shrugged. "Men may be violent, Officer Dodge, but let's face it— women are cruel."

Chapter 11

The man sat at a table outside a coffee bar at Faneuil Hall, frowning first at his double mocha latte, then at the scenery around him. What the hell had happened to this place? The Faneuil Hall of his memory had cutsey little boutiques, old Irish pubs, and lots of cheesy souvenirs. Now he was staring at The Disney Store, Gap, and Ann Taylor. The historic market had become a fucking suburban mall. There was progress for you.

The man grunted, sipped his double

mocha latte, and promptly grimaced. For the record, he'd been waiting a decade to try this drink—watching TV characters, rock stars, and movie actresses sip double-soy this or tall nonfat mocha that while hanging out in chic little coffee shops. You wore tight clothes, sipped your super-caffeinated beverage, then drove off in your Eddie Bauer SUV, Jennifer Aniston–looking wife sitting next to you, golden retriever panting in the back. Welcome to the American Dream.

Well, all these years of wondering later, the man had his answer—double mocha lattes tasted one step above cat piss. He was not picturing SUVs, soccer games, or perfectly mowed lawns. He was thinking how the hell had he gotten suckered into paying so much money for something that tasted so positively bad? It was tempting to return to the coffee counter. He would stand right in front of the black-haired cashier with her numerous facial piercings and sullen attitude. He'd never say a word. Just stand. Stare. She'd give him his money back in sixty seconds or less.

Then she'd hustle out back for a desperately needed smoke, rattled without being one hundred percent certain why.

He would like to see her face then. More than anything else in the past quarter century, he'd missed the look of a young girl's face filling with fear. The way her eyes would dilate, pupils growing dark as the rest of her face turned to ash. And then that moment, that sublimely erotic moment, when the true horror would wash across her features, when she would realize it was no longer a vague, unidentified sense of fear. When she would realize that he really *was* going to kill her. That she belonged to him now and there was nothing she could do.

The man had been locked up eight thousand three hundred and sixty-three days. He'd gone into the slammer barely a day over twenty. Sure, he'd been oversized, freakishly strong, and, as his neighbors had testified at his trial, "frighteningly strange." But, he'd still been a kid.

Now, as of a few hours ago, at the ripe old age of forty-four, he'd become a bona fide civilian again. He knew the parole board assumed that age would mellow him, just as quality time within concrete walls had supposedly eradicated his baser instincts.

Surely, after nearly twenty-five years in prison, he'd be a good boy now.

He thought about it. Nah. Truth be told, he mostly felt like killing someone.

Two girls walked by. Eighteen, nineteen years old. One of the girls caught him watching. She flipped him off, then gave a little twitch of her hips as she sauntered by, jeans so low and tight they appeared painted on her ass. He muttered a single word under his breath, and the girl suddenly picked up her pace, dragging her startled friend behind her. Smiling, the man let them go. It almost made up for the bad coffee.

He'd started his Walpole stint in PC, protective custody, for "snitches and bitches." It was a double-bunked dorm-room–like situation, technically medium security. "Don't screw this up," his court-appointed attorney had told him sternly. "For a guy like you, this is as good as it's going to get."

First night, his bunk mate had curled up in the corner and begged him not to rape him. The man had stared at the sniveling mass in disgust. He did *not* jitterbug.

Second night, the bunk mate started crying and the man gave in to his baser impulses and beat the little shit unconscious.

That at least shut him up. It also gained the man an infraction. And a reputation.

He didn't know it then, but the hawks were already watching, the prison scuttlebutt working overtime. His act of hostility got him kicked into general pop, then the real adventure began. A white guy had two choices in prison: join the Aryan brotherhood for protection against the blacks and the Hispanics or find God. God's protection was a little less certain inside the cement walls of Walpole. The man (boy) became a neo-Nazi.

He got an education. How to poke holes in the drywall of his cell, then patch them up with toothpaste and modeling paint to hide the drugs. How to pass off cigarettes, cocaine, heroin, you name it, using the rolled cuffs of his pants. How to fasten razor blades to the metal frame of his bunk, or inside the tank of his toilet, to catch the fingers of inexperienced guards.

How to live surrounded by dirty, filthy, angry men. How to piss in front of an audience. How to take a dump in front of an audience. How to sleep through certain half-realized screams, while knowing to wake for others. How to pass day after excruciating day inhaling stale, overprocessed air that stank of urine and Windex.

He still didn't learn quite enough. They caught him the second year. Boston Red Sox were trying to make the World Series and the guards were glued to the TV. The Hispanics came out of nowhere and "bungled" him good. Guards said they never saw a thing. So did his two fellow neo-Nazis, who never took their eyes off the game.

He was big, he was strong, he was mean. He managed to break various ribs, noses, and wrists of his eight attackers. They got his kidney with a homemade shank, dropping him like a stuck rhino and leaving him to bleed out on the floor.

One of the white guys came over then. "Baby rapist," the neo-Nazi said and spat on the man's face.

He began his plotting, lying twisted on a cement floor, his blood pooling up around his face.

The prison officials weren't stupid. Put him back in general pop and he was as good as dead. Put him back in PC and someone else was as good as dead. So what to do?

Stick him in solitary confinement, the only place left. It took the man only one week to realize his sack-of-shit lawyer had been right after all—medium security had been as good as it was ever going to get for a guy like him.

Now he passed his time alone in a six-by-eight cell. He was allowed out one hour a day, to exercise in a penned-in yard the size of a dog kennel or attend to personal hygiene. From a rectangular window about the same size as his face, he could watch leaves turn from green to gold to brown. Watch trees go from full to bare to covered with snow. Watch the seasons pass painfully slow, month after month, year after year.

Best he could look forward to now was to become a "runner," a prisoner who tends to the housekeeping for the cell block, in return for a slightly larger cell. Yeah, it was the goddamn glamorous life for him. Biggest thrill in the world was turning on the TV to stare at Britney Spears.

So much time. To sit. To brood. To plot what should happen next.

Prisons were about power. Power was about money. He was hated, he was feared,

and now, he was patient. Hoarding cigarettes, building his stash. Waiting for new
blood to enter the cement walls, someone
who would care less about what he did and
more about what could be done.

It took him eight years. The lucky candi-
date was a kid, not much older than the
man had been in the beginning, except this
kid was all skinny limbs and acne-spotted
face. Turned out he'd been making indecent
movies starring the little girls in his mother's
daycare. The kid went straight to PC, where
he sat bug-eyed each night, knowing he
didn't stand a chance and waiting for the
bogeyman to get him.

The man got to him first. Slipped some
money to a guard who in turn slipped the
kid the man's note, signed by "Mr. Bosu." A
bit more money, a few more notes, and the
kid was greased and ready to go. Mr. Bosu
had convinced him. If the kid was planning
on surviving, he needed to strike first and
strike hard. Build a rep, now, these first few
weeks, and everyone would leave him
alone.

The kid bought the preaching; Mr. Bosu
graciously offered more mentoring. How to
make a shank, how to conceal it. How to ex-

tract the sharpened piece of metal quickly and strike with surprise. Oh, and how to pick a target.

The man didn't care about the Hispanics. Fuck 'em, they'd kill any white guy just for sport. Mr. Bosu had bigger game in his sights.

It went down on a Thursday. In the cafeteria. Porno Kid was serving the meal to the other maximum security inmates. The right two white guys got in line. Kid said wait, he needed to get fresh food. He went around, no one really paying attention.

He dropped the first neo-Nazi before the guy ever made a sound. Second had just brought up his tray in bewilderment and the kid was at his throat.

The man heard stories later. How the kid, one hundred and fifty pounds soaking wet, was surprisingly strong. How he sprung on the two white supremacists like a spider monkey, teeth bared, eyes feral while he slashed away at their necks. The arterial spray shot eight feet. Guys already sitting down didn't know if the red on their shirts was from the two flailing white guys or the marinara sauce on their overcooked spaghetti.

Pandemonium ensued. Fellow neo-Nazis springing from their tables and, like the thick-headed Neanderthals they were, going after the nearest Hispanic, versus doing anything about the long-armed kid still carving up their fellow gang members.

Guards burst into the cafeteria, wielding heavy mattresses and firing knee knockers at anyone stupid enough to stand. Place went to full lockdown, alarms screeching, sirens whirling while the kid stood up in the middle of the carnage, held up the metal shank in his bloody fist, and shrieked, "So don't you buttfuckers ever *think* about touching me!"

It was a glorious moment, the man thought. He was shocked and pleasantly pleased with his prodigy. Two days later, the kid disappeared of course. Lot of blood in the laundry room, but no sign of a corpse. Word on the street—don't eat the meat loaf.

The state assembled a task force to look into "gang issues" at the prison after that. And the warden made them sit through a video on "racial sensitivity." Afterwards, everyone made a real point of saying, "No, it's really about *you,* not your fucking race,"

right before they beat the shit out of someone.

The man got to feel good for a few days,
before going back to his exciting life of
watching paint dry.

Now, however, there were whispers and
rumors about the mysterious Mr. Bosu. He
had friends, he had connections. This Mr.
Bosu, no one was quite sure who he was,
but even behind bars, he could get things
done.

The man was satisfied. From within the
harsh recesses of solitary confinement, he
had done something special—he'd become
every prisoner's bogeyman.

The man knew now, as he ran each day
around the exercise yard, as he passed his
time doing push-ups and pull-ups and ab
crunches and butt squats, that there would
be life after this. He was going to get out.
He would return to the world. Harder,
smarter, tougher than ever before.

And it would be good.

Once, he'd been a boy. He'd obeyed his
impulses, but he'd made mistakes. Now, he
was a man. He was seasoned. He understood the value of patience. And he knew
the legal system inside and out.

There would be no working at McDonald's for the glorious Mr. Bosu. There would be no life of drudgery, showing up every day for some menial job where he was supposed to be eternally grateful just to have his sorry, felonious ass employed.

He'd served his time. And he was not planning on ever going back to prison.

Oh no, he had quite a vision for himself. A whole career plan, in fact. He'd thought of it even before he'd been contacted by his mysterious Benefactor X, the one who'd arranged his timely parole, the one who'd passed along a certain list of chores.

Mr. Bosu was going to make himself a boatload of money. And Mr. Bosu was going to make it doing what he did best: randomly destroying lives.

The man smiled. He crunched up his disposable coffee cup in a single fist and rose from the table. Now people turned. Now people stared. Then, just as quickly, people turned away.

Mr. Bosu had made one mistake twenty-five years ago. He had let her live.

He did not plan on making that mistake again.

Chapter
12

Catherine drove toward her father's house. Light was failing, another day meeting a premature death as winter reared its ugly head. She was tired. Bone-deep weary in a way that made her grip the steering wheel too tight and twist about in her seat. Jimmy had always teased her when she drove, how she'd be horrible on a road trip, probably falling asleep and killing herself before ever reaching her first stop.

Thinking about him now made her feel a sharp, stabbing pain somewhere deep.

How long had it been since they'd said a kind word to one another? How many years since they'd even bothered to pretend they were in love? She guessed it didn't matter. He'd been a constant in her landscape and she missed him now the way other people might miss a limb. Once she'd been whole. Now she felt curiously incomplete.

She arrived in her father's neighborhood. Her neighborhood. Her parents had bought this house when she was five years old. The split-level ranch sat on a quarter acre, surrounded by other modest homes on other modest lots. Little had changed over the years. Her father maintained the same white siding with Colonial red shutters. Tuesday was garbage day. Saturday, people worked in their yards. And every Wednesday night, her father got together with the McGlashans and Bodells to drink beer and play cards. He'd have stories for her now of their children and grandchildren. Kids she had grown up with who'd gone on to manage grocery stores or work at banks, who drove minivans and now lived in split-levels of their own with tow-headed children and big bouncy dogs. Kids she'd grown up with leading normal happy lives.

She had wondered sometimes, right after it had happened, why it hadn't been one of them. Why couldn't they have seen the blue Chevy? Why couldn't they have been enticed to stop and help look for some mythical lost dog?

God, she hated turning down this street.

She parked her Mercedes in the driveway. Her father had the porch lights on, illuminating the tiny brick walk and four front steps. She took a deep breath, reminded herself to stay on task, and got out of the car.

The cold hit her hard. She shivered uncontrollably. She looked up the street, where night gathered just beyond the trees, forming a dark tunnel from which there would be no escape. She looked down the street and saw the same.

And suddenly, passionately, she hated this damn place. The house, the yard, the 1970s neighborhood. It had been an act of unkind fate that had brought her parents here. And as far as she was concerned, it was a bigger act of conscious cruelty that made them stay.

"It's not the neighborhood," her father had told her mother again and again right after it happened. "It was one man. We move now, and what will Catherine think?"

I would've thought you cared.

She drew in her shaky breath, realized she was close to losing it, and forced her hands into fists. *Think of a happy place,* she told herself a little wildly. Then thought, *Fuck it,* and headed for the door.

Her father was already waiting for her. She came up the steps and he opened the wooden door, leaving her to manage just the screen while he stood patiently to the side.

Inside, he took her coat and, as was his custom, said, "How was the drive?"

"Fine."

"Traffic?"

"Not bad."

He grunted. "Heading in, though, getting back to the city on a Saturday night . . ."

"I'll manage."

He grumbled again about traffic—he didn't like where she lived any more than she liked where he lived—then gestured weakly to the small living room. Carpet was still gold shag, the sofa a brown floral print. Catherine had offered to replace the furniture for him once. He'd shaken his head.

The sofa was comfortable, the carpet durable. He didn't require anything *fancy.*

Catherine moved to the edge of the tiny love seat and sat perched with her hands upon her knees. Entering this room always felt like entering a time warp; she never knew where to look or how to feel. Today she chose a spot on the carpet and fixed her gaze there.

"I need to talk to you about something," she said quietly.

"Are you thirsty? Want something to drink?"

"No."

"I have some soda. Root beer, right? That's what you like."

"I'm not thirsty, Dad."

"What about water? Long drive like that, you must be parched. Let me get you some water."

She gave up arguing. He shambled into the kitchen, then returned with two glasses of water in daisy-printed plastic cups. He took the brown La-Z-Boy. She remained on the love seat. She drank some of the water after all.

"You know what happened," she said at last.

Her father couldn't seem to look at her. His gaze was ping-ponging around the room. He finally found the portrait of her mother, hanging over the mantel, and she thought his face looked old and sad.

"Yeah," he said at last.

"I'm sorry it ended like this. I'm sorry . . . I'm sorry Jimmy's dead."

"He hit you," her father said, the first time she'd ever heard him acknowledge it.

"Sometimes."

"He wasn't a good man."

"No."

"You liked his money that much?" her father asked, and she was shocked by the sudden anger in his voice.

She faltered, her hands shaking harder. She tried another sip of water, but the cup trembled in her grasp. She wished she could just bolt from the room.

"He was good to Nathan."

"He never cared a rat's ass for either of you."

"Dad—"

"You should've left him."

"It's more complicated—"

"He beat you! You should've left him. You should've come here."

Catherine opened her mouth. She didn't know what to say. Her father had never made that offer. He'd never even commented on her marriage. He'd attended her wedding, where he'd shaken Jimmy's hand and told her new husband good luck. After that, he'd been busy with his card games and veterans' groups and routines. He'd appear every Thanksgiving and Christmas at her in-laws', eat some turkey, hand Nathan a present, give her a kiss on the cheek, and that was it, he was gone again, back to the neighborhood that he loved and she abhorred. Sometimes she wondered if things might have been different if her mother had lived. They would never know.

"It doesn't matter anymore," she said at last.

"Guess not." Her father drank some water.

"There's an issue though. The Gagnons, Jimmy's parents, are suing me for custody of Nathan." She brought up her chin. "They claim I'm abusing him."

Her father didn't say anything right away. He drank more water, then twisted the cloudy plastic cup in his hands, then drank some more. The silence dragged on.

Catherine grew bewildered. Where was the wild denial? Where was the leap to his daughter's defense? Sixty seconds ago he'd been claiming she could've turned to him for help for her broken marriage. Now where was he?

"The illnesses?" her father asked at last.

"They claim I'm doing something to Nathan, tampering with his food, I don't know what. They think I'm intentionally making him sick."

Her father looked up. "Are you?"

"Dad!"

"He's in the hospital a lot."

"He's sick!"

"Doctors never found anything."

"He has pancreatitis! Right now. Call Dr. Rocco, call anyone in that damn place." She was on her feet. "He is my son! I have jumped through every hoop I know trying to do right by him. How can you . . . How dare you! Goddammit, how dare you!"

She was yelling now, literally yelling, like a wild woman, with the veins bulging in her neck, and it occurred to her in the back of her mind that this was what she'd wanted to do for days. Ever since Tuesday morning, when she had picked up the phone and heard Jimmy casually discussing with some lawyer his plans to divorce her.

"You're sure she won't get anything?" he'd asked the lawyer. *"I don't want her touching one red cent."*

"No Nathan, no money," the lawyer had assured him. *"It's all taken care of. I can file the paperwork within the hour."*

"I love my son!" she screamed at her father now. "Why doesn't anyone believe that I love Nathan?"

And then she broke. Her legs gave out. She collapsed on the horrible brown sofa, her shoulders heaving, a strange hiccupping sound coming from her throat. She couldn't find herself. She was lost, drowned in some would-be moment, where Jimmy had left her and Nathan had left her and she was back in her rat-infested apartment, no family, no money, all alone. A blue Chevy would turn down the street. A hole would open in the ground. There would be nothing to save her anymore.

Her father was still sitting across from her. He had his gaze locked intently on the portrait of her mother. That finally gave her strength. She pulled herself together, wiping the back of her hand across her dry eyes.

"Will you support me?" she asked quietly.

"You need money?"

"No, Dad." Her voice grew terse again. She forced herself to speak calmly, as if explaining to a child. "There's going to be a hearing. A custody hearing. I met with my lawyer this afternoon. The Gagnons will bring in witnesses to testify that I'm a bad mother. I need my own witnesses who will say I'm a good mother. Or at least," she amended, "that I'm not a threat to Nathan."

"Where is Nathan now?"

"He's in the hospital. He has pancreatitis."

"Shouldn't you be there?"

"Of course I should be there!" She tried taking another deep breath. "But I'm here, Dad, talking to you about Nathan's future, because despite what anyone might think, I don't want to lose my son."

"The Gagnons aren't bad grandparents," he said.

"No. In their own way, I'm sure they love Nathan."

"He's all they have left now."

"He's all I have left, too."

"I think they would provide for him," her father said.

Catherine blinked her eyes, feeling slightly delirious. "I would provide for him, too."

Her father finally looked at her. She was startled by the anguish she saw in his face. "You used to be such a happy child."

"Dad?"

"I got out the home movies. I was cleaning out the attic, going through some stuff. I'm getting some arthritis, you know; it's tough to mount the stairs. So I thought I'd better get to those boxes, get them cleaned out while I still can. I found the old reel-to-reels. Watched them last night."

She couldn't say anything. Tears glistened in her father's eyes.

"You were so pretty," he whispered. "Your hair back in a ponytail, tied with a big red bow. Your mother used to comb it out for you every morning and you'd pick a ribbon for the day. Red was your favorite, followed by pink."

"You were in the backyard. Your birthday, I think, but I didn't see a cake. Other kids were over and we had filled the kiddie pool. You were laughing and splashing in the water, shrieking when I turned on the hose."

"You were laughing," he repeated now,

almost helplessly. "Catherine, I haven't seen you laugh in over twenty years."

Her chest went tight. She thought she should say something. She ended up shaking her head, as if to deny his words.

"Your mother loved you so much." He stood abruptly and turned away from her. "I'm glad she's dead. I'm glad she didn't live to see what would happen next."

"Dad—"

"You're not right, Catherine. You came back to us; God knows we considered ourselves grateful to get you back from that hell. But you're not right. In the end, our little girl died that day, and I don't know who's standing in front of me now. You don't laugh anymore. Sometimes, I'm not sure you feel anything at all."

She shook her head again, but he was nodding emphatically, as if arriving at some destination at the end of a very long trip. He turned back around. He looked her in the eye.

"You should let them have Nathan."

"He's my son."

"They have a lot of money, they'll take good care of him. Maybe they can even find him the right doctor."

"I've been trying to find him the right doctor!"

Her father spoke as if he'd never heard her. "They can get him counseling. That's probably what we should've done."

Catherine rose to her feet. "You're my father. I'm asking for your support. Will you give it?"

"It's not the right thing to do."

"Will you give it!"

He reached out as if to take her hand. She frantically snatched it back. And he smiled at her sadly. "You were a happy child," he said quietly. "Maybe it's not too late. Maybe if you get the right help, you can be happy again. That's all your mother wanted, you know. Even once she got cancer. She never prayed to live. She always prayed just to see you smile once more. But you never did, Catherine. Your mother was dying, and you still couldn't grant her that tiny little curve of the lips."

"You're *mad* at me? Is that what this is about? You're pissed off at me because I couldn't *smile* while my mother was dying? You . . . you . . ."

She couldn't speak. She was beyond words, stupefied by shock and rage. If she could just find the mantel, she could get a grip on the wooden trim and anchor herself. In the next instant, however, she had a clear image of her hand wrapping around the brass candelabra there and using it to bash in her father's head.

In her own detached way, she wasn't sure what surprised her more: the depths of her grief or the strength of her fury.

"Thank you for your time," she heard herself say. She brought her hands to her sides. She forced them to open. She breathed in, breathed out. The calm returned to her. Icy, yes. Barren. But better for her, better for her father, than any genuine emotion could ever be.

Catherine got her coat and very carefully moved toward the door.

Her father stood in the doorway behind her, watching her go down the steps, watching her walk to her car. He raised a hand in parting, and the sheer casualness of the gesture made her dig her teeth into her lower lip to keep from screaming.

Moving with practiced precision, she put her sedan in reverse and slowly backed out of the driveway. Put on the brake, shift to drive, find the gas. She took off down the street, driving too fast and still pursing her lips into a bloodless line.

She needed support. Her lawyer had been very clear. Without some kind of help, the Gagnons would win, they would take Nathan from her. Most likely, she would never see him again.

She would be all alone. And she would be broke.

Oh God, what was she going to do?

She was scattered. Distracted. Desperately searching for answers. That's why she didn't see it, of course. Not until the third or fourth intersection down. Then she finally glanced up, finally looked into her rearview mirror.

Someone had used her own lipstick to do it; she'd left it lying on the console between the seats. It was her favorite OPI color, a deep crimson, the color of a Valentine's Day rose, or fresh-spilled blood.

The message was simple. It read: *Boo!*

Chapter 13

Bobby went home. He had about thirty messages on his answering machine. Twenty-nine were from bloodsucking reporters, each and every one promising to tell his side of the story in return for an exclusive—did I mention exclusive?—interview. The thirtieth was from his LT, inviting him over for dinner.

"Come on over," Bruni extolled into the answering machine. "Rachel's roasted half a cow and is serving it with ten pounds of mashed potatoes. We'll eat too much, make rude bodily noises, and shoot the shit. It'll be fun."

Bruni was a good guy. He looked out for his team, kept them all together. He meant the invitation sincerely and Bobby should go. It'd be good for him, get him out of the house, keep him out of further trouble. He already knew he wouldn't.

He walked away from the blinking machine, into his tiny kitchen. He opened the refrigerator door, eyed the empty interior.

He wanted to call Susan. Say . . . what? *I'm a jerk. I'm an ass. Worse, I'm a killer.* None of it sounded promising. None of it changed anything.

Pizza, he thought. He'd walk to the local pizza parlor, order himself a pie. But thoughts of pizza made him think of beer. And thoughts of beer suddenly had his heart racing and his mouth salivating.

Yeah, that was it. Screw his kindhearted LT. Screw too-perfect Susan. Screw even dark and dangerous Catherine Gagnon, who'd raked her nails across his chest and made him pant like an overeager lap dog. Fuck 'em all. He didn't need people.

He needed a beer.

It occurred to him, in the last functioning

spot in his brain, that if he didn't do something now, *right now,* he was going to end up at a bar. And once he did, he was going to drink.

Bobby picked up the phone. He made a call. Then, before he had time to regret it, he headed out the door.

Dr. Lane buzzed him straight up to her office. Last time he'd seen her, she'd been wearing a suit. Tan pants, squarish jacket, some kind of ivory blouse. Expensive clothes, he'd guessed, but he hadn't cared for the outfit. Looked too mannish, like what a corporate woman with a chip on her shoulder might wear to board meetings. The outfit hadn't gone with her smile.

Tonight, called out on a Saturday to rescue an officer in distress, she wasn't wearing business clothes at all. Instead, given the frigid cold, she'd donned dark brown leggings and a warm, cable-knit Irish sweater that curled up around her neck and set off her long, chestnut-colored hair. She looked like she should be lounging in front of a large stone fireplace with either a good book or a good-looking man.

The image momentarily discomfited Bobby and he found he couldn't make eye contact as he unwound his scarf and hung up his jacket.

"Can I get you something to drink?" she asked, from the doorway of her office. "Water, coffee, soda, hot chocolate . . ."

He went with Coke, refusing her offer of a glass. She took a seat behind her desk. He returned to the wingback chair he'd used on Friday night, balancing on the edge.

"Thanks for the Coke," he said at last.

"You're welcome."

"Sorry if I messed up your plans."

"Not a problem."

"Did you have plans?" he found himself asking.

"I was thinking of going to a nursery and buying a ficus tree."

"Oh," he said.

"Oh," she agreed.

"What about during the day?" he continued like an idiot. "Do anything then?"

She regarded him with open amusement. After his complaint during their last session, he was now using small talk as a stall tactic and they both knew it. For a moment, he thought she might call his bluff, force him to cut to the chase, but then she answered his question. "Honest to God, I did nothing interesting today. Thought about running, decided it was too cold. Thought about cooking, decided I was too lazy. Thought about reading a book, decided I was too sleepy. So mostly, I spent the day contemplating life, then ignoring it. All in all, I'd say it was a perfect day. And yourself?"

"I spent the day ignoring your advice."

"Ah well, not the first time. What did you do?"

He decided he might as well get to it. "Last night I went to a bar."

She regarded him expectantly.

"I ended up drinking."

"A lot?"

"Enough." He took another breath. "I'm not supposed to drink."

"Are you an alcoholic, Bobby?"

"I don't know." He had to genuinely consider her question. He wasn't sure he liked the answer. "Life is better when I don't drink," he said at last.

"I take it you've had some experiences in this area."

"You could say that." He spun the soda can between his fingers. From the distance, her carpet appeared a rich, dark green. He could see now that it wasn't one color, however, but a mixture of many, many threads. Not just green, but giving the appearance of green.

"My father used to drink," he said. "A lot. Every night. Came home from work and headed straight to the fridge to grab a cold one. He said it helped him unwind. What's a few beers after all? Nothing hard-core. My brother and I were just kids. We believed what he said. Though after a while, we all knew it wasn't just a few beers anymore.

"After I joined the Academy, I started doing the post-shift bar scene. Hanging out with the guys, having a few laughs, drinking a few beers. You know, because it helped me unwind. And maybe at one point, I wasn't having just a few beers anymore. Maybe I was having a lot. So many I was showing up late for my shifts the next day. Then one night, I got a call. A buddy of mine had just arrived at the scene of a single-vehicle accident. It involved my father and a tree. In the bad-news department, my father had nailed the sucker going a good forty miles an hour, wrapped his GM truck right around the beech tree. In the good-news department, my father walked away with just a lacerated scalp. Truck was totaled, but he survived."

Bobby glanced up from the carpet. "My father was drunk. Blew a point two on the breathalyzer. No way he should've been behind the wheel of a vehicle; he was goddamn lucky a piece of wood was the only thing he hit. That night scared him shitless. Scared me, too. Kind of like one of those TV commercials: Here's your life. Here's your life with too much booze.

"So we made a pledge. I told him I wouldn't drink anymore if he wouldn't drink anymore. I figured I was doing it to help him. I'm kind of guessing he felt he was doing it to help me."

"And it worked?"

"As far as I know, for nearly ten years we've both stuck to it. Until last night."

"So why last night, Bobby?"

He said levelly, "I could say it was because guys were buying me beers. I could say it was because for the first time in years, I wasn't on call, so I was allowed to have a drink. I could say because after ten years, how much could one beer really hurt? I could say a lot of things."

"But you'd be lying?"

"I keep seeing his face," Bobby whispered. "Every time I close my eyes, I see his face. I did my job, dammit." He hung his head. "Jesus, I didn't think it would be this hard."

She didn't say anything right away. The words just hung there, gathering a weight of their own. He finally brought the Coke to his lips and swallowed. Then he looked up at the ceiling, above the dark paneling of mahogany wood trim, and there was Jimmy Gagnon as clear as daylight. One white male subject holding a gun on his wife and kid. One white male subject appearing genuinely surprised as Bobby's 165-grain bullet slammed into his skull. Do you know how a dead man looks? Startled.

Do you know how other people regard that man's killer? With admiration, pity, and fear.

"Are you thinking of drinking again?" Elizabeth asked quietly.

"Yeah."

"Do you think joining an AA group might help?"

"I don't like talking to strangers about my problems."

"Do you think talking to your father might help?"

"I don't like talking to my father about my problems."

"Then who can help you, Bobby?"

"I guess just you."

She nodded thoughtfully. "There is something you should know," she said after a moment, "before we go any further. . . . I have some previous involvement in this case. I've met with Judge Gagnon."

"What?"

"He wasn't my patient."

"The hell you say." Bobby flew out of his chair. He gazed at her wildly; he couldn't believe this. "Isn't that a conflict of interest? How can you do that? One day you're listening to one guy's problems, the next you're counseling the guy who's suing him?"

Dr. Lane held up a hand. "The judge came to me for a professional opinion. I met with him for thirty minutes. Then I referred him to an associate who I felt would be better able to assist him."

"Why? Why did he come to you? What did he want to know?" Bobby leaned over her desk, jaw clenched, arm muscles bulging.

He was pissed as hell, and he knew it showed on his face.

Elizabeth continued to regard him evenly. "I spoke to Judge Gagnon last night. With his permission, I will share with you what we said. I'm warning you now, however, I don't think it will help."

"Tell me!"

"Then have a seat."

"Tell me!"

"Officer Dodge, please have a seat."

Her expression remained set. After another moment, Bobby grudgingly let go of her desk. He sat back down, picking up the Coke can and twirling it between his fingers. He felt a light fluttering in his chest. Breathlessness. Panic. Damn, he was tired of feeling this way, as if the world had spun away from him, as if he'd never feel in control again.

"Judge Gagnon had gotten my name from an associate. He came seeking specific information about a psychological phenomenon. Perhaps you've heard of it. Munchausen by proxy."

"Shit," Bobby said.

"The judge told me a little bit about his daughter-in-law, Catherine. He wanted to know if someone with her background might fit the profile of a person capable of Munchausen's. Essentially, he wanted me to tell him, sight unseen, if Catherine was either faking his grandson's illnesses or deliberately making the boy sick in order to gain attention for herself."

"And what did you say?"

"I said it wasn't my area of expertise. I said as far as I knew, there wasn't a profile for Munchausen's. I said that if he honestly believed his grandson was in danger, then he should seek immediate professional assistance and contemplate legal action to separate the boy from his mother."

"Is he going to do that?"

"I don't know. He took the name of the person I gave him and he thanked me for my time."

"When was this?"

"Six months ago."

"*Six months ago?* The man sought expert advice for the safety of his grandson, and he didn't bother to act on it for *six months!*"

"Bobby," she said quietly, "I don't know what was going on in that house. More to the point, *you* don't know what was going on in that house."

"No," he said bitterly. "I just showed up

like judge and jury and shot a man. Shit. Just plain . . . shit."

Elizabeth leaned forward. Her expression was kind. "Last night, Bobby, you made a very astute observation. You said, 'Tactical teams don't have the luxury of information.' Do you remember that, Bobby?"

"Yeah."

"More importantly, do you still *believe* that, Bobby?"

"A guy is dead. Is it really such a great excuse to say it's because I didn't know any better?"

"It's not an excuse, Bobby. It's a fact of life."

"Yeah." He crumpled the Coke can. "What a pisser."

Elizabeth shuffled some papers on her desk. The silence dragged on. "Shall we talk about your family?" Elizabeth asked at last.

"No."

"Well, then, shall we talk about the shooting?"

"Hell no."

"All right. Let's discuss your job. Why policing?"

He shrugged. "I liked the uniform."

"Any other family members who were law enforcement? Friends, associates, relatives?"

"Not really."

"So you're the first? Starting a new family tradition?"

"That's me. I'm a wild child." He was still feeling belligerent.

Elizabeth sighed and drummed her fingernails on the top of her desk. "What brought you to the badge, Bobby? Of all the jobs in the world, how did this one become yours?"

"I don't know. When I was a kid, I figured I'd either be an astronaut or a cop. The astronaut thing was a little harder to pull off, so I became a cop."

"And your father?"

"What about my father? He's okay with it."

"What did he do for a living?"

"Drove a front loader for Gillette."

"And your mom?"

"Don't know."

"Do you ever ask your father questions about your mother?"

"Not in a long time." He set down the crumpled can and gazed at her pointedly.

"Now you're asking questions about my family."

"So I am. Okay, you became a cop because the astronaut gig seemed like a bit of a stretch. Why a tactical team?"

"The challenge." He said it immediately.

"You wanted to become a sniper? Were you always into guns?"

"I'd never shot a rifle before."

He'd finally surprised her. "You'd never fired a rifle? Before joining the STOP team?"

"Yeah. My father collects guns, does some custom work. But those are handguns, and frankly, my father's not big into shooting anyway, he just likes working on pistols. The machinery. The beauty of a really nice piece."

"So how did you become a sniper?"

"I was good at it."

"You were good at it?"

He sighed. "When qualifying for the tac team, you have to take proficiency exams in a variety of weaponry. I picked up the rifle and I was good at it. Little bit more practice here and there and I scored expert. So my lieutenant asked me about being a sniper."

"You're a natural with guns?"

"I guess." That thought made him un-

comfortable though. He amended it immediately. "Being a sniper isn't just shooting.
The official title is Sniper-Observer."

"Explain."

He leaned forward and spread his
hands. "Okay, so once a month I'm on a
shooting range, making sure my technical
skills are up to par. But in actual field duty,
chances of me being called upon to shoot
my weapon are like one in a thousand—hell,
maybe one in a million. You train to be prepared. But day in, day out, what I do on the
job is observe. Snipers are recon. We use
our scopes and/or binoculars to see what
no one else can see. We identify how many
people are at the scene, what they're wearing, what they're doing. We're the eyes for
the entire team."

"Do you train for that?"

"All the time. KIMS games, stuff like
that."

"KIMS games?"

"Yeah, KIMS. As in 'Kims.' I don't remember what it stands for. It's a title of a
Rudyard Kipling novel or something like
that. It's about observing. You go out on the
field, and the trainer gives you sixty seconds to spot ten things and describe them.

You grab your binoculars and go." He pointed at the Coke can. "I see what appears to be one crumpled soda can, looks new, red and white, probably Coke"—he tipped it on its side—"probably empty. Or, I see something that appears to be a length of wire, approximately eighteen inches long with green coating. It appears cut at one end and I can see the copper core, which is dirty. That sort of thing."

She regarded him with a bemused expression. "So you're professionally trained to notice everything. Does that drive you batty in real life? To notice all the nitty-gritty details everyplace you go?"

He grimaced and shrugged again. "Susan would probably say I don't notice a thing. Last time she got her hair cut, it took me two days to figure it out."

"And Susan is?"

"My girlfriend." He caught himself. "My ex-girlfriend."

"You mentioned her on Friday. I thought you said things were going well."

"I lied."

"You lied?"

"Yeah."

"And that would be because?"

"Because I'd just met you. Because I was feeling uncomfortable. Because . . . hell, take your pick. I'm a guy. Sometimes we lie."

The good doctor didn't seem amused by that statement. "So what happened with Susan?"

"I don't know."

"She just walked away?"

"Not really." He sighed, took a deep breath. "I did."

"You just walked away? Let me get this straight. You haven't talked to your girlfriend about the shooting at all?"

"No."

"Why?"

"I don't know."

"Bullshit." She said it. He blinked. "You're an intelligent man, Bobby Dodge. More intelligent than you like to let on. When you do things, it's for a reason. So why didn't you talk things over with Susan? Did you simply not care?"

"I don't know." He caught himself. She was right; he did know. "I thought she'd be horrified. In Susan's world, cops are the good guys, keeping things safe. In Susan's world, cops don't blow some guy's brains out, right in front of his kid."

"You didn't think she'd be able to handle it."

"I *know* she wouldn't be able to handle it."

"How wonderfully patronizing of you."

"Hey, you asked, I answered."

"Absolutely. And you're wrong, just so you know."

He sat upright. "What the hell kind of doctor are you?"

"Bobby, I'm going to ask you something and I don't want you to answer right away. I want you to think about it real hard before you say anything. Is it in Susan's world that cops are the good guys, or is it in Bobby's world? Is it in Susan's world that cops don't 'blow some guy's brains out,' or is it in Bobby's world? You said once that you were mad. But Bobby, aren't you also horrified?"

His gaze dropped to the carpet. He didn't say a word.

"You've commented several times now that you shot Jimmy Gagnon in front of his son. That seems to really bother you. Who is it in the scenario that you're identifying with? Are you upset for the powerful father dying in front of his child, or are you upset for the helpless child who is watching someone he loves die?"

He kept his gaze on the carpet.

"Bobby?" she prodded.

His gaze finally came up. He said, "I don't think I want to talk about this anymore."

He had his jacket on and was rewrapping his scarf before he spoke again. "Do you think Judge Gagnon could've been right?"

Elizabeth was sitting on the edge of her receptionist's desk, watching her patient bundle up and feeling frustrated. "I have no idea."

"Seems hard to imagine, a woman harming her kid just so she can have attention."

"Munchausen by proxy is not terribly common, but I've read estimates of up to twelve hundred new cases a year."

"What are the warning signs?"

"A child with a prolonged history of unusual illnesses, where the symptomatology doesn't add up. A child whose health is a prolonged cycle of being perfectly well one week, then drastically ill the next. A family with a history of Sudden Infant Death Syndrome."

"I spoke with Nathan Gagnon's doctor today," Bobby said abruptly. "He doesn't have a firm diagnosis for the boy."

Elizabeth was quiet for a moment. Then she said, "Do you think that was such a good idea?"

Bobby gave her a look. "I went. Good idea or not, it no longer matters."

"What are you doing, Bobby?"

"I'm putting on my scarf."

"You know what I mean."

"The Gagnons are suing me for murder. Anyone tell you that? They're using some fancy legal maneuver to charge me with killing their son. In all honesty, Doc, I don't think the concept of 'good' really applies to my life anymore."

"Being charged with murder must be very difficult."

"You think?"

She refused to get sucked into his sarcasm. "Bobby, Thursday night was a horrible tragedy. For you. For the Gagnons. For little Nathan. Do you really think there's anything you can learn now that will make you feel better about having shot a man?"

Bobby stared her straight in the eye. There was a look in his slate-gray gaze she'd never seen before. It left her slightly breathless. It chilled her to the bone.

"I'm going to get her, Doc," he said quietly. "If she's harming that boy, if she set me up to kill her husband . . . Catherine Gagnon may think she knows how to deal with men. But she's never met the likes of me."

He finished up his scarf.

Elizabeth sighed heavily and shook her head. There were things Elizabeth wanted to say to him, but she already knew it wouldn't do her any good. He wasn't ready to listen. Maybe Bobby didn't understand it completely yet, but she knew exactly who he identified with the night of the shooting, and it wasn't the gun-toting father.

"You're not responsible for Nathan Gagnon," Elizabeth murmured softly, but Bobby was already out the door.

Chapter
14

Catherine drove straight to the hospital. Nathan was still asleep, the heart monitor beeping faithfully while morphine dripped slowly into his thin veins. The night nurse didn't have much to report. Nathan remained on intravenous fluids, his temp was down, his pain under control. Maybe tomorrow he could go home, she'd have to consult with a doctor.

Catherine looked down the long, shadowed halls. Machines beeped, respirators hummed, patients thrashed restlessly in their curtained-off beds. But it was still a hospital at night. Too few nurses, too many strangers. Dark corners everywhere.

"Nathan's very sick," she said again.

"Yes."

"I think he needs more nursing care. Is there a private nurse I could hire? Staff of some sort? I'm willing to pay."

The nurse gave her a look. "You know, ma'am, in this mansion, it's just us servants tending the rooms."

"He's my child," Catherine said quietly. "I'm worried about him."

"Honey, they're all somebody's children."

The nurse wouldn't help her. Catherine finally buzzed the doctor on call, but he refused to sign a release. Nathan needed to remain at the hospital. Particularly given his "condition."

And what condition is that, she thought wildly. The infamous condition nobody can identify? Briefly, she contemplated calling Tony Rocco. She could beg, she could plead. Maybe Tony would come down, sign Nathan's release.

And what then? She'd take Nathan home where he'd be magically safe?

Boo! the message had read. *Boo!*

Inside her own car, parked in her father's driveway, written in her lipstick.

She left the hospital, footsteps fast, hands shaking.

At home, she went manically from room to room. The reporters clustered outside her brownstone were gone. Police, too. Where were the vultures when you needed them? Someone else had probably gotten shot tonight. Or maybe a senator had gotten caught with his cute young aide. Even the dubious celebrity of infamy could last only so long.

She checked doors and windows. Turned on lights until her townhouse glowed like a landing strip. The master bedroom thwarted her, however. The police still considered it a crime scene and she wasn't allowed to touch anything. Easy for them to say. They had patched the shattered slider with sheets of plastic. It didn't even block the goddamn wind. How was that going to stop an intruder?

She'd move the bureau. Shove it in front of the slider. Of course, if it was light enough for her to move, it would definitely be light enough for a man to move. Okay then. She'd move the bureau to block the

entry, turn on the outdoor spotlight to illumi-
nate the upper patio, then close the master
bedroom door and nail it shut from the outside. Perfect.

She went downstairs to find Prudence.

"I need your help," she told the nanny
briskly. "We're doing a little rearranging."

Prudence didn't say anything. Years of
training, Catherine thought. Years of very
expensive British training.

They went upstairs. Prudence helped
her push the heavy painted pine bureau in
front of the broken sliding glass door. There
were still some shards of glass on the carpet. Blood, too. Prudence saw all of it and
didn't say a word.

Catherine went down to the laundry room
and dug around until she found the tool kit.
When she started pounding nails into the
outer frame of the bedroom door, Prudence
finally spoke.

"Madam?"

"I saw someone outside," Catherine said
briskly. "Lurking. Probably just a tabloid reporter, looking to make a quick buck. How
much do you think the papers would pay for
a detailed photo of the Back Bay murder

scene? I will not let anyone profit from this tragedy."

Prudence seemed to accept that explanation.

After another moment, Catherine added, "I want to thank you, you know. This has been a terrible time. Heaven knows what you must think. But you've been there for Nathan. I appreciate that. He needs you, you know. With everything that's going on, he really, really needs you."

"Nathan's doing better?"

"He should be home tomorrow." She had another thought. "Maybe if he's feeling up to it, we could all go on vacation. Somewhere warm, with sandy beaches and drinks with little umbrellas in them. We could get away from . . . from all of this."

She finished hammering in the last nail. She tried the door, shaking it hard. It held.

That should do it. She hoped.

"Prudence, if anyone comes to the door that you don't know, don't answer it. And if you see any other . . . reporters . . . please tell me."

"Yes, Madam," Prudence said. "And the lights?"

"I think," Catherine said, still breathing

heavily, "that we'll leave them on for a little bit longer."

Tony rocco had had a long day. Ten p.m., he was finally leaving the hospital. Not bad ten years ago, but he was supposedly at the pinnacle of his career now. At this stage of the game, the hungry residents were supposed to deal with the endless grind of puking kids and snotty noses. He only came in for the big stuff.

His wife liked to remind him of that nightly. "Jesus Fucking Christ, Tony, when are you going to start demanding some respect? Just walk away from that damn hospital. Private practice is where the money is. You could be making three, four times what you're bringing home now. *We* could be making . . ."

He had stopped listening to his wife about five years ago. It had been halfway through a Thanksgiving dinner at his parents' house, when for the first time, honest to God, midway through his mother's rant about his father daring to go play golf with his friends, Tony had looked across the table at his lovely bride of three years and realized that he'd married his mother. It had hit him just like that. A giant thwack to the head.

His mother was a nag. His wife was a nag. And in another fifteen years he'd look just like his father, slightly hunched shoulders, chin tucked against his chest in perfect turtle posture, and selectively deaf in both ears.

He should've divorced her right then, but there were the children to consider. Yeah, his two darling, beautiful children, who already looked at him with his wife's accusing stare every time he was late for dinner.

He found himself thinking of Catherine again. The way she'd first come to him nine months ago. Her fingers brushing up his arm. Her long black hair teasing his cheek as she leaned over his shoulder to study Nathan's medical records.

She'd come to his office one day without Nathan, wearing a long black overcoat. She'd walked into his office. She'd locked the door behind herself. She'd looked him right in the eye and said, "I need you."

Then she'd thrown open her coat to reveal nothing but smooth white skin and tantalizing bits of black lace. He'd taken her right then and there, up against the wall, his trousers around his knees, her legs around his waist.

She'd climaxed so hard, she'd sunk her teeth into his shoulder. Then they'd tumbled to the floor and next thing he knew, she was on her hands and knees and he was riding her from behind, already as hard and horny as a teenager catching his second wind.

Afterwards, when both of them were too exhausted to move, when he could barely summon his receptionist by phone to tell her to cancel all his appointments for the afternoon, he'd seen the contusion on Catherine's left side.

It was nothing, she'd told him. She stumbled against the counter in the kitchen. That day, neither of them had commented on the bruise's perfect palmlike shape.

She'd wept the day she'd finally told him about Jimmy. They'd been in a hotel room in Copley Square. She'd just spent twenty minutes on her knees doing stuff he'd only ever read about in magazines. Now he held her close, stroking her hair.

I need you, she'd whispered against his chest. *Oh God, Tony, you don't know what it's like. I am so afraid . . .*

He should leave this stupid hospital, Tony thought now, walking through the empty parking garage, his footsteps ringing off the cement. He was sick and tired of people telling him what to do—his wife, the head of Pediatrics, a prick like Judge Gagnon. What was the point of working so hard for so many years if he never got to do anything he wanted to do?

He loved Catherine Gagnon. He was tired of all this shit. Screw his wife, screw the kids. He'd drive to Catherine's house right this minute. Tell her he took it back. He was sorry he'd let her down, sorry he'd told her he couldn't help Nathan.

Hell, he was sorry he'd sat in front of some state cop this afternoon, feeling like half a man as he tried to explain how he could love Cat and yet do nothing to protect her from Jimmy. The way that trooper had looked at him . . .

That was it. He would buck the system. He would stand on his own two feet. Just this once, he would do what he wanted to do, and screw the other women in his life.

Tony got to his car. He got out his keys, his hand already shaking in excitement.

It wasn't until he unlocked the door that he finally heard the noise behind him.

The footsteps moved quietly down the hall. Rubber soles treading carefully on white vinyl floors. The soft rustle of curtains. The *beep beep* of heart monitors, the hiss of numerous ventilators.

The nurse was gone, tending someone somewhere.

The hallway was dark and still.

The man tiptoed, tiptoed, tiptoed, until finally, the right room.

A shadow fell across the foot of the bed. Four-year-old Nathan stirred. He turned his head toward the sound. He opened his eyes to drugged half slits.

The man held his breath.

And Nathan whispered, "Daddy."

Chapter
15

Bobby was doomed. His head had finally just hit the pillow when his phone rang again. He didn't think of Susan this time. Instead, his thoughts went straight to Catherine. He'd been dreaming, he realized. He'd been dreaming of Jimmy Gagnon's widow, and she had been naked with her long black hair splayed across his chest.

"I just want to get some sleep," he snarled into the receiver.

"Still feel like playing detective, Officer Dodge?"

It took him a moment to place the voice. Harris, the Gagnons' earnest detective. Bobby's gaze went to the bedside clock. Dial glowed two a.m. Christ, he had to get some sleep. "What?" he asked.

"Got any friends with the Boston PD?" Harris said. "I think there's a crime scene you're going to want to visit."

"Who?"

Harris paused a heartbeat. "Dr. Tony Rocco. Parking garage of the hospital. Don't wear good shoes. I understand it's *messy.*"

Detective D.D. Warren had been with Boston Homicide for over eight years. A petite blonde with a lithe build and killer blue eyes, she worked the Rocco crime scene in slim-cut jeans, stiletto boots, and a caramel-colored leather jacket. *Sex and the City* meets *NYPD Blue.* Lots of the guys were staring. Given that D.D. ate, slept, and breathed her job, none of them stood a chance.

She and Bobby went way back. They'd dated eons ago, when they'd both been new recruits, her starting out for the city, him for the state. They could sympathize with each other's demanding days, without having to be in direct competition. Bobby couldn't remember anymore why they'd broken it off. Too busy, probably. It didn't really matter. They worked better as friends. He appreciated the meteoric rise of her career—she'd probably be lieutenant soon—and she was always interested in his work with STOP.

Now, however, D.D. was peering inside a dark green BMW 450i while chewing her lower lip. Across from her, a crime-scene technician armed with a camera was busily shooting away. The snap and whir of the advancing film echoed across the vast expanse of the cement parking garage and seemed to punctuate Bobby's approaching footsteps.

Garage was a little crowded, given that it was three a.m. Coroner's van, crime-scene van, numerous patrol cars, several detectives' vehicles, and a much nicer sedan Bobby recognized as belonging to the ADA. Lot of cars for a homicide. Lot of attention, period.

Bobby's breath exhaled in frosty pants. He sank his hands deep into the pockets of his down jacket and did his best to blend in. Several heads turned his way. Some faces he recognized, some he didn't. All knew him, though, and despite his best efforts, a buzz was building by the time he arrived at the BMW.

"Hey, Bobby," D.D. said without ever looking up.

"Nice boots."

She wasn't fooled. "Kind of late to be out on the town," she said.

"Couldn't sleep."

" 'Cause your phone was ringing off the hook?" She finally looked at him, blue eyes narrowed speculatively. "You got good ears, Bobby, given that we're doing everything we can to keep this one quiet."

He understood her question, but decided not to answer it. "If I happen to spend the next hour leaning against that concrete support column over there, studying my nails, how much of a problem would that be?"

"I'd say this is strictly a no-manicure zone." D.D. jerked her head left, and Bobby spotted ADA Rick Copley in deep conversation with the ME. Last time Bobby had seen Copley, Copley's men had been engaging in a friendly game of pin-the-shooting-on-the-beleaguered-state-trooper. So yeah, Copley would consider Bobby's presence a big problem.

"Highlights?" he asked D.D. under his breath.

She gave him another look. "When we profile the vic, how many times are we gonna find your name?"

"Once. This afternoon. Met him for the first time today to ask him about Nathan Gagnon."

She processed that, put two and two together very quickly and said, "Ah, shit. He's the kid's doctor?"

"Yeah."

"What else?"

"Had an affair with the boy's mom. Was already being questioned for a possible custody battle to be waged between the parents. Your turn."

She flicked her gaze across the way. Copley was still talking to the ME, but now looking in their direction, a frown marring his pug-nosed face.

"One DOA doctor in the front seat," D.D. murmured quickly, gesturing inside the car. "Looks like he just got his door open and someone nailed him from behind."

"Shooting?"

"Knife."

"Strong," Bobby said, trying to glance inside the car himself, and being blocked by D.D.'s shoulder.

"That's not even the half of it," D.D. said. Copley had started their way.

"You gotta run," D.D. told Bobby.

"Yep."

"But remember, we'll always have Paris." Bobby got the message. "See ya."

Bobby found the stairwell exit just as Copley closed the distance and the first crime-scene tech said, "Holy shit, is that blood?" and the second technician answered, "Actually, I think it's women's lipstick."

Casablanca's was a swanky Mediterranean restaurant in Cambridge. It featured a full martini bar and an eclectic menu targeted toward Harvard's more upscale clientele— namely the well-to-do parents of its Ivy League student population. Bogey's on the other hand was a tiny little diner tucked away just down from the statehouse. It offered twenty-four-hour service, peeling vinyl stools, and an extra-large griddle that hadn't been cleaned in years. Now, this was a place for cops.

Bobby walked all the way there, using the freezing early morning temp to clear the last of the sleep from his head and icicle half his eyelashes. It was shortly after five when he arrived, the sun not even up yet but the diner already hopping. He waited twenty minutes in the egg-and-bacon-scented heat, then finally got to steal a booth in the back. His stomach was growling; he ordered up three fried eggs, half a dozen pieces of bacon, and a butter-soaked English muffin. He wasn't sure if this qualified as a decent meal or not, but it did involve protein. He chased the food down with an extra-large OJ, then started in on the coffee.

He was entering that no-man's-land between food coma and caffeine buzz when D.D. finally walked into the diner. She sported a tight-fitting white T-shirt that announced in scripted red sequins, Felonious. It worked well with the boots.

She slid into the booth, glancing at Bobby's empty plate. "What, you didn't save *anything* for me?"

"What'd you want?"

"Eggs, bacon, French toast. With the

world's biggest OJ. And maybe a side order of pancakes."

"The case that good?"

"Oh yeah. I'm *starved.*"

Bobby walked up to the counter to place her order. When he returned, D.D. was emptying the last of his coffee urn into a mug she'd swiped from the serving station. He returned to the counter, refilled the urn and loaded up on cream. If memory served, D.D.'s appetite ran somewhere between a Marine's and a truck driver's. Lots of cream, lots of sugar, and anything else that was guaranteed to harden an artery.

When he returned to the table, loaded down with coffee and condiments, she finally appeared impressed.

"So, who gave you the heads-up?" she wanted to know, going straight to work on the sugar packets.

"Harris Reed. An investigator. Works for the Gagnons."

"*The* Gagnons? As in Judge and Maryanne?"

"The dynamic duo themselves."

She frowned. "And how'd this Reed know?"

"Didn't say."

"Have contacts inside the department?"

"Probably."

She grimaced. "Police stations. One guy drinks a glass of water and everyone else takes a piss. So the Gagnons are keeping an eye on things?"

"Apparently."

"Interesting." She'd finished sweetening up her brew and now poured in the cream. "And you, Bobby? All things considered, shouldn't you be off fishing or something?"

He spread his hands. "I can't fish."

"I heard about the lawsuit. That sucks."

He didn't disagree.

"Got a lawyer? How bad does it look?"

"Don't know." He shrugged. "Haven't gone attorney shopping yet. Been busy."

She stopped stirring her coffee. "Bobby, you gotta take this kind of thing seriously. If a cop can get pulled into criminal court just for doing her job . . . *this* is cause for concern."

Again, he didn't disagree.

"You have friends, you know. You guys covered for us when you took that call Thursday; no one wants to see you get hosed."

Bobby didn't feel like discussing it. What

was done was done. "So what's up at the garage?" he asked. "What happened to the good doctor?"

D.D. sighed, took a long swig of coffee, and settled back in the booth. "Not sure. For starters, however, I'd say he screwed around one too many times."

"A wronged lover?"

"More likely a lover's pissed-off spouse. Good doctor was attacked from behind. Subject wielded so much force, the blade severed half of Dr. Rocco's neck."

"Messy," Bobby murmured.

"And how. Subject got the doctor leaning forward into his car, so most of the *ewww* is contained in the driver's side of the BMW. Except, the fun didn't end there. The good doctor was kind of, well, *dismembered.*"

"Dismembered?"

"Dis-membered," D.D. said heavily. "We found it in the glove compartment."

"Ouch," Bobby said.

"Ouch," D.D. agreed.

He frowned. That was pretty personal. And an awful lot of activity for a public parking garage. "Got video footage from the surveillance cameras?"

"Looking into it now. Film I have seen is

very grainy and doesn't show much. Whoever did this was thinking. Got the doctor
incapacitated and into his vehicle. Then,
best I can figure it, the killer crawled into the
passenger side. BMW has tinted windows;
it's late at night. Anyone who walks by is
just gonna catch the silhouette of two people sitting in a car. Except one was kind of
dead and the other was getting jiggy with a
serrated blade. People. I swear they've all
seen too many movies."

D.D.'s food arrived. She started layering
the French toast with the fried eggs and
pieces of bacon, her eyes positively gleaming. Then she got her hands on the syrup.

"Gotta be a lot of blood," Bobby said.
"That kind of work . . . I'd think you'd have
splatter everywhere."

"You'd think." She sawed off a bite of
French-toast breakfast sandwich with her
fork and munched away blissfully. "You
were at the scene, Bobby. Picture that big
cold garage, think of the facility it was attached to, and tell me what we got."

Bobby thought back. Under the glare of
the floodlights, the cement floor had appeared smooth and unmarred, not a red
drip in sight. He frowned, considered the

matter again, then suddenly smiled. "A hospital. Surgical scrubs!"

"Bull's-eye. We found a garbage bag filled with bloody scrubs and shoe booties in a dumpster outside of the west-side entrance. It would appear our clever killer donned scrubs, did the deed, then balled up the discarded garments and shoe booties and tossed them tidily away. So most likely he walked into the garage looking like any old surgeon. Once he was done, he waited for a quiet moment, got out of the car, peeled off the garments, and sauntered away."

"You'd get two footprints," Bobby said. "Him exiting the car."

"Found smeared blood outside the passenger's seat. Looks like he wiped up the spot, maybe with part of the scrubs. Didn't get it perfect, but did obliterate any tread patterns. Ingenious little shit."

"Foresight," Bobby thought out loud. "Planning."

"Yes and no. Did take some thought, but everything he needed was on site. So, he didn't have to plan too far in advance. Assuming, of course, that the killer wasn't actually a surgeon, which, of course, given the location, isn't something we've ruled out."

D.D. was halfway through her plate now and positively sighing. "Oooh, that's good. I swear if it wouldn't give me an immediate coronary, I'd come here every day."

"So what about suspects?"

"Funny you should ask."

"You're not thinking me, are you?" He was genuinely startled.

"Should I be thinking you?"

"D.D.—"

"Relax, Bobby. It's your girlfriend we're going after. Catherine Gagnon."

Bobby frowned. The girlfriend comment had been dangled as bait, but he refused to bite. "I don't see it," he said after a bit.

"ADA's office started looking into the widow yesterday. Rumor is, she had a lot to gain from her husband's death. Rumor is, she might have been shopping around for some hired help—or a misplaced fool's heart."

"Copley thinks Catherine approached Tony Rocco about killing her husband?"

"Copley tried to schedule an interview with the good doctor yesterday afternoon. Rocco blew him off."

Bobby nodded, holding his coffee mug between his hands and thinking hard. "If

Tony Rocco was Catherine's ally, why would she kill him or find someone to kill him?"

D.D. shrugged. She wouldn't meet his eye. "Rocco obviously didn't kill Jimmy."

"No," Bobby agreed quietly, "he didn't." He kept gazing at D.D., but her eyes were now locked on her plate.

"But maybe Catherine spoke to Rocco about doing it," D.D. said after a moment. "And maybe she got word that the ADA was looking into it. That would give her motive to want Tony Rocco dead—so Rocco couldn't rat her out."

"But the killer was most likely a male."

"She has looks, she has money. Either one would get her help."

"Help to eliminate the help," Bobby pointed out dryly.

D.D. shrugged. "It's Copley's theory. Me, I'm still going with the jealous spouse. After all, if you were just killing someone to be expedient, would you really engage in postmortem weenie whacking?"

"That does seem more personal."

"Plus there's the message to consider."

"The message?"

"Yeah. Written on the back window.

That's what got Dr. Rocco found; someone leaned closer to read the script."

"And it says?"

" 'Boo.' "

"Boo?"

"Yeah, written in women's lipstick."

"Women's lipstick?"

"Yep. And I'll bet you anything that on Catherine Gagnon this is a particularly killer shade of red."

D.D. polished up her plate. Bobby grabbed the bill.

"Copley's gonna pay you a visit this afternoon," D.D. mentioned.

"Is he flirting, or do you think it's true love?"

"He says that yesterday you and the missus were spotted playing together at the Gardner Museum."

Bobby unfolded the bills from his money clip and started counting out ones.

"It's not good," D.D. continued quietly, "to be seen with the dead man's wife. Makes people talk."

He needed a ten. Didn't have one. Settled on two fives.

"She's trouble," D.D. said.

Two singles should do it for the tip.

"He was going to divorce her, you know, and take full custody of the kid. Sometimes, there's a very fine line between being a destitute ex-wife and being a wealthy widow. Thursday night, Catherine Gagnon crossed that line. In this business, you have to wonder about that sort of thing."

Bobby finally glanced up. "Do you really think she could've set it up? Engineered a fight, arranged for her husband to have a gun, then manipulated everything so that he got shot and she didn't?"

D.D. didn't say anything right away. When she finally spoke, he wished she hadn't. "Did you know her, Bobby? Had you had any contact with her before the call? Even a casual acquaintance, a friend of a friend?"

"No."

D.D. sat back, but her face was still troubled, her eyes watching. Bobby stood up, fumbling to get his money clip back in his pocket and now biting back a curse.

"Bobby," she said after a moment, and something in her voice stopped him. She had an expression on her face he'd never seen before. A certain grim curiosity. For a moment, it appeared she'd changed her mind, but then the question came out anyway, as if she simply had to know.

"When you took the shot . . . was it difficult, Bobby? Seeing a real person, did it make you hesitate?"

It would be easy to be offended, to give her a dirty look, then cut and run. But D.D. was a friend. A fellow cop from way back. And maybe, if he dug deep, Bobby understood her question even better than she did. It was the one thing every cop had to wonder. So much time spent in training, but when it came down to it, in the field, when it was your life, or worse, a fellow cop's on the line . . .

He gave it to her straight.

"Honest to God," he said quietly, "I didn't feel a thing."

D.D.'s gaze fell to the floor. She wouldn't look at him again. And he didn't bother to be surprised anymore. Three days after the shooting, he was finally learning that that's the way these things went.

Bobby nodded at her one last time, and headed out the door.

Chapter
16

Bobby had walked two blocks from the diner when the sleek, black Lincoln Town Car pulled alongside him. A darkened window purred down. Bobby took one look inside and cursed.

"Don't you have a hobby?" he asked Harris Reed, who was slowing down the sedan to match Bobby's walking speed. A string of irritated honks promptly sounded from the traffic behind him.

"Get in," Harris said.

"No."

"My employers would like to talk to you."

"Tell them to file another lawsuit."

"They're very powerful people, Officer Dodge. The right conversation with them, and all your troubles could go away."

"How wonderfully patronizing of them." He picked up his step. "Still walking."

Harris changed tactics. "Come on, Officer Dodge. You killed their son. Surely you can give them ten minutes of your time."

Bobby's footsteps slowed. Harris braked the car. "That's not fighting fair," Bobby said with a scowl. He reluctantly opened the car door. Harris grinned like an asshole.

The gagnons were ensconced at the Hotel LeRoux, a new, high-end hotel across from the Public Garden. Apparently there were too many reporters at their multimillion-dollar Beacon Hill townhouse, so they'd been forced to retire here. Mrs. Gagnon, Bobby was informed, could barely eat or sleep. Judge Gagnon had booked a luxurious penthouse suite, with round-the-clock masseuse, to help ease her nerves.

Harris was chatty about his employers. How the Gagnons were originally from

Georgia, so don't be surprised by their Southern accent. Mrs. Gagnon had been a real, genuine debutante, complete with satin dress and bouffant hair, when she'd met James Gagnon back in '62. The money came from her side, actually. But the judge was an ambitious law student even back then. Her family had approved the match and her daddy was preparing to set up Jimmy at his own law firm.

Sadly, Maryanne's entire family—mother, father, younger sister—died in a fiery car crash a week before the wedding. Needless to say, Maryanne had been devastated. In an attempt to comfort his shattered fiancée, Jimmy had whisked her away from the state. They'd moved to Boston, tied the knot in a small civil ceremony, and made a fresh start.

In the good-news department, they'd gotten pregnant right away. In the bad-news department, their baby, the original James Jr., was born sickly. The infant had died in a matter of months, and James and Maryanne had returned to Georgia for one more funeral, burying their son in the family plot in Atlanta.

Two years later, young Jimmy had arrived, and James and Maryanne hadn't looked back since.

Bobby thought it was creepy they'd name the second child the same as the first. The first boy was Junior, the second, Jimmy, Harris told him. Bobby still thought it was creepy.

Entering the penthouse suite, Bobby's first thought was that the Gagnons knew how to make an impression. The space boasted Italian marble floors, expensive antiques, and a vast bank of windows draped in enough silk to exhaust a worm farm. The high-end hotel suite provided the perfect backdrop for its high-end occupants.

Maryanne Gagnon appeared to be in her mid-sixties, trim but slightly stoop-shouldered, with tight-set platinum blonde hair that was now more platinum than blonde. She wore a triple strand of knuckle-sized pearls around her neck and a rock the size of a golf ball on her finger. Sitting in some dainty French provincial chair in a cream-colored silk pantsuit, she nearly blended in with the draperies behind her.

In contrast, Judge Gagnon dominated the space. He stood slightly behind his wife's right shoulder, tall, in a single-breasted

black suit that probably cost more than
Bobby made in a month. His hair had turned
the color of slate with age, but his eyes remained bright, his jaw square, and his
mouth hard. You could picture this man ruling a courthouse. You could imagine this
man ruling the country.

Bobby had a flash of insight: Weak-willed
Jimmy Gagnon had most likely taken after
his mother, not his father.

"You don't look that big," Maryanne
Gagnon spoke up first, surprising all of
them. She turned her head to look up at her
husband, and Bobby saw her hands trembling on her lap. "Didn't you think he'd
be somehow . . . bigger?" she asked the
judge.

James squeezed his wife's shoulder and
there was something about that quiet display of support that unnerved Bobby more
than the clothes, the room, the perfectly
posed sitting. He studied the marble floor,
the zigzag patterns of gray and rose veins.

"Would you like something to drink?"
James offered from across the room.
"Maybe a cup of coffee?"

"No."

"Anything to eat?"

"I don't plan on staying that long."

James seemed to accept that. He gestured to a nearby sofa. "Please have a seat."

Bobby didn't really want to do that either, but he crossed to the cream-colored sofa, sitting gingerly on the edge and fisting his hands on his lap. In contrast to the Gagnons' perfectly groomed appearance, he wore old jeans, a dark blue turtleneck, and an old gray sweatshirt. He'd crawled from his bed in the middle of the night to view a crime scene, not face grieving parents. Which, of course, the Gagnons had known when they'd sent Harris to pick him up.

"Harris tells us you've met with Catherine." James again. Bobby had a feeling it was his show. Maryanne wasn't even looking at Bobby anymore. Bobby realized after another moment that the woman was crying soundlessly. Her face, carefully angled away, was covered in a glaze of tears.

"Officer Dodge?"

"I've met Catherine," Bobby heard himself say. His gaze was still on Maryanne. He wanted to say something. *I'm sorry. He didn't suffer. Hey, at least you still have your grandson. . . .*

Bobby'd been a fool to come here. He saw that now. James Gagnon had run a sucker play, and Bobby had walked right into it.

"Did you know my daughter-in-law before the shooting?" James was prodding.

Bobby forced his gaze back to the older man. Seemed like everyone was asking that question these days. Firmly, he said, "No."

"You're sure?"

"I keep track of the people I meet."

James merely arched a brow. "What did you see that night? The night Jimmy died?"

Bobby's gaze flickered to Maryanne, then back to her husband. "If we're going to talk about this, I don't think she should be in the room."

"Maryanne?" James said softly to his wife, and she once more looked up at him. Seconds before, she'd been crying. Now Maryanne seemed to draw herself up, to find a reserve of strength. She took her husband's hand. They turned toward Bobby as a united front.

"I would like to know," Maryanne drawled

softly. "He's my son. I was there for his birth. I should know of his death."

She was brilliant, Bobby thought. In four sentences or less, she had cut out his heart.

"I was called out to a domestic barricade situation," he said as evenly as he could. "A woman had called nine-one-one saying her husband had a gun, and the sound of gunshots had been reported by the neighbors. Upon taking up position across the street, I spied the subject—"

"Jimmy," the judge corrected.

"The subject," Bobby held his ground, "pacing the floor of the master bedroom in an agitated manner. After a moment, I determined that he was armed with a nine-millimeter handgun."

"Loaded?" James again.

"I could not make that determination, but previous reports of shots fired would seem to indicate the gun was loaded."

"Safety on or off?"

"I could not make that determination, but again previous reports of shots fired would seem to indicate the manual safety was off."

"But he could've put the safety on."

"Possible."

"He could have never fired the shots at all. You didn't *witness* him firing his weapon, did you?"

"No."

"You didn't *witness* him loading the gun?"

"No."

"I see," the judge said, and for the first time, Bobby saw. This was the preliminary, just a brief taste of what would happen to him when things went to trial. How the good judge was prepared to show that he, Robert G. Dodge, had committed murder on Thursday, November 11, 2004, when he shot the poor, unsuspecting victim, beloved son James Gagnon, Jr.

It would be a war of words, and the judge had all the big ones on his side.

"So what exactly *did* you see?" the judge was asking now.

"After a brief interval—"

"How long? One minute, five minutes? Half an hour?"

"After approximately seven minutes, I saw a female subject—"

"Catherine."

"—and a child come into view. The woman was holding the child, a young boy.

Then the female subject and the male *sub-ject,*" Bobby said emphatically, "proceeded to argue."

"About what?"

"I had no audio of the scene."

"So you have no idea what they said to one another? Perhaps Catherine was threatening Jimmy."

"With what?"

The judge changed his tack. "Or she was verbally abusing him."

Bobby shrugged.

"Did she know you were there?" the judge pushed.

"I don't know."

"There were spotlights, an ambulance arriving at the scene, police cruisers coming and going. Isn't it likely that she noticed this level of activity?"

"She was up on the fourth floor, above street level. When I first arrived, it appeared that she and the child were hunkered down behind the bed. I'm not sure what it's realistic to assume she knew and didn't know."

"But you said she placed a call to nine-one-one herself."

"That's what I was told."

"So therefore, she expected some sort of response."

"Response in the past has been two uniformed officers knocking at her front door."

"I know, Officer Dodge. That's why I find it so interesting that *this* time, she made certain to mention that Jimmy had a gun. A weapon made it an automatic SWAT call, didn't it?"

"But he *did* have a gun. I saw it myself."

"Did you? Are you sure it was a real gun? Couldn't it have been a model, or maybe one of Nathan's toys? Why, it could've been one of those fancy cigar lighters in the shape of a revolver."

"Sir, I've viewed over a hundred pistols of various makes and models in the past ten years. I know a real gun when I see it. And it was a genuine Beretta 9000s that the techs recovered from the scene."

The judge scowled, obviously not liking this answer, but was swift to regroup. "Officer Dodge, did my son actually pull the trigger Thursday night?"

"No, sir. I shot him first."

Maryanne moaned and sank deeper into her chair. In contrast, James nearly grinned. He started pacing, his footsteps ringing against the marble floor, while his finger waggled in the air.

"In truth, you don't really know much about what was going on in that room Thursday night, do you, Officer Dodge? You don't know if Jimmy had a loaded gun. You don't know if he had the safety on or off. Why, for all you know, Catherine started the argument that night. Catherine may have even threatened to harm Nathan. Why, for all you know, Jimmy went into the family safe and got out that gun only as a last resort—so he could fight for the life of his child. Couldn't that well be the case?"

"You would have to ask Catherine."

"Ask *Catherine*? Invite my daughter-in-law to lie? How many cases are you called out to a year, Officer Dodge?"

"I don't know. Maybe twenty."

"Ever fire your weapon before?"

"No."

"And the average length of engagement for those call-outs?"

"Three hours."

"I see. So on average, you're deployed twenty times a year for three hours each episode, and you've managed in all that time to never fire your weapon. On Thursday night, however, you showed up and shot my son in *less than fifteen minutes.* What made Thursday night so different? What made you so convinced that you had no choice but to *kill* my son?"

"He was going to pull the trigger."

"How did you know, Officer Dodge?"

"Because I saw it on his face! He was going to shoot his wife!"

"His face, Officer Dodge? Did you really see it on *his* face, or were you thinking of someone else's?"

In Bobby's heightened state of agitation, it took him a moment to get it. When he finally did, the world abruptly stopped for him. He suffered a little out-of-body experience, where he suddenly drifted back and became aware of the whole sordid scene. Himself, sitting on the edge of the silk-covered sofa, half leaning forward, his hands fisted on his knees. Maryanne, slumped deep into a cream-colored chair, lost in her grief. And Judge Gagnon, finger still punctuating the air with a prosecutorial flourish, a triumphant gleam in his eyes.

Harris, Bobby thought abruptly. Where the hell was Harris?

He turned and found the man lounging in

a dark wooden chair in the foyer. Harris delivered a two-fingered salute: he didn't even bother to hide his smugness. Of course he'd dug up the information. That's how this game worked. The Gagnons paid, Harris dug, and the Gagnons got whatever they wanted.

For the first time, Bobby began to truly understand how helpless Catherine Gagnon must have felt.

"If there's a trial, it's going to come out," Judge Gagnon was saying now. "This kind of thing always does."

"What do you want?"

"She's the reason Jimmy is dead," James said. There was no need to define *she*. "Acknowledge it. She cajoled you into firing."

"I'll say no such thing."

"Fine then. Revisionist history. You showed up, you heard my son and his wife arguing, but it was obvious she started it. She was threatening Jimmy. Better yet, she was finally admitting what she was doing to Nathan. Jimmy simply couldn't take it anymore."

"No one in their right mind will believe I heard all that while sitting in another house fifty yards away."

"Let me worry about that. She murdered my son, Officer Dodge. As good as if she pulled the trigger herself. There is no way I'm going to stand by and let that woman harm my grandson too. Help me, and I'll let your little lawsuit slide. Resist, and I'll sue you until you're a broken old man with no career, no home, no dignity, no self. Consult any lawyer. I can do it. All it takes is money and time." James spread his hands. "Frankly, I have plenty of both."

Bobby rose off the sofa. "We're through here."

"You have until tomorrow. Just say the word and the lawsuit is gone and Harris's little research project is 'forgotten.' After five p.m., however, you'll find I'm no longer as forgiving."

Bobby headed for the door. He'd just gotten his hand on the brass knob when Maryanne's soft voice stopped him.

"He was a good boy."

Bobby took a deep breath. He turned around, asking as gently as he could, "Ma'am?"

"My son. He was a little wild sometimes. But he was good, too. When he was seven, one of his friends was diagnosed with leukemia. That year for his birthday, Jimmy had a big party. Instead of asking for presents, he asked people to bring money for the American Cancer Society. He even volunteered at the suicide hotline while in college."

"I'm sorry for your loss."

"Every Mother's Day, he'd bring me a single red rose. Not a hothouse rose, but a real rose, one that smelled like the gardens of my youth. Jimmy knew how much I loved that scent. He understood that, even now, I sometimes miss Atlanta." Maryanne's gaze went to him, and there was a pain in her eyes that went on without end. "When it's Mother's Day," Maryanne murmured, "what am I going to do? Tell me, Officer, who will bring my rose?"

Bobby couldn't help her. He walked out the door just as her grief finally broke and her sobs began in earnest. James's arms were already going around his wife and Bobby could hear the man as the door shut behind him: "Shhhh. It's all right, Maryanne. Soon we'll have Nathan. Just think of Nathan. Shhhhh. . . ."

Chapter 17

When Catherine got up, Prudence was already gone for the day. Sundays were the nanny's day off and Prudence didn't like to waste a minute. Catherine thought it was just as well. The sun was out, an almost unbearably bright blue sky yawning above, looking the way only a New England sky could look during the crisp days of November. Catherine went from room to room, turning on lights anyway. She thought she might be going a little mad.

Had she slept last night? She couldn't be

sure. Sometimes she dreamed, so that must have involved sleep. She'd seen Nathan, the day he was born. She'd been pushing for three hours. Almost there, almost there, the doctor kept telling her. She'd stopped screaming two hours ago, and now only panted heavily, like a barn animal in distress. The doctors lied, Jimmy lied. She was dying and this baby was tearing her in two. Another contraction. *Push,* screamed the doctor. *Push,* screamed Jimmy. She sank her teeth in her lower lip and bore down desperately.

Nathan came out so fast, he overshot the doctor's waiting hands and landed on the sheet-covered floor. The doctor cheered. Jimmy cheered. She merely groaned. Then they put little Nathan on her chest. He was blue, tiny, all covered in muck.

She didn't know what she was supposed to think. She didn't know how she was supposed to feel. But then Nathan moved, his tiny little lips rooting for her breast, and she found herself unexpectedly blubbering away like an idiot. She cried, huge fat tears, the only genuine tears she had shed since her childhood. She cried for Nathan, for this beautiful new life that had somehow come from her own barren soul. She cried for this miracle she had never believed could happen to her. And she cried because her husband was holding her close, her baby was snuggling against her, and for a fraction of an instant, she did not feel alone.

She'd dreamed of her mother. Catherine saw her standing in the doorway of her childhood bedroom. Catherine lay in her narrow bed, her eyes desperately alert. She had to stay awake, because if she slept, the darkness would come, and in the darkness would be *him.* Forcing her head into his lap. *The smell, the smell, the smell.* Grunting as he rammed himself into her, a camel trying to pass through the eye of a needle. *The pain, the pain, the pain.* Or it would be worse. It would be the days and weeks later, when he didn't even have to force her anymore. When she simply did whatever he wanted, because resistance was futile, because the indignities no longer mattered, because the little girl who'd been thrown into this hellhole didn't exist anymore. Now only her body remained, a dried-up shell going through the motions and feeling only gratitude that he returned to her at all.

Someday he wouldn't. She understood that. Someday, he would tire of her, simply walk away, and she would die down here. In the dark, alone.

There were not enough lights in the house. Three, four, maybe it was five in the morning, Catherine rounded up all the candles. Flashlights were good. The light in the oven. The night-light for the water dispenser in the refrigerator door. The undercabinet lights. The inside-the-cabinet lights. The fires in the two gas fireplaces. She went from room to room, turning them on. She needed light, she had to have light.

She'd dreamed of Jimmy. Smiling Jimmy, happy Jimmy. *Hey, what's a guy gotta do to get a little spritz?* Angry Jimmy, drinking Jimmy, cold Jimmy. *You're sure she won't get anything? I don't want her touching one red cent.*

She'd dreamed of Jimmy so much, she'd bolted out of bed at six a.m. and run to the bathroom to throw up.

Boo, a voice whispered in the back of her mind. *Boo.*

Oh please God, let Jimmy be finally dead.

Now it was nearly nine. Visiting hours at the hospital. Catherine had already called four times. Nathan was awake. She could see him.

Fuck that. She didn't trust the hospital. It didn't offer enough security. She was bringing her son home.

Catherine had her coat, had her keys. One last check of the house. That's right, the candles. She passed through the rooms, blowing out the burning wicks one by one. She was just coming downstairs again when she remembered the Taser. She'd had one in the safe. She returned upstairs to the master bedroom, preparing to arm herself for a war against an enemy that had no name.

Who would write *Boo!* on her rearview mirror? Who would do such a thing?

She didn't like to think about it too much. There were answers out there, and most of them terrified her.

The safe was wide open, the way the police had left it. She gazed inside. The Taser was gone. Rat bastards. They'd probably inventoried it for evidence. Like the Taser was really going to protect her from Jimmy's gun.

She returned downstairs, the anger reinvigorating her and driving her toward the front door. To the hospital, to Nathan. She'd just put her hand on the knob when, from the other side, someone knocked. Catherine recoiled, hand to her chest as if struck. The knocking came again.

Very slowly, she put her eye to the peephole.

Three people stood there. The police.

No, she thought wildly. Not now. Nathan was all alone. Didn't they know that at any time, a man driving a blue Chevy could turn down the street?

Knocking again. Slowly, Catherine opened the door.

"Catherine Gagnon?" the man standing in front asked. His nose was squashed, as if he'd been hit in the face one too many times. It appeared incongruous with his nice gray suit.

"Who are you?"

"Rick Copley, ADA for Suffolk County. I'm here with Detective D.D. Warren, BPD"—he gestured to a beautiful blonde with cheap taste in clothes—"and Investigator Rob Casella, DA's office." He gestured to a particularly grim-faced man who was wearing a dark suit fit only for funerals. "We have a few questions we need answered. May we come in?"

"I'm on my way to see my son," she said.

"Then we'll do our best not to take too much of your time." The ADA was already pushing into her home. After another moment, she gave way. It probably was best to do this now. Before Nathan—or Prudence—returned.

The cheap blonde was looking around the downstairs foyer as if she wasn't impressed. The investigator, on the other hand, was already taking notes.

"I think we'd be more comfortable having a seat." The ADA invited them all to enter the parlor to the left-hand side of the foyer. Catherine finally let go of her purse, shrugged out of her coat. She was watching the ADA most carefully; he was the one in charge.

She wondered what he thought of grieving widows. Then she caught his glance again. His expression was hard, calculating, a predator sizing up prey. So that's the way it was then. For as long as she could remember, Catherine had brought out only the extreme in the male of the species. Men who lusted after women lusted after her more. And men who hated women . . .

She would do better, she decided, focusing her energies on the man dressed for the funeral.

"I'm glad you stopped by," she said firmly, shoulders back, sailing into the room. "I contacted the medical examiner's office yesterday. I confess I was quite startled to learn that I still can't claim my husband's body."

"In these kinds of situations, it takes time."

"Do you have children, Mr. Copley?"

He simply stared at her.

She said quietly, "This is a very difficult time for my son. I would like to finish planning the funeral, so we can both get this behind us. The sooner my son gets closure, the sooner he can begin to heal."

Copley and his crew said nothing. Catherine took a seat across from them all in an antique wooden chair. She crossed one leg over the other, clasping her hands around her knee. She'd chosen her clothes with care this morning: a tea-length black skirt with a heather-gray cashmere turtleneck, belted at the waist. Pearl studs in her ears, her wedding band on her finger, her long black hair knotted at her neck. She was every inch the dignified, grieving widow, and she knew it.

If these people were really going to gang up on the dead man's wife, it would be up to them to start.

"We have some questions about Thursday night," the ADA said finally, clearing his throat and breaking the silence. "Could you review some things for us one more time?"

She merely regarded them expectantly.

"Uhhhh, all right." Investigator Casella had his notebook out and was flipping through the pages. Catherine didn't watch him anymore; she studied the blonde. The DA's office investigated police shootings, not the BPD, so why was the blonde here?

"In regard to the videotapes from the security system . . . we seem to be missing the one from the master bedroom."

"There's no tape."

"There's no tape? It's our understanding from the security company that a camera is installed in your master bedroom."

She regarded Investigator Casella evenly. "It wasn't on."

"It wasn't on?"

"Convenient," the blonde murmured.

Catherine ignored her. "That camera is meant for when we are out. Jimmy had set it up to shut off automatically from midnight to eight a.m."

"That's interesting," Investigator Casella said. "Because according to your earlier testimony, Jimmy came home at ten p.m., so the camera should've still been on."

"True, but it turns out the control panel can't tell time."

"Pardon?"

"Check it," Catherine said. "You'll see that the control panel is currently running two hours ahead, so what it thinks is midnight is really ten p.m." She shrugged. "Jimmy's not very good with electronics. All that 'spring forward, fall back'; I guess he must have messed up the time."

"The security company never mentioned this."

"I don't think he ever told them."

The two men and the blonde exchanged glances.

"You said you and your husband had gotten into an argument," Investigator Casella said finally. "What was it regarding?"

Catherine eyed him coolly. They had covered this before, Friday morning when the blood in her bedroom had still been fresh. She resented the fact that they were making her say it again.

"Jimmy could be jealous, particularly when he'd been drinking. Thursday night, he started in on me about Nathan's doctor. I wanted to take Nathan in to see Dr. Rocco, as Nathan wasn't feeling well. Jimmy thought that was just a ruse so I could see my old lover."

"You were seeing Dr. Tony Rocco?" The ADA again, striving to sound surprised by the news when they all knew he was faking it. The police had their theatrics, she had hers. Which made this whole conversation—what, a Greek tragedy, or a hopeless Shakespearean farce?

She was suddenly more tired than she had ever been in her life. She wanted to see Nathan. She needed to know that her son, at least, was safe.

She answered evenly, "Yes, Tony and I had a relationship. It ended months ago, however, and as I reassured Jimmy, it was solely in the past."

"And where was the nanny, Prudence Walker, when this discussion was taking place?" Investigator Casella picked up the questioning.

"Thursday night is Prudence's night off. Thursday nights, Sunday days."

Casella frowned at her. "But it was pretty late when your husband returned home. You're sure Prudence still wasn't back? Maybe upstairs, sleeping in her room?"

"I believe she spent the night with a friend."

"A boyfriend?" For the first time, the blonde spoke up. She was regarding Catherine sharply. "She often spend Thursday night with him?"

"She's often out all night," Catherine conceded.

"Convenient," the blonde murmured.

Catherine ignored her.

"And your son?" Investigator Doomsday said. "How did he end up being part of the altercation?"

"Nathan had awakened shortly after ten from a nightmare. I had just gone into his room to comfort him, when I heard Jimmy downstairs. I could tell . . . I could already tell that it wouldn't be good."

"What do you mean by that?"

"I could tell he'd been drinking. By the

way he slammed the door. By the way he
started shouting my name. Nathan, of
course, immediately became more frightened."

Not that he said anything. Nathan never
said anything. He'd simply stared at her
with those too-solemn blue eyes, his thin
young body already braced, waiting. Jimmy
was home, Jimmy was drunk. Jimmy was
bigger than both of them.

She had wanted so much more for her
son. That's what she'd been thinking on
Thursday night, when Jimmy slammed the
door, when Jimmy started yelling, when
Jimmy headed for the stairs. She had
looked down into Nathan's eyes and been
terrified by the sight of her own hopeless
gaze reflecting back at her.

"When did Jimmy get the gun?" the ADA
was asking.

"I don't know."

"Where did he get the gun?"

"I don't know."

"He came up the stairs with it?"

"Yes."

"He waved it at you and Nathan?"

"Yes."

"And what did you do, Mrs. Gagnon?"

"I told him to put the gun away. I told him he was scaring Nathan."

"And what did he do?"

"He laughed, Mr. Copley. He said he wasn't the threat to Nathan in this house, that I was."

"What did he mean by that?"

She shrugged. "Jimmy was drunk. Jimmy didn't know what he was saying."

"And what was Nathan doing when all of this was going on?"

"Nathan was . . ." Her voice snagged, she forced herself to continue. "Nathan was in my lap. He had his head pressed against my shoulder so he wouldn't have to see his father. He had his hands over his ears. I told Jimmy I was going to put Nathan to bed in our room. I asked him to please calm down, he was frightening our child. Then I walked past him to our room. The minute I got inside, I locked the door and called nine-one-one."

"Is that when Jimmy fired the gun?"

"I don't remember."

"Neighbors reported two shots fired."

"Did they?"

Copley's eyebrows rose. "You're saying

you're not sure if your husband fired the gun?"

"I wasn't focused on Jimmy at that time. I was focused on Nathan. He was scared out of his mind."

Mommy, are we going to die? Turn on the lights, Mommy. We need lights.

"Did Jimmy ever hurt you or your son before this?"

"Jimmy threw stuff when he was angry. Sometimes . . . We had some troubles in our marriage."

"Troubles in your marriage?" The blonde again, sounding sarcastic. "Uniformed patrols were coming here every other week to respond to complaints. Except things were finally reaching the point of no return, weren't they, Mrs. Gagnon—Jimmy had filed for divorce."

Catherine regarded her coolly. "True."

"He had the money," the blonde pressed. "He had the power. First the guy had been abusing you, now he was setting things up to screw you royally. Frankly, no one here can blame you for being a little pissed off."

"We had issues. It didn't mean we were beyond help."

"Puuuhhhlllleeez. This guy beat you. This

guy yelled and threw things at your kid. Why would you even want to work it out?"

"Obviously, you never met Jimmy."

"Obviously, it didn't matter once you did, because you were still willing to play hide-the-stethoscope with your son's doctor."

Catherine flinched. "That's crude."

"You did see Dr. Rocco in the end, didn't you?"

"Nathan had an attack of acute pancre-atitis on Friday. Of course I saw Dr. Rocco."

"Did the doc miss you? Want you back? Jimmy's gone now. . . ."

"I'm insulted by that insinuation. My husband's body is barely cold—"

"Barely cold? You helped get him killed!"

"How? By being used as target prac-tice?"

The blonde moved to the edge of the sofa. Her questions shot out rapid-fire. "Who started the argument Thursday night? Who first brought up Dr. Rocco?"

"I did. Nathan wasn't feeling well."

"So you decided to mention your past lover to your jealous husband?"

"He was Nathan's doctor!"

"You kept your past lover as Nathan's

doctor when you had a jealous, abusive husband?"

Catherine blinked her eyes, faltered, and tried frantically to regain footing. "Nathan doesn't like new doctors. New doctors mean new tests. I couldn't put him through that."

"Oh, I see. So you kept seeing your old lover as a *favor* to your son?"

"Dr. Rocco is a good doctor!"

"*Is* a good doctor?"

"*Is* a good doctor," Catherine repeated, feeling bewildered.

"Then you must be disappointed he won't be your doctor any longer."

"It wasn't his fault. James Gagnon wields a lot of power. Tony was just doing what Tony had to do."

For the first time, the blonde broke off, frowning. "When did you last see Dr. Rocco?" the blonde asked.

"Friday evening. When Nathan was admitted into the ICU. Afterwards, Dr. Rocco informed me he couldn't be Nathan's doctor anymore. The head of Pediatrics had asked him to remove himself from the case. Instead, he was referring me to a geneticist,

Dr. Iorfino. We have an appointment for Monday."

"And when did you make that appointment?"

"I didn't make the appointment. Tony did."

"Personal touch," the blonde murmured with an arched brow.

"My son is very sick. He needs expert care. And in the medical field it takes an expert to get an expert. If I had called Dr. Iorfino, I would've been put on a waiting list. But Tony could get us right through. Maybe he doesn't have the best ethics in his personal life, but Tony is a very good doctor; he's always done right by my son."

"Sounds to me like you still love him."

"I loved my husband."

"Even when he used you as a human punching bag? Even when he had a gun? Seems to me like you're not making out too badly, Mrs. Gagnon. Now you get all the benefits of the house, the car, the bank accounts, without any of the expensive Jimmy baggage." The blonde's eyes were shrewd. "Why, there's not even anyone around to accuse you of harming your son. You're totally free and clear."

Catherine stood up. "Get out."

"We're going to talk to Prudence, you know. And the nanny before her, and the nanny before her. We're going to go all the way back, until we know every single thing that ever happened in this household."

"Out."

"And then we're going to talk to Nathan."

Catherine stabbed her finger at the door. The three finally rose. "Too bad about Dr. Rocco," the blonde commented casually as they crossed the marble foyer. "Especially for his wife and kids."

"What about Tony?"

"He's dead, of course. Murdered last night. At the hospital." The blonde stopped, staring hard at Catherine's face. For a change, Catherine didn't bother to shield her expression. She was honestly shocked. Then stupefied. Then, just plain terrified.

"How?" she murmured.

"Boo," the blonde murmured, and Catherine froze.

The investigators passed through the doorway. At the last moment, the ADA turned.

"You ever hear of GSR?" Copley asked.

"No."

"It's gunshot residue. Anytime someone fires a gun, traces of GSR end up on their hands and clothing. Guess what we tested for at the morgue, Mrs. Gagnon? Guess what we *didn't* find on your husband's hands or clothing?"

Catherine didn't say a word. Boo, she was thinking wildly. Boo.

The trio headed down the front steps. "One mistake," Copley called back over his shoulder. "That's all I need. One little mistake, Mrs. Gagnon. Then, you're mine."

Chapter
18

Sunday morning. the sun was shining, the air crisp with the promise of winter. Half of the pedestrians in Boston scurried from overpriced shop to overpriced shop, their heads tucked like turtles deep in the folds of their scarves, their hands crammed into the pockets of their coats. Not Mr. Bosu. He walked through the Public Garden with its grand old trees, no coat, no hat, no gloves. He loved this kind of weather. The scent of the decaying leaves. The last gasp of a fading winter sun.

When he was a kid, this had been his favorite time of year. He'd stay outdoors playing long after dark. His parents didn't care.
Being outside was good for the boy, his
father would say, before burying himself
once more in the daily paper.

Not a bad childhood. He really couldn't
complain. He had fond memories of G.I. Joe
figurines and toy cement mixers. He rode
his dirt bike, played well with the other
children. Even had birthday parties in his
mother's gold-colored living room, deco-
rated with the little orange and yellow flowers people thought were absolutely darling
back then.

He heard it was all coming back in fashion now. Retro. That was the word. Mr. Bosu
had been in prison just long enough for his
childhood to once again become cool.

He wondered what would happen if he
returned home. His parents probably lived
in the same house on the same block; hell,
maybe they even drove the same car. If it's
not broke, don't fix it, the senior Mr. Bosu
had always liked to say.

They never visited Mr. Bosu in prison. Not
once. After the day that girl had taken the
stand, pointed at Mr. Bosu, and said, "Yes,

sir, that's the man who grabbed me," his parents hadn't even attended the trial.

He supposed you could say he'd broken his parents' hearts. People like them were supposed to have an ordinary son. One who would join ROTC, end up with a college degree and serve his country on weekends. Then he'd marry an ordinary girl, maybe a younger version of his mother, and she would stand in a vogue *retro* kitchen, whipping up *retro* casseroles while their two point two children played with *retro* toys out back.

Mr. Bosu's fantasies were different. They involved a Catholic schoolgirl in a green plaid skirt and white knee-high socks. She would have her long dark hair tied back in a red bow. She would carry her schoolbooks tight against her just-budding chest. She would say "Yes, sir" or "No, sir." She would have a tight virginal body, untouched by any man, and she would do whatever he wanted, how he wanted, when he wanted.

She would be his forever.

Mr. Bosu hadn't been a dumb boy. He'd kept his fantasies to himself. When he was sixteen, he'd made his first attempt. Approached a girl in a playground, pretending to be looking for his younger sister. The girl hadn't run away immediately, so he'd offered to push her on the swing. The feel of her small bony ribs beneath his hands, however, had led to consequences. His pants had been too tight, no way to hide the results. She'd gotten one look, started to scream, and run all the way home.

Later, her parents had approached his parents about his "inappropriate" behavior. He'd blushed, stammered, lied shamelessly that he'd actually been watching a blonde cheerleader walk by. Of course he hadn't meant . . . He just didn't know how to control . . . Oh gosh, he was just so, so sorry.

Boys will be boys, his father had said, shaking his head and reaching once more for his paper.

After that, he'd been more careful. Taking his parents' car, driving far away from the neighborhood. He practiced and he learned. Nicer clothes were less threatening, particularly given his hulking size. A good story was important. Not candy, everyone warned their children about strangers bearing candy. Better to be looking for a lost sister, lost cat, lost dog. Something a child could relate to.

He learned, he perfected. And one day, he struck.

It was short, messy. Not at all like he'd pictured. Afterwards, he panicked. Didn't know what to do with the body. Finally he'd weighted it down and driven all the way to the Connecticut border, where he found a river.

He'd returned home shaken, disturbed, and interestingly enough, remorseful. He'd watched the news for days, palms sweating, waiting to be discovered.

But nothing happened. Simply . . . nothing. And then the fantasies started again. He dreamed and he hungered and he wanted. Until one day, he'd turned down a street not far from his parents' house, and there had been the girl. She'd been wearing a brown corduroy skirt instead of green plaid, but otherwise, she'd been close enough.

It had been surprisingly simple after that. He'd approached it a whole new way, and it had been satisfying. Right up until that moment when the girl had taken the witness stand.

He'd been young still. He saw that now. He'd been young and he'd made mistakes.

Of course, he'd now had twenty-five years to learn better, and people who didn't think you got an education in prison had obviously never been there.

Mr. Bosu wandered down Park Street until he found the giant Gothic cathedral he remembered from his youth. He sat outside on one of the wooden benches, next to an elderly woman who was feeding bread crumbs to the pigeons. She smiled at him. He warmly smiled back.

"Lovely morning," he said.

"It is, it is," the woman said, and gave a little giggle.

Yesterday, he'd gone on an afternoon shopping binge, courtesy of Benefactor X. The oversized, slightly menacing man from Faneuil Hall was gone. In his place was a classy, middle-aged gentleman who obviously prided himself on being fit. Oh, the wonders of Armani and a decent haircut.

The old woman threw more crumbs at the fat pigeons waddling around their feet. Mr. Bosu tilted back his head and lifted his face to the sun. Damn, it felt good to be outside.

Presently, the church bells started to ring. Grand wooden doors were thrown open.

Families poured down the front steps, first proud fathers, then harried mothers, and then finally screeching children.

Mr. Bosu opened his eyes. He admired dark-haired girls, their long lustrous locks tied back in big white bows. He smiled at the teeming throngs of little blonde princesses, all flouncy white dresses and high-polished Mary Janes. In the vast city block yawning in front of the church, parents were already deep in conversation with other parents while their children ran wild.

Here were five little girls playing tag. Here were two little girls swinging arms. Here was one little girl, already half unnoticed, chasing the scattering pigeons. . . .

"Beautiful, aren't they?" the elderly woman said.

"Nothing so attractive on earth," he assured her.

"Makes me remember my own youth."

"Funny, mine too."

He smiled once more at the woman. She looked a little puzzled, but smiled back. He got off the bench and walked into the sea of young, racing bodies, feeling the breeze of their quick passes like a tingle up his spine.

He walked to the front steps of the

church, ascended to the two large doors, then turned and surveyed his kingdom.

People had a tendency to be wary in the city. But this was a particularly upscale area. A posh little island in the middle of an ocean of concrete. Besides, people grew lax in the comforting embrace of their church. They paid more attention to their earnest networking, or the contest over who was driving the right kind of car or drinking the right kind of coffee. They liked to believe they were keeping watch over little Johnnie or little Jenny out of the corner of their eye. But they weren't. Children wandered away, particularly when their parents were talking to other adults.

Sometimes, they never wandered back.

Mr. Bosu felt a surge, sudden and unexpected. A fierce, rushing appetite that leapt up from his gut and demanded now, now, NOW. He leaned over the steps. He swept his gaze across the screeching, laughing, playing throngs. He was a hawk, circling in the sky. There, no, there, no. There, YES.

One single child. A little girl, maybe four years old, toddling off in pursuit of a dried leaf scattering in the wind. No parental gaze followed her progress. No doting sibling gave chase.

He could walk down the steps now. Moving smooth but casual. Place his bulk between her and the crowd. Herd her a little more right and she'd be behind a tree. Then one last look, left, right, wait for that go-feeling in his gut and scoop her up effortlessly. One blink of the eye and it would be over and done. Child Disappears in Broad Daylight, the headlines would read. Frantic Parents Desperately Search for Clues.

They would never find any. Not when it came to the incredible, powerful Mr. Bosu.

He was halfway down the stairs before he caught himself. His hands found the wrought-iron railing. With genuine effort, he forced himself to take one deep breath. Then another. Then another. Slowly, he relaxed his hands on the railing, his fingers opening up, his hands slowly returning to his sides.

He forced himself to recall last night, the rusty scent of blood, the feel of the blade in his hands, the genuine look of surprise in another, lesser human being's face. It wasn't the same, of course. But it had been more satisfying than he'd expected. Like a pity date. Not his type, not his first choice of entertainment, but action just the same.

Better yet, for the first time in his life, he'd been paid. Up front. In cash. Ten thousand dollars. When Mr. Bosu had been released from prison yesterday, a driver had been waiting for him out front. Mr. Bosu had gotten into the car. A suitcase was waiting for him in the back. Inside was a note, and plenty of cash. The note contained instructions, and with the note came a list. For each target, there was a dollar amount. Now, this was a decent system.

Of course, Mr. Bosu wasn't as stupid as his mystery employer seemed to think. In the note, Benefactor X suggested that things would be easier in the future if Mr. Bosu opened a savings account. Money could be wired directly in, etc., etc. Benefactor X volunteered ways for Mr. Bosu to get ID. Benefactor X even supplied a list of banks.

Benefactor X was an idiot. Banks were monitored. Money transfers were traced. Worse, banks weren't open on Sundays and Mr. Bosu wasn't doing anything for free. He would stick to cash, thank you very much. Nice, thick bundles of dirty green he could strap to his stomach and spend to his heart's content.

Mr. Bosu took the briefcase. His wordless driver dropped him off at Faneuil Hall, handing Mr. Bosu a cell phone containing preprogrammed numbers; that's how they would keep in touch.

Mr. Bosu nodded a lot. He let the driver think he was grateful. Of course, Mr. Bosu knew exactly who his driver was. Most of the guys in the joint knew the go-between by reputation, and of course Robinson's reputation was definitely no match for Mr. Bosu's.

Mr. Bosu didn't say anything, though. As he'd learned in prison, knowledge was power.

Mr. Bosu stuck his hands in his pockets. He started whistling as he sauntered down the church steps and walked one last time through the smorgasbord of running, happy, laughing treats. All in good time.

Now, he was off to find a puppy.

Chapter 19

So how does this kind of thing work?" Bobby was sitting in a small cramped office in Wellesley. He counted four gray steel filing cabinets, one oversized oak desk, and about half a dozen cheap bookcases overflowing with legal reference texts and piles of brightly lettered manila folders. In the two-foot strip of wall space available between the teetering stacks of bureaucracy and the water-stained ceiling, two framed diplomas crookedly announced UNIVERSITY OF MASSACHUSETTS AMHERST and BOSTON COLLEGE.

Bobby tried to picture the office of the lawyers that were representing James Gagnon. It probably didn't look much like this. For starters, he would bet the diplomas came from places like Harvard or Yale. That office also probably came with a receptionist, cherry-paneled conference room, and unbeatable skyline views of downtown Boston.

Harvey Jones, on the other hand, was essentially working out of the attic of an old hardware store. He was a one-man show who'd been practicing law for the past seven years. He had no partners. He had no secretary. Today, at least, he wasn't even wearing a suit.

One of Bobby's fellow cops had recommended the guy. And the minute Harvey had heard Bobby's name, he'd agreed to meet with him. Immediately. On a Sunday. Bobby didn't know if that meant good things or bad things yet.

"So," Harvey was trying to explain to him now, "a clerk-magistrate hearing takes place in front of a judge in the Chelsea District Court. Basically, the plaintiff will bring forth evidence that probable cause exists that you committed a felony. Our job is to refute that fact."

"How?"

"You'll testify, of course, saying why you felt the situation justified the use of deadly force. We'll bring in other officers who were present that night. The lieutenant in charge—what did you say his name was?"

"Jachrimo."

"Lieutenant Jachrimo, we'll want him to testify. Then any other officer who can independently corroborate that you had reason to believe Jimmy Gagnon was going to shoot his wife."

"There isn't independent corroboration. I was the first sniper deployed. No one else saw what I saw."

Harvey frowned, made a note. "Aren't snipers generally sent out in pairs? With a spotter, something like that?"

"We didn't have enough manpower yet."

More frowning, more notes. "Well, we can still go after two things. One, we'll boost your credibility. Bring in the training you've done, have your lieutenant testify as to your expert skills. Establish that you are a well-trained, highly experienced police sniper, qualified to make tough judgment calls."

Bobby nodded. He'd expected that much. Every training exercise performed by the STOP team was heavily documented for just this sort of thing—so someday, if necessary, their lieutenant could prove they were qualified to act as they'd acted. If it's not documented, it didn't happen, the rule of thumb went. Lieutenant Bruni made sure every last thing they did had the proper paper trail.

"Of course," Harvey was saying now, "James Gagnon has politics on his side."

"Being a judge?"

"Being a superior court judge," Harvey said, and grimaced. "As the civil side of the court, a clerk-magistrate doesn't spend a lot of time contemplating what may or may not entail criminal charges. That's what the superior court does. So, think of it from the clerk-magistrate's perspective—here's a judge who's an expert on criminal law testifying that he believes a felony took place. That's going to carry a lot of weight for the clerk-magistrate. If the Honorable James F. Gagnon says it was murder—well then, it must be murder!"

"Wonderful," Bobby muttered.

"But we still have some tricks up our sleeves," Harvey said brightly. "We can hope for a decent ruling from the DA's office—that they've investigated the incident and found the shooting to be justified. That would be huge. Of course," he murmured now, "that's probably why Gagnon filed the motion so fast. It'll take weeks for the DA's office to render an opinion, so Judge Gagnon will try to cram through this motion in a matter of days. Then we're back to his word against your word, with no tie-breaker from the DA."

"Can he move things that fast?"

"If he has the bucks to pay all the attorneys who'll be working overtime, sure, he can do as he pleases. Of course, I'll do what I can to delay. Then again . . ." Harvey looked around his crammed office and Bobby followed his gaze. One-man show versus hordes of top-billing legal eagles. Attic space versus an entire wood-paneled law firm. They both got the picture.

"So he tries to move fast, we try to move slow," Bobby said quietly. "He tries to exert his expertise as a criminal court judge. We hope for a countering opinion from the DA. Then what?"

"Then it gets personal."

Bobby stared at the lawyer. Harvey shrugged. "Basically, it's he said/she said. You're saying you saw a credible threat. The other side is saying you're wrong. To do that, they gotta go after you. They're gonna bring in your family. Were you a violent child, did you always love guns? They're going to dig into your lifestyle—young, single officer. Do you frequent bars, sleep around, get into brawls? Too bad you're not married with kids; it always looks better if you're married with kids. What about a dog? Do you happen to own a cute dog? A black Lab or golden retriever would be perfect."

"No cute dogs." Bobby considered things. "I'm a landlord. My tenant has cats."

"Is your tenant young and beautiful?" Harvey asked suspiciously.

"Elderly woman on a fixed income."

Harvey brightened noticeably. "Excellent. You gotta love a man who helps the elderly. Which, of course, brings us to ex-girlfriends."

Bobby rolled his eyes at that segue. "There's a few," he admitted.

"Which ones hate you?"

"None of them."

"Sure about that?"

He thought of Susan. He honestly didn't know how she was feeling. "No," he found himself saying. "I'm not sure."

"They'll talk to your neighbors. They'll look deep into your past. They'll look for incidents of bias—that you don't like blacks or Hispanics or people who drive BMWs."

"I don't have biases," Bobby said, then stopped, frowned, and got a bad feeling. "The DUI arrest."

"The DUI arrest?"

"Earlier that day. Guy was driving a Hummer while intoxicated. Did a bit of damage, then got bent out of shape when we actually tried to put him in jail. He had an attitude. We, uh, we exchanged some words."

"Words?"

"I called him a rich prick," Bobby said matter-of-factly.

Harvey winced. "Oh yeah, that's gonna hurt. Anything else I should know?"

Bobby looked at the lawyer a long time. He debated what to say, how much to say. In the end, he settled on, "I don't want my father to take the stand."

Harvey regarded him curiously. "We don't have to call him as a character witness if you don't want us to."

"What if they call him?"

"He's your father. Assuming he's going to testify in your favor, they won't call him."

"But if they do?" Bobby insisted.

Harvey was catching on now. "What don't I know?"

"I don't want him on the stand. Period."

"If they know something, Bobby, if they know something you're not telling me, we may not have a choice."

"What if he's . . . out of state?"

"They'll subpoena him. If he doesn't answer the summons, he's in contempt of court and they can pursue legal action against him."

Bobby had been afraid of that. "What if I don't testify?"

"Then you'll lose," Harvey said baldly. "It'll be just their word on what happened Thursday night, and their word will be that you committed murder."

Bobby nodded again. He hung his head. He was looking into the future; he was trying to see beyond one night when he had done, honest to God, what he'd had to do. Nothing looked promising anymore. Nothing looked good.

"Can I win this?" he asked quietly. "Do I really have a chance?"

"There's always a chance."

"I don't have his kind of money."

"No."

Bobby was honest. "I don't have his kind of lawyer."

Harvey was honest back. "No."

"But you think you can pull this out?"

"If we can delay things long enough for the DA's office ruling, and if the DA's office ruling finds that it was justifiable use of force, then yes, I think we can win."

"That's a lot of ifs."

"Tell me about it."

"And then?"

Harvey hesitated.

"He can appeal, can't he?" Bobby filled in the blanks for the lawyer. "If this is the clerk-magistrate, then James Gagnon can appeal to the district court, then the superior court, then the supreme judicial court. It goes on and on and on, doesn't it?"

"Yeah," Harvey said. "And he'll file motions, dozens of motions, most of them frivolous but all of them costing you time and money to refute. I'll do what I can. Call in some favors. I know some young lawyers who will help out for the experience and others who will do it for the exposure. But you're right: this is David and Goliath, and, well, you're not Goliath."

"All it takes is money and time," Bobby murmured.

"He's old," Harvey threw out there.

"You mean one day he'll die," Bobby filled in bluntly. "That's my best-case scenario. Another death."

Harvey didn't bother to lie. "Yeah. In a situation like this, that's pretty much it."

Bobby rose to his feet. He got out his checkbook. He'd had this nest egg he'd been building. Thinking of one day maybe buying more property, or maybe, if things between him and Susan had gone differently, it would've helped with a wedding. Now he wrote a check for five thousand dollars and placed it on Harvey Jones's desk.

According to the good lawyer, that might last a week. Of course, Bobby already knew something the lawyer didn't—if his father took the stand, he would lose.

"Is this enough for a retainer?"

Harvey nodded.

"If I'm going to pursue things," Bobby said, "I'll call you tomorrow by five p.m."

They shook hands.

Then Bobby went home and got his guns.

The fifty-foot indoor shooting range at the Massachusetts Rifle Association in Woburn, Massachusetts, was slow for a Sunday afternoon. Bobby rolled two spongy orange plugs between his index finger and thumb, fit them into the canals of his ears, then adjusted his safety glasses. He'd brought his Smith & Wesson .38 Special, and just for the hell of it, a .45 Colt Magnum.

When Bobby took his proficiency test each month with his rifle, he never took more than one shot. That was it. You took up to an hour, you set up your shot, and then you fired one single bullet. The cold-bore shot. That's because the very first shot out of any gun had the slug traveling down a cold barrel. That slug heated the barrel, which led to slightly different ballistics for every other shot fired.

As a sniper, the assumption was that he'd never fire any of those other rounds. One shot, one kill, so all that mattered, day after day, training exercise after training exercise, was that single, cold-bore shot.

Now, Bobby plunked down six boxes of ammo. The brass casings jingled inside the containers. He opened the first box and loaded up.

He began with the .38, starting at ten feet to loosen up, then moving the target back to twenty-one. Studies claimed that the average police shooting occurred within twenty-one feet, making it a favorite distance for marksmen. Bobby always wondered who did these studies, and why they never bothered to mention if the police were winning or losing in these infamous shootouts.

He started out horribly. Worst damn shooting of his life, and positively embarrassing for someone who'd earned the NRA classification of High Master. He wondered idly if some private investigator was already waiting in the wings to pluck this target for Bobby's upcoming trial. Guy could hold it up on the stand, with its wildly scattered spray of shots: "See this, your honor. And this is from a guy that State says is an *expert.*"

Maybe he couldn't shoot paper anymore. Maybe once you'd shot a real person, nothing else would do.

That thought depressed him. His eyes
stung. He was sad. He was mad. He didn't
know what the hell to feel anymore.

He set down the .38. Picked up the .45.
Set it down and, for a long time, simply
stood there in the cavernous space, pinching the bridge of his nose and fighting for
composure against an emotion he couldn't
name.

Down at the far end, the MRA's gun pro,
J.T. Dillon, was firing away. After a moment,
Bobby stepped away from the shooting line
and, receding into the shadows, watched
the older man work.

This afternoon, Dillon was firing a .22-
caliber target pistol that didn't even resem-
ble a real gun. The handle was a huge
wooden grip that appeared less like a handle and more like a rough-hewn slab of tree.
The barrel was squared off and edged in silver. The capping scope was bright red. All in
all, the piece looked like something out of a
Star Wars movie.

In fact, the custom-fit, superlight Italian-
made target pistol cost upwards of fifteen
hundred dollars. Only the big boys used
these kinds of guns, and in the world of

competitive shooting, Dillon was considered a very big boy.

Dillon was an IPSC competitor—International Practical Shooting Confederation. These guys were considered the martial artists of combat shooting. They were ranked on time and accuracy as they performed various bizarre drills, say, for example, shooting from the saddle, or running through an urban landscape with a briefcase handcuffed to their dominant hand, or shooting their way out of a jungle with an ankle in a splint. The tougher and nastier the drill, the more the competitors liked it.

IPSC shooters always said that bull's-eye shooting, the kind of sniper drills Bobby performed, was like watching grass grow. Combat shooting was where the real action was.

Now Bobby watched as J.T. Dillon loaded the clip of his custom pistol, placed it in his weaker, left hand, and fired off a quick six rounds. Smooth. Controlled. Never blinking an eye.

Bobby didn't have to look at the target to know all six shots were good. Dillon didn't have to look either. He was already reloading his piece.

By now, Bobby had heard all the rumors—that Dillon was a former Marine, dishonorably discharged. That once he used to live in Arizona, where he'd supposedly killed a man. Maybe it was the jagged scar sometimes glimpsed across his sternum. Or the lean, rangy build the years did nothing to diminish. Or the fact that nearing the age of fifty, he could still cut down any man with his dark, forbidding stare.

Bobby didn't know about those rumors, but being a Massachusetts State Police officer, he knew something about J.T. Dillon very few others did: a decade ago, a former police officer and serial killer named Jim Beckett had broken out of the maximum-security Walpole prison. In his brief few months of freedom, Beckett had sliced a long, bloody swath through various law enforcement agencies, murdering a number of state policemen, including a sniper, as well as an FBI agent.

Bobby didn't know all the details, but the way he heard it, the police weren't the ones who caught Jim Beckett in the end. Dillon did. After Beckett murdered his sister.

Now Dillon looked up from his pistol. He met Bobby's gaze across the way.

"That's the sloppiest damn display of shooting I've ever seen," Dillon said.

"I'm thinking of burning the target."

"That assumes you can hit it with a match."

Bobby had to grin. "True."

Dillon peered down his scope and Bobby wandered over. He'd never spoken much to Dillon, though both men knew each other by reputation.

Dillon had pushed the target back to fifty feet. Still using his left hand, he sighted the target. He inhaled. He exhaled. He inhaled one more time and Bobby could feel the man's focus as a sudden physical presence. Dillon's finger moved six times, the flexing of his index finger no greater than the whisper of a butterfly beating its wings against the air. *Boom, boom, boom, boom, boom, boom.* The entire clip was unloaded in three seconds or less.

When Dillon pulled in the target, Bobby shook his head. This time, rather than annihilate the bull's-eye, Dillon had formed a star.

"Show-off," Bobby said.

"Gives me something to bring home to my girls."

"Your daughters?"

"Yep. Two of them. One's sixteen, one's six."

"Do they shoot?"

"Older one, Samantha, she's pretty good."

Bobby read between the lines. If Dillon said his daughter was pretty good, that probably meant she could outgun Bobby. Considering what Bobby knew of teenage boys, that skill could come in handy.

"And the younger?"

"Lanie? Takes after her mother. Can't stand the sound of gunfire. But she has other skills. You should see her ride a horse."

"Nice." Dillon was gathering up his spent casings. Bobby helped him out. The brass was the most expensive part of a bullet. Serious shooters like to reclaim the casings for reuse in their own custom-made ammo. "Married?" Bobby asked now.

"Ten years," Dillon said.

Ten years with a sixteen-year-old daughter. Bobby did the math on that, then gave up. "What does your wife do?"

"Tess teaches kindergarten. And chases

our girls. And tries to keep me out of trouble."

"Sounds like a good life," Bobby said.

"It is."

"Well, I should get back to practicing." But Bobby remained standing where he was. Dillon was watching him, his gaze expectant. Shooters had a bond others didn't have. They appreciated the art, they respected the technique. They understood that snipers didn't get drawn to the craft because they were budding Dirty Harrys or lone gunmen anxious for another shootout at the OK Corral. Bobby did what he did because the skill challenged him, not because he'd ever wanted anyone to get hurt.

"Was it hard?" Bobby asked quietly. "Afterwards, I mean."

"After what? After I shot the man in Arizona, or after I shot Jim Beckett?"

"Either one."

"Sorry to say, son, but I've never killed a man."

"Not even Jim Beckett?"

"No." Dillon smiled ruefully, then flexed out his shoulder. "Though it wasn't from lack of trying."

"Oh," Bobby said, though he hadn't meant to sound so disappointed.

Dillon looked at him awhile, contemplating. Finally, the man gestured around the empty space. "Ten years ago," he announced, "I would never have thought I'd be here. Never thought I'd have a wife. Never thought I'd have two daughters. Never thought I'd be . . . happy."

"Because of Beckett?" Bobby asked.

"Because of a lot of things. Maybe I've never killed a man, but for a lot of my life, I came close enough." Dillon shrugged. "I remember what it's like to sit and wait with your crosshairs sighted on a human head. I know what it's like to will yourself to pull the trigger."

"I didn't think much of it at the time."

"Of course not. At the time, you were too busy. At the time, you were doing your job. It's now, in all the hours and days to come, in all the moments when life gets quiet, that you're gonna find yourself remembering again, wondering for the eleven hundredth time what you could have done differently. If you could have done something differently."

"I keep telling myself it doesn't matter.

What's done is done. No use torturing myself with it now."

"Sound advice."

"So why aren't I taking it?"

"You never will. You wanna talk about regrets? I can talk about regrets, Officer Dodge.
I can give you a whole laundry list of people I
wished I had saved and people I wished I had
killed. Give me five minutes and a bottle of
tequila, and I can destroy my whole life."

"But you don't."

"You have to find something, Officer
Dodge. Something that anchors you, something that keeps you looking forward, even
on the bad days, when you're tempted to
look back."

"Your family," Bobby guessed.

"My family," Dillon agreed evenly.

Bobby looked him in the eye. "So who
really killed Jim Beckett?"

"Tess did."

"Your wife?"

"Yeah, that woman can sure wield a shotgun."

"And she's doing okay with that? Killing
him?"

"Honestly? She hasn't touched a gun
since."

Chapter
20

Catherine arrived at the hospital just in time to find her in-laws standing by the nurses' desk.

"I'm the boy's grandfather," James was saying with his best you-want-to-cooperate-with-me grin. "Of course it's okay for me to take the boy home."

"Sir, Nathan's mother signed the admit papers. I can't do anything without consulting her."

"And it's wonderful that you're so diligent. I commend you. Unfortunately, my

daughter-in-law is extremely busy with funeral preparations right now. Hence, we
were sent to get Nathan. It's the least we
could do during this very trying time."

James tightened his arm around
Maryanne. On cue, she joined him in smiling
at the nurse. Maryanne was a shade paler
than James, dark shadows bruising her
eyes, but still with every hair and pearl in
place. They made an impeccable united
front. The powerful judge and his fragile,
charming wife.

Already, the nurse seemed to be weaken-
ing.

James leaned forward, pressing the advantage. "Let's go see Nathan. He'll be
very excited to go with us. You'll see that
it's all right."

"I should at least consult his doctor," the
nurse murmured, then glanced down at the
admit papers and promptly frowned. "Oh
dear."

"What is it?"

"Nathan's pediatrician, Dr. Rocco. I'm
afraid . . . Oh dear, oh dear." The nurse's
voice trailed off. She was clearly distressed
by what had happened to Dr. Rocco, and
now becoming quickly overwhelmed.

Catherine took that as her cue. She walked up to the desk, gaze going straight to the nurse's name tag.

"Nurse Brandi, so good to see you again. How is Nathan this morning?"

"Feeling better," the nurse said brightly, then glanced nervously from Catherine to James and Maryanne, then to Catherine again.

Catherine decided to solve the dilemma for the woman. She put her hand on her father-in-law's arm. A first-class showman himself, he didn't flinch.

"Thank you so much for helping out," she told James with a warm smile, then flashed the same grateful grin over at Maryanne. "Fortunately, I finished up at the funeral parlor sooner than I expected, so I came to get Nathan myself."

"Really, you shouldn't have," James said. "Maryanne and I would be delighted to watch the boy for a while. You should rest."

"Yes, dear," Maryanne echoed. "You must be exhausted. Let us watch Nathan. We have this wonderful room at the Hotel LeRoux. It will be a great treat for him after all this time in a hospital."

"Oh no. I'm sure after everything Nathan

has been through, it would be much nicer for him to go straight home."

"To the house where his father died?" James asked dryly.

"To the comfort of his own bedroom."

James thinned his lips. He and Maryanne exchanged glances. Catherine turned swiftly to Nurse Brandi.

"I'd like to see Nathan now."

"Of course."

"I'm sure someone must be filling in for Dr. Rocco. Please find that doctor and have him sign the discharge papers so I can take Nathan home." Catherine held up the Louis Vuitton bag she was carrying. "I'll work on getting my son into his clothes."

Maryanne spoke up brightly. "Why don't we get him dressed, darling, while you deal with the paperwork? Surely that will be much faster for everyone."

"Absolutely," James agreed enthusiastically. "Wonderful idea!"

Catherine was getting a pounding headache. She smiled anyway. "That is so kind of both of you, really. But I just miss Nathan terribly; I can't imagine not seeing him right away."

"We also can't wait to see our grandson!"

Maryanne again, so gay, she sounded brittle.

"You're entirely too kind. But Nathan's health is still very fragile. After everything he's been through the past three days, I think it would be best if he just saw me for now—tone down the excitement. Tomorrow, of course, you're more than welcome to come to our home." Catherine put her hand on Nurse Brandi's arm, a little more forceful now, a little more insistent. "Nathan?" she prodded.

"Of course."

The nurse gave James and Maryanne one last uncertain look, then briskly led Catherine down the hall. Behind her, Catherine was keenly aware that her in-laws weren't turning to leave. In fact, at the mention of a replacement doctor for Tony, James had gotten a gleam in his eye.

James and Maryanne never went down without a fight. Most likely, Catherine didn't have much time.

In the curtained-off space, Nathan was sitting up in the hospital bed. His color was better. His abdomen no longer protruded painfully. He still looked tiny to her, lost in a sea of white sheets and black wires. There was nothing quite so grotesque as a hospital gown on a child.

"Baby," she whispered.

Nathan looked up at her with his solemn blue eyes. He said clearly, "Where's Prudence?"

"Today's her day off," Catherine said steadily. "I'm going to take you home. Would you like to go home?"

Nathan looked around the room, at the IV, at the heart monitor. "Am I better?" he whispered, looking suddenly and unbearably uncertain.

"Yes."

He nodded more decisively. "Then I would like to go home."

"Let's get you dressed."

Nurse Brandi removed the IV needle, then pushed aside the heart monitor.

"The discharge papers?" Catherine prompted, her gaze already flicking nervously behind her.

"Of course."

Brandi disappeared down the hallway. Catherine plastered a fresh smile on her face and turned back to her son. "I brought you your favorite outfit. Jeans, boots, the cowboy shirt."

She briskly opened the bag, laying out the clothes on the edge of the bed. Nathan seemed subdued, but finally, he shrugged off his hospital gown.

"Was it a dream?" he asked.

Catherine knew instantly what he meant. "No," she said.

"Daddy had a gun."

"Yes."

"Is he dead?"

"Yes."

Nathan nodded and started to pull on his clothes. He had just finished buttoning his flannel cowboy shirt when James and Maryanne appeared with a man in surgical scrubs in tow.

"Nathan!" James boomed heartily. "It's my favorite cowboy! Ready to saddle up? Your grandmother and I would love to have you come join us at the Hotel LeRoux. Room service, Nathan. All the hot fudge sundaes you can eat."

Nathan regarded his grandfather as if he'd sprouted two heads. James rarely paid Nathan quite this much attention. And in fact, ice cream made Nathan unbelievably ill.

Unperturbed, James turned to Catherine.

The flush of triumph was unmistakable on his face. "Catherine, meet Dr. Gerritsen, head of Pediatrics. I think you two should have a talk. In the meantime, Maryanne and I will stay here with Nathan."

Maryanne had already stepped forward, reaching out a hand toward Nathan. The yearning expression on her face was hard to bear. Did she look at her grandson and see her last link to Jimmy? Or did she merely see another kind of a weapon, a living, breathing tool that could be used to hurt Catherine?

Dr. Gerritsen was trying to gesture Catherine out into the hallway. She refused to budge. All James and Maryanne needed was thirty seconds, and Nathan would be gone. Possession, after all, was nine-tenths of the law.

Dr. Gerritsen finally gave up, stepping into the now crowded space and focusing his attention on Nathan. The pediatrician held a chart in his right hand.

"How are you feeling, young man?" Dr. Gerritsen asked.

"Okay." In fact, Nathan was regarding all four adults nervously.

"According to your chart, everything looks good."

"Where's Dr. Tony?" Nathan asked.

"Dr. Rocco couldn't be here today, Nathan, so I'm helping out. Is that okay?"

The boy merely stared at Dr. Gerritsen. He didn't like doctors, particularly new doctors, and his gaze said he was already suspicious.

"Would you like to go home?" Dr. Gerritsen asked.

A somber nod.

"Seems like a good idea to me, too. I'll tell you what, sport. Why don't you hang out here for just one more minute, while I talk with your grandparents and mother. Nurse Brandi, want to show Nathan how a stethoscope works?"

Nathan already knew how a stethoscope worked. His gaze flew immediately to Catherine, and she could see his growing panic. She did her best to give him a bolstering smile, though the same panic was already rising in her chest.

Nurse Brandi stepped into the space. Dr. Gerritsen, James, Maryanne, and Catherine disappeared back behind the curtain.

Dr. Gerritsen didn't waste any time.

"Judge Gagnon tells me that there is a custody issue with Nathan," the doctor said,
looking Catherine straight in the eye.

"Judge Gagnon and his wife have filed
for custody of Nathan," Catherine replied
evenly. She was desperately eyeing the
head of Pediatrics, trying to get a quick read
on the man. Older. Wedding ring on his left
hand. Happily married? Or bored, egotisti-
cal—ripe for the attentions of a young,
beautiful widow?

"He has concerns for the boy's safety,"
Dr. Gerritsen said. His tone was level. Serious. Very serious.

Catherine abandoned all notions of flirta-
tion. She went instead for the concerned
daughter-in-law, respectful and caring. She
turned her head slightly and said in a low
voice, as if she didn't want to upset her in-
laws, "Judge Gagnon and his wife have recently lost their son. They are wonderful
grandparents, but . . . they're not quite
themselves right now, Dr. Gerritsen. Surely
you understand how difficult this must be
for them."

"We're sharp as tacks and you know it,"
James interjected harshly. "Don't play us for
doddering fools."

Dr. Gerritsen's gaze flickered to James and Maryanne, then back to Catherine. His expression was plainly perturbed. "I don't like being put in the middle of these things."

"I never would have dreamed of getting you involved," Catherine assured him.

"According to Dr. Rocco's records, Nathan falls ill a lot." Dr. Gerritsen added pointedly, "And rather easily."

"Dr. Rocco always took excellent care of Nathan."

Dr. Gerritsen gave her a dubious look. He obviously knew of her relationship with Tony and wasn't fooled. "I don't think you should take the boy home," the head of Pediatrics announced.

Catherine's heart fell. She could feel the panic bubble up in her throat, even as James began to smile.

"Unfortunately," Dr. Gerritsen continued crisply, "I don't have any say in the matter."

"What?" James this time, clearly stunned.

"As of this moment, she's still Nathan's legal guardian." Dr. Gerritsen shrugged. "I'm sorry, Judge Gagnon, but my hands are tied."

Maryanne started shaking her head, a

woman suddenly coming awake only to find herself in the middle of a very bad dream.

"Exigent circumstances," James countered quickly. "You felt there was an immediate and compelling threat to the boy, justifying sending him home with his grandparents."

"But I don't know that there's an immediate and compelling threat."

"The boy's health history. You yourself said it was suspicious!"

"He needs us," Maryanne said plaintively. "We're all he has left."

Dr. Gerritsen flashed Maryanne a sympathetic look, before returning his attention to James. "Suspicious, yes. Definitive, no."

James was clearly furious now. "She is a threat to that child!"

"If I was a threat to Nathan," Catherine interjected levelly, "why would I keep bringing him to the hospital for medical care?"

"Because it's what you do!" James barked. "Using your own child to gain attention for yourself, so you can play the role of the tragic mother. I tried to warn Jimmy, I tried to tell him what you're doing. Harming your own son. It's disgusting!"

"But I don't need to play the role of the

tragic mother anymore to get attention, do I, James?" Catherine looked her father-in-law in the eye. "Now I'm the grieving widow."

James growled, an unexpected snarl of frustration and fury in the back of his throat. Catherine feared for a moment that the man might leap forward, that he might actually wrap his hands around her throat. That would be a change of pace. Jimmy had always been so sloppy with his rage. His father, on the other hand, was cold.

"James, darling?" Maryanne was whispering. "Is she getting Nathan? You said it wouldn't happen. How can that happen?"

James put his arms around his shaking wife. He pressed her against him, comforting her with one hand, even as he continued to give Catherine a dark, angry stare.

"This isn't over," he said clearly.

"It is today."

Dr. Gerritsen had had enough of the family drama. The doctor was already gesturing Catherine back inside the curtained-off space. "I'm sorry, Judge Gagnon, but there is nothing I can legally do to stop Mrs. Gagnon from signing out her son. If circumstances change, I'll be happy to help you. But until then . . ."

Dr. Gerritsen shrugged; Catherine ducked around his arm. She didn't bother to flash James a triumphant smile over her shoulder. She didn't dare look at Maryanne's grieving face.

She simply bundled Nathan up in his coat and got the hell out of there.

Nathan was silent for the ride home. He sat in the back of the car, in his car seat, his right hand clutching the shoulder strap. Catherine thought there was something she should say. And then, for a while, she was simply as sad as Nathan that Prudence wasn't working today.

Pulling into a narrow parking space, she went around to get Nathan out of the back. The sun was shining, the afternoon surprisingly warm. She looked down the street and saw several of her neighbors out, walking kids, walking dogs. She wondered if it was strange that she didn't wave to her own neighbors. She wondered if it was stranger that none of them would've bothered to wave back.

Nathan piled out of the car, awkward in his heavy wool coat and new cowboy boots. The coat, a gift from his grandparents, was three sizes too big for him. The cowboy boots, purchased from the baby section of Ralph Lauren, at least fit.

Nathan wouldn't look up. Not down the street. Not at their townhouse. He put his hand in Catherine's obediently enough, but as they got closer and closer to the front steps, his feet began to drag. He shuffled along halfheartedly, kicking at stray leaves.

Catherine glanced up at their front door. She thought of the lobby behind it, then the stairs leading up to their unit. She thought of the master bedroom, with its torn-up carpet, splattered walls, and hastily rearranged furniture. Suddenly, she didn't want to go up those stairs either. She wished, for both of their sakes, that they could simply run away.

"Nathan," she said quietly, "why don't we go to the park?"

Nathan looked up at her. He nodded so vigorously, it made her smile even as her heart ached. They set off down the street.

The Public Garden was crowded. Young lovers, dog walkers, urban families with stir-crazy kids. Catherine and Nathan walked along the water, where the swan boats paddled in the summer. She bought popcorn from a vendor and they amused themselves feeding the milling ducks. Finally they found a park bench at the edge of a clearing, where children the same age as Nathan, but twice his size, ran and tumbled and laughed in the now waning sunlight.

Nathan didn't even try to join them. At the age of four, these were the lessons he'd already learned.

"Nathan?" Catherine said quietly. "Now that you're home . . . some people are going to need to talk to you."

He looked up at her, his face so pale, she felt compelled to run her finger down his cheek. His skin was cool and dry, the face of a boy who spent too much time indoors.

"Do you remember Thursday night?" she asked softly. "The bad night?"

He didn't say a word.

"Daddy had a gun, didn't he, Nathan?"

Slowly, Nathan nodded.

"We were fighting."

Nathan nodded again.

"Do you remember what we were fighting about?" Catherine was holding her breath. This was the wild card, of course. How much did a frightened four-year-old remember? How much did he understand?

Reluctantly, Nathan shook his head.

Catherine released her pent-up breath. She said lightly, "All the people need to know, honey, is that Daddy had a gun. And that we were terribly scared. They understand the rest."

"Daddy's dead," Nathan said.

"Yes."

"Daddy doesn't come home."

"No, he won't come home again."

"Will you?"

Catherine stroked his cheek again. "I will try to always come home to you, Nathan."

"And Prudence?"

"She will come home, too."

Nathan nodded gravely. "Daddy had a gun," he repeated. "I was scared."

"Thank you, Nathan."

Nathan went back to watching the other kids. After a moment, he crawled onto her lap. After another moment, she wrapped her arms around his shoulders and rested her cheek against the top of his ruffling hair.

Chapter 21

When Bobby returned home, not one but three people waited outside his front door. And his day, he thought, just kept getting better and better.

"Shouldn't you be in church?" He asked ADA Rick Copley as he unlocked the door. Then he held up a hand. "Wait, I know: you already sold your soul to the devil."

Copley scowled at Bobby's attempt at humor, then followed Bobby inside his first-floor unit. Behind Copley came D.D. Warren, careful not to look Bobby in the eye, and behind her came an investigator from the DA's office whom Bobby vaguely remembered from the initial shooting interrogation on Friday morning. He couldn't recall the man's name.

Investigator Casella was the magic answer, provided by Copley thirty seconds later as the ADA made introductions in the middle of Bobby's family room. The space was small, the furniture well broken in and currently cluttered with an assortment of empty take-out food boxes and piles of napkins. All three looked around, no one sure where to sit.

Bobby opted not to help them out. As far as he was concerned, these were not people he wanted getting too comfortable in his home.

He went into the kitchen, grabbed himself a Coke, and came back into the family room without bothering to ask if anyone else wanted something to drink. He pulled out a wooden kitchen chair and had a seat. After a moment, D.D. shot him a dry glance, then set about moving pizza boxes until the trio could plunk down on his ancient sofa. They promptly sank down four inches. Bobby used the Coke to cover his smile.

"So," Copley said, trying to sound very authoritative for a man who now had his chin propped up on his knees. "We need to follow up on some questions from Thursday night."

"By all means." Bobby waited for Copley to start from the very beginning, making Bobby retell his story yet again and seeing what kind of details they could ferret out to trip Bobby up. Copley's first question, then, surprised him.

"Did you know that Catherine and Jimmy Gagnon were big supporters of the Boston Symphony?"

Bobby tensed. His mind was already racing ahead, and what he saw, he didn't like. "No," he said carefully.

"They attended a lot of the concerts."

"Is that right?"

"Fund-raisers, cocktail parties. The Gagnons were real active in those circles."

"Good for them."

"Good for your girlfriend," Copley corrected.

Bobby didn't say anything.

"Susan Abrahms. That's her name, correct? Plays the cello with the orchestra."

"We've dated."

"We had a nice conversation with Susan this afternoon."

Bobby decided to take a long sip of his Coke now. He wished it were a beer.

"You went to a lot of functions with her," Copley said.

"We dated two years."

"Seems strange to think that in all that time, at all those functions, you never met Catherine or Jimmy Gagnon."

Bobby shrugged. "If I did, it never made an impression."

"Really?" Copley said. "Because Susan remembered both of them just fine. Said they met on a number of occasions. Sounds like the Gagnons were regular groupies when it came to fine music."

Bobby couldn't resist anymore. He glanced in D.D.'s direction. She not only refused to meet his gaze, but she was practically staring a hole through the carpet.

"Detective Warren," Copley spoke up crisply, "why don't you tell Officer Dodge what else we learned from Susan Abrahms?"

D.D. took a deep breath. Bobby figured at this point, he already knew what was coming next. And now he remembered something else—why he and D.D. had broken up in the end. Because for both of them, the job always came first.

"Miss Abrahms recalls you meeting the Gagnons at a function eight or nine months ago. Catherine, in particular, asked you a lot of questions about your work with the 'SWAT' team."

"Everyone asks me about my work," Bobby said evenly. "People don't meet a lot of police snipers. Particularly in those kinds of social circles."

"According to Miss Abrahms, you made a comment later that you didn't like the way Jimmy was looking at her."

"Miss Abrahms," Bobby said with emphasis, "is a very beautiful and talented woman. I didn't care for how a lot of guys looked at her."

"Jealous?" Investigator Casella spoke up.

Bobby didn't take the bait. Instead, he finished up his Coke, set it on the table, then leaned forward, resting his elbows on his thighs. "Did Miss Abrahms mention how long this alleged encounter lasted?"

"Several minutes," D.D. said.

"I see. So, let's think about this. In my day job, I probably meet fifteen new people a shift, so with twenty shifts a month, that's what? Three hundred new people a month? Which in the course of nine months, means twenty-seven hundred different names and faces crossing my path? Is it really so strange then, that I don't remember meeting two people I spoke with for a matter of minutes at some high-society function where frankly everyone in the room is unfamiliar to me?"

"Hard to keep all the rich pricks straight?" Investigator Casella deadpanned.

Bobby sighed. He was starting to get annoyed now. Not a good thing. "Never had a bad day at the office?" he asked Casella irritably. "Never said anything you later came to regret?"

"Susan Abrahms had some concerns about your relationship," D.D. said quietly.

Bobby forced his gaze from Casella. "Yeah?"

"She said you'd seemed distant lately. Preoccupied."

"This job will do that to you."

"She wondered if you were having an affair."

"Then I wish she would've said something to me."

"Catherine Gagnon is a beautiful woman."

"Catherine Gagnon has nothing on Susan," Bobby said, and he meant it. At least he thought he did.

"Is that why you were bothered by Jimmy paying attention to her?" Copley spoke up. "Jimmy had money, looks. Let's face it—he was much more her type."

"Come on, Copley. Did I kill Jimmy Gagnon because I was jealous of his attention toward my girlfriend, or did I kill Jimmy Gagnon because I was fucking his wife? Three days of questioning later, you can do better than this."

"Maybe it's both," Copley said crisply.

"Or maybe I honestly don't remember ever meeting either of the Gagnons. Maybe I went to those functions simply to support my girlfriend. And maybe I have better things to do with my time than remember every random stranger I've ever met."

"The Gagnons make an impression," Casella said.

Bobby was already waving him off. "Find me one person who ever saw me and Catherine Gagnon alone. Find one person who ever saw me and Jimmy exchanging

words. You can't. Because it never happened. Because I really don't remember either one of them, and when I killed Jimmy
Gagnon Thursday night, it was purely because he had a gun pointed at his wife. Take
a life to save a life. Didn't any of you ever
read the sniper's manual?"

He broke off in disgust. He got up, not
caring anymore how agitated he appeared,
and started to pace.

"Understand you've been drinking," Copley persisted.

"One night."

"I thought one night was all it took for an
alcoholic."

"I never said I was an alcoholic."

"Come on, ten years without a drink . . ."

"My body is my temple. I take care of it;
it treats me right." He looked at the ADA's
definitely softer middle. "You should try it
sometime."

"We're gonna nail her," Copley said.

"Who?"

"Catherine Gagnon. We know that somehow, some way, she was behind it."

"She arranged for me to kill her husband?
Murder by police sniper? Come on . . ."

Copley had a calculating gleam in his

eye. "You know, the Gagnons used to have a housekeeper."

"Really?"

"Marie Gonzalez. Older woman, very experienced. Worked for the Gagnons for the past three years. Know why she was fired?"

"Since I didn't know they had a housekeeper, I obviously don't know why she was fired."

"She fed Nathan a snack. Part of her tuna sandwich. The boy—who is twenty pounds underweight, by the way—was hungry. So Marie gave him some of her sandwich. Nathan wolfed down the entire half. And Catherine fired Marie the very next day. No one other than the nanny is supposed to feed anything to Nathan. Not even if he's starving."

Bobby didn't say anything, but the wheels were once again turning in his mind.

"We're going through the other nannies now," Copley said, almost casually. "So far, it's a string of strange and sordid stories. How Catherine would disappear for long periods of time. How no sooner did she reappear than Nathan would be sick again. Then there were the soiled diapers she demanded be kept in the refrigerator—"

"Soiled?"

"Filled with shit, to be exact. For six months, each and every one of them went straight into the fridge. Then there were the diets—lists of things he wasn't allowed to eat, lists of things he could only eat. This, combined with strange minerals and herbs and supplements and drugs. I tell you, Officer Dodge, I've been in the business fifteen years, and I've never seen anything like this. No doubt about it, Catherine Gagnon is abusing her son."

"Do you have proof?"

"Not yet, but we'll get it. The security camera was her first mistake."

They were baiting him again. He still couldn't stop himself from asking, "The security camera?"

"For the master bedroom," D.D. supplied. "It was turned off Thursday night. Except according to the security company, that's not possible."

"I don't get it," Bobby said honestly, finally standing in one place and rubbing the back of his neck.

"The security camera in the master bedroom was set to turn off at midnight; instead, it magically shut down at ten p.m.

Catherine gave us some song and dance about the control panel messing up the time. But we talked to the security company. Tuesday, when Jimmy filed for divorce, he contacted the company directly. He told them he had a situation at home— he wanted to be able to monitor the rooms without someone manually overriding the cameras. So the security company reset the whole system, then gave him a new code. As of Tuesday, the control panel was in proper working order, and more importantly, the only person who could alter the system was Jimmy Gagnon."

"So he shut off the camera in the master bedroom?"

"No," Copley said. "He didn't. She did."

"But you just said she couldn't—"

"She couldn't. Which I bet you anything she didn't know, until ten o'clock Thursday night, when her plan went into play. I bet she stood in front of that control panel for ten minutes, trying to figure out why she couldn't override the system, and slowly getting desperate. She has to be in the bedroom. You of all people should know why."

Bobby opened his mouth to protest, but then abruptly, he got it. He got the whole sordid theory. He shut up and simply waited for Copley to finish his spiel.

"You had to be able to see them, Officer Dodge. You had to be able to see Jimmy, who has no history with firearms, suddenly threaten his wife and child with a gun. The big questions, of course, are what got him going, and what—or who—put that gun in his hand. Now that's the kind of stuff Catherine can't afford for us to see. That's the kind of stuff she *doesn't* want caught on their home security system. So it comes to her. She advances the control panel's clock two hours, and boom, her work is done. The camera thinks it's midnight, and automatically shuts off. She's clever, I'll give her that. Almost too clever for her own good."

Copley switched gears. "Did you mean to help her, Officer Dodge? Were you just flirting a little at a cocktail party, bragging about your life with the STOP team, trying to make yourself sound good? Or did it go deeper than that? Few little rendezvous later, maybe this whole thing was actually your idea."

"For the last time, I don't remember ever talking to her!" Bobby shook his head, frustrated, fed up. He couldn't even bring any kind of concert event into focus in his mind.

Frankly, the functions bored him. He attended on autopilot, pasting on a smile, shaking hands, and counting down the minutes until the evening was done and he could go home, take off the penguin suit and get Susan into bed.

But then, all of a sudden, he did remember something. *"What's the most common kind of call for a team like yours? Bank robberies, hostage situations, escaped felons?"*

"Nah. Around here it's mostly domestics. Drunk guy gets all pissed off and starts threatening his own family."

"And that's a SWAT call?"

"If the guy is armed, you bet it is. It's called a domestic barricade, where the family members are considered hostages. We take those calls very seriously, especially if there are reports of shots fired."

It had been a Mardi Gras party, with all the symphony patrons floating around in elaborately feathered masks. Jimmy and Catherine Gagnon had stopped by to congratulate Susan on her performance. Catherine had had her black hair piled on top of her head and was wearing a formfitting gold dress and exotic peacock mask. At first glance, Bobby had been aware of a

certain visceral-level response to the stunning costume. Then he'd been too busy
watching Jimmy devour Susan with his
eyes to pay Catherine much attention.

He'd ended up breaking off the conversation abruptly, leading Susan away with
some flimsy excuse or another. Later, they'd
shaken their heads at Jimmy's obvious display, feeling that vague sense of moral superiority one couple gets when they meet
another couple who is obviously more
glamorous, more successful, and more
fucked up.

Bobby hung his head. Ah shit, he did not
want to remember this now.

"We're going to get her," Copley repeated. "And you know Catherine's not the
kind of woman to take the fall. First sign of
real danger, and she's going to cry me a
river. You don't want to get caught in that
deluge, Officer Dodge."

"Got a deadline?" Bobby shot back,
stung. "Let me guess. It's tomorrow by
five."

Copley scowled at him. "Now that you
mention it—"

"Yeah, well, there we go. Tomorrow it is.
I'll give you a call." Bobby gestured them

up, off his dilapidated sofa and out his front
door. D.D. was regarding him strangely. He
wouldn't look her in the eye.

"One last thing," Copley said, halting in
the door frame. "Where were you last night,
between ten p.m. and one a.m.?"

"I was killing Tony Rocco, of course."

"What—"

"I was sleeping, you piece of shit. But
thanks for insulting me in my own home.
Get out."

Copley was still in the doorway. "This is
serious business—"

"This is my *life*," Bobby said and
slammed the door.

Chapter 22

Robinson made the mistake of answering the phone. Not a good thing these days. Now Robinson had to deal with the caller, and the caller was not happy.

"His instructions were to make it look like an accident or, at the very least, random bad luck—say a carjacking. Carving someone up with a butcher knife does *not* appear accidental!"

"I told you I couldn't control him."

"The police are crawling all over this. That's going to make things a goddamn mess."

"I don't think he's worried."

"Why? Because he's the world famous 'Mr. Bosu'? What the hell does that mean?"

"It's a piece of exercise equipment."

"What?"

"Both Sides Up ball," Robinson supplied. "BOSU ball. It's flat on one side, domed on the other. You balance on it to do squats, or place the domed side down for push-ups. Makes for a good workout inside a confined area."

"You're telling me I've hired a man who thinks he's a piece of exercise equipment?"

Robinson said seriously, "I'm telling you you've hired a man who doesn't mind pain."

The caller was silent for a moment. So was Robinson.

"Is he prepared for the next assignment?" the caller asked finally.

"Working on it now. Of course, there's been a minor wrinkle." Robinson spoke carefully.

"Minor wrinkle?"

"Mr. Bosu has some new terms: Instead of ten thousand dollars for the new job, he expects thirty."

The caller actually laughed. "He does,

does he? The man just *fucked up his very first assignment.*"

"I don't think he sees it that way."

"Did he at least open a bank account?"

"Mmm, no."

"No?"

"Mmm, he prefers cash."

"Oh, for the love of God. You tell Señor Psycho a few things for me. One, I don't have that kind of cash lying around. Two, he'll get ten thousand dollars and not a penny more. Frankly, he should be happy I'm willing to pay that much, given that we both know I'm only asking him to do something he already wants to do."

"I don't think he's into negotiation."

"Life is negotiation."

Robinson took a deep breath. No way around it now. "Mr. Bosu sent a note. It says if you want results, it will cost you thirty grand. It says if you *don't* want results, it will still cost you thirty grand. It says Mr. Bosu knows where you live."

"*What?* You haven't told him anything, have you? I thought you picked him up in a rental car, gave him a stolen cell phone. There should be no way for him to trace—"

"I think he's bluffing. But I can't be positive. I have my contacts. Maybe he has his."

The caller was quiet, breathing hard. Angry? Or fearful? It was hard to be sure.

"I would pay him the money," Robinson said very seriously. "Or, I would get the hell out of town."

The caller took a noisy breath. "Tell him there will be no new terms. Tell him I got him out of jail, I can sure as hell put him back."

Robinson was silent for a moment.

"What?" the caller prodded.

"Well, to put him back in jail . . . you kinda gotta catch him first."

Another pause.

"Shit," the caller said.

"Shit," Robinson agreed.

Mr. Bosu had a puppy. He'd had to buy it from a pet store, not his first choice but about all that was available to him on a Sunday afternoon. The shop, with its crowded shelves, cheap linoleum floors, and vaguely antiseptic smell, had given him the heebie-jeebies. Given that just forty-eight hours ago he'd been a victim of incarceration, looking at a bunch of puppies and kitties plopped down in tiny wire cages hadn't done much for him either.

He'd planned on hanging out for a while. Pet stores on a Sunday afternoon, filled with fluffy kitties, soft puppies, and oodles of milling kids, what wasn't to love? But the dispirited air of the place made him cut and run.

Mr. Bosu bought a beagle-terrier mix. The tiny, ecstatic puppy was all white with giant brown patches over each eye, dangling brown ears, and thumping brown tail. He was the cutest little bugger Mr. Bosu had ever seen.

For his new charge, he acquired a leash, a small carrier that resembled a duffle bag, and about five dozen chew toys. Okay, so maybe he'd gone overboard. But the puppy—Patches, maybe?—had gnawed on his chin and nuzzled his neck so enthusiastically, Mr. Bosu pretty much bought anything and everything the puppy so much as sniffed.

Now he had the puppy on the leash and they were both trotting merrily down Boylston Street. The puppy—Carmel? Snow?—appeared absolutely thrilled to be out in the

fresh, fall air. Come to think about it, Mr.
Bosu was happy, too.

Mr. Bosu and the puppy—Trickster,
maybe? Come on, how could you have a
puppy without a name?—reached the street
corner. Mr. Bosu got out the map tucked
into his pocket. A woman paused beside
him. She was blonde, beautiful, and
dressed entirely in the fall collection of
Ralph Lauren. She gave him a stunning
smile.

"What a beautiful puppy!"

"Thank you." Mr. Bosu looked around the
woman. No kids in tow. He was disappointed.

"What's its name?"

"I just bought him fifteen minutes ago.
We're still getting to know one another."

"Oh, he's adorable." The woman was
squatting down now, oblivious to the people trying to walk all around them. She
scratched the dangling brown ears. The
puppy closed his eyes in true puppy bliss.
"Your first dog?" the woman asked.

"I had another when I was a kid."

"Do you live in the city?"

"At the moment."

"It won't be easy to have a puppy in an apartment."

"Fortunately, my job allows me to make my own hours, so it won't be so bad."

"You're really lucky," the woman gushed. She was eyeing his Armani sweater and obviously liking what she saw. He flexed just for the hell of it, and her smile grew. "What do you do?"

"Kill people," the man said cheerfully.

She laughed, a full, throaty sound. He bet she practiced that at night, just for guys like him.

"No, really," she said.

"Yes, really," he insisted, but then softened the words with a smile. "I would tell you more," he said, "but then I'd have to kill you, too."

He watched her work it out. Was she amused, frightened, or confused? She glanced at his Armani sweater again, then the puppy—Trickster, he was starting to like Trickster—and decided to go with amused. "Sounds exciting. Very hush-hush."

"Oh, it is. And you?"

"Recently divorced. He had money, now I'm spending it."

"Congratulations! No kids to worry about?"

"Fortunately not. Or maybe unfortunately. There's a lot more money in child support."

"Indeed unfortunate," he agreed. Her eyes were warm, practically glowing as they caressed his chest.

"Maybe we could have dinner sometime," he said. Those were the magic words. The woman whipped out a card with her name and number like a seasoned pro. He slid it into his pocket and promised that he would call her.

Trickster was now peeing on a newspaper stand. Not quite so attractive, so Mr. Bosu tugged on the puppy and they headed on their way. He eyed the map again. Six blocks later, they were there.

It was a lovely street, tiny, tucked deep within a maze of roads in downtown Boston. Clearly residential here. The lower level offered a corner grocer, florist, a tiny deli. Upstairs were the apartments. He counted from left to right until he found the number he was looking for. Then he eyed his notes once more.

Okay, all was well.

He found a bench by the corner grocer.

He tapped the empty place beside him and Trickster jumped up, curling up beside his leg. The puppy made a long, soft sigh, obviously winding down from another hard session of busy puppy work.

The man smiled. He still remembered his first dog, Popeye. A cute little terrier his father had brought home reluctantly from some guy at work. Neither of his parents had been into dogs, but a boy needed a dog, so they brought home a dog. Mr. Bosu was given its complete care and his mother learned to sigh and blink hard when Popeye chewed up her favorite shoes, then went to work on the plastic-covered sofa.

Popeye had been a good dog. They'd run together through the neighborhood, playing endless games of fetch and diving through big piles of leaves.

Mr. Bosu knew what people expected of a guy like him, but he'd never hurt his dog. Never even thought about it. In the silent, little house where he grew up, Popeye had been his best friend.

It lasted five years, until the day Popeye rushed into the street after a squirrel and got flattened by Mrs. Mackey's Buick sedan. Mr. Bosu remembered Mrs. Mackey's horrified

scream. Then watching his little dog twitch-
ing in the throes of death. There had never
even been a question of bringing Popeye to
the vet. It had been that bad.

Mr. Bosu had wrapped Popeye in his favorite T-shirt. Then he'd dug a hole in the
backyard, burying his dog himself. He
hadn't cried. His father had been very proud
of him.

Mr. Bosu went to bed early that night, but
never slept. He lay wide-eyed in his twin-
sized bed, wishing his dog would return to
him. Then he had an idea.

He left the house shortly after one a.m. It
didn't take him long. People parked their
cars in the street, and in a neighborhood
like his, no one ever locked the doors. He
popped the hood. He used a screwdriver.
Punched a few holes. In the end, it was simple and neat.

They said Mrs. Mackey never saw it coming. One minute she was braking for the intersection, the next she was sailing right
through the stop sign. The oncoming traffic
nailed her at thirty miles an hour. Gave her a
concussion and broke several of her ribs,
not to mention her hip.

Didn't kill her though. Damn Buick.

Still, it wasn't a bad effort from a twelve-year-old. Of course, he'd gotten much better since then.

Now Mr. Bosu eyed the apartment window up on the second floor. Still no sign of movement. That was okay. He could wait.

He leaned back against the bench. He closed his eyes against the warm sun. He let out a long, low sigh, very similar to Trickster's. Then he scratched his puppy's ears.

Trickster thumped his tail appreciatively. Just a man and his dog, Mr. Bosu thought.

Yeah, just a man, his dog, and his hit list.

Chapter
23

Bobby went for a run. Daylight was failing.
The sunny fall afternoon had come to an
end, and the evening loomed dark and cold.
Heading out the door, he found himself automatically grabbing his neon yellow running jacket, and that filled him with a sense
of relief that was hard to explain. Even after
everything he'd been through, his subcon-
scious wasn't trying to kill him just yet. He
wondered if he should call Dr. Lane and give
her the good news.

He hit the streets, pounding down one

long city block and up another. The streets
were quiet, people tucked in their homes,
preparing for another work week. Lone cars
zoomed by here and there, illuminating him
briefly before sweeping past.

He planned on running to the old Bath
House, an easy five-mile loop from his
home. But the Bath House came and went,
his feet still churning pavement. He arrived
at Castle Island, then swept around the
shore's edge, running into the dark.

He wanted to blame James Gagnon for
his current mood. Or Catherine Gagnon or
even bloodthirsty ADA Rick Copley, so eager to sink his chops into a good, juicy
homicide he already had saliva dripping
from his teeth.

But in all honesty, he knew what his
mood was all about. Tonight, he was thinking about his mother.

It had been so long ago now, he didn't
know if the face he recalled was actually
hers or some composite carefully crafted
by his mind. He had a vague impression:
brown eyes, dark hair curling around a pale
face, the scent of White Shoulders perfume.
He thought he remembered her squatting
before him, saying urgently: *I love you,*

Bobby. Or maybe that was merely a product of mental fiction. Maybe she'd actually said, *Don't stick your hand in the light socket, son* or *Don't play with guns.*

He didn't honestly know. He'd been six when she'd left. Old enough to hurt, young enough to not understand. *Your mother's gone and she's not coming back.* His father had announced it one morning over break-fast. Bobby and George had been chomp-ing away on the sugarcoated Apple Jacks their mother always refused to buy, and as a kid, that had been Bobby's first thought— *Wow, Apple Jacks every day.* His father didn't seem upset, George was nodding solemnly, so Bobby went along.

Later, he'd lie in bed at night, a crushing weight building upon his chest that would still be there when he woke up in the morn-ing. Then there'd been the night he'd heard George yelling at their father. Then there had been the subsequent trip to the emer-gency room.

After that, no one in their house had spo-ken of his mother again.

For a long time, Bobby had hated his father. Like George, he'd blamed him for everything. His father who said too little and drank too much. His father who could be very quick with his fists.

When George had turned eighteen, he'd hightailed it out of the state, and he wasn't ever coming back. Maybe that was their mother in him. Bobby would never ask.

But for Bobby it was different. Time did change things. His father changed. Bobby changed. And so did Bobby's impressions of his mother. Now he thought less and less about all the good reasons she had to leave, and wondered more and more why she'd never tried to make any contact. Didn't she miss her two sons at all? Didn't she feel at least a little bit of ache, a little bit of emptiness, where all that love for her children used to be?

Bobby's side hurt. He felt a stitch, growing rapidly as his breath heaved in painful gasps. He picked up his step, running anyway, because anything had to be better than standing alone with these kinds of thoughts. If he kept moving, maybe he could outrun his memories. If he kept running, maybe he'd exhaust his mind.

Twelve miles later. Winded. Sweat-soaked. Chilled.

He finally headed for home. Footsteps tired now, but mind still churning.

He wished he could turn back the clock. He wished he could pull his finger off the trigger the second before he sighted Jimmy Gagnon's head. He wished, in fact, he'd never even heard of the Gagnons, because now, for the first time, he wasn't sure anymore what he'd seen, or why he'd done what he'd done, and that was the most frightening thing of all.

Three days later, Bobby wasn't afraid that Catherine Gagnon was a murderer. He was afraid that he was.

Bobby ran home.

He called Susan.

She wanted to meet at a coffee shop. They settled on a Starbucks downtown. Neutral territory for them both.

He spent too much time picking out his clothes. He ended up with jeans and a long-sleeved chambray shirt he remembered too late Susan had given him for Christmas. Finding his wallet, he ran into a photo of them hiking together, and that sent him into another emotional tailspin.

He exchanged the chambray shirt for a dark green jersey and headed for the Pru.

Business, he told himself. It was all about business.

Susan was already there. She'd selected a small table tucked away behind a towering display of silver-and-green logo mugs. Her hair was pulled back in a clip at the nape of her neck. Long blonde strands had already escaped, curling around her face. The moment she saw him, she started tucking the loose tendrils behind her ears, the way she always did when she was nervous. He felt an immediate pang in his chest and did his best to ignore it.

"Evening," he said.

"Evening."

They suffered an awkward moment. Should he bend down and kiss her on the cheek? Should she stand up and give him a friendly hug? Hell, maybe they could shake hands.

Bobby expelled another pent-up breath, then jerked his head toward the counter. "Gonna get a coffee. Need anything?"

She gestured to the giant, foam-topped mug in front of her. "I'm fine."

Bobby hated Starbucks. He stared at the

menu with its dozen different espresso drinks, trying to figure out how you could make so much money off a coffee shop that offered hardly any plain old coffee. He finally settled on a French roast the perky cashier assured him was dark but smooth.

Bobby took the oversized mug back with him to the table, noticed that his hands were shaking slightly, and frowned harder.

"So, how have you been?" he asked at last, setting down the mug, taking a seat.

"Busy. The concert and all."

"How's it going?"

She shrugged. "The normal amount of panic."

"Good." He took a sip of his coffee, felt it sear a bitter trail all the way to his gut, and missed Bogey's with a passion.

"And you?" Susan asked. She still hadn't touched her drink, just kept turning it between her palms.

"Bobby?"

He forced his gaze up. "I'm hanging in there."

"I thought you would call on Friday."

"I know."

"I read the paper, and I was so . . . sad. I was sad about what happened and how that must feel for you. All evening on Friday I'd thought you'd call. Then Saturday morning, I thought to check your drawer. Imagine my surprise, Bobby, when I discovered it empty."

His gaze went to the tower of coffee mugs; her eyes bored into his face.

"You've never been the most approachable man, Bobby. I used to tell myself that was part of your appeal. The strong, silent type. A regular macho man. Well, I'm not finding it very appealing anymore, Bobby. Two years later, I deserve better than this shit."

The unexpected curse startled Bobby into looking at her again.

Slowly, she nodded. "Yes, I swear, sometimes I even break things when I get mad. In fact, in the past two days, I've broken quite a few things. It gave me something to do before the investigators came."

Bobby raised his coffee mug. Christ, his hand was shaking.

"Is that why you finally called, Bobby? Not out of concern for me, but because of curiosity over what the investigators said?"

"Both."

"Fuck you!" Her control disintegrated.

She was nearly crying now, pushing at her eyes with the heels of her hands, trying desperately not to make a scene in public, but failing.

"I was wrong to walk out on you on Friday," he offered awkwardly.

"No kidding!"

"It wasn't something I planned. I woke up, I looked around . . . I panicked."

"Did you think I couldn't take it? Is that what this is about?"

"I thought . . ." He frowned, not sure how to put it in words. "I thought you deserved better than this."

"What a crock of shit!" Whatever he'd just said, it was the wrong thing, because now she was shaking with rage. She let go of her coffee mug and stabbed a finger at him instead. "Don't you put this on me! Don't you get all high and noble, Neanderthal male just trying to protect his little woman. That's bullshit! You ran away, Bobby. You never even gave me a chance. The going got rough and you split, plain and simple."

Bobby's own temper started to rise. "Well, excuse me. Next time I've just shot a man, I'll be sure to put your feelings first."

"I *cared* about you!"

"I *cared* about you, too."

"Then why are we sitting here yelling at each other?"

"Because it's all we have left!" He regretted the words the moment he said them. She sat back, clearly stunned, deeply hurt. But then she started to nod, and that hurt him, so they were even.

"You've been waiting for it to end since the minute it started," she said, her voice soft, her hands back to rotating her coffee mug.

"We've never had much in common."

"We had enough to last two years."

He shrugged, feeling even more awkward, and hollow now, in a way he couldn't explain. He wished this scene were over. He wasn't so good with the leaving. He was better when the people were already gone.

"Ask me what you're going to ask me, Bobby," Susan said wearily. "Quiz your *ex*-girlfriend on what she told the police."

He had the good grace to flush.

"I honestly didn't remember meeting them," he said curtly.

"The Gagnons?" She shrugged. "Personally, I think they make quite an impression."

"Was it only that one time that we met?"

"I've met them several times at a variety of functions, but the big shindigs . . . I think you only met them that once."

Bobby felt it was important to say this: "I didn't pay much attention to her."

Susan rolled her eyes. "Come on, Bobby! She's a gorgeous woman. And with that gold dress and the exotic mask . . . Hell, even I thought about sleeping with her."

"I didn't pay much attention," Bobby repeated. "I was too busy watching him watch you. That's what I remember. Some man ogling my girlfriend, right in front of me and his wife."

Susan didn't look convinced, but she finally nodded, cradling her mug. "Does that bother you?"

"What?"

"You knew Jimmy Gagnon. You thought bad things about him. Then later, you killed him. Come on, Bobby, that's gotta gnaw at your gut."

"But I didn't remember meeting him until after you mentioned it to the police."

She was silent for a moment. "If it helps any, from what I read in the paper, it sounds like you saved that little boy's life."

"Maybe," he said bleakly, and then, simply because he needed to say the words out loud, "I think the family is going to get me."

"The family?"

"Gagnon's parents filed a lawsuit against me. They're going after me for felony murder. As in, if I'm found guilty, I go to jail."

"Oh Bobby . . ."

He frowned, surprised by how tight his throat had grown, then picked up his coffee and took another bitter sip. "I think they're going to win."

She closed her eyes. "Oh Bobby . . ."

"It's funny. The whole time I've had this job, I've always been so certain. Of what I do, of what I see. Even Thursday night. I never had a doubt. I sat there, lined up my shot and pulled the trigger. Then I told myself I didn't have any other choice.

"What a load of horseshit," he expelled now. "As if in fifteen minutes or less I could really know or understand what was going on inside a family."

"Don't do this, Bobby."

"Do what?"

"Give up. Blame yourself. Crap out. It's what you do. You're one of the smartest guys on the force, but you never became a detective. Why is that?"

"I like being on STOP—"

"You gave up. You and me, a great two years together. But here we are, doing an awkward farewell in the middle of a coffee shop. I don't think we don't have enough in common. I don't think this has to end. But I also know it's over. Because you gave up."

"That's not fair—"

"You're a good guy, Bobby, one of the best I've ever known. But there's something dark in you. Something angry. For every step forward, you take two steps back. It's as if half of you genuinely wants to be happy, but the other half won't let go. You want to be angry, Bobby. You need it, somehow."

He pushed his chair back. "I should be going."

Her gaze was dead-on. "Yes, run away."

"Hey, I *do not* want to go to prison!" He was suddenly impatient. "You don't understand. The truth doesn't matter to a guy like Judge Gagnon. He can take any fact and twist it to be what he needs it to be. If I want to get out of jail, I gotta trade in another life. And I won't do that."

"Catherine Gagnon," Susan guessed softly.

He thinned his lips, not denying it, and Susan slowly but surely shook her head.

"I don't know, Bobby. Sounds to me like you remember Catherine better than you think. Sounds to me like she made quite an impression."

"Not at the cocktail party," he countered harshly, "not when you were with me."

Susan had always been smart. "Oh God, Bobby, what exactly was it that you saw on Thursday night?"

Chapter
24

Catherine didn't know what started to spook her. She and Nathan were downstairs in the family room. It was nearly ten o'clock, well past Nathan's bedtime. He didn't seem to want to head upstairs, however, and she didn't have the heart to make him. He lay on the floor amid a mound of pillows, only his head visible above the pile. She'd put in his favorite movie, *Finding Nemo*. So far, he'd watched it twice.

Catherine spent too much time glancing

at the clock, wondering when Prudence would be home.

Finally, just to keep busy, she started messing around in the kitchen. Nathan wasn't allowed chocolate. Instead, she heated up a mug of vanilla-flavored soy milk. He accepted the mug wordlessly, his eyes glued to the TV.

"How does your stomach feel?"

He shrugged.

"Are you hungry?"

Another shrug.

"Maybe you'd like some yogurt."

He shook his head, pointedly staring at the TV.

Catherine retreated once more to the kitchen. Now that she was paying attention, they desperately needed groceries. Soy milk was low, soy yogurt, too. Nathan ate a special gluten-free bread, nearly gone. His organic peanut butter, almost wiped out as well. She started working on a list, then remembered that they had an appointment with the new doctor tomorrow afternoon and paused.

She headed back out of the kitchen, past the bar, and stepped down into the sunken family room.

"Nathan, we need to talk."

Reluctantly, Nathan turned his TV-glazed stare onto her.

"Dr. Tony can't be your doctor anymore."

"Why?"

She hesitated, fully planning on telling the truth, then looked at his drawn face and lost her courage. "Dr. Tony thinks you need a special doctor. A super-duper doctor. One with superpowers."

Only four years old, Nathan gave her the look of a born skeptic. God, why wasn't Prudence home yet? Sure, she had the whole day off, but did she have to stay out all night too? Didn't she know how much Catherine might need her? Catherine tried again.

"Tomorrow, we're going to see a new doctor. Dr. Iorfino. His specialty is little boys just like you."

"New doctor?"

"New doctor."

Nathan looked at her. Then he very deliberately held up his mug of soy milk and poured it out onto the carpet.

Catherine took a deep breath. She wasn't mad at Nathan—not yet—but she felt a growing, displaced rage toward Prudence, who had abandoned her, thereby forcing her to handle this scene.

"That wasn't very nice, Nathan. Only bad boys dump their milk on the rug. You don't want to be a bad boy."

Nathan's lower lip was starting to tremble now. He jutted it out, nodding furiously. "I'm bad! And bad boys don't go to doctors!"

He had tears in his eyes. Big, unshed tears, that hurt a mother even worse than angry sobs.

"Dr. Iorfino's going to help you," Catherine insisted. "Dr. Iorfino is going to get you well. Make you a big kid, so you can play with all the others."

"Doctors don't help! Doctors have needles. Needles don't help!"

"Someday they will."

Nathan looked her right in the eye. "Fuck doctors!" he said clearly.

"Nathan!"

And then, "I know what you're trying to do," he said in a sly, nasty voice she'd never heard before. "You're trying to kill me."

Catherine's heart stopped in her chest. She headed back into the kitchen, hoping Nathan wouldn't see how badly her hands were trembling. You're in control now, she

kept telling herself. This was the true con-
sequence of Jimmy being dead. No more
excuses, no more escapes. Buck stopped
with her now. She was in charge.

She got a roll of paper towels and returned to the family room. Nathan looked a
great deal less certain. His chin was tucked
against his bony chest, his shoulders were
up around his ears.

He was waiting for her to hit him. It's what
Jimmy would've done.

She held out the roll of paper towels. After another moment, Nathan took it.

"Please wipe up the milk, Nathan."

He remained hunched.

"You know what? You do half, I'll do half.
We'll do it together." She took the roll back,
briskly ripping off sheets. After another moment, he did the same. She got on her
hands and knees. This intrigued him
enough to emerge from his cocoon of pillows. She started blotting. "See, it comes
right up."

Slowly but surely, he followed suit.

When they were done, she took the pile
of soggy paper into the kitchen and threw it
away. In the family room, Nathan ejected

the movie. He sat in the middle of the soy-stained rug, still looking small and forlorn.

It was bedtime. Both of them stared at the dark shadows looming at the top of the stairs.

"Mommy," he whispered, "if I go to so many doctors, why don't I ever get better?"

"I don't know. But someday we're going to figure it out, and then you'll get to run around just like all the other kids. Come on, Nathan, it's time for bed."

He reached up his arms. She gave in to his silent request. For a split second, he hugged her hard. For a split second, she hugged him back.

And then, at that moment, she knew what was wrong.

The draft of air. Very cold, very crisp, very *outside* air drifted down the stairwell. It ruffled Nathan's fine brown hair. And it carried with it the unmistakable odor of death.

For a change, Bobby wasn't asleep. He'd given up on it. Fuck sleep, fuck healthy foods, fuck moderate exercise. He'd taken everything Dr. Lane had told him to do and tossed it out the window. Now he was pacing his family room on exhausted, rubbery legs, gnawing cold pizza, guzzling a liter of Coke, and working himself into a state.

He had messages on his answering machine. A lot from reporters. A few from his team. Bruni invited him to dinner again. Two guys from the EAU asked if he wanted to meet. Everyone calling to check up on the psycho shooter cop. He should be grateful, appreciative. Once on the team, always on the team, that's what they said.

He was resentful. He didn't want their calls, he didn't want their attention. Frankly, he didn't want to be the psycho shooter cop, the unfortunate sniper who'd discharged his weapon in the line of duty and now was screwed for the rest of his life. Fuck the team, fuck camaraderie. None of the rest of them had their butts on the line.

Yeah, he was feeling good and sorry for himself now.

He thought about calling his brother in Florida. Hey, Georgie boy, it's been what, ten, fifteen years? Just thought I'd give you a ring. Oh yeah, I blew some guy away the other day and that reminded me of something. What exactly happened with Mom?

Or maybe he'd call Dr. Lane instead.

Good news, I haven't had a drink today. Bad news, I fucked up everything else. Say, if you have a chance to save yourself by ratting out someone else, should you do it? Or is that the kind of thing that'll just drive you insane?

He couldn't stand himself in this kind of mood, so edgy he felt as if he were going to burst out of his own skin, so ragged he could barely think. Honest to God, he needed to shoot something.

Instead, his phone rang. He picked it up and he wasn't even surprised anymore.

"This is Catherine," a husky female voice whispered straight out of his dreams and into his ear. "Come over right away. I think someone's broken into my house. Please, Officer Dodge, I need you."

Then the phone went click and the sound of dial tone filled Bobby's ear.

"Intruder, my ass," Bobby muttered, but then he shrugged. The call solved one problem for him. Now he had an excuse to get his gun.

Driving by the Gagnon residence, Bobby expected to feel a creepy sense of déjà vu.

He didn't. Thursday night it had been all lights, cameras, action. Now, nearly midnight on a school night, the dignified brick neighborhood was quiet, discreet, a proper lady gone to bed with curlers in her hair.

He looked around for a patrol car and was slightly surprised none were about. He would've bet money Copley was having the BPD keep close tabs on Mrs. Gagnon.

Bobby parked twelve blocks away, at the movie theater by Huntington Ave. He made a note of the late shows and when they started. The cool, detached part of his mind found it interesting that he was already building an alibi.

Making the dozen-block hike to Back Bay, the saner part of his mind tried to reason with him. What was he doing? What did he honestly think was going to happen? He didn't buy Catherine's intruder story for a minute. Instead, he was thinking of what Harris had told him. *She's going to call you again. She's going to tell you that you're the only hope she has left. She's going to beg you to help her. It's what she does, Officer Dodge; she destroys men's lives.*

Would she try to seduce him? Did he care if she did? His career was already in the toilet. He'd had his first drink in ten years and just this evening he'd officially ended things with the woman who was probably the best damn thing that had ever happened to him.

He was footloose and fancy-free. He was feeling reckless, and yeah, more than a little self-destructive. A sordid rendezvous sounded just about right. He could already recall the warm, cinnamony scent of her perfume. The way her fingernails had felt, raking lightly across his chest.

It didn't take too much for his mind to fill in the rest. Her long, pale legs wrapped around his waist. Her strong, lithe body writhing beneath his own. He bet she moved like a pro, moaned like a pro. He bet she was the type of woman who'd do just about anything.

So Harris had been right all along—Jimmy'd been dead only four days, and Bobby already couldn't wait to fuck his wife.

He walked into the neighborhood, head down against the cold, hands thrust deep into the front pockets of his down jacket. A dozen bad seduction scenes ran through his mind, each more sordid than the last.

Then he looked up, saw the fourth-story window, and felt the air freeze in his chest.

Holy shit!
Bobby started to run.

Catherine was downstairs in the lobby. She was curled up at the base of the townhouse's elevator, Nathan pressed tight against her chest, his face buried against her neck. Bobby barely had time to register the irony of it—that this is how Catherine and Nathan had looked on Thursday night, that every time he met this supposed child abuser, she was cradling her son—then he was vaulting for the stairs to her second-story unit, gun in hand.

"You hear gunshots, get out. Head straight for your neighbors', bang on the door, and tell them to call the cops."

He didn't wait to see if she nodded, but bounded up the stairs.

Bursting low and fast through the open front door, he came to an immediate crouching halt beside a fake ficus tree, breathing hard, realizing he was moving too fast, too heedlessly, and now trying to regroup. Face-to-face confrontation was really no different than sniping. The winner was usually the guy who could control his adrenaline the best.

Bobby took another deep breath and steadied his nerves. He'd never been inside the Gagnons' townhouse. Four stories, he'd been told on Thursday night. The Gagnons occupied the top four stories of a five-level townhouse, with the top story being converted to cathedral ceilings.

So he needed to head up.

He gazed around the marble-tiled foyer, identifying what appeared to be a formal parlor to his left and a vast, open expanse of family room and kitchen directly ahead. His back pressed against the wall, two hands holding his nine-millimeter dead center against his chest, he approached the parlor first.

He led with his gun, ducking in low and sweeping the dark, shadowy space. Finally satisfied that it was empty, he departed, closing the door, then moving the fake tree in front of it: he didn't want someone doubling back behind him.

He hit the family room and kitchen next, though he was relatively sure that area would be secure. Too many lights, too much vast, open space. If someone was still in the townhouse, they wouldn't hide here.

For protocol's sake, he cleared the

pantry, the walk-in closet, and the laundry room. That left him with the stairs.

He could smell it now. Wafting down the dark, shadowed space. No lights here. Just steps leading to a thicker gloom, and thanks to the unmistakable odor, a bitter, unhappy end.

His heart was pounding again. His palms sweating. He turned his focus inward. Part of the moment, but outside the moment. A predator on a trail. A calm, well-oiled machine doing what it was trained to do.

He drifted up the stairs silently, patient footstep after patient footstep. He came to a small, dark landing. Closed doorway to his left. Open doorway straight ahead. He went through the open doorway first, the smell noticeably fading as he entered the room. He didn't snap on the overhead light—the sudden rush of illumination would leave him exposed—but instead used the dim light seeping through two windows to make out his surroundings. It was a small living suite: bathroom, bedroom, playroom. Nathan's space, judging by the murals of cowboys and bucking broncos decorating the wall. He checked the closet, checked the shower, even thought of the toy chests.

Finally satisfied that no intruder lurked in the shadows, he picked up a discarded shirt of Nathan's and hung it on the doorknob as he shut the door behind him.

Closed-door time. A little riskier, but he was finding the zone now, each movement smoother and more controlled than the last. Go low, turn sideways to present less of a target, open the door and slide inside in one fluid motion.

Another suite of rooms, equally dark. Strictly utilitarian now. Queen-sized bed, old eighties loveseat, hand-me-down bedroom furniture. The nanny's quarters, he'd bet. Functional, but not fancy. He was almost sorry he didn't find anything here. Because that left only one place. The vaulted fourth floor. The infamous master bedroom.

Very carefully, Bobby headed up the stairs.

The smell was unmistakable now. Sharp, acrid. Bobby's gun had slipped lower. He wasn't holding it as tightly. Somehow, he didn't think he was going to need it anymore. What had happened in the master bedroom was all about presentation. That's what he'd seen from the street.

The door was wide open. No overhead

lights. But candles. Dozens and dozens of flickering little candles, all framing the scene.

The body hung from the rafters in front of where the glass sliders used to be. The plastic had been removed, letting in the breeze. The candles flickered. The body swayed creakily.

Bobby walked around. And the pale, stricken face of Prudence Walker slowly twisted into view.

Chapter
25

I need to call it in."

Bobby and Catherine were speaking in hushed tones in the parlor. Bobby had shut up the master bedroom. Then, after a second pass through the residence, he'd escorted Catherine and Nathan back inside; the BPD detectives were going to want to question them at the scene.

Now, Nathan sat in the living room, staring slack-jawed at the TV as his eyelids slowly began to droop. The kid would be asleep in a matter of minutes. Better for him. Better for all of them.

"I don't understand. Prudence hanged herself?"

"So it would appear."

Catherine was still bewildered. "Why would she do that?"

He hesitated. "There was a note," he said at last. "She claimed she was despondent over Jimmy's death."

"Oh, please! Pru didn't give a rat's ass about Jimmy. And he certainly didn't pay attention to her. Let's just say they weren't each other's type."

"Are you saying . . . ?"

"Pru was a lesbian," Catherine supplied impatiently. "Why do you think I hired her? Anyone else, no matter how old, always ended up in Jimmy's bed, if only just for sport."

Bobby sighed. Ran a hand through his hair. Sighed again. "Shit."

"There's more in the note, isn't there?"

"It says she couldn't go on living, knowing who really killed Jimmy." He looked Catherine in the eye. "Her note very clearly targets you."

Catherine expelled her opinion of that in one simple word: "James!"

"You think your father-in-law killed your nanny?"

"Not personally, of course, don't be stupid. But he hired someone, or hired someone to hire someone. That's the way he always works."

"You're accusing a judge of murder?"

"Of course I am! You don't understand. This is perfect for him. The police come, they read the note, and they arrest me. Then James turns up just in time to take custody of Nathan."

Bobby tried to sound reasonable. "Mrs. Gagnon—"

"Catherine! I am *not* my mother-in-law."

"Look, the judge has already started legal action against you. I think we both can agree that given his money and connections, it's only a matter of time before he wins. Why would he even bother to take a chance with murder?"

"So he can have Nathan tonight."

"Mrs. Gagnon—"

"Catherine! You don't know what he's like. James wants total, utter control. Of the money, of Nathan, of me. Who do you think told Jimmy I was abusing Nathan? Who did you think probably first suggested divorce? The judge has never liked me. Maryanne has never liked me. And now they're going to take Nathan, and they're going to get all the money, and I'll have *nothing*! I'll be all alone."

Catherine's gaze took on an unhealthy light. He had only a second's warning, then she was across the room, striding toward him. Her touch was light, yet the minute her thumb came to rest in the open V of his shirt, his body went hard and the air froze in his lungs.

She reached down and very deliberately raked her nails across his thigh.

"I can do things," she murmured. "Things you've only watched in cheap pornographic movies. Tell me the truth, Officer Dodge: Aren't you tired of the same old, same old? Haven't you always wondered what it would be like to meet a woman with whom you no longer had to pretend?

"Want to rip open my sweater and pinch my nipples? Do it. Want to bite my neck, pull my hair? I don't mind. You don't even have to call me later or make fake proclamations of love. You can take me right here and now, we'll do it doggy style on the floor, or I can bend over on the couch, or maybe you don't want to fuck at all. Maybe you're more oral. That's fine by me. Or maybe"—her throaty voice changed, grew more calculating—"you'd prefer a fantasy."

Her hand tightened suddenly on his crotch, squeezing his balls. He flinched like an uninitiated schoolboy, then, in the next instant, surged against her touch. She laughed huskily, her left hand stroking him hard while her right hand feathered back his hair.

"Would you like the sweet Catholic girl? I'll wear the plaid skirt and knee-high socks. You can have the ruler. Or do you like wild and wicked? Black leather, stiletto boots, cowhide whips. Ever done a sixty-nine? Ever gone round the world? Tell me, Officer Dodge, what do you secretly dream about?"

He said, "Stop."

She merely laughed and worked him harder. "Oooh, it must be something very special. Bestiality maybe? I can put on a horse tail, utter a few good neighs while you mount. Or is it worse than that? Homo-erotic? Or maybe . . . Some men like it when I reenact for them. Would you like that, Officer Dodge? I can act out for you every single thing he ever made me do. I'll be the little girl and you can be the pe-dophile."

He didn't get it at first. He was too lost in the moment, the darkness in her finding an unexpected match in the darkness in him. He did want to rip off her clothes. He wanted to throw her down. He wanted to possess her in a way that was violent and raw. He felt as if he'd been pretending his entire life, and only now, in this moment, did he finally feel an emotion that was real.

But then, the full meaning of her words penetrated. A shudder moved through him, cold as ice. He grabbed her right hand, grabbed her left, and twisted them behind her back.

"Don't," he said harshly.

"Ooh, you *do* like it rough."

"Catherine, what happened to you . . . it wasn't your fault."

Her eyes widened. In the shadowed room he could see her pupils grow large. She jerked savagely out of his grip. Then she slapped him.

"Don't talk about things you know noth-ing about!"

Bobby didn't say anything. He was breathing hard. So was she. She spun away from him, walking haughtily across the space. Her gray sweater fell off her shoulder, exposing the black lace of her lingerie. She tugged at the fabric impatiently, still not meeting his eye.

There was something he should say right now, but he couldn't get the words out. He was too rattled, seeing not the woman in front of him, but the little girl who'd been trapped down in the dark.

The desire was long gone now. He felt drained, almost detached. Harris had been right. The little girl who had been cast down into that pit was not the same girl who had finally crawled her way to the top.

"Fine," Catherine announced crisply from across the room. "You don't want to play nice, I won't play nice. Call the police. By all means, tell them to come here. Let them see you in my home. I'll confess that we're lovers. Have been for months. The whole shooting, in fact, was your idea. Jimmy didn't even have a gun. I had it. I fired the warning shots for the neighbors to hear. Then you showed up, claimed he had a gun, and blew him away. It'll be your word against mine, Officer Dodge. How do you feel about doing twenty-five to life?"

"By tomorrow at five p.m.," Bobby said steadily, "if I don't tell the world that you were threatening your husband on Thursday night, Judge Gagnon has promised to put me in jail."

Catherine chewed on her bottom lip furiously. "I'll tell them Prudence was sleeping with you, that's why she hanged herself!" She stabbed her finger at him. "You! You're the one she alludes to in the note. You're the one she knows killed Jimmy, and it broke her heart because you're the love of her life."

"That story would work better if Prudence had hanged herself."

"What?"

He finally took pity on her. "There's no bruising around her throat. No burn marks from the rope, no broken fingernails from frantic clawing at the knot. Hanging's messy business. Prudence is too clean."

"I don't . . ."

"Someone killed her. Most likely snapped her neck. Then brought her to your bedroom and set the stage."

Catherine paled. She swayed slightly on her feet. "Boo," she murmured. "Boo."

"What?"

"Nothing."

"The point is, Catherine, I saw that right away. The BPD detectives will, too."

"What if they think I killed her?"

"Prudence had thirty pounds on you. There's no way you single-handedly strung her from the rafters."

"What about the note?"

"If the hanging's not a suicide, then the note's not a suicide note. By definition, all of its contents are in doubt."

"Oh," she said in a small voice.

"Prudence was murdered, Catherine. It's time to call the cops."

He headed out of the parlor toward the family room, where he'd seen a phone. Catherine stopped him halfway through the doorway.

"Bobby . . ."

He turned. For the first time since he'd met her, she appeared genuinely uncertain, genuinely fragile.

He regarded her levelly, as curious as anyone what she would do next. She was cold and calculating, no doubt about it. If he hadn't told her the truth about the nanny's death, she would've sold him out. Maybe, in time, she still would. But he couldn't bring himself to hate her. He kept seeing that little girl again, which was maybe her biggest trick. She could play the victim, even while staging her next plan of attack.

"You understand . . ." She gave up on the apology, waving her hand instead. "I can't lose Nathan. I can't."

"Why'd you fire the housekeeper for feeding him?"

She didn't seem surprised he'd heard the story. "Tony Rocco had ordered a strict diet—no wheat, no dairy. Dairy by-products are in everything from cereal to tuna fish. It was simpler to order people not to give him snacks. Unfortunately, not everyone saw it that way."

"And the poopy diapers in the fridge?"

"Fecal matter collections to rule out cystic fibrosis. Jimmy kept throwing them out, however, so we had to do it many times."

"People say the boy is sicker when you're around."

She said tiredly, "Nathan is sick all the time, Bobby. Maybe people just notice it more when they have someone around to blame."

"So he really is sick?"

"Yes."

"But Jimmy didn't believe you."

"No. Jimmy's parents told him I was the root of all evil, and as time passed, Jimmy loved me less and believed them more."

Bobby still had to think about it. "All right," he said quietly, and went to find a phone.

Chapter
26

D.D. wasn't happy to see him again. He'd called her direct and she was on-scene in twenty minutes, wearing a leather jacket, stiletto boots, and a scowl. The crime-scene techs followed close on her heels.

"You're a fuckin' idiot," she growled as she stormed through the door. "One suicidal fuckin' idiot."

"Careful. Kid." Bobby jerked his head toward the front parlor, where Catherine now had Nathan fast asleep in his nest of pillows. Bobby didn't know how the kid could sleep through all the chaos, but then, he didn't know anything about kids.

D.D. grimaced. She disappeared upstairs to view the scene for herself. He waited patiently in the foyer, leaning against the wall. More uniforms were coming in now. One fresh-faced kid set himself up discreetly in the entranceway, where he could watch Bobby standing in the foyer and Catherine sitting silently in the parlor. Periodically, Bobby would look over at the rookie and yawn mightily. It was fun to watch the rookie struggle not to yawn back.

Fifteen minutes later, D.D. returned, jerking her head toward a quiet corner. He obediently followed her over for the sidebar. They both understood they had to talk sooner versus later—it was only a matter of time before Copley stalked onto the scene, drawn by the fresh scent of blood.

"What the hell are you doing, Bobby?" D.D. demanded without preamble.

"She called, said there was an intruder in her house and asked me to come over. What was I supposed to do?"

"Call BPD."

"You think they would've taken her seriously? Thanks to Copley, most of the department seems to have her pegged as a murderer."

"Not your concern, Bobby. Your career is your concern, and just to enlighten you, these little stunts don't help you out."

"Funny how many people suddenly care about my career," he murmured.

"Bobby—"

"I didn't think there was an intruder," he said.

D.D. finally quieted. Now that he was getting serious, her temper calmed. "What'd you think?"

He shrugged. "That it was a ploy. That she wanted to talk to me alone. That she was probably going to lobby me for one thing or another."

"About the shooting?"

"Yeah."

D.D. grunted. "Better reason for you not to have come."

"Of course. Officer should have no contact with the victim's family postincident. Think I haven't read the manual? I've read the manual."

"So why did you come?"

"Because I shot this woman's husband, and what the manual doesn't tell you is that leaves you feeling all torn up inside, and yeah, desperate for answers, or maybe even just for someone to say, 'Officer, you did the right thing. Officer, I forgive you. Officer, you can go on with your life now, it's gonna be okay.' "

D.D. expelled a breath. "Ah Jesus, Bobby—"

Bobby cut her off. He didn't want to hear it anymore. "I received a call from Mrs. Gagnon shortly after ten-thirty," he said crisply. "Upon arriving in Back Bay, I parked my car and walked the rest of the way here. Halfway down the block, I saw the silhouette of a body hanging in the fourth-story window. You can say I moved a little quicker.

"Upon entering the lobby of the townhouse, I encountered Mrs. Gagnon and her son curled up on the floor in front of the elevator, obviously fearful. After instructing Mrs. Gagnon and her son to stay put, I took the stairs up to the front entrance of her residence. I entered armed with a fully loaded nine-millimeter, which I am licensed to carry. I conducted a full sweep of the residence, level by level, finishing in the master bedroom, where I walked through the open door to find the body of Prudence Walker swinging from the rafters.

"After reading the note resting upon the mattress, I exited the room, careful not to disturb anything and closing the door behind me with the cuff of my shirt. I then came downstairs and notified Mrs. Gagnon that it was time to call the police."

D.D. mimicked his stilted professional tone back to him. "And how did Mrs. Gagnon react to the news?"

"She appeared startled that Prudence would hang herself."

"What did she say?"

"That since Prudence was a lesbian, it was highly unlikely that she was Jimmy Gagnon's lover."

"Really?" That caught D.D.'s attention. She made a note. "Do you have confirmation?"

"Well, we could ask Prudence," Bobby said dryly, "but she's dead."

D.D. rolled her eyes. "What else did you and *Mrs.* Gagnon discuss?"

"She was concerned about what the police would think of the note. In particular, she and her in-laws are engaged in a custody battle over her son and she feared the police might use the note as an excuse to remove Nathan from her custody."

"Reasonable fear."

"I told her the police were smart enough to realize that the suicide was staged."

"You fucking did not!"

"I fucking did."

"Jesus H. Christ, Bobby, why the hell didn't you hand her evidence to destroy as well?"

"If I hadn't told her that, she wouldn't be here right now, D.D. She'd have grabbed the kid and fled."

"And you would've stopped her."

"How? By pointing my gun at her and her four-year-old son? Somehow, I don't think she would've taken me seriously."

"You had no right to give away details of a scene. You deliberately hampered the progress of this investigation—"

"I called you in. Without me, you had nothing."

"With you, we have nothing."

"No, you have a name."

"What name?"

"James Gagnon."

D.D. stopped, blinked her eyes several times, then peered at him in genuine confusion. "Judge Gagnon? You think he killed Prudence Walker?"

"Catherine thinks he did. Or hired some-one to."

"Why?"

"To implicate her in the death of her husband. Ask around, D.D. It's no secret that Judge Gagnon is real distraught over the death of his son. And it's no secret he blames Catherine."

"For God's sake, Bobby, he's a superior court judge—"

"Who just yesterday invited me up to his hotel suite, where he offered to drop all criminal charges against me in return for my promise to testify that on the night of the shooting, I heard Catherine deliberately pro-voke Jimmy into pointing the gun."

"You don't have audio."

"I mentioned that. The judge said not to worry about it. He'd take care of it."

"He'd take care of it?"

Bobby shrugged. "All he needs is one other guy who was at the scene to say he heard what I heard. The judge has long arms and deep pockets. I'm guessing I'm not the only one receiving his outreach."

"Shit," D.D. said heavily.

"I have a deadline—five o'clock tomor-row," Bobby said quietly. "I can lie about Catherine and watch my legal troubles go away. Or I can tell the truth, in which case, the judge will seek to bury me."

D.D. squeezed her eyes shut. "Politics and murder. Great, great, great." She opened her eyes. "Okay, so what are you going to do?"

He was honestly offended. "You shouldn't have to ask."

"I didn't mean it that way."

"The hell you didn't."

"Bobby—"

"We were friends once. I still remember it, D.D. Do you?"

She didn't answer right away. Which was answer enough. Bobby pushed away from the wall. "Investigate how you need to investigate, D.D. But if you want my two cents, Tony Rocco and Prudence Walker are both dead for the same reason."

"Because they knew Catherine Gagnon."

"Because they were *allies* of Catherine Gagnon. I spoke to Dr. Rocco the day he died—he fervently believed Catherine wasn't harming Nathan. Catherine trusted him as Nathan's doctor, just as she trusted

Prudence to help with Nathan. Now she has no one."

"She has a father," D.D. pointed out.

"Really? I'd send a few patrol cars in his direction. Maybe he's next."

"To be attacked by a knife-wielding butcher or to mysteriously hang himself? Come on, Bobby, the MO's don't even match!"

"He's isolating her."

"*He's* a well-respected judge who doesn't need to resort to murder. By your own admission, he's got money, influence, and an intimate knowledge of the legal system. Face it, Bobby: if Judge Gagnon wants custody of his grandson, he's going to end up with custody of his grandson. He sure as hell doesn't need to resort to murder."

"Five o'clock deadline," Bobby said. "The judge wants me testifying tomorrow and he obviously prefers possession of his grandkid tonight. The judge is in a hurry." He grimaced. "I wonder what's up."

D.d. interviewed Catherine next, sequestered in the front parlor. Bobby wasn't allowed in the room. He roamed the foyer, trying to catch Catherine's muffled replies through the closed parlor door, and wondering why Copley still hadn't shown his ugly mug.

Catherine and Nathan had been out most of the day. Bobby caught that much of Catherine's report. The security system had been set when she'd left; it was still set when she returned. No, she hadn't seen Prudence all day; she assumed the girl had left before she'd gotten up that morning. No, she didn't know much about the girl's local associates or friends. Prudence had a cell phone; that's what Catherine used to reach her. No, she had not tried to contact Prudence all day; she hadn't had a reason.

Catherine didn't know where the candles had come from. She didn't know where the rope had come from. A ladder had also been discovered. Maybe from their storage unit in the basement? She didn't know much about these things; the basement was Jimmy's domain.

Last time she'd been in the master bedroom had been the night before. She'd been concerned about security, so she and Prudence had moved the dresser in front of the broken slider. She hadn't known that anyone had moved it away, and she doubted Prudence would've done so—the dresser had been too heavy for either of them to move it alone.

At this point D.D. asked dryly if the bedroom security camera was on—or did it still not know how to tell time?

Catherine responded stiffly that she hadn't touched the security system at all, but she knew for a fact there would be no video footage from the master bedroom—the police had seized all the tapes.

Having achieved conversational stalemate, D.D. switched to more neutral ground.

Prudence had worked for her for six months, Catherine supplied. She'd been referred by an agency in England. Yes, Catherine had based part of her decision to hire her on the fact that Prudence was gay. Just because she'd come to terms with Jimmy's incessant infidelity didn't mean she was going to encourage him.

She had thought Prudence was an excellent nanny. Quiet, hardworking, discreet. No, the girl had not seemed particularly upset about what happened to Jimmy. Did that seem odd to her? Well, the British were known for their reserve.

Prudence had been more concerned about Nathan's health, as she should be.

Had Prudence visited Nathan in the hospital? No, Nathan had been in the ICU, where only family members were allowed.

But Nathan had been in the hospital for the past two days. So what had Prudence been doing? Her employer was dead, her charge was in the ICU. What was Prudence doing?

For the first time, Catherine hesitated. She didn't know.

Had she seen Prudence? Not really. Catherine had been out a lot—she'd been with Nathan at the hospital.

Had she talked to Prudence? Not much.

So in fact, Prudence could have been quite upset about Jimmy's death. Prudence could have understandably been terrified about staying alone in a house where a man had been shot. Maybe she'd even harbored a secret crush on Jimmy. He'd been charismatic, charming, handsome. Or maybe, she'd overheard a few things. A girl that quiet, that discreet . . . Maybe she knew more than she was saying about Thursday night, and that had left the girl extremely upset.

So upset, Catherine countered quietly, that she'd snapped her own neck?

Bobby could pretty much hear D.D.'s mental curse through the door. D.D. would be writing up a report this evening; his name would not be mentioned favorably. And with her would go the other few allies he had within the BPD.

Isolation, he thought. Of himself, of Catherine. He wanted to think it was due to choices of his own making. Or was Judge Gagnon really that good?

The interview wound down. Little more D.D. could ask. Little more Catherine would tell.

The door finally opened. D.D. stalked out, looking even angrier than when she'd stalked in. Bobby didn't bother to try to apologize.

He slid up beside her, just as she was walking out the door.

"Get the fuck out of my way, Bobby—" she started.

"I know how the murders are connected," he said. She wasn't going to ask, so he supplied on his own: "Overpowering a grown man and snapping a young girl's neck.

Whoever did this is very big and very strong."

D.D. whirled on him with surprising vehemence. "She's leading you around by the tail between your legs. She's turned you from a good cop into a fucking idiot. Well, you'd better be enjoying the sex, Bobby, because this is the end of your damn career."

Chapter
27

Two a.m. the whole world was sleeping snug as bugs in their beds. Mr. Bosu thought he'd like to join them. Unfortunately, Trickster had other ideas. The puppy was currently whining in the bathroom, scratching at the door. A part of Mr. Bosu thought, Fuck it. It was only his second night in a real bed on real sheets, for chrissakes. He could spread out his arms and legs. He could bury his face against the mattress and not smell the stink of piss. Like hell he was getting up for some sniveling little dog.

The other half of his mind was relentlessly
logical—he was already wide-eyed. Had
been for hours. Might as well take care of
his dog. Who knew that when he finally got
out of the joint, he wouldn't be able to stand
the quiet?

Life was so unfair.

Mr. Bosu got out of bed. He threw on his
five-hundred-dollar trousers. He opened the
bathroom door. Trickster came shooting
into his arms, wriggling ecstatically and licking at his chin.

"Yeah, yeah, yeah." He tried to sound
gruff. Trickster kissed half of his face, and
Mr. Bosu's grumpiness melted once and for
all. He supposed he'd slept enough the past
twenty-five years. Now he was a free man,
hanging out with his dog.

"Outside it is." He snapped on Trickster's
leash and headed out the door. Mr. Bosu
had selected a Hampton Inn tonight, nice
but not that noticeable. He'd be just another
guy in a suit, passing through. Here today,
gone tomorrow, not even worth remembering.

Trickster found a good bush in the parking lot, squatted and ejected a shockingly
strong spray. No one was about at this hour.

What the hell. Mr. Bosu unzipped his
trousers and joined him. A man and his dog,
taking a leak. Made him feel better about
things.

Which was good, because earlier this
evening, Mr. Bosu had been feeling blue.

The day had been disappointing. Produc-
tive but . . . flat. He'd found the girl. He'd
watched her exit the identified apartment.
He'd fallen in step beside her and struck up
a conversation using the dog. Everything
had gone smooth as silk. Except . . .

She hadn't been taken in by his new
clothes, for one. He'd seen no spark in her
eyes, no iota of interest. It had actually
started to piss him off. He looked pretty
damn good, you know. Good enough, at
least, for some lady he'd never met to want
to meet him for dinner. But here was this
young girl—and no beauty contestant at
that—barely giving him a second glance.

In fact, after a brief pat of Trickster's ears,
she'd been on her way.

Flustered, he'd had to do a quick two-
step to catch up. Funny thing about spending twenty-five years in the slammer—you
don't think so good on your feet.

The stupid cow was walking away. He

couldn't make a scene, but couldn't let her go. After all, she was never going to believe he just magically crossed her path again later. No, this was it. He'd selected his strategy and now it had to work.

It had come to him halfway across the street. What did he know and love? Kids. What did a nanny know and love? Children. He started spouting off about his two point two kids and the lack of good daycare. Boom, he got her attention back.

Turned out Prudence Walker was looking for a change of employers. Interestingly enough, she found her current family "kind of frightening." Apparently, when the father of the family is killed pointing a gun at his wife and child, it doesn't make the childcare provider feel too good about things.

Not that the father was sorely missed. Wandering hands when it came to the nanny, violent drunk when it came to the family. Guy sounded like a real loser. Rich, though, which would explain why he maintained a house in Back Bay while the other losers went to prison. Again, life was unfair, yada, yada, yada . . .

Mr. Bosu grew tired of hearing about the father. He wanted to know about the mother. He wanted to know about Catherine. . . .

Real piece of work, said the nanny. Mrs. Gagnon pranced around in impossibly high heels—a woman her age, bloody well ridiculous. (Mrs. Gagnon was beautiful, Mr. Bosu translated in his head, more beautiful than the young nanny, and twice as sexy.)

Too many rules, too. Boy can't eat this, boy must eat that. "Poor bugger can't weigh more than a blade of grass," the nanny prattled on. "Seems to me, she should be grateful for anything he wants to jolly well stuff down his face."

The mother was cold and arrogant. Held herself too high, put on airs. The woman didn't work, didn't tend the house, didn't raise her own son, and yet she was never home. Probably kept too busy by all her various boyfriends.

Mr. Bosu didn't have to talk anymore, just said "Oh no" or "Oh yes," in an appropriately sympathetic voice. The girl had worked herself into a state, obviously having kept too much locked inside. He found now that, with just the slightest nudge, he could steer her back to Catherine, that *dreadful* woman who did such *dreadful* things to her *poor, poor* son.

And then, briefly, he felt the old magic again. The sun was shining. Trickster was prancing. They were walking along, a regular bounce in their steps as his nerve endings prickled to life and the world took on a slow, surreal feel. This was Mr. Bosu prowling the urban jungle. This was Mr. Bosu, closing in beautifully, magnificently, on his prey.

Thirty thousand dollars, he was thinking. Wow, who had ever known he could get paid for this shit.

Corner bus stop now. The nanny came to a halt, suddenly seeming to realize how long she'd been talking and that he was still with her. For the first time, she appeared uneasy.

He thought he should make his move then. Invite her home to meet the wife and kids. Just around the corner. Make some kind of excuse to get her all alone.

He looked into her eyes, and in that moment, the fantasy left, the colors bled out of the world, and his adrenaline rush came to a crashing halt. She wasn't buying it. In fact, far from being taken in by his beautiful clothes and adorable puppy, she was beginning to frown.

He wavered on a precipice. Let her go. Walk away. No one would be the wiser.

But then he understood it was too late.

She knew Catherine. She'd talked about Catherine. From that moment on, her fate was sealed.

He looked up the street. He looked down the street. The girl opened her mouth.

He grabbed her left arm, spun her back against him, and wrapped his other arm around her neck. A small squeak. Yes, no, please don't. One snap, and she collapsed weightless against him. He cradled her into his arms, nuzzling the side of her neck as if they were lovers.

Then he smelled it on her skin. Sex. Sweaty, lustful, recent. Adult.

The desire washed right out of him. He was left supporting the dead weight of an uninteresting body, while Trickster tugged on the leash and whined curiously.

It was just plain work after that, and not even fun work. Having to lug the body out of view without calling too much attention to himself. Realizing he'd really screwed up now—he was supposed to have used his powers of "persuasion" to make the girl write a note. Well, that ship had sailed. He'd have to write it himself in his best young girl's script—yeah, like the police wouldn't see right through that.

No doubt about it, his employer wasn't going to be happy. And this, right on top of the small little issue of "overkilling" his last assignment.

Mr. Bosu began to get truly resentful. If killing was so damn easy, his employer should do it himself. Honest to God, a little murder and mayhem wasn't everything it was cracked up to be. Take right now, for example. Mr. Bosu was tired. Mr. Bosu wanted dinner. Hell, he wanted a good drink.

Instead, he was standing on a street corner with a corpse, forced into faking a make-out session simply so he didn't look ridiculous.

He had to force his brain into thinking fast once more.

Okay. He propped the dead nanny in a stairwell. Nice and peaceful, a girl just catching a snooze in the sun. Then he went around the block and, taking a chance he didn't like, hot-wired a car. This would be the end of things, he thought morbidly. He'd get away with murder, but get busted for auto theft.

Back to the main street. Now double-parked with a stolen car. Waiting for traffic to pass, then trying to get a body into the front seat of the car without attracting too much attention. "Oh, honey, you have to stop drinking so much," he announced loudly in an exasperated tone. Just because no one appeared to be around didn't mean no one was listening.

Finally, he had puppy, dead nanny, and the stolen car out on the road. Now he had to get the body to the right place at the right time for the right moment.

Shit, he'd engineered jailhouse killings that had taken much less work than this. Good thing Benefactor X had coughed up the extra dough, because this was certainly well beyond ten thousand dollars' worth of work. Thirty grand wasn't even seeming like such a bargain anymore.

He got on the cell phone and reached his contact. Turned out his timing wasn't too bad. Residence was clear, he was good to go.

Short drive later, Mr. Bosu arrived at a

house he'd been fantasizing about visiting for the past six months, ever since he'd gotten the first phone call, ever since his mysterious employer had reached out and brought hope to Mr. Bosu's world with one magic touch.

One twist of the nanny's key, and Mr. Bosu walked inside the townhouse. He inhaled the scent of the air, searching for a hint of her perfume. He couldn't linger. Not today, but oh, oh, to be so close . . .

When he walked up the stairs, he thought of her. When he unfolded the ladder, strung up the rope, and wrestled a fat girl's corpse, he pictured her delicate face. And when he arranged every single candle, lighting them tenderly, he once more remembered his hands around her neck.

He had squeezed. Each and every day he had squeezed. And each and every day, at the last minute, he had stopped. There would come a day when he wouldn't. They had both known that. There would come a day when the desire would be too strong, and he would simply squeeze out her last painful breath.

But for now, he'd stopped, and each time he'd seen in her eyes a small flicker of relief, before he climbed back up into the light, gave her a cheery wave, and abandoned her once more to the cold, black earth.

Then had come the day when he'd arrived back at their special place, whistling, upbeat, happy—even bringing a Twinkie as a special treat—and found it empty. He'd felt genuine pain, followed by genuine panic. Someone had stolen her, someone had taken her away, he would never see her again. . . .

And then in the next moment, he'd known what had happened. She had escaped. She had left him. After everything he had done for her, all of the care he had given her, all of those moments when he'd held her life in his hands and allowed her to keep on living . . .

The rage that had filled him was unimaginable. He'd returned home, where he'd sat in his room and thought about killing every single person on his street. He would start with his parents, of course. It was the decent thing to do. Kill them off now, before they ever had a chance to realize the monster they'd raised. Then he'd start with his neighbors, be methodical about it—from closest house to the farthest house, he'd work his way down the street.

Gun would be best. Quick, less exhausting. Didn't move him, though. Bullets were death by long distance. He wanted to be close, intimate. He wanted to hear the wet snicker-snack of a knife slitting skin, he wanted to feel the hot rain of someone's life splattering on his hands, he wanted to watch the last glimmer of hope bleed from their face until finally there was only endless, dreadful nothingness.

He should've done it. Should've gone into the kitchen, grabbed a serrated blade, found his mother, and just gotten on with it.

But he hadn't. He'd sat there, and then he'd realized rather idly that he was hungry. So he'd made a PB&J sandwich. Then, on a freshly filled stomach, he'd discovered that all that rage had really left him quite tired, so he'd taken a nap.

Next thing he knew, day had turned into day without him deciding on doing much of anything. Until four days later, when the police had turned up on his parents' doorstep, and that had been the end of him making his own decisions for a very long time.

Now he strung up the nanny, moved the

bureau, and tore back the plastic on the shattered slider. Now he laid the note, awkwardly forged, upon the bed.

The cell phone rang at his waist. Catherine and Nathan were on the move, said his contact. Time to go. He remained in the doorway, his hand fingering the knob, his nose searching for any whiff of her perfume. Did she dream about him? Did she miss him? They say a girl never forgets her first time. . . .

And then, in the next instant, he was seized by divine inspiration. Moving quickly now, to the boy's room. Four minutes, that's all he needed. A quick move here, a quick move there.

The excitement was back. That elusive thrill he hadn't felt since wrapping his arm around the fat girl's neck. Now he had it as he moved swiftly through the boy's room, already picturing the look on Catherine's face.

Three minutes later, he bounded down the stairs, a whistle on his lips. He reset the security, closed and locked the front door, then headed for the lobby. He picked up Trickster, who was waiting for him by the outer doors. They hit the street.

Chapter
28

He said: "I haven't slept in two days. I'm wired, I'm edgy, and I'm thinking of having a drink. I know it's late, but can I come over?"

She said: "I think you'd better."

He arrived fifteen minutes later. She met him at the door.

Dr. Elizabeth Lane had last seen Bobby twenty-four hours ago. The sight of him now filled her with both shock and dismay. His face was drawn, his eyes sunken. Whereas

He was briefly aware of a young boy's voice behind him: "Mommy, look at the puppy."

Then Mr. Bosu faded into dusk.

Back in the Hampton Inn parking lot now, Mr. Bosu gave up on sleep altogether. He was too restless, too keyed up from remembering past events.

Might as well do something useful, he decided.

"Hey, Trickster," he said softly. "Road trip."

once he'd sat in her office with preternatural stillness, now he paced relentlessly, filling the space with manic energy. He was a man on the brink. One wrong step and he'd go over. She was thinking strongly of prescription medication. For now, however, she started with "Would you like a glass of water?"

He said in a rush, "You know that old saying, just because you're paranoid doesn't mean they're not out to get you?"

"Yes."

"Well, I never thought I was paranoid, but now I think they're out to get me."

He wasn't going to sit. Rather than respond to his agitation, she moved behind her desk, finding her chair and clasping her hands neutrally. "Who is they, Bobby?" she asked evenly.

"Who isn't? The judge, the ADA, the BPD, the widow. Hell, everyone wants a piece of me these days."

"The investigation into the shooting has you concerned?"

"The investigation into the shooting?" He stopped, blinked his eyes a few times in confusion, then impatiently waved his hand. "Screw that. No one's waiting long enough

to care about those results. No, they're going to get me tomorrow."

She remained patient. "What's going to
happen tomorrow, Bobby?"

But he'd caught wind of her tone. He
stopped pacing long enough to square off
against her and plant his hands on her desk.
Bobby Dodge stared her straight in the eye,
and Elizabeth was a bit disconcerted to discover that in his current state he frightened
her.

"I am not an idiot," he said intently. "I am
not losing it. No, strike that, I am losing it.
That's exactly why I'm here. But dammit, I
have cause!"

"Would you like to start at the beginning?"

He whirled away from her desk. "Beginning? What beginning? I don't even know
what the hell that is anymore. Was the beginning Thursday night, when I shot Jimmy
Gagnon? Or was the beginning nine
months ago when I randomly met Jimmy
and Catherine at a cocktail party? Maybe it
was Tuesday, when Jimmy filed for divorce,
or maybe it was twenty-odd years ago
when Catherine was abducted by a pedophile. How the hell should I know?"

"Bobby, I would like to help you—"

"But I sound like a fucking psycho?"

"I wouldn't use those words—"

"Gagnon would. Copley would. Christ, it's only a matter of time." He ran his hand through his hair, then looked wildly around her office, like an animal sizing its cage. At the last minute, just when she was beginning to fear the worst, that he would do something rash and hurt himself, or do something dangerous and hurt her, he suddenly took a deep breath and exhaled it long and slow.

Wordlessly, Elizabeth got up and fetched a glass of water. When she returned, he gratefully accepted it and downed it thirstily. She took the empty glass, refilled it, and he drank it again.

"Life has gotten complicated," he said softly. The edge had gone out of his voice. He sounded almost flat now, monotone.

"Tell me."

"Jimmy's father is suing me for murder. But he'll drop those charges if I lie about what I saw on Thursday night and implicate his daughter-in-law. The ADA doesn't think he needs me to implicate Catherine—he's sure she had something to do with the shooting, now he's just trying to decide if I'm in on it, too. At least I had support from my fellow officers, but I sort of screwed the pooch by seeing Catherine, so now they don't trust me either. Oh—and I did have a loving girlfriend, but I dumped her tonight. Told myself I was doing what needed to be done. But honest to God, the whole time, I kept thinking of the dead man's widow."

"You have a crush on Jimmy Gagnon's widow?"

"A crush is feeling tender toward some-one. I don't feel tender toward her."

"How about guilt, then?"

He immediately shook his head. "No. She's not exactly a woman who's grieving her dead husband."

"Lust?" Elizabeth's voice was quiet.

"Okay."

"Do you think she needs you, Bobby?"

He took more time to consider this an-swer. "Maybe. I think she wants me to think that she needs me. But I can't decide how much of that is an act, and how much is the real thing."

"Explain."

"She's a player. She lies, she manipu-lates, she cheats. According to her father-in-law, she married Jimmy for his money. According to the ADA, Copley, she's abusing her kid for attention. According to her, she's the victim. And according to me . . . sometimes I think they're all right. She's self-centered, dangerous, and unpredictable. But she's also . . . she's also sad."

"Bobby, do you think it's smart for you to be in contact with her right now?"

"No."

"But you've seen her. Why?"

"Because she calls."

Elizabeth gave him a look, and he finally had the grace to flush. He pulled the wingback chair closer to her desk. Then, at long last, he sat down. And without having been aware that she'd been holding it, Elizabeth released one very strained, pent-up breath.

"It's not what you think," he said.

"What do I think, Bobby?"

"That this was a run-of-the-mill shooting." He added dryly, "As if there really is such a thing. Look . . . I didn't contact her. I didn't go looking to her for answers. She came to me. And then . . ." He scowled. "Something is going on. The doctor that's been seeing her kid was murdered last night. Tonight, I get called to her house only to find the nanny hanging in the master bedroom. Jimmy wasn't the end, Doc. Jimmy was just the beginning."

"I'm not sure I understand."

"That makes two of us. Everyone around this woman is dying. And now my life is getting sucked into the void. Catherine Gagnon either has the worst luck in the world, or she needs help more than any woman I know."

"So you're helping her? Why, Bobby?"

He frowned, not seeming to understand the question. "Because she needs help. Because it's what people do."

"Bobby, every time you have contact with this woman, it jeopardizes your career. And every time you have contact with this woman, you make it more difficult to put distance between yourself and the shooting. In effect, you jeopardize your own mental health."

"Maybe."

"But whenever she calls, you come. Why do you answer her calls, Bobby?"

He was still frowning. "I'm a cop."

"You're a cop. Which means you know plenty of other people—professionals—you could direct her to, or personally ask to help her. You *don't* have to be the one offering assistance. Isn't that correct?"

He obviously didn't care for that assessment. "I suppose."

"Do you truly believe Catherine Gagnon is in trouble, Bobby?"

"Yes."

"So certain? You said that she was a liar."

"Look, she needs help, I'm trying to help. I don't see how that's so wrong." He stood up again, leg starting to bounce on the floor.

"When was the last time you slept, Bobby?"

"Last night. Three hours."

"When was the last time you ate?"

"I had some coffee earlier."

"Food, Bobby."

His reply was more sullen. "Breakfast, early this morning."

"You went for a run, didn't you?"

He didn't answer this time.

She forced herself to be quiet, calm.

"Fifteen miles," he blurted out at last. Then, he started to pace.

"You're imploding, Bobby. I know you're imploding, you know you're imploding. I have to ask again: Do you think it's such a good idea to be seeing Catherine Gagnon?"

"It's not her," he said abruptly.

"It's not her?"

"No. I think it's my damn mother."

We don't talk about it," he said at last. "Every family has its topics that are off-limits, you know. In my family, we don't talk about her."

"Who's we?"

"My father. My older brother, George." Now Bobby stood in front of one of the framed diplomas on her wall, staring blankly at the glass. "My father used to drink."

"You mentioned that."

"He was a violent drunk."

"He beat your mom and you and your brother?"

"Pretty much."

"Did anyone in your family try to seek help?"

"Not that I know of."

"So your father was an abusive drunk. And your mother left him."

"I didn't see it," he said quietly. "I just heard my brother George yell at my father one night. But I guess . . . My father had gotten really loaded. Then he'd gotten really mad. And he'd grabbed a leather belt and he'd just whaled on my mother. Just . . . whipped her like a dog. I guess George tried to interfere, and my father went after him, too. Knocked him cold. When he came to, my father had finally passed out and my mother was packing a bag.

"She told George she couldn't do it any-more. She said maybe if she left, Pop wouldn't get so mad. She had family in Florida. Together, they picked my father's pockets, then she was gone.

"Later, I heard my father and George ar-guing about it. My father got so mad, he threw George against the wall. George crawled to his feet and he stood in front of my father and he said, 'What the fuck are you gonna do now, Dad?' He said, 'I've al-ready lost my mother.' He said . . ." Bobby's voice grew quieter. "He said, 'What's left?' "

"What did your father do, Bobby?"

"He went after my brother with a knife. He stabbed George in the ribs."

"And you saw this, didn't you, Bobby?"

"I was in the doorway."

"And what did you do?"

He said, "I did nothing."

Elizabeth nodded. Bobby had been six or seven years old. Of course he'd done nothing.

"George went to the hospital," Bobby said. "My father swore that if George would lie, say he was mugged, then he swore he would never drink again. So George lied, my father went to rehab, and none of us ever mentioned my mother again."

"Did that work?"

"Eventually. There were some relapses, some hard times. But my father, he really worked to make it work. I don't know. Maybe my mother's leaving scared him. Or maybe attacking George scared him. But he started to get his act together. He did his best."

"Have you ever heard from your mother, Bobby?"

"No."

"Are you angry at her?"

"Yeah."

"Your father was the one who beat you."

Bobby finally turned, looked her in the eye. "We were just kids. And he was a violent drunk who thought nothing of using belts and knives. How could she have just left us with him? What the hell kind of mom leaves her kids alone with a man like that?"

"Bobby, can you tell me now why you keep seeing Catherine Gagnon?"

He closed his eyes. She saw the shudder that racked his frame. "Because she was holding her son. Because even when Jimmy pointed a gun at her, she didn't give up Nathan."

Elizabeth nodded. She had read his statement from Thursday night. She saw now what he had seen then, and she reached the next logical conclusion, the one he wasn't yet ready to face.

"Oh, Bobby," she said softly. "You are in such a world of hurt."

Chapter 29

The police were winding down their work in Catherine's house. The female detective had left. Bobby, too. Now she saw only a random uniformed officer here and there, doing God knows what.

The space was emptying out, trying to become her home again. She thought she'd feel grateful. Instead, as she watched each crime-scene tech disappear out the door, she felt increasingly anxious, vulnerable. Her home wasn't her home anymore. It had been penetrated, violated in a horrible manner. She wanted to run away. Instead, she stood a lonely watch in the front parlor, desperately trying to earn Nathan a few hours at least of slumber.

He thrashed in the pillows now, his lips mumbling words from an unhappy dream. An outsider may have thought the front parlor was too bright, but she knew the truth. The two burning lamps didn't offer enough radiance for her and her light-obsessed son. At the rate things were going, soon there would not be enough bulbs in the world to grant either of them a respite from the shadows.

She didn't know what to do.

So of course, her father-in-law arrived.

James Gagnon strode into the foyer with his thousand-dollar cashmere coat and impeccably polished shoes. Three in the morning, for God's sake, and he looked like he'd just stepped out of his courtroom.

The young uniformed officer standing in the foyer took one look at him and snapped to attention.

Stand strong, Catherine told herself. Oh God, she was tired.

"Catherine," her father-in-law boomed. "I came the moment I heard."

Catherine moved into the foyer, purposely putting distance between him and Nathan. James rested his hands on her shoulders, the picture of fatherly concern. He kissed both of her cheeks, his gaze already moving hungrily past her, searching for his grandson.

"Of course you and Nathan must come with me immediately. Maryanne and I wouldn't have it any other way."

"We're fine, thank you."

"Nonsense! Surely you can't want to spend another night at the scene of a hanging."

Catherine was very aware of the uniformed officer standing fifteen feet away and listening openly. "Funny, I don't remember calling you with the news."

"No need. One of my colleagues let me know. Dreadful business, of course. I've always said I didn't think it was a good idea to go with foreign nannies. Poor girls. They simply can't handle the pressure. Nathan must be horribly distraught. Let me talk to him—"

He made a move to step forward; she blocked his advance. "Nathan's sleeping."

"Amid all this chaos?"

"He's very tired."

"All the better reason to let him come with me. We have a positively gargantuan suite at the LeRoux. Nathan can have his own bed; he'll get plenty of rest. Maryanne will be delighted."

"I appreciate the offer. However, given that Nathan's already asleep, I think it would be a shame to disturb him."

"Catherine . . ." James's voice remained kind, patient. He said, as if speaking to a very small child, "Surely you're not considering letting your son spend the night at a homicide scene."

"No. I'm considering letting my son spend the night in the comfort of his own room."

"For heaven's sake, there is fingerprint powder everywhere. How are you going to explain that to a four-year-old boy? Let alone the smell!"

"I know what's right for my son."

"Really?" James gave her a smile. "Just as you knew what was right for Prudence?"

Catherine thinned her lips.

There was nothing she could say to that, and they both knew it.

"I hate to state the obvious," James said

now, "but perhaps you don't know what's going on in your own household as well as you think. Prudence was obviously deeply upset about what happened to Jimmy. God only knows how Nathan is feeling."

"Get out."

"Now, Catherine—"

"Get out!"

James still wore that horribly paternal smile upon his face. He tried to clasp her shoulder; she whirled on the policeman still in attendance.

"I want this man gone."

"Catherine—"

"You heard me." She pointed a finger at the officer, who was blinking his eyes in shock at being dragged into the middle of this scene. "This man is not welcome in my home. Escort him out."

James was still trying. "Catherine, you're upset, you're not thinking clearly—"

"Officer, do I need to call your superior? Escort this man from my home!"

The young man pushed away from the wall, belatedly springing into action. As he stepped forward, James's voice dropped to a low octave, heard only by her ears.

"I'm running out of patience, Catherine."

"Out!"

"Mark my words, things for you are only going to get much, much worse. I have so much power, Catherine. You have no idea . . ."

"I said get out!" She was screaming. The noise woke Nathan. He started to cry.

The officer finally crossed the room. He put his hand on James's elbow, and the judge had no choice but to comply.

He said out loud, for the officer to hear, "I'm dreadfully sorry to have upset you, my dear. Of course, Maryanne and I only want what is best for our grandson. Perhaps in the morning, when you're thinking more clearly . . ."

Catherine pointed stiffly toward the open door. James tilted his head forward in chilly acknowledgment. A moment later, she stood alone, listening to the sobbing hiccups of her hysterical son.

One battle at a time, one battle at a time . . .

She entered the parlor and picked Nathan up from the pile of pillows. He flung his thin arms around her neck, gripping hard.

"Light, light, light," he sobbed. "Light, light, light!"

"Shhh . . . shhh . . ."

The foyer wasn't going to work anymore. Too dark, too strange. Her son needed deep, undisturbed sleep in an overly bright room where all the lamps could chase the demons away. Where he could finally relax. Maybe she could, too.

The police officer had already returned. No doubt James had told the man there was no need to walk him out. He'd go, not make any trouble. He was merely trying to help his family. His daughter-in-law was not quite stable, you know. . . .

Catherine took a deep breath. With her arms wrapped tight around Nathan, she looked the officer in the eye and announced, "I'm taking him to his room. I'm closing the door. He's going to sleep. I'm going to sleep. Whatever else you people need, it can wait until morning."

"Yes, ma'am," the officer said, sounding only slightly sarcastic.

Catherine turned away from him and, before she could lose her courage, mounted the stairs.

The smell was dissipating now, probably

carted off with Prudence's body; she had seen the girl's corpse roll out the door on a metal gurney. Her mind hadn't come to terms with it yet, hadn't reconciled the image of Prudence sitting on the floor reading to Nathan with Prudence zipped up in a black body bag. The concept of Prudence dead remained abstract to her. It seemed more like the girl had gone out on her day off and had simply chosen not to return.

It was easier for Catherine this way. Not so much because she was attached to the girl—in all honesty, she'd cared for Prudence no more and no less than the others. But the nature of the killing—neck snapped, body hanged from the rafters of Catherine's bedroom—led to horror beyond imagining. It implied an intruder in Catherine's home. It implied a man targeting her and the people around her. It implied that if she didn't surrender Nathan as her father-in-law demanded, she would be next.

She thought of James's soft-spoken threat. That he would make life miserable for her. That he had all the power. That she was nothing.

She thought, almost bitterly, he should tell her something she didn't know.

Right before she'd met Jimmy, she'd sunk so, so low. Her mother was dead, her life empty. Day after day she spent standing in a department store, spritzing perfume and trying not to flinch as man after man hit on her. She would study all the male faces, wondering which ones touched their children inappropriately and which ones beat their wives. Then she'd go home to her cockroach-infested apartment and dream of a darkness without end.

There came a morning when she just couldn't do it anymore. Couldn't stand the thought of spending one more day in a state of such perpetual fear.

She'd crawled into the tub. She'd gotten out a razor. She'd started to slice her paper-thin skin. And the phone rang. Without giving it a second thought, she'd crawled out of the tub to answer it. Ironically enough, it had been a telemarketer. Someone asking her if she wanted to buy life insurance, which had made her laugh, and that had made her cry, and while she'd stood there, sobbing hysterically into the ear of a very flustered salesperson, she'd seen the ad flash across her TV screen.

Feeling alone? Feeling like there is no way out? Feeling like no one cares?

A suicide hotline number had scrolled across the screen and, driven by a survival instinct she didn't even know she had, she'd slammed the phone down on the tele-marketer, then dialed the number.

Thirty seconds later, she was listening to the calmest male voice she'd ever heard. Deep, soothing, funny. She had curled up on the floor and listened to him talk for an hour.

That's how she'd met Jimmy, though she hadn't known it then. Hotlines had proto-cols. Handlers were not to give out too much personal information. But they could ask questions, encourage their troubled callers to talk. So he did, and so she did, about her dead-end job, her apartment, her mother.

It wasn't the next day, that would've been too obvious, or even the day after that.

But Jimmy came to the department store where she worked. He found her, he flirted with her, he wooed her. And she found her-self strangely moved by this charming young man with his incredibly calm voice.

He'd asked her out. Much to her own surprise, she'd said yes.

It wasn't until months later that he admitted to her what he'd done. That he'd been
so moved by her call, he'd felt compelled to
find her in person. Please don't tell anyone,
he begged prettily. Oh, she could get him in
so much trouble. . . .

At the time, she'd found it romantic. This
man had moved heaven and earth to find
her. Surely it was a sign. Surely it meant he
loved her. Her life was finally looking up.

It was only later, after they were married,
maybe that one Monday evening when
she'd commented on his drinking and he'd
shocked her by slapping her across the
face, that she'd started to wonder. What
kind of man used a suicide hotline to pick
up girls? What did that say about what he
was looking for in a prospective mate?

Like his father, Jimmy had liked power.
He'd liked to remind her that she'd be nothing without him. He'd liked to tell her that
he'd scooped her out of the gutter, and he
could damn well throw her back.

Sometimes, when Jimmy spoke, she actually pictured Richard Umbrio, standing
way above her, haloed by daylight as one

arm held up the wooden cover that would soon be sealing her in. "Better make my next welcome even more exciting," he'd tell her gleefully. "Because otherwise, you never know when I might decide not to visit. I've given you this much, Cat. You never know when I might take it all away."

Jimmy had never wanted to save Catherine. He'd simply wanted to extend her programming.

Well, she now thought matter-of-factly, she had shown him.

In Nathan's room, she snapped on the overhead light. Two sixty-watt bulbs blazed from the ceiling. It wasn't enough, however. For her, for Nathan, it would never be enough.

"Cowboy," Nathan murmured sleepily against her shoulder. Obediently, she went to that night-light first. Snap.

Nothing.

She frowned, tried it again. No light magically illuminated the cowboy's cheery face. Bulb must be burnt out. She went to the night-light beneath it, the traditional clam. Click.

Still nothing.

Maybe a blown fuse? The police with all

their spotlights and recorders, maybe they'd overloaded the system. She crossed to the dresser, Nathan's weight growing heavy in her arms. Two table lamps. One had a cactus as its stem, the other a bucking bronco. She tried both, fingers shaking slightly, breathing accelerated.

Nothing. Nothing.

Okay, lots of options. Plenty of options. What was the point of having a neurosis if you didn't do it properly? Nathan's room offered six night-lights, three table lights, and two standing lamps. The overhead light worked, which meant there had to be electricity to at least part of the room. She just had to find those outlets, get those lights humming.

She moved quicker now. Nathan was lifting his head from her shoulder, as if sensing her agitation.

"Mommy, lights!"

"I know, sweetheart. I know."

The damn bear lamp didn't work. Two hundred bucks, she'd found it in Denver and mailed it home as a gift. The antique brass desk light, five hundred dollars from a tiny little shop on Charles Street, also out of commission. She moved to the standing

lamps, halogen bulbs, the kind that illuminated the entire ceiling.

Nothing.

More night-lights now. Small little specks
of radiance, topped with stained-glass im-
ages, or a red plastic Elmo, or a beaming
Winnie-the-Pooh. They had to work. At
least one or two or three. Dear God, something in the monstrous room had to break
up the dark.

She was breathing too hard, panting
really. Nathan pushed rigidly away from her
body, arching his spine in growing distress.

"Light, light, light!"

"I know, I know, I know."

Fuck the room. It was too big, too vast.
What did two people need with a space this
huge? She cradled her son close and bolted
for his adjoining bath. Quick flick of the finger and she snapped on the overhead light,
waiting for the white-tiled space to come
brilliantly into view.

Nothing.

She clicked again. Then again. Hysteria
was coming now. She could feel it bubbling
up in her throat.

Nathan kicked in her arms. "Mommy,

Mommy, Mommy, where are the lights? I want light!"

"I know. Shhh, baby, shhh."

It came to her. His closet. The small walk-in space boasted two more sixty-watt bulbs. They could curl up on the floor, taking refuge in a puddle of illumination. It would get them through the night.

"Nathan, love, we're going to have an adventure."

She rubbed his back, trying to calm him, as she whirled out of the bathroom and bolted for the closet. She rolled back the mirror-paneled door, reached in her hand, and found the switch. Click.

Light. Bright, brilliant, wondrous light. It flooded the scene, reaching glowing tendrils to each dark corner, shoving back the shadows. Lovely, lovely light.

Catherine took one look inside the closet, then she stuffed her hand in her mouth to muffle the scream.

They were there, in the middle of the floor, right where she would see them: every single bulb, from every single light. They'd been taken out, then arranged into one simple, three-letter word.

BOO

Catherine forced her son's face back down into her neck. She stumbled away from the closet. She careened down the hall, clambered down the stairs. In the foyer, she grabbed her coat, her purse, her car keys. Didn't look at the uniformed officer. Didn't bother to talk.

She burst out of the front door of the townhouse. "Light, light, light," Nathan was sobbing.

But there was no light. She understood it better than anyone. Now it was just her and Nathan, alone in the dark.

Chapter 30

You told me you and your father had made a pact about drinking," Elizabeth said. "I believe you mentioned an incident with him driving under the influence and that scaring him into sobriety."

"I lied."

"Do you lie often?"

Bobby shrugged. "For certain things, you need a ready explanation. Saying my father attacked my brother with a knife isn't an explanation I feel like giving. Besides, the DUI incident happened. It was one of my

father's relapses—sobriety wasn't exactly a
one-step plan for him. More like one step
forward, two steps back. And around that
time, I was having my own issues. So yeah,
we made the pact."

"I see. So you lied to me, but in your own
mind, it was a lie containing the truth."

"Something like that."

"Uh-huh. And as a child, every time you
had a bruise, I imagine you had an 'explanation' for that. And every time your father
couldn't attend a school function or embarrassed you in front of your friends, another
'explanation,' which may or may not have
contained a kernel of truth?"

"Yeah, okay. I see your point."

"You say your father is better, but it
seems to me that thirty years later you're
engaged in the same old patterns, including
telling lies."

He didn't answer right away. She thought
he was working on a good line of defense,
but then he surprised her by announcing
quietly, "My father would agree with you."

"He would?"

"He joined AA eight years ago, and for
him, it's been like discovering religion. He's
big on atonement. Wants to acknowledge

what he did. Wants to talk about the old
days, ask for forgiveness. My brother,
George, won't take his calls. As for me . . . I
just want to forget. My father was who he
was, and now he is who he is. I don't see
the point of dwelling on it."

"Bobby, aren't there times when you are
very, very angry? Angrier than you probably
should be?"

"I guess."

"Aren't there times when you look at the
future, and you feel an overwhelming sense
of hopelessness?"

"Maybe."

"And aren't there times when you feel as
if everything is out of your control?"

He looked at her, clearly captivated.
"Okay."

"That's why you need to talk to your
father, Bobby. That's why your father needs
to talk to you. Your family has changed, but
it hasn't healed. Part of forgiving your father
is also giving yourself permission to hate
him for what he did. Until you do that, you're
not going to move forward, and you're not
honestly going to love him for who he is
now."

Bobby smiled, a wan expression in his

tired face. "I hate my mom, isn't that enough?"

"Your mom's the easy target, Bobby. Once she left, you had to love your father; he was the only caretaker you had. But you also feared and loathed him for how he treated you. Hating your mother resolved the conflict. If what happened to you was her fault, then it was okay to love your dad. It's called displaced rage. Thirty years later, you have a great deal of it."

"Is that why I point guns at people I've never met?" he asked dryly.

"I don't know, Bobby. Only you can answer that question."

Bobby steepled his fingers, splaying his fingertips against one another. He said abruptly, "Susan said I was angry."

"Susan?"

"My girlfriend. My ex-girlfriend. When we were talking tonight . . . she said I deliberately shortchanged my life. That I held on to my anger. That I needed it."

"What do you think?"

"I'm driven." His voice picking up, he said almost hotly, "Is that such a bad thing? The world needs police officers. The world needs guys like me, perched on rooftops with high-powered rifles. Without me, Catherine Gagnon and her son might be dead. Doesn't that count for anything?"

Elizabeth didn't say anything.

"The rest of the world expects us to be all-knowing. But I'm just a guy, okay? I'm doing the best I can. I got called out to a scene. No, I didn't remember the Gagnons, and even if I did, what the hell do I know about them and their marriage? All I could do was react to what I saw, and what I saw was a man pointing a gun at his wife and child. I'm not a murderer, dammit. I had to kill him!"

Elizabeth still didn't say anything.

"What if I'd delayed? What if I'd watched it and done nothing? He could've shot his wife. He could've shot his son. And that would've been my fault, too, you know. If you shoot, you're screwed; if you don't shoot, you're also screwed. How am I supposed to win? How the hell am I supposed to know what to do?

"He was pointing his gun. He had his wife in point-blank range. And then he got that look on his face. I've seen that look. Oh my God, I've seen that look too many times, and I'm so tired of other people getting hurt.

You can't believe the blood. . . . You can't believe . . ."

Bobby's voice broke. His shoulders were moving, giant, dry sobs, and then he was twisting away from her, mortified by his own outburst, seeking the back of the chair with his hand, clinging to it for support.

Elizabeth didn't move. She didn't go to him. She sat there and let emotion heave through him in raw, violent waves. He needed this. After thirty-six years, a little emotional outburst was long overdue.

He wiped at his face now, hastily drying his cheeks with the back of his hands.

"I'm tired," he said roughly, half apology, half excuse.

"I know."

"I need to get some sleep."

"You do."

"I got a big day tomorrow."

She said bluntly, "This is not a good time in your life to be making major decisions."

He laughed. "You think Judge Gagnon cares about that?"

"Can you get away from the situation, Bobby? Take a little break?"

"Not with the DA's office conducting a

formal investigation. Besides, there's too much going on."

"All right, Bobby. Then sit down again. Because there's one more topic we need to cover before you go. We need to talk, *honestly,* about Catherine Gagnon."

Catherine and Nathan were in the lobby at the Ritz. She knew they must look odd. A woman, a small child, no bags, checking into a hotel at this hour. She didn't care. Nathan was literally shaking in her arms, his distress apparent in his pale, wide-eyed face. Pancreatitis, she was already thinking again. Or an infection, or chest pains, or God knows what. His health always deteriorated when he was under stress.

She fumbled with her purse, trying to get it on the counter while still holding Nathan in her arms. A hotel clerk finally appeared, looking surprised to see someone at this hour.

"Ma'am?"

"I'd like a room, please. Nonsmoking. Anything you've got."

The man raised a brow, but didn't comment.

A few clicks of the keyboard and he announced they did have a room available. King-sized bed, nonsmoking. Would she like a crib?

She passed on the crib, but asked for a toothbrush and toothpaste, as well as three extra lamps. The lights didn't have to be anything fancy, they'd take whatever they got.

Catherine produced a credit card. The hotel clerk swiped it through the machine.

"Ummm, could I see some ID?"

Catherine was stroking Nathan's back, trying to soothe his trembling. "Pardon?"

"ID. Driver's license perhaps. For security purposes."

Catherine was perplexed, but obediently dug into her purse. She produced her license, and for the longest time the hotel clerk gazed at the photo on the ID, then back at her.

"Ma'am, are you aware that this credit card has been reported stolen?"

"What?"

"Ma'am, I can't take this card."

Catherine stared at him as if she'd never heard English. She wanted a room. She wanted a beautiful room in a fancy hotel where bad things couldn't happen. Surely if you were surrounded by silk drapes and down pillows, monsters couldn't find you.

"Perhaps your husband . . ." the hotel clerk suggested kindly.

"Yes, yes, that's right," she murmured. "He lost his card not that long ago. I didn't realize the company would cancel both."

She knew this wasn't Jimmy's doing, however. He'd never possessed this level of finesse. This was her father-in-law. This was James. *"Things for you are only going to get much, much worse. . . ."*

"Do you have another card?" the man asked.

"Umm . . . let me look." She opened her wallet, staring blankly at her collection of plastic. She had an Amex and two more platinum cards. She could hand them over, but she thought she already knew the results. James was thorough. And the more cards that were rejected, the more reason the hotel clerk would have to be suspicious.

She checked her cash instead. One hundred and fifty dollars. Not enough for the Ritz.

She gave it one last try, hoping her voice didn't sound as desperate as she felt. "As you can see from the address on my driver's license, I live just around the corner. Unfortunately, there's been a terrible incident this evening and my son can't sleep in our home. We just need a place to crash for a few hours. I don't have another credit card, but tomorrow, I swear to you, I'll bring a check."

"Ma'am, we need a credit card to release a room."

"Please," she murmured.

"I have so much power. . . . You have no idea . . ."

"I'm sorry, ma'am."

"He's only four years old."

"I'm sorry, ma'am. Surely you have some family that could help you?"

She turned away. She didn't want this stranger to see her cry.

Walking across the lobby, she saw an ATM. Fatalistically, she got out her bank card. Inserted it. Entered her PIN.

A message flashed across the screen: "Please contact your nearest bank branch. Thank you."

The machine spat her bank card back out, and that was it. No cash, no plastic. She'd been trying to stay one step ahead, but still her father-in-law had outmaneuvered her. How far could she get on one hundred and fifty dollars in cash?

Catherine took a deep breath. For one instant, she heard the weak little voice in the back of her mind. *Just hand over Nathan.* If she played her cards right, she bet she could get James to write her a check. No, scratch that—she'd get cash. Or better yet, a wire transfer. How much was a son worth? One hundred thousand, two hundred thousand, a million?

She wasn't a good mother. The authorities weren't as wrong as she would've liked. She didn't know how to love the way other people loved. She didn't know how to feel the way other people felt. She had gone into a hole a happy little girl; she'd emerged a hollowed-out shell of a human being. She was not normal; she merely did her best to imitate the normalcy she sensed in others.

So she'd gotten a husband, she'd had a child.

And now here she was, thirty-six years old and still terrified of the dark.

Catherine pulled out her cell phone. She dialed a number. It rang for the longest time, then a male voice came on the line.

"Please," she whispered. "We have no place else to go."

Do you think Catherine Gagnon was abused by her husband?" Elizabeth asked.

"Yeah."

"Do you think she deserved it?"

"What the hell do I know?"

"Come on, Bobby. You have anger toward your mother, you have anger toward Catherine. Part of that anger is the belief these two women could've done something differently. That they should've kept themselves from being victimized."

"I watched her," he said abruptly. "Some nights, my father would walk through the door, obviously already liquored up, and I'd watch her start in on him. *Been drinking again? Jesus, just one night couldn't you be a decent man and think about your family. . . .* Come on, we all knew what was going to happen next."

"He'd hit her?"

"Yeah."

"Did she fight back?"

"Not physically."

"But he'd hit her. And then?"

Bobby shrugged. "I don't know. He'd get mad, then eventually he'd pass out."

"So if he started out by getting *mad* at your mother as you say, he'd take his aggression out on her, then pass out."

"I guess."

"So he wouldn't hit you or your brother?"

"Not if we stayed out of the way."

"Do you think your mother knew this?"

He paused, appeared troubled. "I don't know."

"A woman's love for her husband is a very complicated thing, Bobby. So is her love for her children."

"Yeah, she loves us so goddamn much she just can't wait to call."

"I can't comment on that, Bobby; I've never met your mother. For some women, however . . . some women might feel too ashamed."

"I thought we were talking about Catherine," Bobby said.

"All right. Do you think Catherine provoked her husband?"

"She's capable of it."

"And Thursday night?"

He resumed pacing again. "Maybe. It doesn't make sense. But then again . . ." He looked at Elizabeth. "It's the fact that we had met before, that we had spoken, that bothers me. Sure, I didn't remember her, I'm confident of that. But she asked me questions about the job, questions about how and when a tactical team would be deployed. Why those questions? What was she thinking?"

"You said she's manipulative."

"Exactly. But at the same time . . . could she have pulled it off? I sure as hell wouldn't have gone anywhere near the trigger if Jimmy hadn't been holding a gun. So she'd have to engineer a scenario that would make him get a pistol, and then she'd have to risk herself and her son in a standoff with an armed drunk."

"Dangerous," Elizabeth observed.

"Ballsy." Bobby shook his head. "If it was just her in that room, I could see it. But I don't think she'd risk her son."

"You don't believe Catherine is abusing Nathan?"

"No."

Elizabeth arched a brow. "You sound very certain of that."

"I am."

"Would it bother you to know that I'm not

as certain? In fact, the more I learn about
Catherine Gagnon, the more I'm deeply
concerned about the relationship between
her and her son."

"You and everyone else."

"She's self-centered, you've said that
yourself. And she's a victim of abuse, and
we know these things tend to have patterns."

"I'm a victim of abuse, too," Bobby said
stiffly. He added almost defiantly, "And we
just established that I like to lie, too."

"Bobby, look me in the eye. If Catherine
Gagnon felt herself at risk, if Catherine
Gagnon felt herself or her lifestyle seriously
in jeopardy, do you honestly believe there's
a line she wouldn't cross? A person she
wouldn't sacrifice to save herself?"

He stared at her mutinously.

But Elizabeth wouldn't drop it. For his
sake, she couldn't drop it. "You don't believe it, Bobby. That's another reason you
can't let Thursday night go. Because, deep
in your heart, you believe Catherine is *capable* of engineering the shooting of her husband. You're just not sure how she did it."

"He was an abusive asshole!"

"How do you know?"

"She said—"

"She lies."

"Dr. Rocco saw the bruises!"

"Who is Dr. Rocco?"

He flushed, chagrined. "Her ex-lover."

Elizabeth let that sink in. Then, abruptly, she switched gears. "Why did you see Susan tonight?"

Bobby was clearly startled. "Because I felt like I owed it to her. After two years together . . . I should at least say goodbye in person."

"What did she say?"

He shrugged. "Not much. I mean, we'd already broken up. What was left to say?"

"Did that disappoint you?"

"I don't understand."

"When you went to meet her tonight, did you really want to finalize the end of the relationship, Bobby? Or did you secretly wish for something else? Did you wish that she would fight for you? Did you wish that she would beg you to stay? Did you wish, deep down inside, that she would love you so much she would not let you go?"

"I would never . . ." But he couldn't continue the protest. Caught off guard, stripped of his own defenses, he finally couldn't tell a lie. He whispered, "How did you know?"

"Someone you loved once left you and never looked back. Now, all these years later, you're still waiting for people to leave, Bobby. In fact, the longer a woman stays, the more anxious it makes you. So you engineer little scenarios, little tests. The woman will either fight for you or she'll leave you. Either one eases your anxiety. At least temporarily."

"Jesus," he said quietly.

"When Catherine calls, you tell her to leave you alone, don't you?"

"Yeah."

"But she doesn't go away. She fights to see you. She tells you she needs you. She reminds you of her poor, sick son, and when you do show up, she makes sure you see her and Nathan together. For some men, I imagine she plays the sex card. But your female fantasy isn't a woman in black lace. Your fantasy is a woman who would never—ever—abandon her child."

Bobby closed his eyes. She could see the dawning realization in his face, because slowly, but surely, he appeared horrified.

Elizabeth leaned forward. "One more

time, Bobby: Do you think Catherine Gagnon may have caused her husband's death?"

He murmured, "Yes."

Elizabeth nodded slowly. "Then you have to let her go, Bobby. You have to stop seeing her. Because if Catherine Gagnon is a predator, then surely you realize now that you make the perfect prey."

It was three a.m. when Bobby finally made it home. No lights were on in his unit. Just his answering machine blinked a frantic red dot in the night.

He slumped into one of the hard wooden chairs in his kitchen. He felt wrung out, drained, not an ounce of emotion or intelligence left. For the longest time, he simply sat there and watched the message light blink.

Slowly, he reached out and hit Play.

His lieutenant. A guy from the EAU. A hang-up. His father. Two more hang-ups. Silence.

Bobby leaned forward onto the kitchen table and used his hands to pillow his head.

Three hang-ups on the message tape. Catherine, he thought.

He squeezed his temples. Get her out of his head, get her out of his head. Don't let her mess with him like this. Sitting in Dr. Lane's office, it had all made perfect sense. Yet here he was, an hour later, alone in the dark, and already thinking of Catherine.

Was she all right? How was Nathan holding up, and where would they go? Not to her in-laws, that much was clear.

Maybe she had another lover. Why not? She'd certainly wasted no time coming on to him. Woman like that, not the type to go at it alone. Probably had a sugar daddy in every port. Maybe she was already lining up another doctor. Or, more likely, a lawyer. Yeah, she needed a big gun to take on Judge Gagnon.

He bet she could find someone pretty quick. Right clothes, right time, right twitch of the hip.

He wished he could hate her. But he didn't. Catherine was doing what she needed to do to survive. And he understood that too well.

If someone else had taken the call on Thursday night, a sniper whose father had never smacked his mother, a sniper who'd never grown up watching that look of hopelessness bloom on another person's face, would Jimmy Gagnon still be alive?

Would Catherine Gagnon now be dead?

None of them would ever know.

Bobby buried his head deeper into his arms. His breath exhaled as a broken, exhausted sigh.

He did his best not to dream.

Chapter
31

Mr. Bosu was trying hard to be a better employee.

Currently, he was watching the faintly lit home of a fifty-thousand-dollar man. No doubt about it, this job was going to be tricky.

For starters, the house sat in the middle of a densely populated neighborhood. Secondly, a sticker on the front window advertised the ADT security system. Third, a light was on in the house, which surprised Mr. Bosu. Given the late hour, he'd assumed the occupant to be asleep.

No way around it, for this job, Mr. Bosu was going to need some help.

He eyed Trickster, who was curled up fast asleep in the front seat of the stolen car. As if sensing his look, the puppy opened one eye and yawned mightily.

"I need an accomplice," Mr. Bosu said.

Another puppy yawn.

"Do you think you could play dead? Just hang around looking half asleep. Yeah, like that."

Trickster had already dropped his head back into his paws and had closed his eyes. Mr. Bosu stroked the puppy's ears meditatively, his sausage fingers delicate on the puppy's small head.

Briefly, the thought came to him: Faking wasn't foolproof. If he really was striving to be a dedicated employee, he shouldn't take unnecessary chances. One small twist and he could snap Trickster's neck. It would be swift, painless, the dog would never feel a thing. And with fifty thousand dollars, he could get a lot of new puppies.

His hand stilled on the back of Trickster's head. He felt his fingers dig into the scruff of the dog's fur. Soft. Silky. Fragile. Everyone had to die sometime.

He pulled his hand away. He slid the knife from the strap at his ankle. He looked at Trickster one last time, then shoved up his linen shirtsleeve above his elbow and slit his forearm.

Blood gushed forth, a dark, red welt. Mr. Bosu wiped the blood onto his fingers, then smeared it onto Trickster's white haunch.

"It's okay," Mr. Bosu told him. "I'll give you a bath as soon as we get home. Now hang on. Things are about to get interesting."

He put the car into reverse. He eased down the block, lights off. Then his hand returned to Trickster's head, steadying the dog, steadying himself.

"One, two, *three!*" Mr. Bosu flipped on the car's headlights. His foot slammed down on the accelerator and the car shot up onto the curb in front of the target home. Mr. Bosu drove straight onto the lawn, screeched the brakes, and let out a giant "Holy crap!" just for good measure.

He grabbed Trickster and bolted out of the car, leaving it parked in the middle of the yard, its headlights pointing into thin air.

"Oh no," he groaned loudly. "Oh no, oh no, oh no."

Mr. Bosu scrambled across the lawn and knocked furiously on the fifty-thousand-dollar man's front door. Mr. Bosu was breathing hard, sweat rising on his brow. He'd pulled his sleeve back down, but drops of blood were leaking through the fine linen fabric. Excellent.

He banged again, hard, insistent, and the porch light abruptly snapped on.

"Help, help, help," Mr. Bosu said. He glanced down at Trickster, pleased with the matted, bloody look of the dog's white fur.

The door finally cracked open, stopped by a metal chain. The guy was careful, Mr. Bosu would give him that.

"Sir, sir, so sorry to disturb you," Mr. Bosu exclaimed in a rush. "I was just driving by when a dog darted in front of my path. I tried to avoid him, I swear I did, but I nailed him pretty good. Please, I think he's hurt."

Mr. Bosu held up the bloody bundle.

The fifty-thousand-dollar man's reaction was instantaneous and admirable. It would also be his downfall.

"Quick!" the man said. "Bring him in."

The chain was dropped, the front door

opened. The man wasn't wearing a robe as Mr. Bosu would've expected, but apparently was dressed for work.

"I thought I heard a commotion," the man said, already leading the way into the house.

With a slight kick of his foot, Mr. Bosu had the door shut securely behind him.

"Are you a vet, do you know a vet?" Mr. Bosu babbled. His eyes swept the home, getting the lay of the land. He followed the man to the back of the house, where a light blazed. They entered a narrow kitchen, circa 1950s. It boasted a small breakfast nook where an old table was totally covered in stack after stack of paper.

"I was up late working," the man commented absently. "Must've dozed off."

"What do you do?"

"ADA. Here, let me look at the dog, see how bad it is."

Mr. Bosu finally relinquished his hold on Trickster. It made it easier for him to reach down and grab his knife. When he straightened, the man had Trickster propped up on the counter and was inspecting him thoroughly for damage.

"I see blood," Rick Copley reported. "Funny thing is, I can't find a source."

"Really? Maybe I can help with that."

Mr. Bosu was big, Mr. Bosu was heavily armed. Copley was fast, however, and seemed to know plenty of fancy footwork.

First time Mr. Bosu lunged forward, Copley dodged left. The ADA let go of Trickster. The puppy bounded onto the floor, scampering across the linoleum and disappearing into the family room.

Neither man paid any attention to him. Copley was already up on the balls of his feet, not wasting any time with denial. Mr. Bosu was pleased. After the day he'd had, he was in the mood for a really good fight.

The ADA was a thinking man. A thinking man would want a phone, so he could notify his colleagues of his distress. Sure enough, Copley dove for the cordless receiver on the edge of the table. Mr. Bosu flashed forward and had the satisfaction of drawing first blood.

Copley danced back, now holding his sliced forearm. The ADA was starting to sweat.

"What do you want?" he demanded.

"Peace on earth."

"You need money? I have three hundred dollars in my wallet."

"Please, you're worth a hundred times that dead."

"What?" The ADA was taken aback by the news. He lost focus. Mr. Bosu lunged again. Copley whirled at the last minute, but was a hair too late; Mr. Bosu nicked his ribs.

The ADA ran for the family room. And Mr. Bosu gave chase.

It was a small house. Not many places to run, not many places to hide. Copley found a lamp, a bookend, a sofa cushion. He danced, he whirled, he dodged.

Mr. Bosu had fifty pounds on him and a much longer reach. For him, the end was never in doubt. Copley hit and tossed and ran. And Mr. Bosu kept coming, herding the man away from the front door, forcing him deeper into his own home, where he slowly but surely became trapped by the very walls that were supposed to protect him. A man's home was his castle. For Rick Copley, it became his execution chamber.

Mr. Bosu finally got the smaller man cornered in his own bathroom, trapped against the tub. After that, it went quick.

In the aftermath, when the bloodlust finally stopped thundering in Mr. Bosu's head, when his breathing eased, when his heart decelerated, he finally became aware of many things at once: His shin hurt. His shoulder where he nailed a doorjamb, the side of his head where Copley finally got lucky with a lamp.

His left forearm also throbbed. Pain from his own self-inflicted wound. It occurred to him now that the cut was still bleeding, possibly leaving splatters on the floor as he'd moved. He tried to look for telltale spots, but given the mess . . .

The house was destroyed. Books and paper and gutted pillows and, well, blood, lots and lots of blood, just plain everywhere. If he had bled onto the floor, it was now so mixed up with other fluids maybe the lab guys would never be able to sort it out. Honestly, he didn't know. Forensics wasn't his strong suit. He only knew what he'd seen on TV.

He retreated to the kitchen, carefully washing his hands and arms. His five-hundred-dollar leather dress shoes were now slick with blood. He took them off, made an attempt at rinsing them, then grimaced at the results. Note for the future: blood ruins dress shoes.

He went in search of the laundry room.

On top of the washer, he found a bottle of bleach. He carried it back into the kitchen, where he poured half the bottle down the sink. He'd seen an episode once where blood had gotten trapped in the drainpipes, then been traced by the savvy crime tech.

Mr. Bosu was a registered sex offender. That meant his prints, his blood, and his DNA were all on file.

He applied the rest of the bleach to a dish towel, then went to work on the blood trail winding through the house. He couldn't get all the blood up, so he worked on smearing it instead, obliterating tread patterns and, in some cases, paw prints. In hindsight, he should've grabbed more surgical scrubs from the hospital. Those had been handy.

Mr. Bosu finished up in the bathroom. Helluva mess there. He threw the towel in the bathtub, on top of Copley's body.

Four-thirty in the morning. Mr. Bosu was officially tired. And, come to think of it, hungry.

He went in search of Trickster, finding the puppy huddled beneath the bed.

"It's okay," he told the quaking dog. "All done now. All done."

He held out his hand. The puppy obediently crawled forward, then nuzzled Mr. Bosu's fingertips. Mr. Bosu picked up his dog and patted him comfortingly on the head. Trickster had peed on the rug. Oh well. Couldn't be helped. Besides, he'd never seen a show where the crime-scene tech had traced dog piss.

"You're a good boy," Mr. Bosu told his bloody dog. "Tomorrow for dinner, I promise you steak!"

Mr. Bosu was just plotting his exit when the phone rang. He stopped, wondering who'd call at this hour, then listening mesmerized as the machine picked up.

"Copley, it's D.D. We've just wrapped up the Gagnon residence—surprised I didn't see you there. Some things have come up." Deep breath. "I'd like to talk about Trooper Dodge. I have some concerns about his involvement with Catherine Gagnon. You may . . . you may have been right about things. Give me a call when you have a chance. I'll be filling out paperwork for the next few hours."

Phone clicked off. Mr. Bosu walked into the kitchen to stare at the blinking answering machine. Then his gaze fell to a pile of paperwork. He glanced at the summary report, the list of names, and for the first time, he got it. What he'd just done and why.

Then, on the heels of that thought . . .

"Trickster," he murmured, "I think I know how to make Benefactor X very, very happy."

The brilliant Mr. Bosu went to work.

Chapter
32

Bobby woke up Monday morning with light hammering against his eyelids. His neck ached. His shoulder throbbed. At some point in the early morning hours, he'd made it from the kitchen table to the dilapidated couch. Now he was sprawled facedown in musty cushions, his right arm dangling over the edge, and half a dozen springs jammed into various parts of his body.

He sat up slowly, biting back a groan. Jesus, he was too old for this shit.

He rose to his feet, stretching his arms above his head and wincing as nerve endings prickled to life. Daylight poured through the front windows, high and bright. He staggered into the kitchen and searched for a clock.

Ten a.m. Shit! He'd been out seven hours. His first decent sleep in days. And an absolutely stupid thing to do, given the five p.m. deadline. He needed food. He needed a shower, he needed a shave. He had to move, he had to . . . do something.

He headed for the bathroom, then belatedly remembered the messages on his answering machine. He should check in with his LT. Probably call his lawyer. Maybe call his father.

And say what?

Bobby stepped into the shower. He stuck his head beneath the stinging spray. He needed clarity. He needed alertness. He needed strength.

Halfway through, it came to him.

Bobby sprang out of the shower, and headed for the phone.

"Hey, Harris," he said a minute later, dripping water all over the carpet. "Let's meet."

*   *   *

Robinson was humming. Not being musically inclined, it wasn't a pretty sound. Robinson hummed incessantly, however, when suffering from a bad case of nerves.

Robinson had a police scanner. All night long, it had been picking up chatter regarding a scene at the Gagnon residence. It didn't sound good.

Now Robinson wasn't taking any chances. There came a time when a body had to put safety first. This was definitely one of those times.

Robinson packed up quickly. Attached to the toilet tank was a waterproof box filled with various credit cards and fake IDs. The box went into the bag. Then came clothes. Taser. Handgun. Little spiral-bound notebook.

That was it.

Place was a rental. Robinson didn't own furniture and had never bothered to supply so much as a doily. The less you owned, the less you had to lose. And the less that could be held against you.

Five minutes later, Robinson stood by the back door, holding the match.

One last hesitation. A tiny moment of

regret. This was to have been the job. The big job. Increased risk, no doubt about it, but oh, the payoff. The beautiful lure of cold hard cash. After this job, Robinson would've finally hit easy street. We're talking a white sandy beach, fruity frozen drinks, and clear blue water that would've gone on without end.

Robinson sighed. And tossed the match.

No apologies, no looking back. You took a job, you did your best. But you always put your own interests first. And Robinson's interests said it was now time to get the hell out of town.

Robinson stepped outside, looking up the street, then down the street. Coast was clear.

Robinson walked to the car parked halfway down the block. Bag went into the trunk, then Robinson slid into the driver's side. First thing Robinson noticed was a tiny white and brown puppy curled up in the passenger's seat. Then a giant form filled the rearview mirror.

"Morning, Colleen," Mr. Bosu said. "Going somewhere?"

*   *   *

Catherine didn't sleep. She sat in a chair in her childhood bedroom, watching Nathan finally succumb to exhaustion in the corner of her old twin bed. Her father had taken her in without protest. He'd wordlessly provided the extra lamps. Then he'd stood in the doorway while Nathan had tossed and turned, crying out with terror at things only he could see. Catherine had quietly sung a song she barely remembered but that came back to her now as she returned to her old home. Her mother used to sing it to her. Back in the good old days before a man came looking for a lost dog.

She sang to Nathan, and when she'd looked up again, her father was gone.

Later, after Nathan had fallen into a brief slumber, she'd found her father downstairs. He was sitting in his old recliner, looking at nothing in particular.

She told him about Prudence. He didn't comment. She told him about Tony Rocco. She told him the police thought she'd arranged for Jimmy's death and that her father-in-law would stop at nothing to get Nathan.

When she was done, her father finally spoke. He said, "I don't understand."

"It's James, Dad. James Gagnon. He thinks I hurt Jimmy and now he's determined to take custody of Nathan."

"But you said a police officer shot Jimmy."

"A police sniper did kill Jimmy. James thinks I staged it somehow. Like I wanted Jimmy to go after me with a gun, like I forced him to threaten Nathan and me in front of the cops. James is crazy with grief. Who knows how he thinks."

Her father was frowning. "And this upset the nanny so much she hanged herself?"

"She didn't hang herself, she was murdered. Her neck was snapped. I told you that."

"That makes no sense."

"What makes no sense? That a woman can be murdered? Or that a woman can be murdered in my house?"

"There's no call for getting snotty, Catherine."

"Someone is trying to kill me!"

"Let's not rush to conclusions—"

"You're not listening! James wants possession of Nathan. He's obviously hired someone to kill anyone and everyone who might be willing to help me. If I don't surrender Nathan soon, I may be next."

Her father said stubbornly, "Seems to me a man as well bred as the judge hardly has to stoop to murder."

Catherine opened her mouth. She looked at her father's implacable face, then abruptly closed her mouth again. It was no use. Her father lived in his own world. He wanted to believe in the sanctity of a neighborhood, in weekly rituals such as Wednesday night poker and Sunday afternoon barbecues. He'd never been cut out for a reality where little girls could be abducted walking home from school and where the person you feared the most was the man sharing your bed. He hadn't known how to help her when she was a child; he certainly didn't know how to help her now.

She rose quietly to her feet, thinking wistfully of Bobby Dodge. She could give him a call. . . . A shiver moved through her. A slight, unexpected tingling of the spine. She didn't recognize the sensation and it left her feeling vaguely uncomfortable.

She found herself remembering his face. She had been touching him, she'd been working him, she'd been winning. And then . . . He'd looked at her. He'd looked at her and he'd honestly *seen* her. And that had ruined everything.

Catherine returned upstairs to her son.

Nathan was starting to fret again, whipping his head from side to side. She stroked his cheek until he calmed. Then she kneeled next to the bed, feathering back her son's soft brown hair.

"I'll always believe you," she murmured. "When you're older, you can tell me anything, and I'll believe."

The phone calls happened shortly thereafter.

The first call came on her cell phone at nine a.m. It was the receptionist from Dr. Iorfino's office, confirming Nathan's three o'clock appointment. By the way, the doctor wanted to speak with Catherine at length. Maybe she could come by earlier, at one p.m.? No need to bring Nathan. In fact, it would be better if Catherine came alone.

Catherine hung up, her heart already pounding in her chest. Nothing good ever came out of meetings where the doctor wanted to see you alone.

She was still trembling when she heard her father's phone begin to ring downstairs.

Five minutes later he materialized in her doorway. He had a look on his face she'd

never seen before. Shell-shocked, border-
ing on shattered.

"That was Charlie Pidherny," he murmured.

"The lawyer?" Charlie Pidherny had been
the DA who'd handled Catherine's case.
He'd retired nearly a decade ago; she
couldn't recall having heard from him since.

"He's out," her father said.

"Who's out?"

"Umbrio. Richard Umbrio."

"I don't understand."

"They paroled him, on Saturday. Except
according to Charlie, they don't release of-
fenders without proper notification, and
they don't release them on Saturday morn-
ings. It must be a mistake. That's what happened. Some kind of mistake."

Catherine was still staring at her father.
Then, realization hit, hard and visceral.

*Hey, honey. Can you help me for a sec?
I'm looking for a lost dog.*

Catherine bolted from the bedroom. She
made it to the toilet just in time.

Nathan, she thought, Oh God, Nathan.
Catherine threw up until she dry-heaved as
the tears poured down her face.

Chapter
33

Bobby met Harris Reed at Bogey's. Even a high-priced private investigator could appreciate a good diner. Harris went for the double cheeseburger, extra onion, extra mushrooms. Bobby ordered a sausage and cheese omelet.

Harris was in a good mood, taking big bites of his dripping burger and chewing enthusiastically. No doubt he thought Bobby had arranged this meeting to announce his submission; he'd surrender to Judge Gagnon's master plan and do whatever was required.

Bobby let the investigator get halfway through his burger before dropping the bomb.

"So, quite a scene in Back Bay yesterday," he said casually.

Harris's jaw slowed, his teeth taking a momentary pause from grinding beef. "Yeah."

"I hear the nanny hanged herself. What's the word from your contacts?"

Harris swallowed. "My contacts say you were at the scene, so you'd probably know better than them."

"Maybe I do." Bobby waited a moment. "Are you curious?"

"Should I be?"

"I think you should."

Harris shrugged. He was doing his best to retain his casual demeanor, but he'd set down his burger now and was wiping his hands with the oversized paper napkin. "So the nanny hanged herself. These girls are young, doing a tough job a long ways from home. Given everything else, maybe it's not surprising."

"Come on," Bobby goaded softly. "You can do better than that."

"I don't know what you mean."

Bobby leaned forward. "Did Judge Gagnon ask you for a name? Someone capable of doing 'odd jobs'? Or maybe someone who knew someone who could take care of things? Or did you get personally involved? I'd like to think you're too smart for that, but then again . . ."

"I don't know what you mean—"

"Come on! You knew about the Rocco scene before the blood hit the pavement. You were listening. You were waiting. Why? Because you thought something like that might happen. How good is the judge's money, Harris? How far were you willing to go?"

"I think I'm done eating."

Harris moved to stand. Bobby grabbed the man's hand, and slammed it against the table.

"I'm not wired," he said intently. "I'm not looking to nail you. I just want a little exchange of information. Man-to-man. You could use a new friend, Harris. Your old ones are putting you in a tough place."

"Nothing personal, Dodge, but at the rate things are going, associating with you hardly does me any favors."

"Her neck was snapped, Harris. Someone broke Prudence Walker in half as if she were nothing but a toothpick. Can you really sleep at night with that on your conscience? Can you really look me in the eye and tell me you don't feel a thing?"

Harris was starting to sweat. His gaze dropped to Bobby's hand, still pinning his wrist in place.

"The cops are gonna start putting two and two together," Bobby said. "Why did a doctor end up butchered in a parking garage? Why did a nanny go out on her day off and wind up dead? Two murders is too many; that's why it was so important that Prudence's death look like suicide. Is there an end point to this game, Harris? Because you and I both know once you start killing, it's hard to stop."

"I didn't give the judge any information," Harris said abruptly. "As a matter of fact, he's the one who came to me with a name."

"What name?"

"Colleen Robinson. Asked me to check her out. I didn't understand at first, but then I got her background report. According to several sources, she has a reputation for getting things done."

"A female assassin?"

"No, no, no. Colleen specializes in . . . hooking people up. You need this, someone else needs that, she makes it happen. She was a small-time player—spent time in prison for grand theft auto. Built a network while she was in there, and has been moving on up ever since." Harris shrugged. "I ran the report. I gave it to the judge. He seemed satisfied."

"I want her name and address."

"I have a cell phone number. Knock yourself out."

Bobby finally released Harris's hand. "At the first crime scene, there was a message, 'Boo.' What does that mean?"

"I don't know. Frankly, I'm guessing you need to ask that question of Miss Robinson. So I take it you're not accepting the judge's little deal."

"Nope."

"She that good of a fuck?"

"I wouldn't know."

Harris snorted. He moved to get up from the table, rubbing his wrist self-consciously, then catching the gesture and sticking his hand in his pocket. He said stiffly, "Needless to say, if the judge asks, we never had this conversation."

"Fine by me, though personally, I think you should do a better job of screening your clients."

"Let me tell you something: the ones with the money are always the ones with something to hide. We start screening and we'd be bankrupt in a year."

Harris took a step toward the door, but then at the last minute, did a little about-face.

"The Prudence thing . . . What happened to her, yeah, that pissed me off." He gazed at Bobby, his lips pressed into a hard thin line. "You want to hear something funny? The judge claims he and Maryanne are from Georgia. Met there, married there, then came to Boston, looking for a fresh start. Now here's the funny part: I did a bit of digging. I can find record of James— schooling, his graduation, the law firm where he used to work. Maryanne Gagnon, on the other hand, doesn't exist."

"What?"

"No birth certificate, no driver's license, no marriage license. Before 1965 there was no Maryanne Gagnon."

"But that doesn't make any sense."

Harris merely smiled. "Like I said, Dodge,

it's the ones with money who are always fucked up."

Twelve-thirty p.m., Bobby left the diner. He flipped open his cell phone. Million and a half reasons he shouldn't call her. He dialed the number anyway.

"I know who the judge used to hire the killer," he said.

"I know who the killer is," Catherine replied. "Richard Umbrio."

It took him a moment to place the name; then, he was genuinely startled. "Are you sure? How?"

"Paroled on Saturday morning. Except they don't release inmates on Saturday."

"It would take someone with very high-level contacts to do such a thing," Bobby filled in.

"Yes," she said quietly.

"Where are you now?"

"Off to see the new doctor; he asked me to come in at one."

"This is the specialist Dr. Rocco recommended?" Bobby asked sharply.

"Yes."

"I'll meet you there."

*   *   *

He braced himself for the sight of her. He re-
played his conversation with Dr. Lane in his
mind: Catherine was smart, tough, extremely manipulative; he was a man with issues. Catherine was on the defensive, deep
in survival mode, and capable of anything;
he was a man who should know better.

Walking into the discreet, high-end lobby
of the doctor's office, he was still struck
dumb.

She stood alone in the corner, wearing
last night's clothing. The black skirt was
rumpled. The gray cashmere sweater had
seen better days. Her face was pale, her
eyes bruised. She had her arms wrapped
tightly around her waist, too thin, too tired,
and too small to be carrying this much
weight on her shoulders.

She looked up, saw him, and for the
longest time, they simply regarded each
other across the empty room.

He thought of when he'd seen her at the
Gardner Museum, just two days before.
Catherine's slinky black dress. Her pencil-
thin heels. Her strategic positioning in front
of an erotic blue painting. Everything she'd

worn, everything she'd done, everything she'd said, had been perfectly planned and elaborately staged. That had been the Catherine Gagnon a man should fear.

This woman, he thought, wasn't.

He crossed the room. "Nathan?"

"He's at my father's." She cleared her throat. "We had to go there. Last night. My credit cards have been canceled. Same with the ATM. I called the bank this morning. They won't let me access any of the accounts, as apparently they are all in Jimmy's name."

"The judge," Bobby said softly.

"Umbrio has been in my home," she whispered. "I went to put Nathan to bed, and none of the night-lights worked. We were so scared. . . . I went to the closet. And there on the floor, all the little bulbs: *Boo.*"

"Catherine—"

"He killed Tony. He killed Prudence. Soon, he'll kill me, too. It's what he promised to do. It's what he's always wanted. Day after day. You don't understand." Her hand had come up. It was compulsively rubbing her throat.

"Catherine—"

"I've been alone too long in the dark," she whispered. "I can no longer find the light."

He took her in his arms, and she collapsed, her hands grabbing the folds of his shirt, her body trembling uncontrollably. She was small, tiny really, of no significant weight against his chest. And he could feel her exhaustion now, rolling off her in waves, night after sleepless night of doubt, terror, fear.

He wanted to tell her it would be all right. He wanted to tell her he was here now, he would take care of everything. She would never have to be frightened again.

Too many other men had made the same silly promises. He knew better. So did she.

He reached up a hand and stroked her hair.

And for just one moment, she pressed herself hard against his chest.

The door opened. A receptionist appeared. "The doctor will see you now, Mrs. Gagnon."

Catherine straightened, pushing away. Bobby's hand dropped back to his side.

She turned toward the hallway first; he fell in step behind her. Right before they passed through the door, however, she paused one last time.

"I never said I didn't harm Jimmy," she said. And then they walked into the doctor's office.

Chapter
34

Mr. Bosu was exhausted. He remembered now: the glorious, nerve-zinging euphoria that always accompanied a good plan. The way, for example, he'd felt high as a kite the minute he'd lured twelve-year-old Catherine into his specially equipped car. Or the way he'd felt coming up behind that gel-slicked doctor in the empty parking garage. One quick flick of the knife . . . the rush of endorphins. The sheer, giddy *thrill* of warm, red blood, oozing across his hands.

But what went up must come down.

Which brought the second half of the equation: body-slamming crash. The moment the endorphins and adrenaline bled out of your system and left you absolutely, positively done. He could lie down on the hard ground right now and sleep for days.

Unfortunately, he had work to do.

First stop, a small convenience store. Puppy Chow for Trickster. An interesting high-energy drink called Red Bull for him. According to the can, Red Bull would *give him wings.* Given the tasks Mr. Bosu had left to perform, that couldn't hurt.

Exiting the convenience store, he patted the trunk of Robinson's car. "Here's to you," he said, holding up the drink can in a mock toast. "Thanks for negotiating that pay raise, and hey, no hard feelings. Business is business."

Since Robinson was dead, she couldn't very well reply. But Mr. Bosu remained appreciative. Thanks to her, he had a better set of wheels, some unexpected documents, and a lovely infusion of cash.

He slid into the driver's seat, polishing off his drink.

"Hey, Trickster," Mr. Bosu said. "Now, things are about to get interesting. . . ."

* * *

Dr. Iorfino was a bit of a shock after Dr. Rocco. The geneticist was tall, thin, and balding. With his oversized glasses and hooked nose, he reminded Bobby of pictures of Ichabod Crane—and not the Johnny Depp version, but the classic portrait of the gaunt country schoolteacher from *The Legend of Sleepy Hollow.*

The doctor ushered Bobby and Catherine into an impressive office, boasting a massive cherry desk and two huge windows overlooking the city of Boston. Apparently, there was a bit of money in genetics. Dr. Iorfino also appeared to be a neatnik. In contrast to Dr. Rocco's office, no loose papers were in sight here. In fact, the man's desk offered only a flat-screen monitor and a single manila folder.

Dr. Iorfino took the black leather seat behind the desk, then indicated the two empty chairs across from him.

"Catherine Gagnon," Catherine introduced herself, holding out her hand.

"Ah yes." The doctor shook her hand belatedly, then turned to Bobby curiously.

"Bobby Dodge," Bobby provided. "Friend of the family."

"Interesting," the doctor murmured.

Bobby shrugged. He wasn't as convinced that it was interesting to be a friend of the family, but the doctor was already flipping open the manila file.

"I'm pleased you could meet with me," Dr. Iorfino said. "I felt it was important that I share my findings with you before I saw Nathan."

"Findings?" Catherine looked confused. "How can there be any findings? You haven't seen Nathan yet."

Dr. Iorfino blinked owlishly. "Dr. Rocco didn't tell you?"

"Tell me what?"

"When he approached me about Nathan's case, he sent me the boy's whole medical history, as well as blood and urine samples. So I could begin testing our theory."

"Theory? What theory?" Now Catherine sounded nearly panicked.

Bobby leaned forward. "Mrs. Gagnon's been through a lot the past few days, Doctor. Maybe you should start at the beginning."

"Well, yes. I suppose. That horrible business with Dr. Rocco, of course. Oh well, and yes, Mrs. Gagnon's own husband. Quite right." Dr. Iorfino shuffled the papers inside the file, cleared his throat. "Dr. Rocco contacted me several months ago regarding Nathan. Did he mention that, Mrs. Gagnon?"

"No."

"Hmm. I see. Well, given Nathan's symptoms—first the fever, vomiting, growth failure, retarded development of motor skills, now the obvious hepatic glyconeogenesis, galactose intolerance, and medically resistant hypophosphatemia—he began to suspect a particular syndrome. So he asked me to perform an in-depth analysis of Nathan's chromosomes."

"Glyconeogenesis," Catherine repeated awkwardly. "Galactose intolerance? I don't know what those are."

"Dr. Rocco has been treating Nathan as if he's had food allergies, correct? Asking you to substitute soy products for dairy, following a diabetes-mellitus-like diet of small meals with low sugar/carbohydrate intake?"

"He thought Nathan might be allergic to

milk. And his blood sugar levels are too high, so he's been on a low-carb, high-protein diet."

"Correct, that's what the records indicate. However, as you can attest, even after a year of this regimen Nathan has failed to make significant progress. Tests show increased levels of glucose in the body, which in turn is leading to the accumulation of glycogen in the liver, pancreas, and kidneys—"

"He's not improving," Catherine agreed.

"Mrs. Gagnon, Nathan doesn't have food allergies. He does, however, have a mutation in the GLUT2 gene. In short, he suffers from a rare but well-defined clinical entity known as Fanconi-Bickel syndrome."

Catherine expelled a short breath. "You know what's wrong with him?" You know what's wrong with my son?"

"Yes. Basically, due to a genetic defect, your son does not correctly metabolize glucose and galactose—"

"Galactose?"

"The sugars in milk. Pulling Nathan off dairy products certainly helped, but the fact remains too much sugar is being built up in the filters of his kidneys, leading to a host of problems, including, if we don't start proper treatment, kidney disease."

"There's a proper treatment? You can fix it, this Fanconi-Bickel?" Catherine's eyes were growing bright, nearly feverish.

"There is no cure for Fanconi-Bickel, Mrs. Gagnon," Dr. Iorfino said patiently. "But now that we have a diagnosis, we can start an appropriate regimen that will mitigate many of the complications Nathan is experiencing. And with proper treatment and diet, your son can lead a fairly normal life."

"Oh my God," Catherine said. "Oh my God." She put a hand over her mouth. She eyed the doctor wildly, then stared at Bobby, and then in a rush of emotions burst into tears. "He's going to be okay. Finally, finally, after all these years . . ."

"Thank you," she sobbed to Dr. Iorfino. "After all the tests, all the wondering and doubt . . . you have no idea how good it is to finally know what's going on."

Dr. Iorfino actually blushed. "Well, you don't have to thank me, per se. It's Dr. Rocco who put the pieces together. Fine bit of analysis, I must say. Fanconi-Bickel is very rare, and hardly ever seen around these parts."

"A genetic disorder," Catherine murmured, belatedly wiping at her eyes. "Random bad luck. Who would've thought?"

But Dr. Iorfino was frowning now. "Fanconi-Bickel isn't exactly random, Mrs. Gagnon. It's an inherited defect, mostly seen in males." Matter-of-factly, he stated: "It's what you find in families with a history of incest."

For a moment, Catherine didn't speak. She appeared too stunned to react to the news. In contrast, for Bobby, the pieces were finally coming together.

"But Jimmy and I weren't related," Catherine protested. "My family is from Massachusetts; his family is from Georgia. We knew our parents, there is no way—"

"It's not you," Bobby said.

She turned to him, still confused. "But who?"

"The Gagnons. The judge and his wife. It's why they left Georgia. It's why she doesn't exist—because, of course, they had to give her a new name. And probably why there is no marriage license—they never would've passed the blood test."

He turned to Dr. Iorfino. "Can genetic defects skip a generation?"

"Absolutely."

"And can two interrelated parties still have a healthy child? Or would the children have to have the defect?"

"No, there could be healthy offspring. Think of the royal families of Europe in centuries past. Many of them married first cousins, and still had relatively healthy offspring. But inbreeding weakens the gene pool. Sooner or later . . ."

"So James and Maryanne get together. Say they're first cousins." Bobby frowned, glanced at Catherine. "Harris said Maryanne's family died before the wedding. What about James's family? Have you ever heard talk of other relatives? Grandparents, aunts, uncles, anyone?"

"No, Jimmy said his parents came from small families. There was no one left alive."

"So James and Maryanne meet. God knows her family couldn't have been wild about the idea, but then they died. Problem solved. James and Maryanne move up here, start fresh with a new name for Maryanne, new past for both of them. Have a son."

"Jimmy's older brother," Catherine whispered. "The one who died young."

"Maybe Nathan isn't the first Gagnon male to show signs of Fanconi-Bickel. Harris said James Junior was a sickly baby."

"Fanconi-Bickel varies in its severity," Dr. Iorfino provided. "In a very severe case—"

"But Jimmy didn't have signs of any . . . disorders," Catherine protested.

"Again, inbreeding doesn't guarantee genetic disaster, Mrs. Gagnon, it just makes it more probable."

"A ticking time bomb," Bobby said quietly.

"Oh my God, poor Nathan . . ." And then, Bobby could tell she had reached the same conclusion he had, because her eyes suddenly widened with a fresh look of horror. She turned toward him. "But if Nathan has this syndrome . . . if others find out that Nathan has this syndrome, then . . ."

He nodded grimly. "Yeah. This is why the judge is so determined to get custody. Whoever has Nathan has the key to unlocking the Gagnons' deepest, darkest secret. And that's something worth killing for."

Chapter

35

As he walked out of Dr. Iorfino's office to the lobby, Bobby's cell rang. He grimaced, but Catherine merely pushed him toward one corner of the lobby.

"I need to call my father, anyway," she said. "I'll tell him we're ready for him to bring Nathan."

Bobby nodded, giving Catherine some space as he flipped open his phone. It was D.D. She sounded strange.

"Where are you? I've been trying to reach you all morning."

"I had things to do. What's up?"

"Are you with her?" D.D. asked.

Bobby didn't have to ask who D.D. meant. It was implicit in her tone.

"D.D., what do you want?"

"Where are you?"

"You answer my question, then I'll answer yours."

There was silence. Bobby frowned, trying hard to interpret that silence. He didn't get very far.

"Got ballistics back on Jimmy Gagnon's gun," D.D. said. "The nine-millimeter was fully loaded. Not a single cartridge missing from the clip. No GSR on the barrel, handle, anything. It was never fired."

"But I thought . . ." Bobby paused, struggling to get his bearings. He could feel the danger, but he still couldn't see it coming.

"But what about the reports of shots fired?" D.D. filled in.

"Yeah."

"Fascinating development. Last night, when we were at the Gagnon residence cutting down the nanny's body, one of the crime-scene techs bumped the bureau. Guess what had been taped to the underside of the top, inside a drawer? Guess what then fell down?"

He got it now. He closed his eyes. He turned away from Catherine completely, because he couldn't look at her and hear this news. "A second gun."

"Also nine-millimeter. Recently fired. Two bullets missing from the clip."

"Prints?"

"Her prints, Bobby. Her gun, registered in her name, loaded with the bullets purchased by her, according to the gun dealer. Jimmy Gagnon never fired a shot Thursday night. She did."

Bobby tried to make the words sink in. Then tried to tell himself it didn't matter. Jimmy abused her, she had cause. Or maybe, Jimmy abused her, and she was just looking out for her son. He didn't know. He tried on the thought as many ways as he knew how. He was still left cold and empty.

"Did you tell her how to do it, Bobby?" D.D. asked now. "Is that how it played out? You met her at the cocktail party. Decided to trade in your current blonde for a more exotic model. Catherine's a big step up, I gotta give you credit for that. Did she promise you money, or was it all for love?"

"It didn't happen like that."

"No? So it was just sex? She used your body, and you shot your mouth off in the postcoital glow?"

"D.D., I only met Catherine for one brief moment at that party. I never saw her again until Thursday night."

"Catherine framed you, Bobby. She fired the gun, she set the stage. If we did have audio, I bet it would be filled with all sorts of venomous things she yelled at Jimmy to keep his anger high, to keep him waving that pistol. After that, it was only a matter of time."

He didn't protest anymore. He had squeezed his eyes shut. It still didn't stop him from seeing what he didn't want to see. Jimmy Gagnon's head in his sights. His finger, squeezing the trigger.

"I just don't get it, Bobby," D.D. said quietly. "So maybe she could get you to take out Jimmy. Maybe you even thought it had to be done. But what in the world could she have said to make you turn on Copley? Jesus, Bobby, he was one of our own!"

"What?"

"We both know he was on to you. It was only a matter of time. But still, you could've

pled down, Bobby. You're a law enforcement officer with a distinguished career. So
you made a mistake. You still had options.
You didn't have to do . . . God, Bobby, a
knife? I wouldn't have even thought you had
it in you."

"D.D., I have no idea what you're talking
about."

"One more time, Bobby, where are you?"

But he already knew better than to answer. Something had happened to Copley.
A knife. Umbrio probably. Except they
thought he did it, and if his fellow law enforcement officers thought he did it . . .

You didn't go after an expert-ranked police sniper with a pair of handcuffs.

Jesus Christ, he was in a world of hurt.

"D.D.," he said urgently. "Listen to me.
Saturday morning a man was released from
prison. His name is Richard Umbrio. Look
him up: you'll find he was the same man
who kidnapped and raped Catherine
Gagnon twenty-five years ago. You'll also
discover that he wasn't due for parole.
Judge Gagnon arranged it. He set it up.
He's using Umbrio to kill the people close to
her."

"Copley wasn't close to her."

"I don't know why he killed Copley! Honest to God . . . You said knife. Umbrio used a knife at the Rocco crime scene. Umbrio's the one who killed Tony Rocco, as well as Prudence Walker."

"Copley wasn't dead, Bobby. He used to be a boxer in college. Did it surprise you how much he put up a fight? Did you think it would get that messy? Well, he still had the last laugh. As he lay in the bathtub, bleeding out, he left us one last clue. He wrote your name, Bobby, in his own blood."

Shit, Bobby thought.

"Colleen Robinson," he said quickly, trying to get out as much as he could. "She's a middleman, hired by Judge Gagnon to hire Richard Umbrio. Pull the judge's financial records, track down Robinson. You'll find corroboration of what I'm saying. The judge did it, D.D. He's desperate to cover up evidence of his and Maryanne's incest. Contact Dr. Iorfino, he'll tell you all about it."

"Turn yourself in, Bobby."

"I can't."

"For the last time—"

"If I'm behind bars," he said simply, "there's no one left to protect Catherine."

"Goddammit, Bobby—"

He flipped the phone shut. He turned away. Then he was crossing the room, powered by grief and rage. Catherine was still on the phone, face pale, eyes wide.

He grabbed her shoulders and, before he could stop himself, shook her hard.

"What the hell did you do?"

"Bobby—"

"Did you think I wouldn't care? Did you think I wouldn't mind being used as a tool for murder?"

"It doesn't matter, it doesn't matter."

"The hell it doesn't! You used me. You lied to me. You set me up to kill another human being."

"I didn't have any other choice! Bobby, please listen to me—"

"Shut up!" he roared.

And then she slapped him. Across the face. Hard. His ears rang. His eyes blinked. The shock rocketed through him, and for an instant, he found his own arm pulling back. He could see himself in his mind's eye, swinging forward, smacking her back. She would fall, cut down by the blow. And he'd, what . . . lord it over her? Feel triumphant in his physical superiority? Watch her cower, as his mother used to cower, alone on the kitchen floor?

His arm came down. The roaring subsided in his brain. He came back to himself. Saw that he was still gripping Catherine's shoulder with one hand, and that his fingers were squeezing mercilessly while the tears poured down her face.

He let her go so abruptly, she stumbled.

"He was going to take Nathan away from me," she said. "He was going to leave me with nothing simply because he could. You don't know what it's like, Bobby, to have nothing."

"You had no right—"

"It never would've worked if he hadn't hated me. That's the real trick to manipulation, you know. You can never make someone do something they really don't want to do. You can only make them do what was already in their heart."

"You don't know that."

"I saw his face, Thursday night. I looked into Jimmy's eyes, and, in that one instant, I knew I was dead."

"Liar."

"Bobby, I didn't thank you for killing him,"

she said steadily. "I thanked you because you saved my life."

He couldn't talk anymore. He was too heartsick.

"Bobby." Her hand came up. Tentatively, she stroked his arm. He flinched at her touch. "I need you. You have to help me."

He laughed hollowly. "What, already got in mind someone else to kill?"

"Just now, when I called, my father didn't answer his phone, Bobby."

"So what?"

"Richard Umbrio did."

Chapter 36

Mr. Bosu had no problem finding the neighborhood. This had been his first request when initially contacted by Robinson. He wanted to know everything about Catherine. Her home, her family, her husband, her son. He got a list of every job she'd ever had. He demanded photos and driver's license information and details down to her grocery shopping list and her favorite restaurant. Some of the information had been boring. But most had intrigued him.

The fact that her parents had never

moved—that had genuinely fascinated him. Mostly, because he was willing to bet the last penny he would soon be making that his own parents were sitting in the same old house, on the same old sofa, staring at the same old living room from all those years before. They were two peas in a pod, he and Catherine. He had not expected that in the beginning, when he had randomly plucked her off the street with an abbreviated scream and scattering of schoolbooks. It had come to him slowly, day after day, as he continued to let her live. She was the only person in the world who could truly meet his needs. She was the only person in the world who knew the real him.

The day he'd arrived to find her gone was the worst day of his life.

But that was okay. He was going to correct all that real soon.

Mr. Bosu was whistling when he pulled into the driveway. He was still whistling when he got out of his car.

"Stay put," he told Trickster. "This time around, I'm flying solo."

He mounted the steps, banged on the door.

He heard the voice from the other side, wary and cautious. "Who is it?"

Mr. Bosu smiled. He flipped open the ID he'd found on Colleen and waved it briefly in front of the peephole. Enough to give the impression of possessing an official ID, without giving away the actual photo.

"Detective Bosu," he announced. "I'm afraid, Mr. Miller, I have some bad news about an old case. We should talk right away."

"Is it Richard Umbrio?" Frank Miller asked.

"Yes, sir."

Catherine's father unlocked the door. And Mr. Bosu walked right in.

It turned out that Frank Miller was no dummy. Mr. Bosu wasn't sure what he'd expected. Maybe someone smaller, more shrunken, more beaten by the lousy blow delivered to his family earlier in life. Someone more like his own dad.

Instead, Frank Miller was tall, erect, trim. Active for his age, no doubt prided himself on living alone.

He took one look at Mr. Bosu's hulking

build, older, fleshed-out face, and promptly paused.

"Don't I know you—?" he started. Then recognition struck. The older man's eyes went wide. Much faster than Mr. Bosu ever expected, Frank Miller pulled back his right arm and nailed Mr. Bosu in the eye.

"Shit," Mr. Bosu gasped, staggering back, belatedly trying to cover his face. The old geezer didn't wait. He went for Mr. Bosu's kidneys. Got him with a good three or four jabs that would definitely have him coughing up blood later tonight.

Miller launched his right hook again. Enough was enough. Mr. Bosu held up his meaty hand. He caught Miller's blow in his palm. Then he wrapped his fingers around the older man's hand and bore down hard.

The blood drained out of Miller's face. And for the first time, fear appeared in his eyes.

"Tell me where the boy is."

Miller didn't speak.

"I know you have him. She had nowhere else to go. Of course she brought him to you." Mr. Bosu forced back Miller's hand now, bending the wrist until the man's knuckles nearly touched his own forearm. Miller went bug-eyed with the pain.

"You can tell me sooner, or you can tell me later. But I'm going to get the information. The only question is, how much will you suffer?"

"Fuck . . . you," Miller said. Then he surprised them both by kicking Mr. Bosu in the kneecap. Mr. Bosu went down. Startled, he released his grip on the man's hand, and Miller promptly bolted for the kitchen.

Mr. Bosu sighed. There was only one thing left to do. He got out the knife.

Mr. Bosu entered the kitchen just as Miller reached into the utility closet. Mr. Bosu had a split-second warning, then he was staring down the barrel of a shotgun. He didn't wait. He sprung forward, left arm outstretched to grab the gun barrel and force it up, even as Miller fumbled with the trigger. The gun didn't go off and Mr. Bosu didn't expect that it would. Few people left a loaded shotgun lying around the house, particularly given the presence of a child.

Miller's retrieval of the gun told Mr. Bosu something else. The utility closet was only inches from the back door. Surely Miller had had enough time to run out, flee to safety. Instead, he'd chosen to take a stand.

The boy was somewhere in the house. That's why Miller hadn't run. He couldn't bring himself to leave his grandson.

Noble, Mr. Bosu thought idly, as he drove the serrated blade into the soft spot beneath the man's ribs. Miller made a curious wet sound. Not a scream. Not a groan. Almost a sigh. A man who knew what was coming next.

"Sorry to hear about the wife," Mr. Bosu said. "Otherwise, I would've done her next."

He pulled the knife over and up. It didn't take much after all. The old man collapsed, a shriveled husk on the kitchen floor. Mr. Bosu remembered to step back more quickly this time. He didn't want to ruin a second pair of shoes.

He washed up in the kitchen sink, grimacing at the sight of blood still staining his shirtsleeve and now fresh splatters on his pants. No doubt about it, he was a mess. He rinsed the knife before returning it to the sheath wrapped around his calf. Then he went to search the house.

He found the boy upstairs, in a room dec-

orated with faded pink and purple flowers.
As he pushed open the door, the boy said in
a hopeful sort of voice, "Mommy?"

Mr. Bosu smiled. First time he'd seen the
boy was in the hospital the night he went after the doctor. That night, the boy had called
him Daddy. It was nice to know Mr. Bosu
could be so loved.

He pushed all the way into the room and
the boy sat up on the bed. For a moment,
they regarded each other soberly. The boy
was small, pale, and sickly. Mr. Bosu was
huge, heavily muscled, and stained with
blood.

"So," Mr. Bosu said at last, "would you
like to see a puppy?"

The boy held out his hand.

As they were leaving the house, the
phone rang. Mr. Bosu didn't have to be a
psychic to know who it would be. He picked
up the phone.

"Dad," Catherine said.

"Catherine," Mr. Bosu said.

"Oh my God."

"Hey, Cat. Your son says hi."

Chapter
37

We're going to need a gun," Bobby said.

Catherine didn't reply. She was in a state of shock, her gaze unfocused as she followed him blankly down the stairs. He'd made a conscious decision to bypass the elevators. The hospital had security officers. Would they already be on the lookout for him, maybe lying in wait in the lobby?

He remembered what he'd told Dr. Lane only hours before: Just because you're paranoid doesn't mean they're not out to get you.

"They took Jimmy's guns," Catherine said abruptly, panting a little as Bobby rushed them downstairs. "He kept them in the safe. An officer took them all away."

Except for the one she'd hidden in the bureau, Bobby thought, but now was not the time.

"I have three handguns and a rifle at home, but I'm pretty sure they already have officers positioned at my front door." He frowned, hammered down another long flight, and found a solution. "My father. Pop. Maybe they haven't reached him yet."

There was no cell signal in the stairwell. Bobby had to wait until they reached the lobby. He spotted two security officers positioned by the main doors. They didn't seem to be watching for anyone in particular, but Bobby didn't feel like taking a chance. He grabbed Catherine's hand and pulled her down the side hallway. They emerged out a smaller entrance into a busy side street. Perfect.

"Grab a cab," he ordered.

"I have a car—"

"And the police know your plates."

She went to work on the cab. He flipped open his cell phone and pressed the speed-dial button for his father. Pop picked up on the second ring.

"Pop, I need a favor."

"Bobby? Two guys came here earlier. Looking, asking, making a lot of nasty suggestions."

"I'm sorry, Pop. I can't talk, and I can't explain. I need a gun, though, and I don't have time to drive out to your place."

"What do you want?" his father asked.

"Handgun. Nothing fancy, but plenty of ammo. Are they watching you?"

"You mean the two guys in suits across the street?"

"Shit."

"They told me you're in over your head."

"I'm still swimming."

"I saw on the news. . . . They're flashing your photo, Bobby, saying you're wanted for questioning regarding the murder of a local ADA."

"I didn't do it."

"Never thought you did."

"Do you trust me, Pop?"

"Never had a moment's doubt."

"I love you, Dad." And that comment, probably more than any other, scared them both.

"Where?" his father asked quietly.

Bobby thought of Castle Island.

Thirty minutes later, his father met them there.

Mr. Bosu was also on the phone. Winding his car through the maze of back streets in downtown Boston, he was semi-lost, but not quite worried about that yet. The boy sat quietly in the front seat. He was a good boy, passive, obedient. He already reminded Mr. Bosu of his mother.

Trickster was on the boy's lap. Nathan was stroking Trickster's ears. Trickster was nuzzling Nathan's hand. Mr. Bosu smiled at them both indulgently as his call was finally picked up.

"Good afternoon!" he boomed into Robinson's cell phone.

"Who is this?" the man asked.

"Mr. Bosu, of course. And this is Judge Gagnon, I presume."

The good judge, aka Benefactor X, was obviously flustered. "Who . . . what—"

"Do you prefer me to use the name Richard Umbrio? I would think on an open phone line, you wouldn't, but I don't care. Either way, you owe me money."

"What are you talking about?" the judge demanded.

Mr. Bosu glanced over at the boy. Nathan was regarding him curiously. Mr. Bosu grinned. He meant it to be friendly. Maybe he'd spent too much time among felons after all, for the boy promptly turned away, focusing intently on the dog. Trickster licked his chin.

"You owe me two hundred and fifty thousand dollars," Mr. Bosu said matter-of-factly.

"What?"

"For your grandson." Mr. Bosu had finally found the side street he wanted. He turned onto a row of grand old homes in the middle of Beacon Hill.

"That is not funny—"

"Nathan, my good boy, tell your grandfather hi."

Mr. Bosu held out the phone. Nathan called out, "Hi."

"You monster!" the judge boomed. "Where the hell are you?"

And Mr. Bosu said merrily, "Right at your front door."

*   *   *

Bobby's father wanted to join them. Bobby lost ten precious minutes explaining to his father that it was too dangerous, that Pop was a custom pistolsmith and not a trained marksman, etc., etc., etc.

In the end, Bobby got rude, grabbing the gun, loading up Catherine, and climbing impatiently into the front seat of his father's car. Bobby drove away, with the image of his father standing lost and alone captured vividly in the rearview mirror.

Bobby's hands were tight on the wheel.

"Where do we start?" Catherine asked.

"Your father's house."

"Do you think . . ."

"I'm sure Nathan is all right," he tried.

She gave him a feeble smile, but the tears were building in the corners of her eyes.

"My father and I have always fought," she said quietly. Then she turned her head away from him to cry.

Frank Miller's house looked quiet from the front. Door was closed. Blinds were drawn. Nothing and no one stirred. Bobby cruised

by once, saw no police in the neighborhood, and rounded the block.

He parked on the corner, instructing
Catherine to take over the wheel. "You see
him," he said, no need to define *him,* "just
hit the gas and get the hell out of here."

"And if he has Nathan?"

"Then hit the gas and aim for clipping
Umbrio's kneecaps. He'll go down, you can
grab your son."

She liked that idea. It infused color into
her cheeks and put a spark in her eyes. She
took over the driver's seat with a look of
pure determination, while Bobby rechecked
the gun his father had given him, then
headed down the street.

The front door was unlocked. That gave
him the first hint. Walking into the living
room, the heavy, rusty scent told him the
rest. He checked the whole house just to be
sure. But it was empty. Umbrio had come
and gone, leaving nothing but a corpse in his
wake.

Bobby couldn't bear to look too closely
at Catherine's father. The gray hair, the bent,
sprawled form, already reminded him too
much of Pop. He saw the shotgun on the
floor and picked it up, recovering a box of

shells from the yawning closet. The man had put up a fight. He'd held his ground for his grandson.

He'd tell that to Catherine, see if that gave her any measure of comfort for all the days to come.

Bobby exited with the shotgun, jogging back to the car, unbearably aware of time. Umbrio had now had Nathan for nearly an hour. Sixty whole minutes. There was no telling what a man like that could do with so much time.

But he didn't think Umbrio had killed the boy—at least not yet. If that's all Umbrio wanted, Bobby would've found Nathan's body with his grandfather's. No, when it came to Nathan, Umbrio had something much grander in mind.

And that thought left Bobby chilled to the bone.

He dialed 911 as he approached the car.

"Body found, male deceased, definite homicide," he reported, and rattled off the address. He flipped his phone shut just as the 911 operator asked him to hold, opening the car door and sliding into the passenger seat.

Catherine looked at the shotgun, then at his face.

Her face was pale; she struggled briefly, then got it together. "Nathan?"

"No sign of him. I'm sure he's still all right."

"Okay," she said, but her voice was clearly strained, barely holding it together. She took a shaky breath. "Where?"

"I think it's time we go straight to the source."

"Walpole?"

"No. Your father-in-law."

Mr. Bosu was extremely pleased with himself. He parallel-parked the car in front of the Gagnons' prestigious townhouse, address courtesy of Colleen's records, and prepared to hear the judge hastily renegotiate terms.

Instead, over the phone, the judge had started to chuckle.

"Let me get this straight," the judge was saying, "you want two hundred and fifty thousand dollars or you'll do what?"

Mr. Bosu glanced at the boy next to him. Interestingly enough, he couldn't bring himself to say the words with the boy sitting right there.

"I think we both know what," Mr. Bosu said primly. He peered out the window, scowling at the townhouse. Place looked dark. Deserted. For the first time, Mr. Bosu began to wonder about things.

"I don't care."

"What?"

"You heard me. The boy was a problem I was going to have to take care of sooner or later. In a curious sort of way, you've now done me a favor and I thank you."

"I don't want your gratitude," Mr. Bosu said with a scowl. "I want your money!"

"I'm calling the police," Judge Gagnon announced silkily. "I'm telling them you, a convicted sex offender, kidnapped my grandson. Then I'm bringing every FBI agent, state police trooper, and pissant local sheriff down on your ass. I'd start running, *Mr. Bosu.* You don't have much time left."

The phone clicked off. Mr. Bosu sat there, stunned. What the hell? The man would even sell out his own grandson?

Mr. Bosu got out of the car. He forgot about Nathan sitting in the front seat, he forgot about the bloodstains on his shirt. He reached the front door of the townhouse and banged hard. Nothing. He rang the doorbell. Then, in a fit of temper, he banged and kicked on the solid oak door with all his might.

The house was empty. Abandoned. Deserted. As in, rats were always the first to abandon ship.

Mr. Bosu was breathing hard. His forearm throbbed from the earlier cut. He was also starting to feel nauseous, a junkie coming down hard from a fix.

He took a few seconds and thought long and hard about things.

So the judge was taking care of the judge. To hell with paying Mr. Bosu, and to hell with saving his grandson.

That was it. Mr. Bosu was officially pissed off. He didn't even care about the money anymore. Now, it was the principle of the thing.

Nobody crossed Mr. Bosu. *Nobody.*

Mr. Bosu returned to Robinson's car. The boy sat in the passenger seat, tickling Trickster's ears.

"Say, does your grandfather have a second home?" Mr. Bosu asked casually.

The boy shrugged, played with the dog.

"Anyplace he likes to go in particular? You know, his own special place?"

Another shrug.

Mr. Bosu grew impatient. "Nathan," he said sternly, "I'm supposed to be returning you to your grandfather. Don't you want to see your grandfather?"

"Okay."

"Then where the hell is he?"

The boy looked up at him. He said promptly, "At the Hotel LeRoux."

Mr. Bosu smiled. He put the car in gear. "Nathan," he said seriously, "when the time comes, I'll make sure you never feel a thing."

Chapter

38

I don't understand," Catherine was saying. "You think my father-in-law hired Umbrio?"

"He used a middleman, Colleen Robinson, to make the arrangements. Umbrio got paroled in return for agreeing to perform a few favors."

"So why am I still alive?"

"Because killing you isn't as important as discrediting you."

"Come again?" She blinked her eyes.

"The judge hates you. Hates you for

Jimmy, hates you for marrying into the family. But mostly, I think, he hates you for Nathan. As long as you continue to press about Nathan's health, you're on the verge of uncovering his and Maryanne's secret."

"If I died, I wouldn't be a threat anymore."

"No. But Dr. Rocco would be. And maybe your father would be. There would always be those who'd observe Nathan's poor health and wonder. Unless, of course, they already had a reasonable explanation for why Nathan was sick."

"I was poisoning him," she filled in. "I was a bad mom."

"Exactly."

"But once he won custody of Nathan . . ." She frowned. "Wouldn't the fact that Nathan didn't magically get better become a problem?"

"I don't think the judge planned on letting that become a problem," Bobby said quietly.

"You think he would really harm his own grandson?"

"I think," Bobby answered grimly, "the man may have already killed his own son."

*   *   *

It turned out a luxury hotel made a pretty good fortress. Sure, Mr. Bosu valet-parked his car. Sure, he strolled right in with Nathan, and even Trickster, because who was going to say no to a cute boy and his puppy?

That didn't solve his problem. He didn't know what room the judge was in, and the pretty young desk attendant was polite, but firm about the hotel's policy of not giving out such information. She could call Judge Gagnon for him, she could notify Judge Gagnon that he had guests, but without the judge's permission, she could not let the guests go to the judge.

Mr. Bosu had already determined another problem. According to the boy, the judge had described a luxury suite in the hotel. That meant the upper floors, which required a special keycard inserted into the elevator. Assuming the judge was staying in a penthouse suite, Mr. Bosu would not be getting up there any time soon.

It was perplexing. A dilemma, and Mr. Bosu was getting very tired now. He suddenly missed his nice clean bed at the Hampton Inn. Hell, he even missed his prison cot.

He and the boy walked outside, where Mr. Bosu had another Red Bull and contemplated things. The bloodstain on his shirt bothered him; the suspicious stare of the twerpy doorman bothered him. The whole fucking world bothered him.

Then Mr. Bosu had an idea.

He downed his Red Bull. He walked Nathan back into the hotel lobby and took him straight to the receptionist's desk.

"This is Nathan Gagnon, grandson of Judge Gagnon," he announced in his most cordial voice. "If you call up, you'll find the judge is expecting him. Unfortunately, I've received a bad cut—" Mr. Bosu flashed his bloody arm, "and I need to seek medical attention. Do you have someone who could escort Nathan upstairs to his grandparents? They'd greatly appreciate the boy not being left alone."

The receptionist smiled at him. "Of course. One minute, sir."

She dialed the room. Mr. Bosu held his breath. Surely the good judge couldn't refuse his grandson, particularly if the boy was coming up alone.

"Mrs. Gagnon?" the receptionist said brightly. Mr. Bosu exhaled. The wife. Perfect.

"Yes, we have a fine young man here, Nathan Gagnon. . . . Yes, your grandson. What a handsome boy, too. We'll send him right up with a bellhop. Do you know Nathan has a puppy? Not a problem, ma'am, but we do have a form we'll need filled out. Excellent. I'll send that up, as well. Thank you."

The receptionist put down the phone, the perky smile still on her face. "Mrs. Gagnon is very excited to see her grandson. If you'd like to depart, sir, we can take it from here."

Mr. Bosu graciously thanked the woman. He even shook Nathan's hand. "So happy I could get you to your grandparents, young man. The puppy's name is Trickster. Your mom wanted you to have him as a surprise."

"Mommy?" the boy asked hopefully.

"Trust me, you'll be with her soon enough."

This pacified the kid, and he nodded his head vigorously while clutching Trickster against his chest. Then the bellhop came over, admiring the fine boy, admiring the fine dog, and all was well.

They headed for the elevator. "The penthouse suite," the bellhop was telling Nathan.

"That sucker's bigger than my house. You're gonna love it up there."

The elevator doors opened. Mr. Bosu turned. The receptionist was attending someone else, the bellhop was busy with Nathan. . . .

Mr. Bosu bolted for the stairs. He sprinted up three levels, bam, bam, bam, taking the stairs two at a time. Then he burst onto the third floor—blissfully empty—where he pounded the elevator button. The elevator came to an immediate halt.

The doors opened. The bellhop appeared surprised to see Mr. Bosu standing right there.

"Weren't you in the lobby—"

Mr. Bosu seized the young man by the shirt and jerked him into the hall. One quick snap and the man crumpled to the floor. Mr. Bosu grabbed the man's jacket, snatched the man's master key—a card hanging from a chain around his neck—and stepped back inside the elevator.

Nathan was staring at him. The boy's eyes were solemn and wide.

"My mommy warned me about men like you," the boy said.

Mr. Bosu grinned his full, awful grin. "Yeah, I bet she did."

Entering the hotel LeRoux, Bobby watched for security guards while Catherine did the talking.

"James and Maryanne Gagnon," she told the receptionist.

"They're expecting you?"

"Tell them it's about their grandson."

"Nathan?" the receptionist asked brightly.

Catherine became hyperaware. So did Bobby. "You've seen Nathan?" Catherine asked sharply.

"Why, yes. Just ten minutes ago. One of our bellhops escorted him upstairs."

"Was he with a man?" Bobby broke in. "Big, maybe looked like he'd been in a fight?"

"Yes, he mentioned he'd been hurt—"

They didn't wait to hear the rest. "That man is a convicted pedophile," Catherine screamed. "He kidnapped my son earlier today. Call the police *and get us upstairs*!"

* * *

The receptionist was flustered. She wanted to call for security. She wanted to dial the room. She needed permission, she needed help. She clearly didn't know what to do.

Bobby was already in front of the elevators, stabbing at the buttons, pacing wildly.

"Fine, call the room!" Catherine pleaded. "Dial the room number now. Get them on the phone, please, go ahead."

The overwhelmed receptionist picked up the phone. She punched in a four-digit number. Catherine blatantly memorized it. Thirty seconds later, however, the receptionist was more confused than ever.

"No one's answering. I don't understand. Why, just a few minutes ago—"

A sudden, sharp scream. The elevator doors opened. A well-dressed man and woman came stumbling out.

"There's a body!" the woman wailed. "There's a body on the third floor."

"It's a bellhop," the man said. "I'd swear someone snapped his neck."

Pandemonium broke out. Now security guards did come running, bellhops, too. The parking valet went sprinting by Bobby.

Bobby grabbed the man's arm, then flashed his badge.

"Police. Give me your pass key. *Now!*"

The bewildered valet turned over his pass key. Bobby jerked his head at Catherine.

They bolted into the elevator, slammed the key into the slot, and headed for the penthouse floor.

"You look for Nathan," Bobby said. "I'll take care of Umbrio."

"What about James and Maryanne?"

Bobby shrugged. "If they're working with Umbrio, then they're probably safe. If they're against Umbrio, then we probably don't have to worry about them anymore."

"Oh God . . ."

"Let's go," Bobby said.

Mr. Bosu knocked once. He went for a childlike rat-a-tat.

The door opened, and, without bothering to wait, Mr. Bosu slammed his fist into the man's face. There was a wet crunching sound. Then the man sprawled onto the vast marble floor.

"Hey, Judge," Mr. Bosu said. "Remember me?"

He was still smiling when Nathan's teeth sank into his hand.

Stepping out of the elevator, Bobby's first glimpse was an open doorway and a fresh corpse. He reached back one hand to steady Catherine, then realized he was wasting valuable energy. With Umbrio on the premises, one body was the least of their concerns.

"Shhh," he ordered in a low voice. "Let's not announce ourselves before we have to. We need whatever advantage we can get."

The place was quiet. Eerily quiet. Bobby didn't like it. He expected screams or scrambling footsteps or a child's excited yells. There was nothing. Absolutely nothing. It made the fine hairs rise up on the back of his neck.

They stepped into the marble foyer and Catherine's heels promptly rang out like shots. They both drew up short, Catherine's dark eyes wide with distress.

"Off."

She removed her heels.

Bobby stepped forward and inspected Harris. The investigator's nose had been shattered, bone fragments driven up into his brain. It had happened so fast, the man had never even unbuttoned his jacket or reached for his gun. One minute he'd answered the door, the next, he was dead.

Bobby shook his head. In his own way, he'd started to like Harris.

Bobby reached inside the investigator's jacket, and removed the man's nine-millimeter from the shoulder holster. He flipped off the safety, then gave the piece to Catherine. Still no other sounds in the suite.

"Something's wrong," she whispered.

"No kidding."

And then . . . Musical chimes. The notes were haunting, distant. A slow lullaby drifting from the back of the suite. A music box. Maybe a child's toy. Bobby didn't know, but the high, tinny notes strained the heavy air.

He looked at Catherine, whose face had gone white.

"What is that?" Her tone was getting strident again. He motioned, *Easy,* with his hand.

"I don't know. Hold it together, Cat. Nathan needs you."

She nodded, taking a deep shuddering breath. After another moment, Bobby motioned to the wall, and Catherine fell in step behind him.

Time gave Umbrio the advantage, Bobby realized now, to separate them, to ambush them. The suite was too big for Bobby to control, and Catherine was too inexperienced to help. Whatever happened next would need to happen fast.

Cautiously, he led them from the foyer into the empty sitting room. Given the force of Umbrio's entry, anyone in this room had probably run for cover.

A hallway loomed through an arched expanse on the left. Another loomed on the right. Apparently, the sitting room acted as the central area for the two wings of the suite. Bobby hesitated. Catherine tapped his hand and pointed to the left.

"The music," she mouthed.

He nodded, understanding. It was difficult to pinpoint the tinny notes, but they appeared to still be coming from the left.

He took her hand. They edged, single file, down the hall.

Then they heard a scream. Shrill, high-pitched, distinctly feminine.

"Maryanne!" Catherine gasped.

They bolted down the hall.

Chapter
39

Bobby processed everything at once. Three open doorways, three bedrooms. He ran by the first, then the second, and came sprinting into the third just in time to see Maryanne staggering back.

"James, James, James," the woman was sobbing. "Oh God, James!"

Bobby looked down, registered a bloody body, and in the next minute, sensed, more than heard, the movement behind him.

"Look out!" Catherine's cry, farther down the hall.

He tried to turn, tried to get the gun up.

Umbrio caught him in the shoulder. Bobby felt a stunning blow. The force whirled him around, knocked him off-balance. He fought desperately to retain his footing. He had an image out of the corner of his eye, something silver and red.

Knife, he managed to think. Knife, coming for him.

Then he heard a gunshot. A split second later, plaster exploded beside his head.

Bobby fell down. Umbrio, however, stopped and turned.

"Why, Catherine," the large man said, "what a pleasant surprise to see you here."

Umbrio grinned. There were flecks of red all over his face. Blood, maybe from James, maybe from Bobby. It gave the murderer a feral look.

Catherine brought up the nine-millimeter again. She was using two hands, trying to take a stand. Her arms shook so badly, however, she couldn't aim. She pulled the trigger wildly and the bullet nailed the wall an inch from Umbrio's shoulder.

Umbrio smiled again. He took a step forward. "Oh, Catherine, Catherine, Catherine."

Blood poured down from Bobby's shoulder, mixing with the sweat on his palm. His right arm didn't want to move, his fingers didn't want to contract. He shifted the gun to his left hand and squeezed the trigger.

The gun exploded, the shot sailing wildly by Umbrio's knee. The surprise attack from the rear drew the big man up short. He took in Catherine, still trembling in front of him, and Bobby, badly wounded behind him. Bobby was already taking aim again. The floor was an awkward position, but he could make it work. He hadn't spent years practicing weak-hand drills for nothing.

Umbrio seemed to realize that Bobby was down but not out at the same time Bobby centered his second shot on the big man's chest. His finger tightened on the trigger, just as Umbrio sprang through the doorway, vaulting down the wide arched hall. Catherine belatedly fired a dozen times behind him, hitting two pictures, an antique sofa table, and about nine inches of plaster. Umbrio disappeared into another room.

"Shit!" she cried.

She arrived in the bedroom, still shaking uncontrollably and now reeking of gunpowder. Her eyes were dark saucers in her pale face, her hair a disheveled mess. But she was still standing, still bearing her pistol, and Bobby thought she looked gorgeous as hell.

Now she saw the blood pouring down Bobby's shoulder. "Oh no!"

"Who is that man?" Maryanne cried. "And where is Nathan?"

Catherine got Bobby into a sitting position. Good news, Umbrio had missed a major vein. Bad news, he'd injured the joint and now Bobby's right arm dangled uselessly at his side.

"I don't understand," Maryanne was babbling. "The receptionist called. Nathan was coming up, and I was so excited. I wanted to get the door, to be the first to greet Nathan, but James said no, let Mr. Harris get it. Then the door opened and I heard an awful noise, like a crunch. James yelled at me to run, so I ran. Then James pushed me into this bedroom, told me to get into the closet and not come out no matter what happened. So I hid. Then came the sound of footsteps.

"I thought it would be Mr. Harris, or

maybe James. Instead, the closet door opened and that hideous man was staring at me. He was smiling. He was holding a knife and smiling. What kind of man does such a thing?"

Bobby and Catherine didn't answer. Catherine had pulled a pillowcase from the bed and was now tying it awkwardly around Bobby's shoulder.

"James suddenly appeared. He hit the man over the head with a bookend. Really hard. I've never seen such a thing. But that horrible man, he didn't even blink. He just turned around and he looked at James . . . Oh my God, James knew!" Maryanne sobbed. "You could see it on his face, he knew what was going to happen next. 'Run, Maryanne,' he said. So I did. And I heard noises. I heard the most awful noises. I tried so hard not to hear those sounds. Except then it became quiet and that was so much worse. I couldn't take it anymore. I had to see James. Oh, my poor, poor, darling James . . ."

She crumpled to the floor beside the body. She clutched her husband's limp hand. And his fingers very slowly curled around hers.

"James!" Maryanne wept. "James! He's breathing. Oh my darling, you're still alive!"

"Shhh," Bobby and Catherine said instantly. "He's going to come back."

"Who's coming back?"

"Richard Umbrio."

"Isn't that the man who kidnapped you, Catherine?" Maryanne was bewildered. "That was years ago. What would he possibly want with us?"

"Maryanne," Catherine said steadily, "where's Nathan?"

The closet was dark, but not totally dark. Nathan couldn't stand totally dark, especially now, when he was already really scared. He'd let the puppy go. He wished he hadn't done that now. He missed its warm little body, its sandpaper tongue licking reassuringly at his hand.

Now he was very much alone.

He'd seen the bad man do bad things. Then he'd heard his grandfather holler, "Run!" so he'd run. The other way. Far from everyone, because he didn't like his grandfather, who kept demanding Nathan go home with him, even when it was clear his mommy didn't want him to.

So Nathan dropped the puppy and ran in the other direction, away from everyone, including the bad man.

Then he'd seen this closet, with the shuttered door. It was small, filled with blankets and pillows and piles of bedding. He wished he were bigger. He wished he were stronger. He wished he were a normal healthy boy, because a normal healthy boy could probably climb all the way to the top of the closet, where he could hide above the bad man's head.

But Nathan couldn't do that. So he simply dug his way to the back of the tiny space. He closed the door. He covered himself with down pillows and did his best not to sneeze.

Now he waited. All alone. In the dark.

The bad man was coming.

Nathan whispered, "Mommy . . ."

Catherine had finished tying the pillowcase around Bobby's bleeding shoulder. It looked and felt ridiculous, but it was the best they could do. Both handguns rested next to

Bobby on the bed, within easy reach if Umbrio should return. Looking at Bobby's mangled shoulder, however, Catherine wondered if the guns would really do much good.

Next, Catherine crossed to James, still prostrate on the floor. Blood pooled beneath him while from his lungs came an ominous whistle, like a balloon losing its air.

Maryanne had his head on her lap, her hand stroking his cheek. She was crying huge soundless tears. As Catherine approached, Maryanne raised her head. Her gaze was beseeching, but there was nothing Catherine could do. The judge was dying. They all knew that.

The judge gazed up at Catherine. For the longest time, the two simply stared at one another.

Catherine waited to feel something. She *wanted* to feel something. Triumphant. Victorious. Satisfied. But all she felt was an emptiness that went on without end.

"I know what you did," Catherine said at last, her voice curiously flat. "A geneticist finally diagnosed Nathan—my son suffers from a rare disorder that only occurs in families with a history of incest."

Maryanne made a small squeaking sound, belatedly covering her mouth with her hand. Catherine looked at the woman. And then she finally felt an emotion—icy cold rage.

"How could you not tell me? The minute Nathan showed signs of illness, how could you not think—"

"I'm so sorry—" Maryanne began.

"Are you cousins?" Catherine interrupted angrily.

"Half siblings," Maryanne confessed, then threw out in a rush, "But we were never raised together, we never even knew each other as brother and sister. After James's mother died, his father sent him off to military school, you see. They had a bit of a falling-out, and James decided to stay up north. But as the years passed, my father finally made an attempt at reconciliation. He invited James back to visit his new family. I was turning eighteen. My parents threw a magnificent party. And then I saw the most handsome man enter the room. . . ."

James's hand spasmed in hers. Maryanne immediately bent to brush his cheek, but there was something in the tender gesture that now left Catherine feeling sickened. They had been *siblings*?

"He murdered your family," Catherine told Maryanne.

"Don't be ridiculous. There was an accident—"

"James made that 'accident' happen, Maryanne. He arranged for your whole family to die, just so he could have you. Like he killed your firstborn so the doctors would never discover your little secret. Like he released a convicted pedophile to murder Nathan and me. Why do you think everyone around you dies, Maryanne? Can you really be so naive?"

Catherine's voice had risen dangerously. Maryanne shook her head against the onslaught, while on the floor, James moaned feebly.

"I . . . loved her," the man rasped out.

"Love?" Catherine spat. "You murdered innocent people. Was it easy the first time? Tamper with your father's brakes, tell yourself accidents happen."

"You don't . . . understand."

"After that you were free to come up to Boston, make a fresh start where no one would ever know your dirty little secret. Except then you had a child. And genetics found you out. Did your first son have Fanconi-Bickel, as well? Maybe a very severe case. Always sickly, always suffering."

"I don't understand," Maryanne whispered brokenly. "Junior died of SIDS."

"Or because someone pressed a pillow over his face."

"James?" Maryanne whimpered.

"I . . . love you," the judge said again, but there was something pleading in his tone now. Something even more damning than guilt. Maryanne started to cry again.

"Oh no . . . oh no, oh no, oh no."

Catherine, however, wasn't done. "You turned Jimmy against me. You filled his head with awful ideas, and forced me to do unspeakable things. How dare you! We could've worked together to help Nathan. Maybe we could've been happy."

"My son," James said clearly, "was always . . . too good . . . for you."

"James!" Maryanne gasped.

"You idiot," Catherine said coldly. "You released Umbrio, and now he will kill us all."

"Police . . . will come," the judge murmured.

But then, from down the hall, they all

heard Umbrio's voice: "Nathan, Nathan, Nathan. Come out wherever you are."

Bobby said quietly to all of them, "Not soon enough."

Mr. Bosu was tired of this game. Coming to the judge's hotel had seemed a good idea. Threaten the judge in person and get a little money, or hey, kill the judge in person and get a little satisfaction, that had been the plan. Mr. Bosu was flexible.

But nothing had turned out that way. Yes, he'd gotten to exercise a little vengeance. But that hadn't felt as good as he'd expected. Maybe even murder got boring after a while. He didn't know. But the wife was still running around and the kid was running around and now Catherine was here and, with her, another man.

Mr. Bosu wanted to feel excited. But mostly, he just felt tired. Screw killing all of them. He'd settle for one last target. The one that would inflict the most damage of all.

He wanted the boy.

Just the boy.

Then he was out of here.

Mr. Bosu had already completed a search of the left side of the palatial suite. He'd found the master bedroom, raided the wife's jewelry box, and found a wad of cash. Now, he turned his attention to the right-hand side of the suite. If he were a four-year-old boy, where would he hide?

Someplace cozy, someplace dark. No. Wait. The boy had all those dozens of night-lights. The kid was scared of the dark.

Mr. Bosu's eyes fell upon the louvered door of the hall closet. Of course. Mr. Bosu began to smile.

Chapter 40

We need a plan," Catherine said. Her gaze fell to Bobby. He nodded, struggling to sit up straighter on the bed.

"What are we going to do?" Maryanne whimpered forlornly from the floor. "James is injured. You're injured. What are we going to do?"

"I can fire a gun just fine," Bobby said levelly. "I drill with my left hand all the time."

Catherine nodded. She picked up both nine-millimeters off the bed and handed him one. "All right. You take a gun, I'll take a gun."

"You can't shoot worth shit," Bobby said seriously.

"Well then, I'll just have to make sure I get close enough. Do we hunt him? Is that how this game is played?"

Bobby immediately shook his head. "I don't want us split up. Two against one is better odds, plus I don't want the risk of one of us accidentally hitting the other with cross fire."

"We're not going to have much element of surprise, two of us blundering down a hall."

"No, we won't. Which is why we're going to make him come to us."

"And how do we do that?"

Bobby looked her in the eye. "Well, Catherine, you know him best."

She nodded slowly. "Yes," she said after a moment, "I guess I do."

Mr. Bosu was on the prowl. He spotted the target. He yanked back the closet door. He thrust deep with his knife. And ripped into a pile of terry cloth towels. What the hell?

"Shit!" Mr. Bosu roared.

He tossed out the pile of towels. Then the

shelf of toilet paper, then a collection of bathrobes. Empty, empty, empty. Where was the boy?

"Shit!" he roared again.

But then he saw it. Farther down the hall, another louvered door. Mr. Bosu stalked forward.

"Richard."

The voice stopped him, the name, too. Mr. Bosu turned, feeling slightly confused. It had been years since anyone had called him Richard. Prison guards didn't use it, neither did his fellow inmates. He was Umbrio or, in his own mind, Mr. Bosu. He had not been called Richard in over twenty years.

Catherine stood alone at the end of the hallway. Taller than the image implanted in his mind, and yet in many ways still the same. Those dark, dark eyes. That tangled mass of black hair. He wished she were wearing a red bow.

Pity that girls should grow up at all.

"Catherine," he said, and gestured with his bloody knife. "Did you miss me?"

He grinned at her. She had her shoulders back and her head up, trying to appear strong. But he could see how hard she was breathing by the rapid rise and fall of her chest.

She was terrified.

That old feeling came back to him, nostalgic and swift. It was twenty-five years ago, and he was scrambling through the woods, heading happily for a small clearing made distinct only by the large piece of plywood that appeared to be lying on the ground. Next to it were a tall stick and a section of chain that, only upon closer inspection, became a ladder.

He raised the plywood, supporting its edge lean-to style on the stick. Then he was leaning over the gaping hole, preparing to drop down the chain.

Her face appeared below in the gloom. Small, pale, dirt-streaked. Desperate.

"Are you happy to see me?" he called down. "Tell me you're happy to see me."

"Please," she said.

He flew down the ladder, grabbing her into his arms. "What shall we do today?"

"Please," she said again, and just the sound of that word made his heart burst in his chest.

"Are you going to beg?" Umbrio asked

now, genuinely excited. "You know what I like to hear."

"No."

"You should. I'm going to kill you and your son."

"No."

"Come now, Catherine. You of all people know how powerful I am."

"You put me in a hole for twenty-eight days, Richard. I put you in prison for twenty-five years."

Mr. Bosu scowled. He didn't like that thought. In fact, he didn't care for this whole conversation. He took a step forward. Catherine held her ground. He took another step, then came to a sudden halt. Wait a minute.

"Show me your hands," he ordered.

She obediently lifted them up.

"Where's the gun?" he asked suspiciously.

"I gave it to Maryanne. I already tried it and you and I both know I can't shoot."

He frowned, still not liking this. "So you're just going to attack me with your bare hands."

"No."

"What then? Why'd you come out? Why'd you leave the room?"

"To buy time for my son. The police are going to come, Richard. They're going to be here any minute. And frankly, I don't care if you hack apart every inch of my body, just as long as you don't touch a hair on Nathan's head."

"Oh." He considered it. "You know what? It's a deal."

He sprang forward and Catherine bolted down the hall.

Catherine ran. Not too fast. That was the hard part. Her heart was pounding, her nerve endings screaming. Adrenaline pumped through her veins and commanded that she run, run, *run.*

But she had a role to play. They all had a role to play, and this was suddenly the biggest stage of her life.

She could hear him thundering down the hall behind her. In all of her nightmares, Umbrio rarely had a face. He was a giant black shadow, an impenetrable force that always mowed her down. She was tiny and insignificant. He loomed like a dark, vengeful God.

She had tried telling herself over the years that it was a child's perspective on things, a young girl versus a grown man, a child versus an adult. But seeing him now, she realized she'd been wrong. Umbrio was huge, a muscled mountain of a man. He had terrified her then, and he terrified her now.

So much of her life he'd taken from her. So many pieces of herself, which had gone into that hole and never emerged again.

Now she ran from him. She ran and she cried, out of fear, out of sadness, out of rage. She hated Richard Umbrio. And she missed the woman she might have become if they'd never met that one horrible day.

He was closing in. She picked up her pace, letting her control slip, letting the panic kick in. He was upon her, he was reaching for her. He was going to grab her by the neck and throw her to the ground and then . . .

She burst into the sitting room. Her gaze flew to the coffee table. Bobby was lying behind it, his nine-millimeter propped up on the edge as a makeshift rifle stand, his left hand on the trigger.

"Now," he ordered.

She dropped like a rock. Behind her, Umbrio came to a screeching halt. He waved his arms wildly, trying to slow his own momentum.

Bobby pulled the trigger. Pop, pop, pop. One-two-three.

And Umbrio fell like an oak, crashing to the ground. His hand twitched. Then he was still.

Catherine pulled herself up shakily. Flat on his back on the floor, Umbrio was staring at her. Blood creased the corners of his mouth. He smiled.

"Now what?" he whispered.

She didn't understand.

Then he grabbed the corner of her skirt.

Catherine screamed. Beside her, she heard Bobby pull the trigger but receive only an empty metal click. The guns, Catherine realized. She had swapped them when handing them out, with Bobby receiving the one she'd already fired a dozen times. Bobby swore violently just as Umbrio heaved forward and grabbed Catherine's knee with his big meaty fist.

Then Catherine simply stopped thinking.

Umbrio was going to get her. His hands

would wrap around her throat. He would squeeze and she would die, just as she was supposed to have died twenty-five years ago. She was in the hole. She was in the ground. She was all alone.

Vaguely she was aware of movement. Bobby was on his feet. Yelling something. She couldn't hear. The room had lost sound. The moment had lost crispness.

Umbrio now had his hand on her hip. He was crawling his way up her body, leering at her with a mouth of bloodstained teeth as his right hand reached for her throat.

She fumbled frantically. And then she found what she'd been looking for, stashed beneath the sofa.

Umbrio's fingers were closing around her neck.

Bobby was rising beside him, arm swinging back.

And Catherine shoved the barrel of the nine-millimeter right into Umbrio's mouth. For one split second, he appeared very, very surprised. Then she pulled the trigger.

Richard Umbrio was quite literally blown away.

He collapsed as a massive weight upon

her smaller body. And Catherine started to weep.

Bobby pulled the body away. His arm went around her, cradling her against his chest. "Shhh," he murmured. "Shhhh, it's all right now. It's over. It's all done. You're safe now, Cat, you're safe."

But it wasn't over. It wasn't done. For a woman like her, it would never be done. There were still too many things Bobby just didn't know.

She cried, feeling her first real tears streaking down her face. Bobby stroked her hair. And she cried harder because she knew, better than he did, that it was only the beginning of the end.

The police came. Hotel security, too. They burst through the door in a flash of badges, guns, and shouts. In contrast, Bobby quietly surrendered his gun to D.D., who took the nine-millimeter from Catherine as well. Medics came for the judge. An EMT tended Bobby's shoulder. The coroner's assistants carried Harris and Umbrio away.

They were still inventorying the damage

when a uniformed officer finally located Nathan.

The little boy appeared in the hallway, clutching a rumpled puppy against his chest.

He saw Catherine, who'd been forcefully detained on the sofa despite her pleas to look for her child.

"Mommy?" he said clearly, in the growing din.

Catherine stood. She moved toward her son. She held open her arms. He released the puppy, flying into her embrace.

"Mommy," Nathan said, and burrowed his head against her shoulder.

Bobby smiled at them both. Then D.D. finished reading him his rights and led him away.

Epilogue

January was an ugly month. Thermometer hovered around ten degrees. The wind contained a cruel bite that went straight for the bones.

Bobby didn't mind it that much. He strode down Newbury Street, wool cap pulled low, scarf tight around his ears and the rest of him buried deep in his down jacket. Tiny white lights twinkled merrily on the rows of trees lining the street. Store windows still boasted bright holiday colors and hints of frivolous retail treats.

New Englanders were a hardy lot, and even on a day like today, people were out and about, enjoying the city and taking advantage of fresh winter snow.

Bobby had reached a benchmark of his own today. He'd had his last meeting with Dr. Lane.

"So how were the holidays?" she'd asked him.

"Good. Spent it with my father. We went out. Two bachelor men, no sense cooking."

"And your brother?"

"George never returned Pop's call."

"That must have been hard on your father."

"He wasn't wild about it, but what can you do? George is a big boy. He'll have to come around on his own."

"And you?"

Bobby shrugged. "I can't speak for George, but Pop and I are doing okay."

"Which, of course, brings us to your mother."

"You always want to talk about my mother."

"Industry habit."

He'd sighed, shaking his head at her persistence. But of course they were going to talk about his mother. They *always* talked about his mother. "Okay. So, I asked my father some questions about her, like you and I discussed. Pop did his best to answer. We, uh, we actually had a conversation about that night."

"Was that difficult?"

He spread his hands. "More like . . . awkward. You know the truth? That one big apocalyptic night? Neither one of us remembers it too well. Seriously. I was too young. Pop was too drunk. And maybe— I'm guessing here—but maybe that's why we can move on and George can't. He still sees what happened. Honest to God, even when we try, Pop and I can't."

"Has your father tried contacting your mother?"

"He said he did, years ago, as part of his program. He reached her sister in Florida. She said she'd give my mom the message. He never heard anything again."

"So you have an aunt?"

"I have an aunt," Bobby said matter-of-factly, "and two living grandparents."

Dr. Lane blinked. "That's news."

"Yeah."

"How does that make you feel?"

"Oh boy," he rolled his eyes, laughing a little at the trite phrase, but it was a strained laugh. "Yeah," he admitted finally with a sigh, "yeah, that's a tough one. To know you got family out there and they've never even tried to reach out . . . it hurts. How can it not hurt? I tell myself it's their loss. I tell myself a lot of things. But okay, it sucks."

"Have you thought of contacting them yourself?"

"Yeah."

"And?"

"And I don't know. I mean, I'm thirty-six. Seems a little old to be reaching out to Grandma and Grandpa. Maybe if they don't want to reach me, I should take the hint."

"You don't really believe that, Bobby."

Another shrug.

"So what's really going on?" Dr. Lane had gotten to know him pretty well.

He sighed, stared at the floor. "I think maybe it's a matter of politics. My mother's in Florida. George is in Florida. We never hear from him, we never hear from her. I think maybe the family split. George abandoned Pop, but gained Mom. I didn't abandon Pop, so . . ."

"You think as long as you're close to your father, your mom won't contact you."

"That's my guess."

Dr. Lane nodded thoughtfully. "It's possible. Although I would suggest it would be healthier for you and your mother to have your own relationship, regardless of your father."

Bobby grinned wryly. "Well, you know, feel free to write her a note." His smile faded. He shrugged again. "Life is what it is. I'm trying to do as you suggested—focus on controlling the things I can control, and letting go of the things I can't. I can't control my mom, I can't control my grandparents, I can't control George."

"That's very wise of you, Bobby."

"Hell, I'm a regular sage these days."

She smiled at him. "So, moving right along. Work?"

"Start next week."

"Excited?"

"More like nervous."

"That's to be expected."

He considered things. "I was cleared for shooting Jimmy Gagnon and I was cleared for killing Copley, so that's all good. But I broke with the ranks. My involvement with

Catherine, the way I handled the investigation . . . I burned a lot of bridges there. Part of being on STOP is being a team player. There are a lot of guys who now doubt my ability to be part of the team."

"And what do you think?"

"I miss the team," he answered firmly. "I miss my job. I'm good at it, and if I have to prove myself again—well, I'll prove myself again. I'm not afraid of a challenge."

"But I'm curious, Bobby. Do you consider yourself a team player?"

"Sure. But being a team player shouldn't be an excuse for acting stupid. If the whole team is leaping off a cliff, should you join them, or, for the sake of the team, should you stand up and say, 'Hey, guys, stop leaping'? With all respect to D.D. and the other investigators, they didn't understand what was going on with the Gagnons. I did. So I followed my conscience. And I'm fine with that. Frankly, that's what a good cop should do."

"Why, Bobby, you've come a very long way."

"I'm trying."

Her voice grew quieter, so he knew what

she was going to ask next. "Do you still dream about him?"

"Sometimes."

"How often?"

"I don't know." His own voice had grown soft. He no longer looked at her, but studied her framed diploma on the wall. "Maybe three, four times a week."

"That's better than it was."

"Yeah."

"Are you sleeping?"

"Some. That road . . . it's gonna be a long one."

"Do you think there will be a time when you won't think of Jimmy Gagnon?"

"I killed the man. That's a heavy burden to bear. Especially knowing there might have been mitigating circumstances. Especially . . . well, you know, that's precisely the problem. Even after two months, I'm still not sure what happened that night."

"The police aren't pressing charges against Catherine?"

"No evidence."

"I thought you said they found a gun in the dresser in the bedroom."

He shrugged. "But what does that prove? She fired two shots in her own home?

There's no law against that. The decision to kill Jimmy was mine and mine alone. I'm the one who saw his face. I'm the one who pulled the trigger."

"Do you hate her?"

"Sometimes."

"And the other times?"

He smiled wryly. "The other times I'd just as soon keep to myself."

Dr. Lane shook her head. "She's a dangerous woman, Bobby."

"No kidding."

"Well, I think we're all set for now. I've signed off on the paperwork and sent it over to Lieutenant Bruni. Of course, you're always welcome to call me."

"I appreciate that."

"Good luck to you, Bobby."

And he said genuinely, "Thanks, Doc. Thank you very much."

He was at the end of Newbury Street now, arriving at the Public Garden. Children were running through the maze of trees, trying to catch snowflakes on their tongues. Adults were out, too, bundled up against the cold.

Some watched the kids. Others walked an assortment of exuberant dogs.

Bobby didn't see them right away. When he finally did, he was pleasantly surprised.

He crossed to Catherine, beautiful as always in a black wool coat and deep purple scarf and gloves. Nathan wasn't sitting beside her. For a change, he was chasing after two other kids, the puppy hot on his heels.

"I almost didn't recognize him," Bobby said as he took a seat.

Catherine glanced up at him, flashed a smile, then went back to watching her son. "Two weeks suddenly makes a big difference."

"I take it the new diet is working out."

"The power of high-fructose corn syrup. Turns out glucose and galactose are processed by the GLUT2 gene, which in Nathan's case is mutated. Fructose, however, is transported by GLUT5, so his system can absorb it much more readily. Now he's not only getting more calories, but he's finally getting an energy source his body can use to grow."

"Catherine, that's excellent."

She smiled again, but then her expression, as it often did these days, grew more somber. "He'll be on a restricted diet all of his life, and even then, he's going to have issues. His body doesn't absorb nutrients the way it should. He'll always have to monitor his health, and God knows all the complications still to come."

"But the two of you are pros."

"I wish I would've found the cause sooner. I wish I would've gotten him better help earlier. I wish . . . I wish so many things."

There was nothing to say to that. Given the past two months, they both had their share of regrets. "Any word on the house?" he asked at last.

"Already sold."

"Jesus, that was fast."

"There's a waiting list for Back Bay. Even at these prices."

Bobby shook his head. Catherine had listed her residence at four million. He'd never understand where people got that kind of money. "So what's next?"

"I'm thinking of Arizona. Someplace warm, where Nathan can play outside every day. Someplace where no one has ever heard of James Gagnon or Richard Umbrio.

Someplace where Nathan and I can both start fresh."

"And Maryanne?"

"She's devastated about what James put us through. I think she'd like a fresh start, too, and more time with Nathan. On the other hand . . . you know, she really loves James. Even after everything, I don't think she can bring herself to leave him."

James was in a coma. Between the blood loss and damage to his internal organs, his system had shut down. Doctors didn't think he'd ever regain consciousness. Mostly, they were surprised the man was still alive.

"Maybe someday," Bobby said.

Catherine nodded. "Maryanne likes Arizona. She mentioned they'd always talked about buying a home out there. So maybe, afterwards . . ."

His turn to nod. Now they both watched Nathan. The boy's cheeks were flushed, his breath coming in frosty pants. Trickster nipped at his heels and all the children laughed.

"The nightmares?" Bobby asked quietly.

She smiled wanly. "Only half a dozen a night."

"You or him?"

She smiled again, but the look was sad. "Both. You know what's funny? I don't dream of Umbrio. First time in my life, I no longer fear a stranger turning down the street. I dream of Jimmy. That last look on his face. And sometimes, in the middle of the night, I hear Nathan calling out for Jimmy, as well."

"Ouch," Bobby said.

"Ouch," she agreed. She paused. "When we get to Arizona, I think I'm going to find a specialist. Someone who can help Nathan with the trauma. And maybe someone who can help me, too."

"I think that would be a great idea."

"You could come with us."

"What, and give up all this cold?"

Her hand clutched his. "Bobby, I'm scared."

"I know."

"Do you not want to work? I can support you—"

"Don't."

She turned away, immediately embarrassed, but he softened the blow by stroking her cheek.

"You're the most special woman I know, Catherine," he said. "You love your son, you finally stood up to Umbrio. You're going to be okay. Both you and Nathan. It just takes time."

"If I'm so special," she challenged in a muffled tone, "why don't you come with us?"

Bobby smiled. He pulled his hand away from her, clasping his fingers on his lap. He looked at Nathan, running and laughing with the other kids, and then he said the only thing left to be said: "Got a call from Detective Warren the other day."

Beside him, Catherine immediately stilled.

"She's been working the connection between Judge Gagnon and Colleen Robinson—looking for phone records, financial transactions, anything to tie the two together. The judge was a smart man. D.D. can find records of cash withdrawals but no indication of where the money went. And when it comes to phone records, D.D. can't find evidence of a single call. Not from the judge.

"But she found two calls from you."

Bobby turned and looked at Catherine. In her cool gaze, he saw a wariness that told him more than any words.

"Turns out, Colleen Robinson had a bad

time of it in prison. Getting out, she joined a female support group for post-traumatic stress syndrome. You might know the group, Catherine. According to the counselor, you attended some of the meetings."

"I tried out group therapy once," Catherine said levelly. "But that was ages ago. Before I met Jimmy. Surely you don't expect me to remember one woman from so many years ago."

"Maybe you didn't. But maybe she remembered you." Bobby shook his head, bouncing his fingertips off one another. "I've been turning over the pieces in my mind all week. On the one hand, I don't think you had the connections to get Umbrio out of prison. But once you knew he was out, that the judge had pulled those strings . . . Did Colleen give you a call? Is that how it worked? Maybe she wanted some sort of payoff, or maybe she was just trying to be helpful, give you a warning. Of course, a warning wouldn't help you, would it? Umbrio was legally paroled. And the police were too busy suspecting you of murder to be interested in offering you protection. No, you were all alone, backed into a corner. Is that when the idea came to you, Catherine?

That you could use the judge's own weapon against him?"

"Richard Umbrio murdered my father," Catherine said steadily. "How dare you suggest I had anything to do with him. For heaven's sake, he killed Tony and Prudence. What incentive did I have to engineer such a thing?"

"You didn't, not for Tony and Prudence. I suspect Judge Gagnon was the one who paid Umbrio for those targets. But Rick Copley, on the other hand . . . the ADA was going after you, Catherine. If he had his way, you would've lost Nathan."

Catherine thinned her lips mutinously. She said nothing.

"And then there's the judge himself," Bobby continued quietly. "A man so cautious, so clever, he left behind no phone or financial records that tie him to Colleen or Umbrio. And yet Umbrio headed straight for him. How did he know to go after Judge Gagnon, Catherine? Who gave him the judge's name?"

"You would have to ask Umbrio."

"I can't, Catherine. You killed him."

She didn't say anything more. Because she had no defense, or because she didn't think he'd believe her if she did? He doubted he would ever know the answer to that. When it came to Catherine, he doubted he would ever know the answer to a lot of things.

"Dr. Lane told me something early on," he murmured. "She said that, for a woman like you, when it came down to protecting your world, there wasn't any line you wouldn't cross. It's true, isn't it, Catherine? To protect yourself against Judge Gagnon, you were willing to deal with the likes of Umbrio. Through Colleen Robinson, you paid money to the devil himself."

He paused a heartbeat. "Rick Copley," he said quietly, "was a very fine man. So, I think, was your father."

Catherine didn't speak, but he thought he saw tears in her eyes.

"I hope," she said after a moment, "that someday, when you have your own child, you will never know what it's like to fear for his life."

"You had other people to help you, Catherine. I *helped* you."

She finally looked at him. "But I didn't know that in the beginning, did I?"

She rose off the bench, still regal, still ungodly beautiful, and even knowing what he knew, he found himself holding his breath.

"D.D.'s a good detective," he said softly.

"My son is safe. For that, no price is too high."

"You really believe that, don't you?"

She smiled crookedly. "Bobby, it's the only thing that keeps me sane at night. I'll miss you in Arizona."

"Goodbye, Catherine."

Catherine retrieved her son. Bobby sat on the bench, snowflakes falling on his face, and watched them walk away.

After another moment, D.D. emerged from the white van parked down the street. She sat down heavily on the bench beside him.

"Told you you wouldn't get anything," Bobby commented.

She shrugged. "It was worth a try."

He reached inside his jacket, and went to work on the wires.

"You think she's honestly moving to Arizona?" D.D. asked. Then she added, "I can always extradite her when the time comes."

"Sure."

"I'm going to get her, Bobby."

"It hardly matters."

D.D. scowled. "What do you mean by that?"

"All she'll ever need is one man appointed to the jury, then Catherine will never spend so much as a day behind bars." Bobby rose off the bench. "Face it, they don't make 'em like her anymore."

"Thank God," D.D. muttered.

Bobby smiled. He stuck his hands into his front jacket pockets and headed home.

Author's Note and Acknowledgments

As always, I'm deeply indebted to many folks for helping make this book happen. The following list of people kindly and patiently offered me expert opinions. Of course, any mistakes and incidences of artistic license are my responsibility alone.

For information on law enforcement sniping and tactical units, I would like to thank: Lt. Cary Maroni, Trooper John Bergeron, and Major Marianne McGovern of the Massachusetts State Police; Special Agent James Fitzgerald, FBI; and Lt. James Swanberg,

Rhode Island State Police. I also pass along my sincerest appreciation to several other law enforcement professionals who wished to remain nameless; you know who you are.

Next up, the legal department. My deepest gratitude to Sarah Joss, Assistant Attorney General's Office; Bill Loftus, Civilian Investigator, Suffolk County DA's Office; Jerry Stewart, ADA, Suffolk County DA's Office; Detective Sgt. Richard Clancy, Boston PD, Suffolk County DA's Office; and Patrick Loftus, Defense Attorney.

For medical research, I couldn't have done without the wonderfully devious minds of Margaret Charpentier, Clinical Assistant Professor, College of Pharmacy, University of Rhode Island, and Kelly L. Matson, Clinical Assistant Professor of Pharmacy Practice, University of Rhode Island.

I'm also deeply indebted to my very good friend, Dr. Greg Moffatt for his insights into post-critical incident counseling as well as overall homicidal tendencies. And of course, where would I be without great friend and fellow writer Betsy Eliot, who spent a grand afternoon taking me all over South Boston, and siccing me on her relatives. You're the best, Bets!

In the fun news department, I'm very pleased to announce the first ever winner of the Kill a Friend, Maim a Buddy Sweepstakes. Many people entered, but only one could win the magnificent opportunity to have the person of his or her choice die in my novel. So here's to Jillian Zizza, winner of the contest, and to Jillian's dear friend, Colleen Robinson, whom she nominated to be the Lucky Stiff. Both will be receiving free signed books to celebrate this great honor!

If you would like to nominate yourself, or someone you love, to die in my next novel, never fear. Kill a Friend, Maim a Buddy will begin again in the fall. Check out www.LisaGardner.com for more details.

Finally, to Kate Miciak, quite honestly the most brilliant editor a girl could have. To Melinda, Barbara, Kathleen, and Diana, for serving once again as brilliant proofreaders.

To Brandi, because we all know I couldn't
have done it without you. And to my husband and my very own Tuesday's child, for
filling my world with grace.